Pushing back the branches of the tall shrubs Ann was about to step out onto the sidewalk when she heard another loud crack.

Her shoulder . . . her left shoulder.

'Oh, God,' she cried. Her mind began spinning, and she couldn't catch her breath. Instinctively her hand flew to the spot where the pain was, and she touched something wet. When she brought her hand to her face and saw the blood, she screamed. 'I've been shot! God help me . . . someone's shooting at me!'

She heard an engine roar, tires squealing, and smelled the distinctive odor of burning rubber . . .

Even though Ann was desperately trying to scream and draw attention to herself, she could hear her own words mumbled against the sidewalk. Like boiling water poured over her back, she felt the hot blood spreading, dampening her blouse . . . She was going to die. But she couldn't die. It wasn't fair. She'd already paid her dues in suffering. Her precious child . . . he needed her. She was all he had in the world.

Nancy Taylor Rosenberg received a BA in English and worked as a photographic model before studing criminology and joining the Police Department. She has served as an Investigative Probation Officer in Court Services for the County of Ventura, where she handled major crimes such as homicide and multiple-count sex-related offences. Nancy Taylor Rosenberg is married with five children and lives in California.

Also by Nancy Taylor Rosenberg

Mitigating Circumstances
Interest of Justice
California Angel
Trial By Fire

FIRST OFFENCE

Nancy Taylor Rosenberg

ORION

An Orion paperback
First published in Great Britain by Orion in 1994
This paperback edition published in 1995 by Orion Books Ltd,
Orion House, 5 Upper St Martin's Lane, London WC2H 9EA

Second impression 1995
Third impression 1995

Copyright © 1994 Literary Inventions

Published by arrangement with Dutton, an imprint of New American
Library, a division of Penguin Books Inc

The right of Nancy Taylor Rosenberg to be identified as
the author of this work has been asserted by her in accordance with
the Copyright, Designs and Patents Act, 1988.

A CIP catalogue record for this book is available
from the British Library.

ISBN: 1 85797 739 4

Typeset by Deltatype Limited, Ellesmere Port, Cheshire

Printed and bound in Great Britain by
Clays Ltd, St Ives plc

This one is for the gang:
Forrest and Jeannie, Chessly and Jimmy,
Hoyt, Amy, Nancy, and my husband,
Jerry Rosenberg

Acknowledgements

I must give credit where credit is due. Michaela Hamilton, my marvelous editor at Dutton Signet, played a large part in making this book what it is. Mike, you are not just an editor, you're a great friend and an excellent taskmaster. You always manage to get me to put forth the extra effort.

Also, I must express my gratitude to my agent, Peter Miller, of PMA Literary and Film Management, Ltd., for his tireless efforts on my behalf, and to Jennifer Robinson, also of PMA, another friend and adviser. I would also like to thank the entire staff of Penguin USA, including Peter Mayer, Marvin Brown, Elaine Koster, Lisa Johnson, John Paine, and many more. Particularly, I would like to thank the hardworking and supportive sales staff.

A special note of gratitude to my publicist and close friend, Alexis Campbell, for all her diligent efforts.

Last, this book was written in tribute to the thousands of dedicated probation and parole officers, a job of little glory and much toil. You not only make the world a great deal safer, you bring reason and impartiality into the troubled waters of our criminal justice system.

Chapter 1

The courtroom was armed and waiting. Assistant district attorney Glen Hopkins was making notes in his file and sipping a cup of coffee while the defense counsel, Harold Duke, glanced at his watch anxiously. Two court clerks and a uniformed bailiff were staring straight ahead like statues. A probation officer, Ann Carlisle, an attractive woman with short blond hair and classic features, had her head braced in her hand and intermittently glanced over at the well-built district attorney, wanting to catch his eye.

Judge Hillstorm took another look at the clock and then glared at the defense attorney. Originally from Georgia, the white-haired judge still spoke with a distinctive southern accent. 'Your client is late, Mr Duke,' he chided. 'This here hearing was scheduled for four o'clock. In exactly sixty seconds your client will forfeit his bail, and a bench warrant will be issued for his arrest.'

Harold Duke, a small, wiry man, gulped and swallowed. He turned toward the double doors for the hundredth time and then let out an audible sigh of relief when they were thrown apart by a lanky, long-haired young man wearing black jeans, a black shirt, and black leather boots with jangling chains and fake spurs. He strode into the courtroom as if he owned it, marched straight to the counsel table, and flopped down in the chair between his attorney and the probation officer. Duke's relief quickly dissipated when he saw the entourage that followed.

The judge had the gavel in his hand and had opened his mouth to call the court to order when he froze. Four striking young girls pranced into the courtroom, each one flashing a smile at the judge. They looked like recycled hippies: bell-bottom pants, bare midriffs, breasts bulging and jiggling, platform shoes, long straight hair. They slipped into the back row and huddled together.

Following them was a tall, handsome Chinese man in his early twenties. He rushed up to the defendant at the counsel table, dropped down on one knee, and whispered something. As soon as he was finished, he took a seat several rows up from the girls, glancing back and smiling at them over his shoulder.

Judge Hillstorm's face flushed, and he slammed the gavel down to call the courtroom to order. As he did, the back doors opened again and another attractive young man, this one with blond hair, burst through the doors, scanned the courtroom, and then quickly took a seat next to the young Chinese man.

'Well,' Judge Hillstorm said nastily, 'now that we're all assembled under the big top, why don't we try a little law on for size? People versus James Earl Sawyer II.' He nodded his head at the probation officer, and the sentencing hearing was officially on record.

'Mr Sawyer spent six days in custody subsequent to his arrest and prior to the court's setting bail,' Ann Carlisle said, her words clearly enunciated as always. 'According to the felony disposition, the defendant should receive credit for time served of twelve days, pay a fine of one thousand dollars, and be placed on twenty-four months probation. Since the original charge was a felony and involved narcotics, it's our recommendation that the defendant be placed on formal probation with full drug and search terms.'

'I see,' the judge said slowly, turning toward the district attorney. 'Mr Hopkins.'

At that moment Glen Hopkins was leaning over the counsel table, gazing across the room at Ann Carlisle. He was a tall, muscular man in his late thirties. His face was more rugged than handsome; fine lines radiated out from his eyes and clustered around his mouth from too much time spent in the sun. Raised in Colorado, he had once ridden bulls on the rodeo circuit. That wildness of spirit had not left him, either. No matter how expensive or well tailored his suits were, he always looked uncomfortable in them, constantly pulling his starched collar away from his neck as if it were strangling him.

Ann Carlisle flushed when she realized he was eyeing her. Several months ago, after a year of fencing and flirting, she had finally given in to his advances. Sex with him was an adventure, she had quickly found out. Knowing he could see her long legs under the table, Ann slowly crossed and uncrossed them. Then she stiffened her back and stared straight ahead, annoyed at herself for having such thoughts in the courtroom.

'Mr Hopkins, we're in session here. Could you please give us your full attention?'

'What? Oh,' the district attorney said, instantly collecting himself and facing the judge, a sly smile on his face. 'I think Ms Carlisle is mistaken. We agreed on the fine and the credit for time served but not supervised probation. The negotiated disposition states summary probation.'

Judge Hillstorm looked down at his file and riffled through the papers. 'Ms Carlisle, do you have a copy of this agreement?'

Ann looked up. 'Yes, Your Honor, I have the documents right in front of me, but the agreement only states twenty-four months probation. It doesn't specify summary or formal. My agency is recommending formal.'

'It was an oversight,' Hopkins said impatiently, speaking to Ann instead of the judge. 'The typist just failed to type the word "summary" next to the word "probation." '

'Mr Duke,' the judge said, 'would you like to comment?'

The diminutive attorney stood formally to address the bench. 'This is a first offense, Your Honor, and my client is an earnest young man who unfortunately bowed under peer pressure. He has never used drugs before and is preparing right now to enter college. All he did in this matter was accept what he thought were 'smart pills' from a stranger, not knowing they were controlled substances or in fact hallucinogens. This same individual then told Mr Sawyer that they would help him concentrate at a higher level. Mr Sawyer, after ingesting these –'

'Mr Duke,' the judge said, interrupting the attorney's dissertation, 'we're only discussing one point here, and we wouldn't be discussing even this point if there hadn't been an oversight. I mean, you are aware that this case has already been settled? You're not in the wrong courtroom, are you?' Hillstorm smiled as chuckles acknowledged his wit.

'Of course not,' Duke said, shifting his shoulders uncomfortably.

'Well, then,' Hillstorm said, 'this is what we're deciding: will your client be on summary probation to this court, basically unsupervised, or will he have a probation officer? Once we determine that, we can all go home.'

Duke continued, his voice carefully modulated, showing no hint that he was annoyed. 'There's no reason to submit my client to supervised probation.'

Judge Hillstorm played with his glasses, taking them off and then putting them back on again while he made his decision. 'James Earl Sawyer,' he finally said, 'in case number

A5349837, I hereby sentence you to twenty-four months *modified* probation. As a condition of this here modified probation, you will have what we call drug terms, and you will pay a fine of five thousand dollars by October 23rd, exactly one year from today. Now, I know this here fine is more than this agreement stated, but the agreement between you and me was that you were to appear in this court promptly at four o'clock and you failed to honor that agreement. That,' Hillstorm said, chuckling, 'is what we call breach of contract. Running this operation costs what a young fellow like you'd call *big bucks*. As for your probation, you'll have to report once a month to your probation officer, Ms Carlisle. She's the pretty little lady sitting right next to you. Do you understand?'

'Yes, I understand,' Sawyer answered stiffly, not looking at Ann, whose mouth was open in outrage.

'This court's adjourned, then,' Hillstorm said, standing and quickly exiting the bench down the back stairs.

As soon as the judge disappeared, the court reporter began folding up her machine and the court clerks bolted from the room. Ann remained at the table, incredulous. Hillstorm had done it again. The old judge had developed an annoying habit of making up the rules as he went along. A judge could modify the terms of a person's probation, but there was no such thing as modified probation per se, and Ann did not supervise probationers. Judge Hillstorm, however, was a dinosaur. He thought every offender should have his own private probation officer. It simply wasn't possible. The field supervision officers now handled only the most serious offenders, and their caseloads were still mammoth and unmanageable. This was the second time Hillstorm had done this to Ann, sticking her with a probationer to supervise personally, and she was hopping mad. Her desk was piled sky-high with files as it was.

'What did that mean?' Jimmy Sawyer asked her. 'You know, what the judge said?'

Ann looked over her shoulder – let the man's attorney explain it to him – but like everyone else, Harold Duke had made a run for the hills. Everyone, that is, except Glen Hopkins. The district attorney was still seated at the counsel table, packing files in a large black litigation case, a scowl on his face.

'I guess it means I'm your probation officer, Jimmy,' Ann said, her expression making it clear that she was not happy about the situation. 'Call me tomorrow to set up an appointment, okay? Then I'll get your terms and conditions typed and go over them with you.' She picked up her files and started to leave.

Sawyer held out a hand to stop her. 'I understand about the probation part. But the drug terms – what does that mean?'

'It means you have to urinate in a bottle once a month anytime I ask you. If the test comes back dirty, you go to jail for a violation of probation.' He flinched as she bore in on him. 'You also have search terms. They go along with the drug terms. That means I can come out to your house and search for narcotics without notice, anytime I wish. Any more questions?'

'Yeah,' Sawyer said, his face ashen. 'You mean you can just walk in my house anytime you want? Isn't that a violation of my constitutional rights?'

'What constitutional rights?' Ann said harshly. 'You're on probation now, Jimmy, you don't have any rights.'

As she headed down the aisle, Glen Hopkins fell in beside her. 'Can you believe it?' she said. 'Hillstorm did it again. I wanted this guy supervised, but I didn't want to be handcuffed to him for life. That stupid old fart.'

Outside the courtroom, Ann stopped and turned to face the district attorney. 'And your office simply has to stop busting felony drug charges down to misdemeanors. Sawyer had a ton of dope on him, and an extensive juvenile record, and he ends up convicted on a paraphernalia charge.' She gave him a querulous look. Normally he hated to settle for a lesser count. 'Give me a break, Glen. Why don't you just give the guy a medal and the address of every elementary school in the city so he can ply his trade? He's a damn dealer.'

She looked over and saw that Jimmy Sawyer had trailed closely behind and was listening to every word they said. Their eyes met briefly before Ann turned her back on him. A moment later, she heard Sawyer's chains and spurs clanking down the hallway.

'It was his first adult offense,' Hopkins said softly, his eyes following Sawyer down the hall. When he turned his gaze onto Ann, his voice was unusually sharp. 'Look, I don't like it any more than you do. Tell me one person who works harder at putting these people away than I do, huh? But you have to look at the big picture, Ann. We've got four murder trials in progress, seven rapes, and God knows how many gang-related shootings and stabbings. We can't take the time to try every first offense that comes through the doors any more than you can supervise them.' He frowned as he recalled something, then went on. 'I thought you'd be overjoyed that I asked for summary probation. You really threw me for a loop in there, Ann.'

Ann stepped back, a bit off balance. They had frequently debated the inadequacies of the criminal justice system, yet Glen had never fired off like this. As in the courtroom, he was always cool and loose, making his points effortlessly. Ann was the one who got hot and started hammering at him, just as she was about to do now.

'That's a crock and you know it. By the time a person gets his first conviction – not his first arrest, mind you, but his first actual conviction – he may have committed dozens of crimes. Just look at Sawyer's juvenile record.'

'It's sealed, Ann,' he said, shrugging, regaining his cool.

'You know we can't use it. Most of the charges were dismissed anyway. Look, if you don't want to deal with Sawyer, just carry the case on the books and ignore him. That's what all the other probation officers do.'

'Well, I certainly don't,' Ann said, her eyes narrowing. 'Sawyer will be sorry he was ever born by the time I get through with him. I'm going to crawl right up his asshole. Hillstorm wants him supervised? Believe me, he'll be supervised. If he so much as dispenses an aspirin, I'll drag him back to court.' As Ann leaned back against the wall, though, she looked at her lover and saw his face shift into hard lines. Suddenly she realized she had been pushing him too hard. 'I'm sorry, Glen. I just needed to let off steam.' She laughed. 'Guess I'd make a lousy prosecutor. Good thing I never went to law school. If I lost a case, I might go over and punch someone out.'

'Oh, yeah?' he said, not really listening, rubbing his temple as if he had a headache.

Ann became concerned. 'Are you all right? Is something bothering you? You seem . . .'

Glen loosened the knot on his tie, grimacing as he did so, as if he wanted to yank it off. 'I'm fine, Ann.'

She saw a glint of perspiration across his forehead and upper lip. 'Well, you don't look fine.'

'It's Delvecchio,' Glen said sourly.

Ann waited until four or five people passed. 'I thought that case was going well. Did something happen?'

Hopkins raised his eyes and shook his head. 'Fielder declined to file on the homicides: insufficient evidence.' Robert Fielder was Glen's boss, the elected district attorney of Ventura County.

Ann put her hand over her mouth in dismay. Randy Delvecchio was on trial for raping four women, all in their sixties or seventies. Although they had as yet to prove it, the district attorney's office and the Ventura police department were certain he was responsible for two unsolved homicides, also of elderly women. They had been brutal, savage slayings, and Glen was determined to put this man away. His fervor was understandable, Ann had thought, for he was very close to his elderly mother, a justice on the Colorado supreme court.

A sea of people swirled around as another court spilled out for the day. Wanting privacy, Ann took Glen's hand and led him across the hall, through a heavy steel door to the landing of the fire stairs.

'You're going to get convictions on the rapes, though?' she said, her voice echoing in the stairwell. 'Isn't that what you told me just the other day?'

'I want the homicides, Ann. I can't let maniacs kill people and get away with it.'

'It's just a case, Glen,' she said, trying to get him to look at her. Just then she noticed that Glen's hair had fallen forward onto his forehead, and she reached over and tenderly brushed it away.

'It's not just a case,' he said, flinging his hand up to brush her away. 'One of the victims was my high school English teacher. Shit, these women are the same age as my mother.'

No wonder he was tense and distracted, Ann thought, wanting to comfort him. Because she was handling Delvecchio on an underlying offense, a violation of probation, and would also be assigned the presentence report following conviction, Ann was not only familiar with the case, she would have considerable influence at sentencing. 'Just get the rapes,' she said firmly. 'With the enhancements for the weapons and a recommendation for consecutive sentences on the sodomies, I'll recommend at least twenty years.'

'He'll be out in ten years,' Glen responded. 'And that's if he gets the full boat. The judge may impose the midterm and then he'll be out in five years. Delvecchio's only twenty-six, Ann.'

She moved closer and ran her fingers along the lapels of his jacket, wanting to coax him out of his funk. 'He'll get the max, Glen. The court always follows my recommendations. You know that. He was even on probation at the time of the rapes. That's an aggravating factor.' Seeing the tension in his face ease, Ann carried it a step further. 'And don't forget, he's an African-American with an established record.'

Glen smiled weakly. 'You really believe the court imposes higher sentences on minorities, don't you?'

'Of course,' Ann said. 'I know it for a fact, Glen, and it makes me sick, but hey, when they're guilty of crimes as nasty as these, it can work in our favor.'

The smile on his face expanded, one corner of his lip curling up and exposing a tooth.

Luring him on, Ann idly trailed her hand over the metal railing for the stairs, then ran it down the side of her neck, stopping right over her breasts. 'Guys like Jimmy Sawyer glide through the system because they're white or their families have the bucks to buy a first-rate defense,' she said, her hand now circling her breasts seductively. 'But believe me, Delvecchio is going to sit in prison for a long time.'

Even though Glen was still smiling, he shook his head. 'You're wrong, Ann. The only reason minorities get stiffer sentences is that they commit more serious crimes. Hey, I believe in the system, remember?'

'Yeah,' Ann said playfully, 'you're the last Boy Scout. You showed me that on the beach last week.' With her foot, she kicked the toe of his boot.

Glen chuckled. 'I'd rather be the last Boy Scout than the Angel of Death. I hear that's what they call you at the jail.'

Ann stiffened. 'Where did you hear that?'

'From one of the deputies. He says you go over there and sweet-talk those animals, get them to tell you all kinds of incriminating shit. Then you turn around and use it to aggravate their sentences. Is that true?'

'Of course not,' she said quickly. 'My God, they're criminals. I wouldn't be surprised at anything they say about me.'

Glen tilted his head and winked. 'Oh, come on, Ann. I know it's true.'

Ann tried to keep a straight face, even though she wanted to break out laughing. She was cautious, however, about admitting her private war on crime: getting criminals to talk, tell her things they had never told anyone else. It was a skill she had honed for years. Defense attorneys frequently tried to cry entrapment, but not one of Ann's cases had ever been overturned on appeal. Just as some officers generated hostility and apprehension, Ann had a disarming, innocent way about her that garnered trust almost from the moment she walked into an interview room.

She was turning to leave when Glen pulled her into his arms. 'I need you, Ann,' he said in an urgent tone she was starting to know well.

'I have to get back to work,' she said, her breath catching in her throat, memories of the last time they had made love igniting her body. Glen had taken her to the movies and slid his hand up her dress. By the time they'd walked out of the theater, Ann was both wildly excited and mortified at the thought that someone might have seen them. Glen had driven straight to the beach and talked her into making love in the open. Conservative Ann, who people said looked like a schoolteacher in her pastel sweaters and white cotton blouses, had discovered a side of herself she'd never known existed. And Glen made it all seem so natural. Hemmed in a stuffy courtroom all day was agonizing, he told her. Passion should be spontaneous, even a little dangerous – not delegated to a bedroom.

'You don't have to go back to work,' he said, his voice low and sexy.

'I have a report to dictate,' Ann said, gently pushing him away.

'Please, Ann, I want you,' he said, placing his hands on her buttocks and pressing her even closer to his body. 'You're begging for it,' he said, emitting a husky laugh. 'You should see the look on your face.'

'No, Glen,' she protested, looking up and meeting his mouth and then trying to slip away. 'Don't do this . . . not here.'

'I can't wait,' he said, keeping her close, his eyes dancing in anticipation. 'No one's going to see us.'

She could feel his chest expanding and contracting, feel his erection through her clothing. She should never have brought him here, never acted so suggestively. It was just so new and exciting, she thought, this feeling, this man.

Fingers tickled the back of her thighs. Hands slid the hem of her skirt over her nylons covertly, an inch at a time. Ann felt the cold surface of the wall against her buttocks through her panty hose as he raised her skirt to her waist.

'I hate panty hose,' Glen panted, his fingers inside now, ripping right through the nylons to reach the spot between her legs, touching her, stroking her.

'Please, Glen,' Ann said, torn now between her urge to run and her growing desire to do anything and everything he wanted.

He kissed her neck again along her collarbone, then sucked her left breast right through her silk blouse, leaving a small wet spot. Ann laughed nervously. 'You're incorrigible.'

Opening his jacket, Glen leaned his torso into her and pulled her head gently onto his shoulder. The sound of their clothes rustled up and down the stairwell. He began rubbing the small of her back. 'Relax, Ann. Look at me. I like to watch your face when you get turned on.'

Ann's mouth was open and her eyes closed. If she didn't

open them, she thought, then she could possibly forget where they were. 'I can't,' she protested, her eyes springing open. 'Someone's going to see us.'

'Yes, you can,' he whispered. 'You loved it the other night on the beach.'

'Not here,' she said, eyeing the surroundings. Everything in the stairwell was painted gray, like the interior of a battleship, ugly, industrial. Huge rolled ducts laced across the ceiling. They must have just painted the whole area recently, because Ann could smell the paint.

'Oh,' she exclaimed, feeling him push inside her.

Lifting her legs, Glen held them as he moved inside her slowly and sensuously. 'I adore you, Ann,' he said, finding her eyes and probing there. 'You know what turns me on the most?'

'Mmmmm,' was the only sound she could make. His words were falling around her while she responded with her body, pushing forward to meet him.

'You look so prim and proper . . . that little gap between your front teeth.' Ann's legs were locked around his waist now, and he placed a palm over her stomach, right above her pubic hair. 'But down here you're hot,' he said sensuously. 'Incredibly hot.'

Holding her breath, Ann was adrift, her inhibitions stifled by her state of arousal. She didn't cry out, but she felt a jolt of liquid pleasure and her body trembled and then stiffened. Silent and intent, Glen began moving faster, her lower body striking the wall again and again until he exploded inside her.

All at once Ann heard a noise and looked up just as the door leading out into the corridor slowly closed. 'Glen . . .' she said, panic rising.

Ignoring her, he kissed her on the mouth and pinned her arms against the wall, chuckling while she tried to twist away. Then he released her arms and sighed, running his fingers through his hair and looking around in a daze.

'Christ, Glen, someone opened the door. Someone saw us.' She shoved her skirt down, saw her nylons in shreds where he had ripped them. 'The door just closed. Why did I let you talk me into doing this?' she said, her face flushed and damp with perspiration.

'Great, wasn't it?' Glen said, slumping back against the wall. Then he saw the alarm in her eyes and became alert. 'Are you serious? Someone saw us?' He quickly zipped up his pants, shoving his shirttail in at the same time. 'Who? Did you recognize them?' His tie had been flipped over his shoulder, and he pulled it back down, smoothed his hair, and straightened his jacket. 'You just imagined it.'

'No, Glen,' Ann insisted. 'I saw the door closing. If it was closing, it had to have been open. It's too heavy to open by itself.'

She glared at him as she would at an errant child. Although he was concerned, she could see that he was also titillated by this public exposure. When she spoke, her voice was low but cutting. 'I have a son, Glen. I can't afford to carry on like this in public, subject myself to ridicule. Especially not here at the courthouse.'

He tried to take her in his arms, but she pushed him away and reached for the heavy fire door.

'Don't you think David has been through enough?' she tossed out, her voice shaking. 'He certainly doesn't need to hear that his mother is screwing in the stairwell at the courthouse.'

'Ann,' Glen said, trying to get her to calm down, 'even if someone did see us, it's not going to get back to David. Aren't you overreacting? So, maybe it was a risky thing to do, but it's not a four-alarm fire.'

She sighed, letting the tension go. He was right. There were more serious things to be concerned about. David was one. 'I just want him to accept you, get to know you, before he finds out we're sleeping together. And he will, Glen. He might even suspect it now. He's very observant for a twelve-year-old.'

Glen held up his hand, irritated. 'It's not like I haven't tried,' he said.

They stood there facing each other without speaking. Ann felt sorry for him. He'd made every effort to gain her son's approval. A week ago, she'd casually mentioned that Tommy Reed, a homicide detective and old friend, was taking her son to a Raiders football game. Glen had insisted on tagging along. Not only had the boy remained aloof, barely acknowledging Glen's presence, but Reed and David had purposely excluded Glen from every conversation. Glen had even bought David a Raiders pennant, but when the game was over, David had left it on the stadium bench, telling Glen that he didn't like pennants. Ann had scolded him, but beyond that there was little she could do.

Ann knew she had to give the man credit. Faced with a hostile kid and a woman recovering from the loss of her husband, most men would have walked away. 'David will come around, Glen. We just have to give him time.' She glanced at her watch, reaching for the door handle again. 'I've got to go.'

With that, she touched a finger to his lips in a mock kiss, smiled, and walked through the door.

Back in her office, Ann went into an interview room and dictated her report. By the time she finished and returned to her desk, most of the other probation officers had already left for the day. She thought of calling David and telling him she was running late, but after the frenzied coupling in the stairwell, she was in a strange mood – pensive, inert. Picking up her briefcase, she had decided to forgo the call and leave when her gaze landed on her husband's picture on her desk. Setting the briefcase down, Ann brought the photograph close to her face. He would always look like this, she thought. No gray hair, no wrinkles, not a day older. Sometimes the only image she could remember was the one she was holding.

The time had come, she decided, sucking in a breath and then letting it out slowly. She opened her desk drawer and gently slid the glass frame inside, knowing this was a significant moment. Funny, she thought, sometimes milestones in a person's life came and went in the most mundane ways. A picture placed in a drawer. A letter tossed in a mailbox. A key removed from a key chain.

Thank God for Glen's persistence, she thought, grabbing her briefcase and heading for the elevators, feeling lighter and younger than she'd felt in years. Without Glen she would still be mired in the past, sitting home alone every night feeling sorry for herself. Seven times over the past year, the district attorney had asked her out, and each time Ann had turned him down. But he was patient and polite, expressing his concern for her and her son each time they spoke, and he continued to ask until she finally said yes.

'Yeah, sure,' Ann said, chuckling at herself as she pushed the button on the elevator to go down. Now that she knew him, she wondered if her repeatedly turning Glen down was what had fueled his interest. Who cares? she thought. Glen might be brash and a little wild in some ways, but he made her feel alive. Now all she had to do was get her son to let go and move forward with his life.

That could take some doing, though. The boy was as stubborn as his father.

A highway patrol officer, Hank Carlisle had been nick-named 'Bulldog' by his fellow officers. Although he had been six feet tall, his stockiness had made him appear closer to the ground. He had worn his light brown hair in a military-style crew cut, but the 'Bulldog' handle developed because of his thick neck and small, cunning eyes. That and his explosive temper. Ann had accepted her husband's fierceness as an assurance of security. Unlike the average police spouse, she hadn't worried about him getting injured on the job. Of course, Ann's father had been a police captain, and Ann herself had started her career as an officer with the Ventura police department. She wasn't exactly the run-of-the-mill police wife.

She'd always seen Hank as indestructible. She even used to crack jokes around the office that it was the people on the streets that she worried about, not her husband.

Then, four years ago, the incomprehensible had occurred: Hank Carlisle had simply vanished off the face of the earth.

His police cruiser had been found abandoned alongside the interstate just beyond the Arizona–California state line – that long, dusty stretch of road highway patrol officers call no-man's-land. The car doors as well as the trunk of the police unit had been left standing wide open, and no blood or other evidence was found in the vehicle. He'd made no radio transmissions the hour prior to his disappearance.

The investigators had put it together only one way. Sergeant Hank Carlisle had made a routine traffic stop that summer night four years ago, probably to issue a speeding citation. The motorist he'd stopped had been a wanted criminal. Knowing the policy of the highway patrol was to check wants and warrants on all traffic stops, the person or persons had jumped Carlisle as he walked back to his unit to use his radio. The most likely scenario was that he had been struck from behind with something heavy, the butt of a weapon perhaps. Then when he was unconscious, he had been disarmed, transported to some unknown location, and executed.

After months of digging in the miles of barren, sandy earth, the authorities had failed to locate the body. They'd used dogs, helicopters, and the most sophisticated aerial photography, and had canvassed the area on foot and in four-wheel-drive vehicles. But they had found nothing. No body, no evidence, not a single thread they could pursue.

Ann had suffered through grueling interviews from highway patrol investigators, question after question about their marriage, their finances, their friends and associates. They had to rule out everything, they told her, even the possibility that her husband had purposely staged his own disappearance for some reason they had as yet to uncover.

Thank God, Ann thought now, as she stepped off the elevator, the ruling of foul play had been officially entered in the file. The ruling was important for more reasons than her peace of mind. Although the department had been issuing Ann small checks each month from Hank's retirement fund, it had not yet released his life insurance money. She could use that money to put David through college.

Ann reached her '87 black Jeep station wagon, nearly alone in the vast parking lot. Once she was in the driver's seat, she turned the key in the ignition. There was only a click. 'Damn,' she said, trying it again. Another metallic click; the engine wasn't engaging at all. It couldn't be the battery, she told herself, getting more annoyed by the second. She'd just replaced the battery last week. This time it had to be something even more costly – like the starter. She got out of the car, slammed the door, and stood there trying to figure out what to do.

Glancing back at the court complex, Ann thought of returning to call the emergency road service. For a few moments she just leaned back against the car and let the cool evening air brush across her face, telling herself that she mustn't let little things like this get to her.

Her eyes rested on the windows of the jail, and she watched as shadowy figures moved around inside. The complex took up an entire city block, housing almost every official agency in the county. During the day it was next to impossible to find a parking place, though Ann estimated there were enough slots for five hundred or more cars. The county had also sprung for some decent landscaping. Oleander bushes formed a tall hedge all around the parking lot, filtering the noise from Victoria Boulevard, a major divided thoroughfare in Ventura. Ann thought the bushes were nice, since they softened the concrete and gave her a little greenery to look at from her window.

The road service could only tow her to the nearest garage if it was the starter as she suspected. She decided to walk home. It wasn't that late, and David had probably snacked all afternoon anyway. In the morning she'd ask her supervisor's husband if he would have someone look at her car. He was the service manager of a local car dealership and frequently had had Ann's car repaired for free. Besides, she told herself, her house was only five blocks up Victoria. If she walked briskly, she could be home faster than if she returned to the building and called a cab.

Ann began walking toward the exit that she normally used when driving and then changed course. She'd spotted an opening in the oleanders in the far corner of the lot that would place her right onto the sidewalk for Victoria Boulevard. From there she could walk straight up the hill to her house.

Just as she reached the opening, Ann heard a loud pop and jerked her head around. It sounded like a gunshot. She scanned the empty parking lot and then peered through the foliage to the street. There was nothing. Steadying her nerves, she decided it must have been a car backfiring. People were always mistaking backfires for gunshots. As a cop, she'd responded hundreds of times to such false alarms.

Bending down, she ducked inside the bushes. As her heels sank into the mud, she scowled, thinking her shortcut might not have been such a good idea after all. The automatic sprinklers had just gone off, and the ground was soaked. 'Shit,' she said, squatting down even lower to inspect her shoes. Mud was oozing out around them. She'd have to remind herself to clean off her shoes before she went in the house, or the carpet would be ruined.

Pushing back the branches of the tall shrubs, Ann was about to step out onto the sidewalk when she heard another loud crack.

Her shoulder . . . her left shoulder.

'Oh, God,' she cried. Her mind began spinning, and she couldn't catch her breath. Instinctively her hand flew to the spot where the pain was, and she touched something wet. When she brought her hand to her face and saw the blood, she screamed. 'I've been shot! God, help me . . . someone's shooting at me!'

She heard an engine roar, tires squealing, and smelled the distinctive odor of burning rubber.

Get down, she told herself, but she was unable to move, paralyzed with fear. Stumbling forward, lashing out at the bushes with her hands, Ann fell forward onto the concrete sidewalk, her good arm cushioning her face from being badly scraped. 'I've been shot! Someone help me! Please . . . get an ambulance . . . police . . .'

Even though Ann was desperately trying to scream and draw attention to herself, she could hear her own words mumbled against the sidewalk. Like boiling water poured over her back, she felt the hot blood spreading, dampening her blouse.

She tried to slow her racing heartbeat, tried to find strength inside the panic. The bullet could have struck an artery. Stretching her fingers forward, fighting against the pain and raging fear, she found them resting in a spreading puddle of her own blood.

As her life pumped out on the sidewalk, Ann could hear her internal organs with unnatural clarity: her lungs straining for oxygen, her heart pulsating and pumping, pumping, like the sound an oil rig made. She was going to die. But she couldn't die. It wasn't fair. She'd already paid her dues in suffering. Her precious child . . . he needed her. She was all he had in the world. If there was a God, He just couldn't let this happen.

Cars were zipping by on Victoria Boulevard, the exhaust fumes choking her as she gasped for breath. Without success she tried to make her cries louder, attract someone's attention before it was too late and she passed out. 'Help me . . . please help me . . . I've been shot . . .'

Her face fell back to the cement, the coarse surface scraping her chin. Black spots were dancing in front of her eyes. She was nauseated, both hot and cold at the same time. I can't pass out, she told herself. If she passed out, she would bleed to death for sure.

Gritting her teeth and pushing with all her might, Ann managed to get up on all fours. Then she collapsed again and had to struggle all over.

Ann could hear noises: cars passing, people's voices and laughter, a siren somewhere in the distance, a jet streaking over her head. I'm right here, her mind kept screaming. People were all around her. Why couldn't they see her, hear her? 'Help me!' she cried again, this time louder. 'Please help me!'

Turning her face toward the sound of voices, Ann realized the parking lot for Marie Callender's was right across the divided parkway. People were walking in and out of the restaurant. She was so close – yet not close enough. The traffic, the wide divided roadway, and Ann's position right outside the line of shrubbery made her all but invisible in the darkness.

'Help me!' she called again, fixing her line of sight on a couple with a young child who were about to get into a dark blue station wagon. The woman was laughing and talking to the man, the little boy's hand clasped in her own. Just then the boy turned and looked across the street toward Ann. 'I'm here . . . over here!' she yelled, lifting her head off the concrete. 'I've been shot. Get help!'

While Ann watched in agony, the little boy's mother jerked his hand. Not breaking stride, the family got inside their car and were soon pulling out onto the street. 'No,' she cried, a pathetic wail. 'Don't . . . leave . . .'

She was going to die.

As the puddle of blood increased and the pain intensified, Ann tried to focus on the image of her son's face, use it to fuel herself, give herself strength. Once again she tried to push her weakening body to her feet, blocking out the pain. It's not an artery, she told herself. You're going to be fine. Maybe it wasn't even a bullet. Maybe she'd backed into a jagged metal wire . . . something sharp.

'Stay calm,' she could hear her father say. He'd told her that right after she graduated from the police academy and had seen her first dead body – that of a child. She'd come home and told her father she couldn't do it, wanted to resign. She was too young, too sensitive to be a cop. 'Everyone is sensitive to death. If you weren't sensitive to death, you wouldn't be human. Take some deep breaths and call on your inner strength,' he'd said firmly.

Ann suddenly found herself fully upright. Her vision was blurred and distorted, perspiration streaming from her forehead into her eyes, but she was standing. She knew now what she had to do. She had to make it across the street.

'Are you hurt?' a concerned voice said from behind her. 'Is something wrong?'

'I'm . . . I've been . . .' She tried to hold on, to turn around, to speak. Help was here . . . it was going to be all right now.

Ann felt her strength evaporating. As soon as she felt an arm brush against her side, felt the comforting warmth of another body against her own, she allowed the person to lower her back to the ground.

'You?' Ann mumbled as a disembodied face floated in front of her. Gentle, caring eyes looked down into her own, the most beautiful eyes she'd ever seen.

'Get an ambulance,' a voice yelled so loud she was startled. 'Quick, she's hemorrhaging. She's going into shock. And . . . blankets. Get blankets. Look in my trunk.'

The next second, the voice was calm and soothing, and Ann saw a man leaning over her body, his shirt brushing against her face. 'We have to apply pressure. The bullet struck an artery. Be still and relax. The ambulance is on the way.'

The man moved to the other side of Ann's body, and she felt his hands on her. She kept watching his face, lost in his eyes. From somewhere far away Ann remembered them, knew she had seen them. She was swimming now somewhere between consciousness and blacking out, awake but not really awake – a murky, wavy world, almost as if she were under water. She heard other voices, heard other feet pounding in her direction. All she could see was this face, hear this reassuring voice, feel the warmth of this person's touch on her body.

Through the fog Ann heard a shrill siren piercing the night. With his free hand the man stroked Ann's forehead, gazed down into her eyes again. Hair brushed across her face. 'Your hair . . .' Ann said. It was like a soft blanket.

'You're going to be fine,' the voice assured her. 'The bullet entered near your shoulder.'

Ann strained to see, hear. The face was becoming distorted. She felt a rush of emotion – love – mixed with a feeling of complete peace. 'Hank,' she whispered. 'I knew you'd come back.'

Her eyelashes fluttered and then closed involuntarily. She felt an unknown force pulling her down into the darkness. She desperately held on to the image of the man in front of her, refusing to let it go. It was the only thing between her and the nothingness that was calling. Then she was sinking, unable to hold on. She heard Hank's voice, smelled his body next to her own, recognized his firm touch. Hank was here. Her son would have his father. She could let go.

A few seconds later, she let the darkness take her.

Chapter 2

At fifty, Detective Sergeant Thomas Milton Reed was still a fairly good physical specimen, even if he did say so himself. At six one, two hundred pounds, he had all his hair and only a few strands of gray. He bared his teeth in the mirror. Most of the stains were gone now that he'd kicked cigarettes. Watching Lenny Braddock die of lung cancer had finally done the trick. But the lines in his face would remain. Too many years in the California sun. People said it gave a person character, anyway. If he didn't have anything else, Reed laughed, he certainly had character.

He gave himself this little pep talk a few times a day in the can at the Ventura police department. This year he'd passed the big five-o, and it was every bit as bad as they say. He sucked in his stomach and vowed to go to the gym tonight. There were a lot of younger cops out there, though none of them necessarily tougher and certainly not better. Anyway, he said to himself, tossing the crumpled-up paper towel in the trash can, that's the way I see it.

As soon as Reed cleared the door, he saw Noah Abrams heading down the hall with an alarmed look on his face. Reed almost ducked back in the can, but then he stopped. No gym tonight, Reed thought, knowing he was about to catch a hot call.

'Here,' Abrams said, throwing the keys to a police unit at the older detective. 'You drive. I know you won't let me drive anyway. Ann Carlisle's on the way to County General. Gunshot wound.'

The keys hit the linoleum floor with a ting. All the color drained from the detective's face. By the time the younger officer had gone three feet down the hall, however, Reed had leaned over sideways in one fluid motion, scooped the keys up, and was flat-out sprinting down the corridor leading to the parking lot. 'Where?'

'Government center parking lot. Don't know much . . . just came in,' Noah gasped, running alongside Reed now.

'What's . . . her condition?'

'Dunno. Here's the car. It's the green one.' They both ducked into the unmarked police unit. Abrams slammed the portable light on top of the car and Reed gunned it, screaming out of the parking lot, skidding around the other police units while Abrams flicked through the police bands trying to get the fire department frequency so they could monitor the paramedics who were transporting Ann Carlisle.

Tommy Reed was distraught. This was no ordinary person who had been shot. Ann's father had been his training officer when he was a rookie, his mentor since the first day he'd become a cop. On his deathbed Lenny Braddock had called Reed in and made him promise he would look after his daughter, make certain no one ever harmed her. Ann was impulsive and headstrong, Lenny had always said. One day she was going to get herself hurt. Well, Reed thought, biting down on the inside of his cheek, her father had been right. He slapped the steering wheel, almost losing control of the speeding car, feeling that shaky, hollow feeling inside, the way he felt when things were beyond his control.

'There they are,' Abrams yelled over the siren, hearing the medical lingo on the radio. 'Watch it, Reed, you're busting a hundred. On your right,' he quickly called out, advising the detective he had a side street coming up, a dangerous situation at this speed. If someone was approaching the intersection and didn't hear the siren, there would be no way to avoid a collision and there would definitely be no survivors.

The radio was blasting as the paramedics relayed information to the hospital. Once they cleared the intersection, Abrams killed the siren so they could hear. A few moments later, Reed let up on the gas and his speed dropped down to a more cautious seventy.

Ann was alive.

The bullet had struck an artery but bypassed her vital organs. She'd lost a lot of blood and would more than likely require surgery, but it didn't look critical.

'Siren on or off, Sarge?' Abrams asked, looking over at his partner.

'Off,' Reed said. 'Is patrol on the scene?'

'Five of them and a lieutenant. They were right on top of it when the call came in. The radio room said there's even a D.A. on the scene. They're already calling it a drive-by.'

'Fucking animals,' Reed barked, cutting his eyes to Abrams and then back to the road, his relief turning to outrage. Ann and her son had become Reed's family, particularly since her husband's disappearance. No one played target practice with people Reed called family. Acid rose in his throat. Reaching in his pocket, he found a Rolaid and tossed it into his mouth.

What had begun as an obligation to a dying friend had ended up filling a void in the detective's own life. Even though he'd dated many women through the years, Reed had never felt strongly enough about any relationship to marry. He'd yearned for a family, however, and in many ways he now felt he had one.

Picking up the microphone, he raised the lieutenant at the scene. They were waiting for the forensic people and taking statements from witnesses. No one had seen a suspect or vehicle. All they had seen was Ann down on the ground and bleeding. By the time the paramedics arrived, she had been unconscious. 'Make sure you get in touch with Claudette Landers ASAP,' Reed barked into the radio. 'Get her to pick up Ann's son. He's probably at the house alone right now. Are the press there?'

'What do you think?' Lieutenant Cummings said. 'Like fleas on a dog.'

'Take care of the situation with the kid fast, Pete, or he'll see it on TV. Not the best way to hear your mother's been shot.'

Reed dropped the microphone. He was torn, thinking he should go to the house and pick up David himself. But Claudette was a woman with kids of her own and a very close friend of Ann's. Women were better in this type of situation.

'Look, Sarge,' Abrams interjected, 'why don't you go to the hospital and check on Ann and I'll pick up the kid and drive him to this woman's house? Turn around and take me to the station, and I'll pick up another unit.'

'We're almost at the hospital,' Reed snapped, his voice harsher than he intended. 'As soon as we know Ann's stable, I'll let you get started on the paperwork.'

Having put Abrams firmly in his place, the detective rolled down the window to get some fresh air. Noah had been wanting to get in Ann's pants ever since her husband vanished. If her name so much as fell off Noah's tongue, however, Reed felt like snatching his head off. Why Noah was interested in Ann he had no earthly idea. She was appealing in a fresh-faced way but clearly no raving beauty, and certainly not the type of woman Abrams preferred. He went for flash in a big way: big breasts, stylish hair, sharp clothes. He also had three failed marriages under his belt, and Reed didn't want him within ten feet of Ann Carlisle.

At thirty-seven, Noah Abrams was a handsome man with

chestnut-brown hair, hazel eyes, and a scattering of freckles across his nose and forehead. He had a penchant for hand-painted silk ties. He'd wear the same suit for ten years straight, but he'd cough up a hundred bucks for a single tie. Today he was wearing one with the image of Marilyn Monroe on it.

'Let me ask you something, Noah, now that we're on the subject,' Reed said, coming out of his thoughts. 'Why are you always circling around Ann Carlisle like a damn shark? She's not your type. I've seen the kind of women you take out.'

'I resent that, Reed,' Abrams said. 'Maybe I haven't always had the best taste in women, but I'm not a total jerk. You seem to forget that I've known Ann almost as long as you have. . . .' His voice trailed off and he gazed out the passenger window. When he continued, his voice was low and sincere. 'I really care about Ann, Sarge. Hell, I used to work with her when we were both police cadets. We had some good times back then. Maybe one of these days I'll settle down. If I do, she's the kind of woman I want.'

'Oh, really?' Reed said, shifting around in his seat. 'She's seeing someone anyway, so you can put that out of your mind.'

In reality, Reed thought as little of Glen Hopkins as he did of Noah Abrams. Hopkins was too fast for Ann, with his fancy Rolls and his motorcycle. And the man was a damn cowboy, always bragging about his rodeo days as if anyone really cared. 'After all this with her husband,' Reed said, 'and now someone puts a slug in the poor woman. Isn't life a bitch?'

Abrams hadn't heard a word. He was sitting forward in his seat, bracing himself against the dash. 'Who's Ann seeing? I thought she wasn't dating yet. Why didn't you tell me she was going out?'

'Forget it,' Reed said. He turned into the parking lot for the hospital and cut the engine.

'Will you just tell me who it is, Reed?' Abrams persisted.

'Some D.A.,' Reed mumbled, exiting the vehicle and walking rapidly toward the emergency-room entrance.

Abrams hurried to catch up to him. 'What's his name? How long has she been dating him? I mean, is she serious about this guy?'

Reed stopped cold in his tracks, spun around, and grabbed the other detective by the collar. 'Keep your swarmy moves off Ann Carlisle. *Comprende?* The woman was shot. Can I deal with that right now, huh? Can we forget about your wife-hunting problems? Hell, you've had three already.'

Abrams jerked away, his face flushed. 'Fuck you,' he said. 'I can't even have a conversation with you. I thought we were friends.'

Reed's lips compressed as he stepped onto the mat for the automatic doors. 'After you,' he said to Abrams once the doors swung open. When the younger officer stepped through, Reed gave him a swift kick in the ass and promptly broke out laughing. He was actually quite fond of the younger man.

'What the hell?' Abrams squawked, his hand on the seat of his pants. 'Why'd you do that?'

Smirking, Reed said, 'Just felt like it. Good way to let off tension.' He reached in his pocket for his shield, flipped it, and hung it over his belt.

'Great,' Abrams said sarcastically. 'Maybe I need to let off a little tension too.' He made a move like he was going to kick the detective in return and then stopped. Not on his life. Reed was as tough and as predictable as they came. If Noah retaliated, Reed would knock him down. And it wouldn't even break his stride.

The two detectives leaned against the wall, their toes an inch behind the line that delineated the sterile, restricted area of the surgical section of the hospital. They were staring down at the different-colored floor tiles and wondering if they should leave and come back later.

'What's going to happen,' Abrams said, 'if I step on the green tiles? Will an alarm go off and a gang of nurses jump me?' He chuckled. 'That might be kind of fun.'

Reed looked over at Abrams and growled. Just then a surgeon in a green paper gown, the front of it stained with blood, burst through the swinging double doors.

Reed sprang off the wall and flashed his badge. 'Sergeant Thomas Reed,' he said, then, nodding at his partner, 'Detective Abrams. How is she?'

'She's doing very well,' the young surgeon said. 'The bullet struck a branch of her axillary artery or she would have been up and around already. It didn't strike bone or any other vital organs. We repaired the artery and stopped the bleeding. She'll be fine in a week or so, barring any complications.'

'Did she regain consciousness? Did she say anything?' Reed asked, concern etched on his face.

'Look,' the surgeon said, 'she's not going to be able to give you guys a statement for quite some time. Probably the best thing to do is come back in the morning.'

The doctor started to walk away, and Abrams stepped in front of him. 'This woman is like family,' he said, arching his eyebrows and tilting his head toward Tommy Reed. 'Her father was a captain, and she used to be a cop as well.'

'I see,' the doctor said, his eyes shifting from one man to the other. He hesitated before continuing, 'I was told this might have been a sexual assault. The admitting physician followed protocol and collected specimens, but we couldn't wait for one of your people to get here, and, of course, our primary concern was the hemorrhaging. She regained consciousness for a few minutes when we had her in the operating room, but was more or less incoherent. She mentioned a man's name several times. Hank, I believe.'

'That's her husband's name,' Abrams offered warily.

'Is he here? Maybe he's your culprit.'

Reed stepped closer to the doctor, a look of shock on his face. 'She was raped?' Then he spun around to Abrams. 'See,' he said, poking a finger in the other officer's chest, completely irrational now, 'this is just what I was talking about. Pricks like you who can't keep their damn dicks in their pants. You want to know why I'm protective –'

Abrams knocked Reed's hand away. 'Hell, I didn't rape her. What's wrong with you? Get a grip, Sarge.'

The surgeon cleared his throat, and both men recollected where they were.

'Her husband's dead,' Reed said flatly. 'What made you think it was a rape?'

'There was sperm, but no vaginal trauma, I think.'

While Abrams shook his head in dismay, Reed went after the surgeon. 'What do you mean, you think? Was there sperm or not?' He tossed his arms in the air in frustration, his voice booming in the tiled corridor. 'How're we going to take this to court? What about chain of evidence? Don't you guys know the rules by now?'

The doctor remained calm, even smiling. 'I'm just the surgeon, Officers. The man you should talk to is Richard Ogleby. I think he's still down in the ER. He's the physician who admitted her. We're finishing all the swabbings and collecting other samples now before they move her to the recovery room.'

As soon as the young surgeon took off down the corridor, Abrams said, 'What do you think? Some maniac raped her and then shot her?'

Reed started barking orders now as he walked, his stomach in an uproar. 'Get a patrol unit dispatched over here to pick up the evidence.' He stopped and belched, stuffing his hands in his pockets, trying to find his Rolaids. The situation with Ann was far worse than he had thought. The entire investigation could be compromised now. 'I want to see what they found at the scene.'

'What if she wakes up?' Abrams said, trying to keep his own anger in check. He pulled some antacids from his jacket pocket and slapped them in his sergeant's hand. 'She could give us a description. Without a description we're dead in the water.'

Reed glanced at the mints and then at Abrams, a curious look on his face.

'Occupational hazard, I guess,' Abrams said.

'You heard what the doctor said,' Reed answered, popping a mint in his mouth. 'She's out cold right now.'

'Hey, you're the sergeant,' Abrams said.

'You're damn right I am,' Reed said emphatically. 'And I'll tell you something else, Abrams.'

'Yeah?'

'I'm going to catch the ape who did this and kill him with my bare hands.'

Abrams just nodded, the same steely look in his eyes as in Reed's.

It was one o'clock in the morning and David Carlisle was leaning forward over his knees in the hospital waiting room when Glen Hopkins appeared in the doorway. A stocky young man, far too heavy for his height, David resembled his father: brown hair, olive complexion, squared-off jaw. Only his pale blue eyes were Ann's, but his lashes were darker and more prominent, making his eyes his finest feature. He wore a blue cotton shirt and jeans. One corner of the shirt was sticking out, a few buttons were undone around his waist, and his dark hair was tousled. But it was the hostility shooting from his eyes that made Glen Hopkins pause before speaking.

No tears, no emotion, just a cold, blank stare.

'Hey, David,' Hopkins said softly, sitting next to him on the green vinyl sofa. 'Rough go, huh? I'm sorry about your mother. How are you holding up?'

David immediately stood and crossed the room, flipping on the television set. Instead of returning to his earlier position on the sofa, however, he took a seat on the opposite side of the room.

'They tell me your mother is doing fine, though,' Hopkins said. 'She might have to spend some time in bed, but they assure me she'll make a full recovery. Have you seen her yet?'

When David didn't respond, Hopkins thought of the one thing that might get the little brat's attention. Food. 'Are you hungry? They've got a cafeteria downstairs. We could go get a piece of pie.'

'I'm not allowed to eat pie,' David said over his shoulder. 'Don't you know that by now?'

'Okay,' Hopkins said, glancing at the screen and seeing an old movie playing. Was the kid really watching this or just deliberately being rude? Having already played his ace, Glen was at a loss as to what to do next. When Tommy Reed strode through the door, Hopkins rushed over and pumped the detective's hand.

Reed looked over the attorney's shoulder to David. 'Come on, guy, I'm going to sneak you in to see your mother. She's still in recovery and they don't allow visitors, but I want her to see your handsome mug the minute her eyes open.'

Springing to his feet, David grinned. Then he glanced at Hopkins, and the smile turned to a sneer. 'He's not going in, is he?'

'Ah, excuse us a minute, Hopkins,' Reed said politely. Had to set a good example for the kid, he thought, hitching up his pants. Taking the boy's shoulder, he guided him out the door, and they started walking down the hall together to the recovery room. 'You know, David, you shouldn't be so hard on your mother's friends. He's not *such* a bad guy, is he? I mean, your mother wouldn't like him if he was that big of a knucklehead.'

'He's a creep. I hate him. And he's not just my mom's friend. You're my mom's friend.' Raising his eyebrows, the boy looked Reed in the eye. 'I'm not stupid, you know. I know the difference.'

Okay, Reed thought, they were on the same wavelength on this one. David didn't like Hopkins any more than he did. They continued walking, the boy trying to stay in step with the detective, having to almost jog to do so. Already short of breath because of his weight and aversion to exercise, David grabbed Reed's arm.

'Will . . . Mom be okay, Tommy?' he said, his voice breaking with held-back emotion. 'You're not lying to me, are you? People always lie to me. Promise me she's going to be okay.'

Reed knew just what he was referring to, the months after his father vanished. He'd been only eight years old then, and they had decided not to tell him about his father until they knew for certain what had occurred. Unfortunately, Ann had taken the deception to extremes, concocting one story after another to explain his father's protracted absence. Only after four months had gone by and every possible lead was exhausted did Ann finally sit the boy down and tell him the truth. But the detective really didn't lay the blame on Ann, even though he had advised her to tell the child the truth a few days after Hank disappeared. It was one of those tragic situations, there was no really good way to handle it. If they told the boy his father was dead and then he surfaced . . .

Well, Reed thought, setting these thoughts aside, that was the past. At present, they had to get Ann back on her feet and find a way to help this poor kid handle another senseless act of violence – one directed at the only person he had left in the world. Reed coughed, his throat suddenly constricted, about to break down himself. David might try to hide his fear, but Reed knew the boy. He was terrified.

'I'm not lying,' Reed said, holding his shoulders and looking him in the eye. 'Listen to me. Your mom will be up and about in no time. Sure, it's terrible that crimes like this happen. No doubt about it. Awful. Just plain disgusting. But let's not dwell on that. Let's just be thankful now that she's going to be okay.' He pulled David into his arms and held him tightly.

Once they reached the door to the recovery room, the detective shoved the boy behind him, opening the door and peering inside to make certain the head nurse was still busy with another patient. He knew Lucy Childers, and she was a stickler for rules. Cop or no cop, she owned the recovery room. Once she had banged Reed on the head with a bedpan when he refused to follow orders. Placing a finger over his mouth, Reed jerked David's hand and pulled him inside the room, walking quickly to Ann's hospital bed.

'Is she asleep?' David said, tears in his eyes. 'She looks so white.'

Reed draped his arm over the boy's shoulders and nudged him closer to the bed, reaching behind him to pull the white drapes closed. 'Talk to her, guy. She's supposed to wake up now. When she hears your voice, she'll wake up for sure.'

David's stubby fingers locked on the railing as he leaned close to his mother's face. 'Mom, can you hear me? It's David. I love you, Mom. Be brave. Be a big girl.' He turned to Tommy. 'That was stupid. I don't know what to say. She used to tell me all the time to be a big boy. Uh, you know,' he said, self-consciously, 'until I got fat.'

'David,' Ann mumbled, her eyes opening to glaring overhead lights and sharp medicinal odors. Even though seven hours had passed, in her mind she was still on the sidewalk. Her eyes darted frantically around the room as reality slowly took hold and she realized she was in a hospital.

Before her eyes settled on David's face, however, the drugs pushed her down and her head sank back into the pillow.

Like slides passing before her eyes, Ann could see the scene on the sidewalk, feel the bullet ripping into her flesh, smell the distinctive odor of blood. But it wasn't the pain that terrified her, it was lying on that sidewalk screaming for help, fearing that no one would ever come to her rescue. She ran her tongue over her cracked lips, tried to swallow but found her mouth too dry. Then she heard someone else talking, but the voice seemed far away. She was safe, she told herself, her fingers closing on the edge of the blanket. She was in a hospital and she was alive. Nothing else mattered.

'Ann, it's Tommy,' the detective said softly. 'And David's here with me. You're in the hospital, honey, and you're going to be fine. We're all here for you.'

David eagerly took his cue. 'Yeah, Mom, we're all here. You're going to be fine. Does it hurt? Where did the bullet go in? Did it come out the other side?'

Reed winced, shaking his head at David. Then he whispered in the boy's ear, 'Try to talk about something other than bullets.'

Ann heard her son's voice but kept slipping back under. David was here. She had to be strong for him. Just thinking of the setback this could cause him chilled her to the bone. 'David,' she called, her eyes still closed. 'David –'

'I'm here, Mom.'

Her mind was spinning, dozens of images coming at her at once. She saw herself holding Hank's picture in her hands, but she couldn't remember where or when. Then she remembered thinking he was there, had actually come to rescue her. Things were so jumbled that she couldn't sort through them. 'Long hair,' she mumbled, remembering the man's hair brushing across her face. 'The man . . . where's the man with the hair?'

Reed sprang to life, thinking Ann could be describing her attacker. 'Ann, did you see the person who did this?'

She shook her head and ran her tongue across her lips again. 'Didn't see the suspect. The man . . . who stopped. Who was he?' She'd been so certain it was Hank. But she knew it was just a hallucination. Of course, she would think of Hank during a crisis. The man had been her husband, her protector.

'The man who stopped was Jimmy Sawyer, Ann,' Reed told her. 'Says he's one of your probationers. When he saw you stumbling on the sidewalk, he stopped. He was trained in first aid. Said his father's a doctor.'

Why? she was asking herself. Her outrage at why someone would do this to her overrode any gratitude she might have felt. Why would anyone shoot her? What had she done? Was it someone just shooting randomly, or shooting specifically at her?

Someone suddenly jerked the curtain back so abruptly that Reed was startled. Lucy Childers, almost as wide as she was tall, her permed gray hair like a Brillo pad, poked the detective in the back with a finger. 'No kids, Reed. You know better than to bring a kid in here.'

Reed's face softened in a mock plea. 'It's her kid, Lucy. Have a heart. I mean, you'd have to be as cold as –'

'That's enough, Reed.' The nurse looked David up and down and then barked in a gravel voice, 'Five minutes more. That's it. I'm counting, Reed. Young people carry all kinds of infections.' She checked her watch to let the detective know she meant business.

Right behind the nurse, Ann saw Tommy Reed's face, and then her heart swelled when she finally focused on David. 'Oh, baby, come here,' she said, her voice barely above a whisper. She tried to turn on her side and then grimaced in pain, but her hand moved to the railing as she reached out for her son.

'Mom,' he said, squeezing her hand in his own. Her other arm was strapped to an IV board. 'I love you, Mom.'

'I love you too, honey. Don't worry. Promise me you won't worry. Everything's going to be fine.' Ann's eyelids would open, flutter, and then close. Fighting with all her strength against the pain, she knew she had to comfort her child. 'The bullet didn't even hurt,' she lied, managing a chuckle. 'It was no worse than a bee sting. That's all, David. I bet I could go home right now if I wanted to.' Ann tried to sit up in the bed, to show him she was okay. 'See,' she said, using her free hand to brace herself to a sitting position, a weak, lopsided smile on her face. Then her head drooped to one side, and Reed put his arm behind her neck, gently lowering her back to the bed.

Reed waved the boy out of the room and remained by Ann's bedside. Where the hell was Abrams, anyway? He'd called Reed after he'd interviewed Sawyer, and the detective had expected him to be at the hospital by now. He wanted him to take David back to Claudette's house.

As soon as the child shuffled out the door, Reed touched Ann's cheek with a callused hand and brushed her hair off her forehead. 'Ann, listen to me. Were you raped? Can you tell us anything about who did this to you?'

'I . . . don't know who did it,' Ann stammered, her face as pale as the sheet, a solitary tear rolling down the left side of her face. 'It hurts so bad, Tommy.'

'I know,' he said, choking up. 'If I could take the pain for you, Ann, you know I would.'

She stared into his eyes before speaking, comforted by the sight of his strong face. 'I didn't see anyone. All I heard was the shots and the car engine.' Her eyes closed and then opened again a few moments later. 'No rape,' she said. 'I wasn't raped, Tommy. I was shot.'

'Did you see a car, Ann?'

She shook her head and then mouthed, 'Nothing.'

Suddenly Reed looked up and saw Glen Hopkins standing at the foot of the bed. How long had he been there? 'She can't have visitors yet,' Reed snapped. 'If you want to be useful, Hopkins, take David back to Claudette Landers's house.'

'But I . . .' the attorney started to protest, then just let it ride.

Ann turned her head toward the sound of the voice. 'Glen,' she said, 'is that you? Oh, God, Glen, I –'

'I asked you to take the kid home,' Reed said to Hopkins between clenched teeth. 'Can you do that for us, huh? We're trying to conduct an investigation here.'

Glen stepped up to Ann's bedside, said a few comforting words to her, and then jerked his head, indicating the detective should step outside. Once they were in the corridor, Glen erupted. 'You're about the biggest asshole I've ever met. I care about her, even if you and her son refuse to accept me. Not only that, I'm an assistant district attorney. Have you forgotten that?'

Reed just shrugged his shoulders. 'I'll take the kid home myself. Wouldn't want you to put too many miles on that fancy Rolls-Royce of yours.'

Glen shuffled his cowboy boots on the linoleum. 'That's the most childish thing I've ever heard of, Reed. The car's twelve years old, and I bought it at a damn auction for twenty grand, for chrissakes.'

Reed stepped right in the attorney's face, his breath hot and foul. 'What did you see out there? You were at the scene right after it happened.'

Hopkins was just as hard in return. 'Your partner already took my statement. Ask him. And you'd better take a close look at your big hero, Reed,' he said nastily. 'Jimmy Sawyer's a drug dealer. He may be your suspect.'

'Sawyer a suspect?' Reed said, his mouth opening in surprise. 'You're joking, right?'

Glen spun around and stomped down the hall, glancing back over his shoulder at the detective. Then he yelled down the hall, 'Joking? I don't think so, Reed. You guys are like the fucking Keystone Kops. Get your act together or I'll have you removed from this case.'

Tommy Reed narrowed his eyes and glared until Hopkins turned the corner and disappeared. Sawyer, he wondered, the guy who saved her? He'd have to ask Abrams what he'd made of the guy. Seemed like a pretty poor suspect as far as Reed was concerned, no matter what Ann's hotshot D.A. thought. People don't put a bullet in a woman and then rush right over and try to save her life. If anyone needed to get his mind set straight, Reed decided, it was Hopkins. This wasn't the Wild West, here – this was Uzi country, sawed-off-shotgun land, 9mm heaven. Around here, people shot you for no reason at all, and they sure didn't hang around to administer first aid.

Several nurses passed in the hallway, and one smiled at the detective. He smiled back, waiting until they rounded the corner to break out laughing. Hopkins was a fool, threatening to get him yanked off the case, strutting around as if he thought he was the one wielding the big stick and the detective was nothing but a lousy cop. Mama's boy, as far as Reed was concerned. Mama probably did all his homework in law school.

Go ahead, cowboy, he thought as he headed to the waiting room to get David, get me removed from the case. The captain had already officially assigned the case to Abrams, claiming Reed was too close to Ann. That was fine with Tommy. The less paperwork he was responsible for, the more time he would have to conduct his own investigation, and he had more contacts on the streets than anyone in the department.

'Hey, kid,' he said, sticking his head into the waiting room. David was sitting straight up in the chair, his head dangling forward onto his chest. The boy was sound asleep.

Chapter 3

Ann was in bed with five or six pillows propped behind her. She had been released from the hospital after only six days, and at the end of the second week she was approaching full recovery. David was munching potato chips and shuffling through his baseball card collection on the floor by her bed. 'One of these days I'm going to save enough money for a Mickey Mantle,' he told his mother. 'Freddy's grandfather bought him a Mickey Mantle last year. Can you believe it? Freddy doesn't even like baseball.'

Ann laughed at the irony of her son's statement. His friend had no interest in sports, but was, like David, a collector. Being surrounded by his favorite objects made David feel secure, and if there was one thing he needed, it was a sense of security. He still wet his bed several times a week, and worried constantly that one of his friends would find out. After years of therapy since his father's disappearance, David was still a disturbed young man.

'It's time for you to get to bed,' Ann told him, smiling. 'And no more chips, honey. Do you know how many calories are in one potato chip?'

If she had done the shopping, there would be none in the house. Glen had dropped by the house earlier with three bags of groceries in his arms. Ann appreciated his kindness, but she'd failed to tell him not to bring over junk food. In the past two weeks, David had packed on another five pounds.

They were a strange pair, this mother and son. David turned to food for comfort. When Ann was under stress, however, she couldn't eat.

'Here,' he said solemnly, handing his mother the bag of chips. 'Maybe you'd better keep these in here so I can't get to them.'

Ann got out of bed, meaning to walk him to his room. She was shoving the bag of chips into her nightstand drawer when she thought better of it and handed them back to him. 'Things have been pretty tough lately. You can go on a diet next week, okay?'

While David changed into his pajamas in the bathroom, Ann ran her hand over his sheets, brushing away a sprinkling of cookie crumbs. She sniffed, checking for the odor of urine. The sheets were still fresh from two days ago, and she was relieved. If David could only make it an entire week, the therapist thought, he might break the bed-wetting pattern.

The tiny bedroom was unbearably cluttered, in contrast to Ann's. The kid was a virtual pack rat. When he was about nine, he'd saved every scrap of aluminum foil he could find, making a silver ball more than a foot in diameter. As there was barely enough space in his room for his twin bed and his small pine desk, Ann had snatched the horrid ball of foil and tossed it into the trash one day while David was at school. This was a pattern. In order to keep his room inhabitable, his mother had to wait until his interest in one set of junk waned and then secretly dispose of it before another set took over the room.

She glanced at the bookcase along his bed. She hoped the model planes would go next. They were impossible to dust, and David hadn't asked for a new model kit in years, not since he glued his finger to his nose with Krazy Glue.

Then a strange sight caught her eye. Since his father's disappearance, David had picked up every book, magazine, and newspaper article he could find relating to UFOs. Although he didn't voice his opinions out loud, Ann knew that he had harbored his own theory that his father had been kidnapped by aliens. It was certainly more agreeable than thinking his father had been viciously murdered and left somewhere in an unmarked grave. If an alien took his father, David must think, an alien could return him.

Since his mother's shooting, however, he had been forced to deal with reality. Yes, she thought sadly, seeing the posters of flying saucers crumpled up on the floor by the trash can. He never voluntarily removed something from his room. 'You really want to throw these away?' Ann asked when he returned from the bathroom. 'I mean, if you don't, you'd better put them in the closet or they're on their way to the dump.'

'Yeah, get rid of them,' David said, flopping on the bed once Ann stood. 'There's no such thing as aliens. And spaceships are dumb. Freddy says they're just trick photography.'

Stroking his hair, Ann bent down and pecked him on the cheek, her heart heavy with emotion. His father had been murdered and his mother had been shot. No child should have to deal with such harsh realities. Guns, Ann thought, shaking her head, eyeing the wall above his bed, lined with sports pennants. When were people going to wake up and get rid of guns? How many more people would have to die before adequate gun-control laws were passed?

'You don't have a Raiders pennant,' she said, crossing her arms now and giving him a stern look. 'Why did you do that to Glen, refuse to accept the one he bought you at the stadium? That was cruel.'

'The Raiders suck,' David said, turning on his side in his

bed. 'I just went to the game to be with Tommy, and then *he* had to come along and ruin the whole day.'

Ann sighed. It was useless to get into another argument over Glen. At the door, she looked back at her son and smiled. 'You liked the chocolate chip cookies he bought for you, though. I saw the evidence in your bed. Remember what I've always told you, David: don't bite the hand that feeds you.'

Abruptly he sat up in bed, a look of urgency on his face. 'Mom, don't go back to work tomorrow. Please,' he begged. 'What if they shoot you again?'

Ann braced herself against the doorframe. 'We went over all this, honey. It was a drive-by shooting. They didn't care if they shot me or someone else. That's good, see. That means it will never happen again.' She started to go to him, make another attempt to assuage his fears but she didn't know anything else to say. 'Go to sleep now. Everything will be fine. I love you, honey.'

Ann padded down the long hall and flopped on her back in the bed, reaching up to touch her sore shoulder. Being in the house the past week had left her surrounded by painful memories of Hank. She glanced around the room, trying to remember what it had looked like when he'd been alive. Her husband had always kept everything freshly painted and repaired. Now the paint was chipped and peeling from the walls, and the roof was shot. But Ann had heeded people's suggestions and tried to make it her room now that he was gone, redecorating the year before in soft pastel colors and floral prints. She didn't like clutter, so there were no knickknacks, but she had purchased lovely cotton fabrics and used them to cover the scratched dresser and nightstand that had once belonged to her parents. Then she'd made dried arrangements with sunflowers and lilies, the same flowers used in the prints, placing them around the room in wicker baskets.

Next to the fresh flowers Glen kept bringing her, though,

the artificial ones looked faded and tacky. The ones on the nightstand he had brought over just today. Ann inhaled their fragrance. Since the shooting she had been pleasantly surprised by the attorney's thoughtfulness and concern. Many men were attentive when things were running smoothly, then conveniently got lost at the first sign of trouble. Glen had proved that he wasn't that type of person. Ann was grateful, and her feelings for him had deepened.

He wasn't anywhere near replacing Hank, though. Right over there, she thought, looking at the dresser, was where Hank used to toss his gun and shield when he crept into the bedroom after a late-night shift. Ann used to have a big ceramic bowl there for just that purpose. Every morning when she got up, she'd pick up his uniform off the floor, checking to see if he could get one more day's wear out of it before she had to send it out to be cleaned. Then she would retrieve his gun from the bowl and lock it in the small floor safe in one corner of the room.

Old habits die hard, Ann told herself. She still caught herself stopping by that one spot on the floor sometimes, just staring down at the place where Hank's uniform used to be. The old safe was covered now with a ruffled print tablecloth and shoved under the window, but Ann still kept her own firearm in it. Probation officers in Ventura County did not carry guns. Since the shooting, she had left the safe unlocked so she could get to the gun in a hurry if she needed it. So many years had passed, David probably wasn't aware the safe was even in the room.

Looking up at the ornate crown molding along the ceiling, she tried to recall the exact age of the house. According to her father, they'd moved here when Ann was three years old. She'd forgotten through the years to ask if the house was new when her parents purchased it, so without a look at the tax assessor's files, she had no way of knowing if other families had ever lived in it. It would seem strange if they had, since the house seemed exclusively her own. Having inherited it from her father when he passed away, Ann and her new husband had moved in right after they got married.

Ann's mother had died when she was eleven years old. She knew firsthand the agony David had suffered over losing his father. But unlike her son, she had known her mother was dying, and she knew where her mother was buried. It made accepting her death a lot easier.

The house had been a sore spot between Ann and her husband. Letting her eyes close, she recalled one fractious time in particular. They'd gone house hunting and found a beautiful four-bedroom home, a new one over by the freeway. David had been two or three years old, and he ran through the empty house making like an Indian on the warpath.

'It's gorgeous,' Ann said, running her hands over the tile countertop in the sparkling kitchen, so different from her father's house with the chipped and stained counter she could never seem to get clean. 'And look at this, a real walk-in pantry.'

'Want to make them an offer?' Hank said, his eyes dancing with excitement.

'What do you mean?' Ann answered, the excitement contagious. 'We can't afford a place like this, not on our salaries.'

Hank swept her up in his arms, whirling her in the air the way he did David. 'Put me down,' Ann cried just before she started laughing.

'Okay,' he said, setting his wife gently back on her feet. 'I've figured it all out. We can get a loan from the credit union for the down payment, then I'll get an extra job working security somewhere on the weekends. We can do it, honey,' he said, smiling. 'I'm going to buy you this house.'

Ann loved it when her husband smiled. His cheeks were full

and he appeared almost jolly, not hard and cold as he did once the uniform and badge came out.

For the next ten minutes, Ann walked around the house, looking in all the closets, checking out all the shiny new fixtures in the bathrooms. 'We could put our bed right against that wall,' she told Hank in the master bedroom. 'Then we could put the television over there. You know, that fourth bedroom would be great for a study. Can you imagine, a real study? I could have a desk and everything.'

'Right,' Hank said, beaming. 'And I could get some guys from work to help me put in a hot tub in the backyard.'

Ann let her gaze drift out the window to the yard, and the excitement began to recede. Nothing but dirt out there. No fence, no yard, no drapes. They'd need more furniture to fill up all the rooms. Ann could see the dollar bills adding up in her mind, see herself sitting at the dining- room table as she did every month paying bills – but if they bought this house, she wouldn't have enough money to pay them.

'No,' she said, connecting with his eyes. 'We can't, Hank. We barely make enough as is, and we don't even have a mortgage. The payments on this house would be close to a thousand a month.'

Hank Carlisle was not a money person. Before he'd married Ann, he'd spent every dime he'd made and had nothing now to show for it. Ann's philosophy was diametrically opposed. People should never spend money they didn't have. It was the first thing her father had taught her.

Hank's face fell. 'So what? I told you I'd work a second job. That alone would make the payment.'

'You're not being realistic, honey,' Ann said to him. 'They take out taxes, withholding. You can't possibly make enough to cover the payment working a few shifts on the weekends. And you hate your job with the highway patrol. You'd detest being a security officer, even if it was only a few hours a week.'

Hank moved close and pulled her against him. 'I want to buy you this house, a brand-new house, a house no one but us has ever lived in. I hate being a cop, baby, but only because I can't buy you all the things you deserve. I don't want to live the rest of our lives in that run-down shit hole of your daddy's. It even smells old.' He stopped and raised his eyebrows humorously. 'Also, you know, David's getting older, and his room is right next to ours. We won't even be able to have sex without him hearing us.'

'It's not that bad, Hank,' Ann pleaded. 'Please, we don't want to go into debt, get in over our heads. We'd need extra money just for the move, and then there's furniture, curtains, higher property taxes, God knows what else. No, Hank, we can't.' And he would want even more goodies, like the hot tub he'd just mentioned. Ann knew her husband – he liked nice things. She pulled away in order to pin him with her gaze. 'We can't afford it, Hank. You don't make enough money.'

Propped up against the pillows, Ann winced at what had come next, wishing she could block the bad memory out of her mind. A few seconds later, the phone rang and she grabbed it, more than ready to set the past aside. It was Tommy Reed.

'Did you know no one's covering my caseload while I'm out?' she told him when he protested her return to work the next day, 'Claudette's even been trying to handle some of the cases herself.'

'I wouldn't worry about that,' Reed said. 'Just worry about your health.'

Ann appreciated all the expressions of concern, she really did. Reed was only the sixth person who had made that statement: just worry about your health, get well, everything will work out. Sounds good, feels nice to say it, not so awful to hear it. Glen had even gone so far as to insist that she take David and go away for a few months, even told her he would foot all the expenses. But for all the good intentions, the people offering words of comfort weren't looking at the situation through Ann's eyes. For the past two weeks she'd been expending carefully guarded sick time with the agency – her paid leave. The county awarded her only a few days paid leave every month, and she had to stockpile it for emergencies. The situation was simple: Ann had no choice but to go back to work.

'Don't worry about me,' she said to the detective, mustering up her customary bravado. 'I'm going stir-crazy in the house anyway. Say, what do you think about that probationer stopping to help me? Jimmy Sawyer. They say if he hadn't known first aid and stopped the bleeding, I might have bled to death. Of all the people, huh?'

Turning off the bedside light, she tossed the extra pillows on the floor, then turned on her side to talk in the dark. 'I promised I'd take Sawyer back to court and get his probation switched to summary so he doesn't have to report every month. Sort of like a reward.'

'Oh, yeah?' Reed said. 'I don't think that's going to work out too well. That's what I called you about. Glen Hopkins is preparing a warrant right now for his arrest.'

Ann bolted upright in the bed. 'What happened? Did he get busted again for drugs?'

'Hopkins thinks Sawyer was the one who shot you.'

'No.' Ann had to stop short, think about this. 'That's ridiculous, Tommy. Why would the man shoot me and then stop to give me first aid? When did Glen tell you this? You don't know Glen that well. He must have been joking. I just talked to him today, and he didn't say a thing about Sawyer or a warrant.' Ann reached over and turned the light back on.

'Look, I'm just repeating what I heard. He believes Sawyer shot you so you wouldn't execute the search terms. You know, Ann, Hopkins might be right. Maybe Sawyer had a big stash in his house and panicked when he realized you could just walk in and bust him. Abrams said your car . . .'

Reed kept on talking, but Ann wasn't listening. Her hand holding the phone was trembling, her heart racing in her chest. She'd accepted this terrible event thinking it was a random act. Now Reed was telling her it was premeditated.

Reed said, 'Did you hear me?'

She had the phone clasped with both hands now. 'But you said it was a drive-by. Even Noah said it was.'

'That was what we originally thought. Like I was saying, Abrams told me today that your Jeep was disabled. The ignition wires were cut, Ann. That doesn't mesh with a random act like a drive-by.'

'Then I was set up. Ambushed. That means they wanted me, Tommy. They weren't just shooting for the hell of it. They were shooting at me.'

The detective paused, trying to gauge her mood. 'Listen, Ann, why don't we discuss this another time? I don't want to upset you.'

'No,' Ann yelled in the phone. Then she lowered her voice, remembering David. 'Tell me everything you know, Tommy. I have to know.'

'Okay,' he said, sighing. 'Glen Hopkins believes Sawyer decided to shoot you the minute the judge issued the order. If you don't believe me, ask him.'

Ann was staring out over the room, reliving the shooting. Every single second was frozen in her mind. As hard as she tried to forget it, suppress it, she knew it would always be there. One word, anything, and the whole night reappeared in blazing color.

'Ann,' Reed said, 'did you and Hopkins go somewhere after Sawyer's hearing and then come back to the courthouse for some reason?'

'No,' she said, puzzled. 'We've already gone over how this went down. Didn't you read the statement I gave Abrams?' When the detective didn't respond, Ann recapitulated the events for him. 'Okay, the hearing lasted maybe thirty minutes. It was supposed to start at four, but Sawyer was late, so that means it must have been around four-thirty when I left the courtroom with Glen.' She paused, not wanting to tell him what had transpired in the stairwell. 'Then I went back and dictated my report. Everyone had left for the day by the time I finished, so I'm guessing it was after five by then. I killed some time in the parking lot trying to decide what to do about the car and then started walking. I assumed Glen had already left, or I would have asked him to drive me home. That's when I was shot. Glen must have spotted me on the sidewalk with Sawyer on his way out of the complex. He told me he stayed late to work up his notes on a case.'

Reed started to tell Ann the truth, that the hospital had conducted a rape exam and established that she had engaged in sexual intercourse on the day of the crime. Then he stopped himself, knowing it would only embarrass her. He had to assume that she had met Glen for lunch that day, and they had snuck in a little afternoon delight. She'd evidently been so heavily drugged the night in the recovery room that she didn't recall him mentioning their original belief that she'd been raped. Once Ann had denied it, there'd been no reason to bring it up again.

'Why did you ask if I left the courthouse?' Ann asked, not certain where he was going with this line of thought.

'Forget it,' Reed said quickly, his tone indicating that he was sorry he'd brought the subject up.

Ann said goodbye, slowly replacing the receiver. She didn't agree with Glen's suspicions about Jimmy Sawyer, but that didn't trouble her. What had her stomach in knots was the fact that the person who had shot her had intended to shoot her, not just anyone, but her. Would whoever it was keep trying until he succeeded?

Feeling a chill, Ann pulled the covers up to her chin and stared up at the ceiling.

From out of the silence erupted David's pleading voice.

'Come back, Dad,' he cried. 'Don't go away. Don't leave me.'

Grabbing her robe off the foot of the bed, Ann raced down the hall to her son's room. 'Wake up,' she said, shaking him gently by the shoulders. 'You're having a nightmare, honey.'

David bolted upright in the bed. His pajamas were soaked in perspiration, and his dark hair was dripping wet. 'He was here, Mom,' he said, his eyes searching the shadows around the room. 'He was standing over my bed. I saw him. I really did.'

Ann sat on the edge of the bed and pulled her son into her arms. She could feel the dampness beneath her and smell the odor of urine. God, she thought, consumed by anguish, why did her child have to suffer this way? 'It's okay, honey,' she said, stroking a thick clump of wet hair out of his eyes. 'You had another bad dream.'

'No,' he insisted, clawing at the edge of his mother's robe. 'Dad was here, really here. He said he was coming back. He said I had to stop you from marrying Glen.'

'Oh, baby,' Ann said, her heart in pieces. 'I'm not marrying anyone, okay? Come on now, let's get you out of these wet clothes, and I'll put some dry sheets on the bed.'

Ann was reaching over to turn on the light when she heard her son quietly sobbing. Instead of putting him through the embarrassment of changing his sheets, she went to the bathroom and got a large towel, making him move so she could put it over the wet spot. Most of the time he got up and changed the sheets himself, placing the soiled ones in the washing machine the next morning.

Climbing into bed with him, Ann pressed his head to her chest. 'I'm going to stay right here, honey,' she whispered, her voice soft and comforting. 'Shut your eyes and think of happy things.'

'Dad's going to think I'm a baby,' the boy sobbed, his entire body shaking. 'He's going to know I still pee in my bed. I have to stop before he comes back, Mom. I just have to.'

Ann held her son, stroking his back gently until the crying stopped and his breathing slowed. After some time the dampness soaked through the bath towel, and she felt as if she were sleeping on a sheet of ice. Pulling the blankets over them, Ann finally closed her eyes and let her exhausted body find sleep.

Chapter 4

Claudette Landers was on a tear, her booming voice bouncing off the walls when Ann walked into the office. 'Get on outta here,' Claudette was yelling at someone. 'I don't want to hear any more pansy-ass complaints.'

Ann grabbed a cup of coffee from the small kitchenette, waited until she saw the offending probation officer scurry off from Claudette's office like a field mouse, and then stepped inside. They called their work spaces offices, but they were constructed out of fabric – upholstered partitions in one enormous room. As a supervisor, Claudette at least had a partitioned area of her own. Ann had to share hers with another probation officer. Phone conversations, business or personal, filtered from one cubicle to another. There was no such thing as privacy.

As the supervisor over adult investigations, Claudette assigned cases to investigators as they came in from the courts, conferred with them on cases – basically approving their assessments and recommendations – and acted as the intermediary between the courts, the district attorney's office, the public defender's office, and other related agencies.

'Well, I'm back,' Ann said. 'Got a minute?'

Claudette smiled. 'Man, am I glad to see your pretty face.

I'm not foaming at the mouth yet, but soon . . . soon. Sit down. How you feeling? You sure you should be back here already? Did the doctors give you clearance to return to work?'

Ann lowered herself into the chair; she didn't lean back, for her shoulder was still too painful. 'I'm weak . . . still sore, you know?' The two women knew each other well enough that Ann didn't have to explain. Yes, she was still in pain, her eyes said. Yes, she was scared. Yes, she had no choice but to return to work.

The contact broken, Ann quickly changed the subject. 'So, what's the problem with Rogers?'

Claudette was a good friend, a fine woman, and one tough cookie. There would be no more talk of Ann's injury, no more gratuitous expressions of concern. At thirty-five, Claudette Landers was a large woman, most of her weight carried in the lower half of her body. Of African-American descent, she was intelligent and articulate, thoroughly respected throughout the county as an outstanding supervisor.

'Little shit is such a bitcher,' Claudette said. 'Every time I assign Rogers a case with more than one count, he cries like a damn baby. Doesn't even know what a bingo sheet is yet and refuses to learn. You hear me, Rogers?' she yelled over the partition, her voice as big as Texas. 'Your mommy should have whipped you when you was a kid, stopped all this complaining shit. Look at Ann here, already back on the job. Now, that's the kind of people we need around here, not a bunch of sniveling crybabies.'

'My mom did whip me,' Rogers yelled back, undaunted and long suffering under Claudette's abuse. 'That's what's wrong with me. Now I've got you for a boss. I'm going to apply for a mental disability if you don't leave me alone, Claudette. Maybe even sexual harassment might work. Then every month when they pay me, they'll deduct it from your check.'

'I wouldn't fuck your skinny white ass if you was the last man on earth,' Claudette quickly retorted.

Chuckles and snide comments from other probation officers rang out and then were replaced with a chorus of voices: 'Welcome back, Ann.'

'Thanks, guys. Glad to be back.' The probation officers in the unit had been very supportive, coming to see her in the hospital, offering to help with David, bringing food to the house.

'I want to take Jimmy Sawyer back to court and get his probation switched,' she said to Claudette once the unit was quiet again. 'What do you think? Do you think Hillstorm will go for it? I more or less promised Sawyer I'd do it.'

'Why in the hell would you do that?' Claudette barked, her dark eyes flashing. 'The D.A.'s office is about to charge him with the shooting and toss him in jail.'

'He saved my life, Claudette,' Ann said. She couldn't believe Glen was really going after Sawyer, with no solid evidence to back him up. Not only that, it was completely unlike him to jump in feet first. He liked cases that led to certain convictions. 'You know Glen Hopkins and I have been dating, Claudette, and he's livid over what happened to me. He must think the sooner he files, the sooner I'll be out of danger. There are no other suspects or leads, so he's going after Sawyer.'

'Maybe the man is right,' Claudette said.

Ann shook her head. 'I'm certain it wasn't him. How many people shoot you and then stop to give you first aid? If he wanted to hurt me, why didn't he just let me bleed to death?'

'Humph,' Claudette said, shifting her ample hips from side to side in the small chair and then lunging forward over the desk. 'No free rides. You know how I feel about that. Besides, Hillstorm will just think you don't want to supervise him. It'll never fly.'

Although Ann respected this woman, she also felt Claudette was being unnecessarily callous. If her supervisor had been the

57

person bleeding on the sidewalk, she would know how Ann felt about Jimmy Sawyer. But Claudette was the boss, and Ann didn't have the strength right now to go up against her. 'You're the supervisor,' Ann said, standing.

Time to take the plunge, she thought, see how bad the damage was in her office. 'Shit,' Ann screamed once she walked into her cubicle. Half the people in the unit, including Claudette, rushed into her office, looks of terror on their faces. Ann glanced over her shoulder at them. 'Sorry. No one's shooting at me but the records clerk.' Ann kicked a big cardboard box out of her way so she had a small path to walk to her desk. 'Look at this place. I knew it would be bad. I never thought it would be this bad.'

Everywhere Ann looked were case files and cardboard boxes. Her ten years with the agency, coupled with her considerable expertise, had left her in the unenviable position of handling only the most complex and serious cases in the system. This meant mountains and mountains of paper: trial transcripts, police reports, preliminary hearing transcripts, criminal histories from other states and agencies, autopsy reports, forensic reports. All of these documents Ann had to read and study. They were tossed and stacked everywhere. On her desk, rising four feet high from the floor, set haphazardly in a plastic basket on top of the metal file cabinet, any second ready to spill over onto the floor.

Ann turned around and saw Claudette still standing there, a concerned look on her face.

'I tried my best, Ann. I really did. I took work home. I assigned it to other people. Just do your best. That's all you can do.' She sighed in weariness.

They were in a sad state at the agency. The cases just kept coming and coming, all of them with deadlines: filing dates, dates for interviews, dates to appear in court, review dates, secondary offense dates. Having more work than they could handle was bad enough, but when everything had a deadline, the pressure escalated to an almost intolerable level.

Once her supervisor had gone off, Ann collapsed in her seat. Her desk was situated flush against a floor-to-ceiling window which allowed her to look out over the parking lot for the complex. Her eyes went immediately to the shrubs on the outer border of the lot, searching for the opening leading to Victoria Boulevard. Then she found it – the exact spot in the bushes where she had stepped through only seconds before she was shot. Earlier this morning, she had made a point to park on the opposite side of the building, not wanting to come anywhere near it.

Grabbing the Delvecchio file, Ann opened it, thinking she could distract herself and forget what she could see out the window. Five or ten minutes passed, but Ann wasn't looking down at the file. She was thinking about that spot, about how much she didn't want to see it ever again. People fought for these desks by the windows, but right now Ann would have preferred to work in a closet.

Without thinking, she stood and walked around her desk, placing her palms flat against the glass. When she saw her hands there, Ann knew why she had done it. She wanted to feel the glass, test the thickness. What she wanted was to assure herself that there was something between her and the spot in the shrubbery.

The next moment questions leaped into her mind against her will. They pounded inside her head like a migraine headache, pressing against her forehead, pushing in at the tender spots at her temples – incessant marching questions – questions she knew she would be asking forever, just as she had with Hank. 'Exactly like Hank,' she mumbled, shaking her head from side to side, wanting to put a stop to it right this very minute.

Where had he been standing when he fired? Why had he

fired at all? What had she done to this person? Who hated her enough to shoot her in the back and leave her bleeding on the sidewalk? On and on the dreaded questions marched, taking on a life of their own.

At last Ann pulled herself from the window and sank again into her chair, looking around at the mountains of paperwork and files, the questions a secondary, whispery voice now. 'Where did that file go I just had in my hand?' she said, talking aloud in an attempt to override the voices.

Where was Hank's body buried? erupted another voice. What had happened that night on that lonely stretch of road? Who had turned her life upside down?

That was the problem when you started asking questions and looking for answers that were not there, Ann thought. One set of questions only led to another.

Around ten o'clock, Ann ran into Perry Rogers on her way back from the coffee room. 'Ann,' he said, a thick file in his hands and a look of frustration on his face, 'I know you just got back and all, but I can't figure this bingo sheet out. This is worse than figuring out my income tax return.'

Ann chuckled. A bingo sheet was what they called the form they used to compute prison terms, and it reminded a lot of people of an income tax form. The state of California had enacted a determinate sentencing law many years back, with specified terms for each crime. 'Sure,' she told him, 'come into my office and we'll go over it right now.'

Perry Rogers was a wisp of a man in his late twenties, so thin and emaciated that he had to sit on a pillow when he was at his desk. Ann had never seen him so much as touch food, and the rumor was that he suffered from an eating disorder. But he was a likable guy, and Ann was always willing to lend a hand to less experienced officers.

'Okay, Perry,' she said once he'd pulled a chair up next to

her desk. 'Give me your bingo sheet and the court order, setting forth the convicted counts, along with your recommendation.'

Rogers handed Ann the entire file and waited while she pored over the particulars. One of the reasons he was encountering so many difficulties, Ann noted, was that the case he was handling involved multiple counts, all sex crimes. Sentencing guidelines for sex offenses had become more complex than those for any other crime. Every year a new law was enacted affecting sentencing. As everyone knew, Ann was the expert at this particular task. She could compute a fifty-count case in her head in a matter of minutes, whereas Rogers and most of the others had difficulty doing it at all.

'Here's where you went wrong,' she told him, pointing at the sheet as she talked, 'this count must be served consecutively, not concurrently, and you put the enhancement for the prior burglary offense in the wrong spot.'

Rogers wasn't following what Ann was saying. 'Why can't the damn judge just figure this out for himself? They make a lot more money than we do.'

This was the sentiment of the majority of probation officers assigned to court services, and Ann had heard this so often she shrugged it off. 'Why don't you see what you come up with now, Perry?' she said, handing him the sheet with her corrections and waiting while he tried to complete it.

Through the years the job had become increasingly more technical. Up until six months ago Perry Rogers had been assigned to field services. In that position he only supervised offenders and filed reports when they violated their probation. Field officers were a different breed from court investigators. Many were negligent in managing their caseloads, came to work in jeans and T-shirts, and seldom had to appear in court on their cases. Now that Perry had transferred to court services, however, his job centered on writing and investigating presentence reports for the court.

'Why did you aggravate this count?' Ann said, looking over his shoulder at the form.

'Because he used a gun,' the man responded.

'But you've already added a two-year enhancement for the use of the firearm. Therefore you can't use it to ask for a higher term. Don't you see?' Ann said. 'That's like double jeopardy. He can't be punished for the same crime twice.'

'Well,' Rogers said, clearly confused, 'his prior record is an aggravating factor, and I've enhanced his term for it. Isn't that the same thing?'

'No, it's not,' Ann said, beginning to get as frustrated as Perry. She knew it was complex, and she felt sorry for the man, but he had to understand the law in order to do his job. 'This enhancement is for one particular prior, this burglary. You've aggravated the crime based on his criminal record as a whole. See the difference?'

Ann glanced at the stack of files on her desk and back to her coworker. She didn't have the time to sit here all day trying to explain it to him. Grabbing the sheet out of his hands and inserting the correct terms, Ann computed it herself and handed it back. 'There you go, Perry,' she said. 'But one of these days you're going to have to take the time to learn it yourself.'

After Rogers had returned to his own cubicle next to Ann's, he started talking again from the other side of the partition. 'It was right over there, wasn't it? You know, where you were shot?'

Without answering, Ann picked up her work and quietly left her cubicle, deciding to find an empty desk she could use temporarily, one that didn't have a window overlooking the parking lot.

At twelve-thirty, Ann heard her name being paged on the loudspeaker system. Collecting her papers and files from the long table in the conference room where she'd been working, she rushed back to her desk to take the phone call.

'Hi,' Jimmy Sawyer said. 'I wanted to see how you're feeling.'

'Oh, Jimmy,' Ann said, recognizing his nasal voice. 'It's nice of you to call. To tell you the truth, I was going to call you this afternoon.' Not wanting to give him the bad news over the phone, Ann suggested he come to the office so they could talk. Then she thought better of it. 'Tell you what,' she said. 'I owe you one. I'll buy you lunch. Why don't you meet me at Marie Callender's?' No matter what anyone said, Ann was grateful that he had stopped to help her. Many people didn't want to get involved, and Ann knew she could have bled to death on that sidewalk.

'Marie Callender's is too far from my house,' Sawyer said. 'Let's meet at the Hilton.'

Ann got to the hotel restaurant, took a table, and was looking over the menu when Sawyer walked in. His long hair was slicked back in a ponytail, and he was wearing Levi's and a white shirt with an embroidered pocket. 'I can't really stay,' he said, not sitting down. 'I have to go. I'm late.'

'You mean you don't want to have lunch?' Ann asked, surprised. 'I wanted to do something for you. I mean, I know it's not much, but . . .'

Sawyer was having difficulty maintaining eye contact, she noticed. He would look at her and then flit away. 'I thought you said you were going to take me back to court, tell them what I did. You know, get my probation switched so I don't have to report every month.'

'Why don't you sit down, Jimmy?' Ann said, studying his face, her assessment of him shifting by the second.

'I can't. I have to go. I have to study.'

'Are you in school?' she asked, confused. She really recalled very little about his case. It seemed like everything that had occurred right before the shooting had simply vanished from her mind.

'No,' he said. 'But I will be by next semester. I have to get my SAT scores up.' He stopped abruptly and rubbed his hands on his jeans. 'I'm going to one of those cram courses. If I don't get my scores up, I'll have to go to a stupid junior college.'

A stupid junior college, Ann thought, compressing her lips in distaste. She knew kids who would love to go to any college. 'That's not so bad. A lot of people do the first two years at a junior college and then transfer to a university. My husband did that, and he later graduated from UCLA with honors.' Mentioning Hank in Sawyer's presence gave Ann a strange sensation. Suddenly the night of the shooting reappeared in her mind. Why had she thought Hank was present that night? Ann knew she'd been delusional, but still it had weighed on her mind. If anyone could dispel this, Ann thought, it should be Sawyer. He had been there. 'Jimmy, can you describe the people who stopped the night I was shot?'

'Some old couple. I don't know. I don't really remember.'

'Detective Abrams told me there were a lot of people that stopped. Did you see a man about my age, crew cut, small eyes, tall, stocky build? Someone that looked like a drill instructor, maybe?'

'Look,' Sawyer said, getting annoyed, 'I was trying to help you. I don't remember.' His anger mounted as he added, 'The cops treated me like I was a suspect or something. Let me tell you,' he said, 'if I had to do it again, I don't know if I would stop.'

Ann swallowed, feeling a pang of guilt. If she didn't talk Glen out of filing charges against him, this poor kid would really be bitter. He'd never help another person the rest of his life.

'That district attorney was there,' Sawyer interjected, as if he could read Ann's mind. 'You know, Glen Hopkins.'

'I didn't mean him,' Ann said.

Sawyer continued, 'Don't they teach those guys first aid? I mean, he didn't seem to have a clue about what to do. All he did was just stand there and look at you like a lame dick. My dad's a doctor, so . . .'

So, Ann thought, Glen wasn't quite as cool in a crisis as he was in a courtroom. Then she thought of an ulterior reason he might be so determined to file against Sawyer. He was her lover and he'd panicked. Sawyer had shown him up.

'Why are you asking me all these questions?' Sawyer said, getting more restless by the second. 'I thought you asked me here to tell me something good, not interrogate me like another cop.'

'I'm sorry,' Ann said, embarrassed. 'I really am grateful for what you did, Jimmy. Why don't you sit down a minute? It's a little difficult to carry on a conversation this way.'

Sawyer was standing next to a large artificial palm tree. He looked behind him nervously and then back at Ann. 'I have to go. I don't want to sit down.'

'Whatever,' Ann said, frustrated by the way he was acting. The waitress had arrived, ready to take their order. 'Are you sure you don't want something? Maybe a soft drink or some ice cream?'

When Sawyer didn't answer, Ann shrugged and started ordering. All the while, though, she watched him out of the corner of her eye. He was staring at a plastic leaf on the palm tree as though it contained the mysteries of the universe. As soon as the waitress left, Ann said his name several times, and he didn't respond. Suddenly the picture came clear. He was high on drugs. Exactly what, she didn't know, but she knew now why he wouldn't eat, why he couldn't sit still, why his palms were sweaty.

Ann always trusted her instincts, and they told her Sawyer was nothing more than just another screwed-up kid on drugs.

He might have stayed straight for his day in court, but Jimmy Sawyer was a user. Peering up at him, she tried to see if his pupils were dilated. 'What are you on, Jimmy?'

'What?' he said, giggling as if she had just said something outrageously funny.

'Are you on drugs right now?' Ann's guess was LSD or speed.

'No way, man. I have to go.' He turned and quickly walked away.

'Hey,' Ann yelled, shooting to her feet. 'Get back here.' He was her probationer. She couldn't let him get away with this no matter what he'd done for her. The last time she'd tried to cut a probationer some slack, the man had taken five hits of LSD and then later stabbed his wife, saying she was a demon from hell. The girl had been only twenty-three years old, and the couple had three tiny babies. Ann didn't take chances anymore. Her responsibilities to both the court and the community were too grave. But Sawyer was already out the door, and Ann was too weak to chase him down.

'What a world,' she said, sitting back down in her seat. She would have to test Sawyer for narcotics. The way it looked, the test would come back dirty and Ann would end up responsible for sending the man who'd saved her life to jail.

Chapter 5

Ann pulled out of the government center parking lot in a white county car, proceeding on a case that was uppermost in her mind. She would contact one of the victims in the Delvecchio rape, the one who had been Glen's teacher. Prior to the brutal attack, Estelle Summer had led an independent and active existence, even though she was in her mid-seventies. According to her children and neighbors, she'd had her own comfortable home, her friends, and her club work. And she'd been a neat, well-groomed woman, pretty for her age. That is, until she met up with Randy Delvecchio.

The rapist had been waiting inside her bedroom closet. Once the woman had walked into the room, he'd sprung out and placed a knife at her throat. Wearing a stocking mask, the attacker forced her onto the floor, frightening the old woman so much that she had defecated in her pants. Randy had been a real sweetheart, Ann thought grimly, even going so far as to get a washrag and clean her up. Once he had done so, he had proceeded to beat her, rape her, and force her to orally copulate him. Then while Estelle lay on the floor, beaten and in shock, Randy had gone to her refrigerator and made himself a ham and cheese sandwich. For dessert, he had flipped the old woman over and sodomized her.

Estelle Summer would never live independently again. The woman had been so terrorized by the assault that she suffered from severe insomnia. Months after the attack, she lay awake night after night, shaking in her bed with fear. She had proceeded to build a fortress around her house, expending all her meager savings to install sophisticated alarms, build fences, hire security officers to stand by her door all night. When that didn't calm her fears, Estelle had boarded up all the doors and windows and refused to leave the house. Her weight had plummeted to sixty-eight pounds. She became incontinent and was forced to wear diapers. Finally her children had placed her in a nursing home.

After thirty years in the public school system, a respected and dedicated teacher, Estelle Summer was unable to enjoy her retirement, her few remaining years on this earth. No wonder Glen was so intent on punishing this man to the full extent of the law.

Ann parked in front of the nursing home, a long brick building set far back from the road, and got out and headed to the entrance. Lovely multicolored pansies were planted along the walkway leading to the front door, but through the open windows Ann could see the hospital beds and wheelchairs.

'I'm here to see Estelle Summer,' she told the nurse in the lobby. An attractive woman in her thirties, the woman had fluffy blond hair, fair skin, and blue eyes.

'Oh,' the woman said, her face blanching, 'are you a relative?'

'No,' Ann said, removing her county identification and flashing it. 'I'm a deputy probation officer. I need to talk to her about a case.'

The woman looked at the identification card and then slowly raised her eyes to Ann's face. 'Ms Summer passed away three hours ago.'

Ann lurched back from the desk, as if pushed by some invisible force. She knew it was fear, but she didn't know why.

She had never even met Estelle Summer. Why was she so stunned by this woman's death? It had to be the shooting, she told herself. She knew now what it felt like to be terrified, helpless, desperate. Estelle had counted on the police to find her attacker and bring him to justice, but before they did, it was too late. Would this happen to Ann? Would they never find the person who had shot her? Would the fear grow and grow until it consumed her every thought?

'Did Ms Summer have a heart attack?' Ann asked, unable to walk away.

The nurse glanced over her shoulder and then back at Ann, standing and leaning forward over the counter. 'No,' she said. 'It wasn't her heart.' The nurse dropped her eyes and started mindlessly rearranging the various items on her desk. Ann could see that her hands were trembling. 'She quit eating,' the nurse said. 'We tried to tube-feed her and she just pulled the tubes out.' The woman looked up. 'You know what she said to me right before she died?'

Ann didn't answer.

A metal chart in her hands, the nurse slammed it down on the desk. 'She said you people were going to let that animal that raped her off, that the jury was going to find him not guilty. That's why she wanted to die. She said she didn't want to be alive when the verdict came in.'

'But that's not true,' Ann protested. 'The trial –'

The nurse flipped her wrist at Ann, dropping back in her seat. 'Trials,' she said, a disgusted look on her face. 'I know all about the big promises you people make. I was raped too. One night two years ago when I was working at County General, I was walking to my car and this guy jumps me and drags me into the bushes. I did everything the cops said: I pressed charges, I went to court.' She stopped and inhaled, almost too shaken to continue. 'He was found not guilty and released. Know how that made me feel?'

Ann slowly shook her head. 'I'm sorry. I'm sure it made you feel horrible.'

'Horrible, huh?' the woman said, her voice loud and abrasive. 'That's not the word I'd use.'

A frail elderly woman suddenly appeared at the counter, a look of confusion on her face. 'I need a size eight, young lady,' she said. 'I want to exchange this dress.' Placing a limp bath towel on the counter, she looked around for a sales clerk to assist her.

'Go on back to your room, Mabel,' the nurse said, handing her back the towel. 'It's almost time for dinner.'

Once the old woman had tottered away, the towel dangling from her hands, the nurse returned to their conversation. 'The doctors wanted to keep that poor woman alive, put her on life support and all. Well, I knew she was already dead from the day she came in here. Estelle died when that guy raped her. He stole her will to live, you know, ripped it right out of her.'

'If you ever want anyone to talk to,' Ann said, handing the woman her business card before leaving, 'I'm a good listener.'

'Yeah,' the nurse said. 'A lot of people listen, but listening isn't going to get it. Tell that to your bosses, huh? Do that for me.'

Emotionally drained, Ann made her way out of the nursing home. No, she told herself on the walk back to the car, squinting in the bright afternoon sun, she would not live the rest of her life in terror. And she would not let this woman's death go unpunished. By his actions Randy Delvecchio had killed Estelle Summer. The nurse was right. He had stolen her will to live.

As she got in her car and cranked the engine, Ann's mind was clocking at breakneck speed. Glen couldn't possibly know yet that Estelle had died. She was a valuable witness in his case against Delvecchio, and her death could conceivably cause them to lose the rape conviction related to her assault.

According to what Glen had told her, they didn't have enough evidence to try Delvecchio on the outstanding homicides. And if he lost even one of the rape counts, he would be devastated.

Turning onto the main thoroughfare, Ann saw a station wagon with the words 'Hughes Funeral Home' on the side enter the alley behind the convalescent home. They were coming to take Estelle Summer away. Ann's hands locked on the steering wheel and her foot depressed the gas pedal, the needle on the speedometer surging as she raced down the street.

Estelle was no longer able to confront her attacker, but Ann certainly could. She glanced at her watch and saw that it was after four o'clock. By the time she got back, Randy Delvecchio should have been returned to his cell.

At the courthouse, Ann headed straight to the jail, eager for the confrontation ahead of her.

Once she had cleared security and had a visitor's badge pinned to her blouse, the jailer led her to a bank of glassed-in booths. 'I told them at the front counter I wanted a face-to-face,' Ann said. 'Didn't they tell you?'

'I wouldn't advise it,' the jailer said, compressing his lips. 'We've had some problems with this inmate.'

'What kind of problems?'

'He jumped one of the other inmates. Doc thinks he's a psycho.'

'Of course he's a psycho,' Ann snapped. 'He's a fucking maniac who likes to rape old women. Go get him, all right? He's just my type.'

'Hey, suit yourself,' the jailer said, shuffling off to get the prisoner moved to a secured interview room, the huge ring of keys on his belt rattling and jangling as he walked down the tile corridor. While he was gone, Ann composed herself. She was going to be sweet as pie to this monster – and then nail him. A few minutes later, the jailer returned and escorted Ann to the door, unlocking it and then locking it again once she was inside.

Ann carried no notebook, pen, or tape recorder. That was how she worked. Prisoners didn't say much when a person wrote down or recorded everything they said. Ann had an excellent memory. That would suffice.

'Hi, Randy,' she said brightly, her voice a few octaves higher than usual. 'Remember me? I talked to you on your bail review. Ann Carlisle with the probation department. How you doing in here? Pretty tough one, isn't it?'

The young man was actually very handsome, almost pretty in a way. His enormous dark eyes were fringed with thick lashes, and his hair was neatly trimmed in a popular style, sort of a boxy, squared-off look. Wearing a jail-issued jumpsuit, he was slouched low in the chair.

'I don't remember you,' he said. 'But I knows I didn't get bail.'

Ann carefully took a seat, watching his eyes. It was dangerous to interview violent offenders alone like this, locked inside a small room with them. Most of the other probation officers opted for the alternative: the prisoner safely behind bulletproof glass. But like tape recorders and notes, glass partitions tended to keep people from opening up. Ann took her chances. If she hit a buzzer, she could attract a jailer's attention – that is, if she could manage to get to the buzzer.

'Randy,' she told him, 'there was nothing I could do for you on the bail review. See, you were already on probation for burglary when these new crimes occurred. That shows the judge that you're not a good risk for bail. That's also why I'm here, to prepare a violation of probation report on the burglary case.'

'They gonna give me probation again?' he said, an expectant look on his face.

'That depends on what the jury says on the rapes, Randy.'
Ann arched her eyebrows, unable to keep herself from striking at least one blow. 'Of course, if they do find you guilty, you'll be going to prison for a very long time. You won't be eligible for probation no matter what I tell them.'

He crossed his arms over his chest, guarded now. 'If I ain't gonna get probation again, why'd they send you?'

'Good question,' Ann said, wondering how many times she'd explained this to inmates facing a prison term. 'Even though I'm a probation officer and you may not be eligible for probation on these rapes, the law states that in all felony convictions, an investigating probation officer must prepare a report. In legal terminology, they call this a mandated report, meaning something that has to be done by law. It's just something probation officers do, another part of our job. Next week you go back for sentencing for the violation of probation. I'm the one who will write a report and make a recommendation to the judge. Then if you're convicted on the rapes, I'll be recommending how much time you should actually serve in prison for those crimes.'

Delvecchio was suspicious. 'Why would you tell them how much time I should do in the joint? Don't the judge do that?'

'He does, but he uses our report to make his decision. Maybe they enacted this law because they thought probation officers understood people like you, people who commit crimes. Does that make sense to you?'

'How do I fucking know?'

Ann leaned forward over the table. 'See, the judge doesn't have time to come and talk to you like this, so I'm doing it for him. Basically, this is your chance to tell your side of the story, Randy, tell the court what your life has been like up until this happened. Things like that. The only thing I don't want you to talk about today is anything pertaining to the ongoing trial. We can't do that just yet, see. Not until the verdict is in.'

'Whose side you on?' Delvecchio said, peering up menacingly.

'Yours, of course,' Ann lied. A few lies with people like Delvecchio didn't cause her to lose any sleep. She had reconciled herself to the fact that they might never find Hank's killer, but there were plenty of men like Delvecchio. As she saw it, someone had to pay.

Seeing the dark look in Delvecchio's eyes, Ann tried to empty all negative thoughts from her mind. She gave Randy another warm, friendly smile. Sure, Randy, she said to herself, I'm your best buddy. 'First, I'd like to start by asking you some routine questions. Is that okay, Randy?'

He nodded. His head slumped toward his chest, his eyes even more hooded and wary. Pretty blond ladies didn't talk to him with sugar-coated voices like this one. He wasn't a fool.

Ann got him off and running, though, by distracting him with a barrage of insignificant questions: questions about his various jobs, his friends, his hobbies. After fifteen minutes of this, she told him a joke, something to get him to laugh. After another interval she dropped in a funny story. Several times she reached out and lightly touched his hand. Each time she was rewarded with a sinister smile, but it was a smile. After an hour of softening him up, she sensed she was about to make a breakthrough. Just a few steps more, Ann told herself, and the door to Rancho Delvecchio would be standing wide open.

'Boy, Randy, I'm thirsty. How about you? Want a cold drink?'

Delvecchio cackled. 'Yeah, get me a Bud.'

Ann tossed her head back and laughed with him, as if he had said something hilarious. Pleased with himself, Delvecchio laughed even harder, slapping his thighs. 'Being a probation officer has its merits,' Ann told him, smiling, then walked over and hit the buzzer. When the guard unlocked the door and looked inside, Ann announced, 'We need a couple cold drinks in here.' She glanced over at Delvecchio. 'Want a Coke or a 7UP?'

Swiping at his mouth with the back of his hand, Delvecchio said, 'Coke, man.'

The guard sneered, but he didn't protest. 'And make sure there's some ice in there,' Ann added. 'It's ninety degrees in this room.'

As soon as the guard returned with their sodas, Ann took a few sips of hers and quickly glanced at her watch. How long had it taken this time? Over an hour. Longer than normal, but Delvecchio was a tough case.

'How old are you?' he asked.

'Guess,' Ann said playfully.

'I don't know. Maybe thirty or something.'

'Nope,' Ann lied, 'I'm forty-three. I look pretty good, don't I?'

'Shit, really? You really forty-three? I think my mom's only forty-three.'

'Sure am, Randy,' she said, her tone serious. 'Now, let's go back to what we were talking about, this business with your mother, since you mentioned it again. You said you're close to your mother, but not that close to your father. My mother died when I was young, Randy, so I didn't get a chance to be close to her. Sad, huh?' Ann said, looking down. A little sympathy right now could go a long way, get her even closer to that door.

'Oh, yeah?' Delvecchio responded, unfazed by Ann's display of emotion, suddenly agitated over something else.

There it was, Ann thought, snapping to attention. Right before her eyes his entire personality was changing. It was like a mask sliding off his face, revealing another person inside. Ann had purposely increased her age, assuming he had a thing for older women. Was this what had set him off, or the questions about his mother? She felt the fine hairs on her arms stand up, but she kept a smile plastered on her face.

Randy leaned down low over the table, his arms folded, his head tilted to one side. 'You're really pretty, you know?' he said, his eyes locked on hers. 'Got a husband?'

'No,' Ann answered under his hot stare. She moved her neck slightly to release the tension, praying he didn't spot the fear. His eyes, she kept thinking. It was all in the eyes. Right behind those dark eyes with the long lashes, rage was just simmering. 'I live alone. Just me and my dog. Do you like dogs, Randy?'

'Sure,' he said, thrown off balance by this change in direction, 'everybody likes dogs.'

Ann beamed innocently. 'I have a German shepherd. You know, a big dog. They say you can tell a person's personality by the kind of dogs they like.' Placing her hands on the table, Ann said, 'Let's play a game just for fun. If you had a dog, what kind of dog would it be?'

Delvecchio became wary all over again. 'Is this some kind of test or something? I don't like tests.'

'No,' Ann said quickly. 'We've been at this for quite a while now, Randy. I thought we'd take a little break. You know, like recess at school.'

'I didn't get to go to school much,' he said, his gaze drifting toward a far corner of the room.

'Oh, no,' Ann said. 'You mean you dropped out?'

'No,' he said, a glint of moisture in his eyes. 'I didn't have no shoes, see, and they wouldn't let me go to school with no shoes.'

'I'm sorry,' Ann said, truly compassionate, watching as he blinked back the tears. Sometimes even with the worst offender, she caught a glimpse of the child he had once been and was saddened. Would Delvecchio be here today, she wondered, if someone had provided him with a pair of shoes? 'Look,' she told him, 'let's play our game. Forget about the past right now. If you had a dog, Randy, what kind of dog would it be?'

Delvecchio narrowed his eyes, but a moment later he relaxed once more. 'I know it wouldn't be one of those little mutts with the bows in their hair. They bite. Those dogs are fucking vicious, man.' He turned his head to the side, and with his other hand he cracked his neck.

'Oh, really?' Ann said, her expression frozen in place, only her eyes expanding. She was getting close, very close. 'A dog bit me one time. Want me to show you?'

'Yeah,' he said, curious, getting into it.

Ann shoved the chair back a few feet from the table and pulled her skirt up above her knees. 'See, right there,' she said, pointing at a nonexistent mark on her thigh. 'A little toy poodle sank his teeth in me. Can you see the scar? Boy, I almost killed him. I kicked the shit out of that damn dog.' Before he could get a good look at what Ann was pointing at, she quickly repositioned her legs under the table and pulled her skirt back down. Delvecchio had been trying to see something, but not what Ann was showing him. Scars were evidently not as interesting as her long legs and the place between them.

Allowed this intimacy, Randy grew animated in a childish way, smiling, moving his shoulders around. He rolled up the sleeves on his jumpsuit and purposely flexed his biceps, showing off for her. He was aroused, Ann could tell. Sitting right there a few feet away from her, he was probably thinking how much fun it would be to place his big hands around her neck and strangle her. A little cheesecake might get him going, but Ann knew it wasn't sex that excited him. Randy Delvecchio was a rapist and a murderer. What turned him on, excited him past the point of no return, was cruelty and intimidation. For Randy Delvecchio, there was no such thing as sex.

'A fucking poodle bit me too,' Delvecchio volunteered, again chuckling and making eyes at Ann. 'Right here by my ankle.' While Ann leaned over to look, he pulled up the baggy pants of his jumpsuit and exposed his muscular calf. 'Hurt like a bitch. I hate those stupid dogs.'

'Was it a white poodle or a black one? I've heard the white ones are the meanest. The one that got me was a white one.'

'Yeah, you're right,' Delvecchio said, smiling so broadly that his crooked teeth were fully exposed. 'They're the meanest. It was a white one, and I think it had a red bow in its hair. Maybe the same dog that bit you bit me.'

Ann leaned back and smiled at Randy Delvecchio, her first genuine smile since walking in the room. She might have wasted an hour in a stifling room with a dangerous animal, but she had what she wanted. The rest of the interview was insignificant. She'd finish it later. Standing, she pushed her chair back to the table and faced him. 'That's it for now, Randy. See, that was painless. You'll be hearing from me in the next couple of days.'

'Wait,' he said, his expression changing to desperation. 'I didn't tell you the most important thing.'

'What's that?' Ann said, hitting the buzzer for the jailer, wanting to get as far away from this creep right now as she could.

He looked Ann right in the eye. 'I'm innocent. I didn't rape no women. I never raped anyone in my life. I don't got to rape 'em. Women love me. I got all the women I need.'

Sure, Ann said to herself, deciding his proclamation of innocence was unworthy of even a response. Everyone in the jail was innocent. As soon as the jailer came, Ann took off down the hall.

When Ann got back to her office, she placed a call to Tommy Reed. After being informed that he was in the field, she asked the dispatcher to call him on the radio and have him meet her at her house.

Only a few blocks away when he got the call, the detective was pulling up to the curb by the time Ann got home. Ann leaped out of her car and rushed to the driver's window, her face flushed with excitement. 'I got him, Tommy.'

'Who?'

'Delvecchio.'

'How?'

'The dog bite. He admitted it.'

The detective's eyes lit up. 'No shit?'

'No shit, and I'll testify. I'm certainly a credible witness. He showed it to me, even told me it was a toy poodle . . . a white toy poodle with a red bow in its hair. Sound familiar? It's on his ankle.'

'There's a lot of white toy poodles with red bows, Ann,' Reed said skeptically. 'And I'll tell you something else. When he was arrested, they went over every square inch of his body. He swore that injury on his ankle was from falling off his motorcycle. His mother even verified his story.' Reed got out of the car and slammed the door, leaning back against it. 'Besides, these homicides occurred over a year ago. Unless it was deep enough to leave a scar, a bite like that would have already healed.' Reed made a little smacking noise with his mouth. Even if he had his doubts, he obviously wanted it to be true. 'He really told you it was a damn poodle?'

'I just said so, didn't I?' Ann was soaring on adrenaline. 'He admitted the scar on his ankle was a dog bite.' One of the victims in the homicides, a grandmother of six, had owned a small toy poodle. The dog had been strangled at the time of the victim's death. Ann had been studying the reports and had come up with the idea that the little dog had probably attacked the killer, and he had choked it in a fit of rage. Reed and some of the other detectives working the case, though, had thought differently. Their assumption was that the dog had been purposely strangled so it wouldn't bark and draw the police.

But Ann knew dogs and poodles, particularly ones that lived pampered lives with long-term owners like the victim. They sometimes developed nasty temperaments, started nipping at strangers. And if the dog had left a permanent scar, as this one evidently had, the lab could still verify that it was made by canine teeth. All they needed was one solid piece of evidence connecting him to the homicides and they would be able to prosecute.

'Look, Tommy, I know you think I'm pissing in the wind, but please, just write it up and shoot it to Glen. He wants Delvecchio bad. You may not know it, but Estelle Summer died this morning. I'm not certain how much her testimony means to the overall case, but if we lose that rape count, Delvecchio will be back on the streets in no time.'

'She died, huh?' Reed said, rubbing his chin. 'Bad break for the prosecution. Has she testified yet?'

'I don't know,' Ann said. 'Listen, get someone from the lab to go over to the jail and take impressions of that bite Delvecchio has and see if we can verify it's from a dog. But don't do it before you tell me. I've got to go back and complete the interview. Once he realizes I set him up, he won't talk and might even attack me.' Ann looked toward the front of her house and saw David opening the front door. He'd probably been watching from the window and wanted to know what was going on.

'What happened to the dog?' she asked Reed.

'How the hell do I know? The animal control people probably picked up the carcass and burned it.'

Ann was irritated, but kept it in check. She waited until David had walked to the curb where they were standing. 'Hi, sweetie,' she said, pulling him into her arms. 'Hey, why don't you let Tommy and me have a few more minutes alone here and then I'll come inside?'

'Why can't I listen?' he protested, his eyes darting from

Ann's face to the detective's. 'What are you talking about, anyway?'

'Go,' Ann said, waving him away. 'We're talking business. You know I don't like you listening to this stuff.'

A sly smile appeared on his chubby face. 'I'll go watch the news then. I think some guy cut a kid's head off, and they're showing it on TV right now.'

Ann's mouth fell open in shock just as David broke out giggling. 'I'm just teasing, Mom.'

'Thank God,' she said with relief, thinking all they needed was another gruesome killer running loose. 'Go on inside, guy. Start working on your homework.'

As he reluctantly shuffled back to the house, the next-door neighbor drove past in a battered Ford and waved out the window. It was a nice neighborhood, Ann thought, although not an affluent one. The houses were older and small. Her house was beige stucco and had a large picture window in front. A huge sycamore in the front yard provided shade in the heat of summer. The grass was high, however, for Ann generally mowed it herself and hadn't been able to do so since the shooting. She made David rake leaves, but she was still too protective to let him handle the lawn mower. Reed spotted the tall grass about the time Ann did and looked embarrassed that he hadn't asked to help her out with the yard work.

'I'll cut your grass this weekend,' he said. 'I'm sorry I haven't already –'

Ann cut him off, unconcerned about her grass, her mind back to the Delvecchio case. She'd provided a possible link to the homicides, and Reed was telling her they'd destroyed the evidence. 'You need the teeth from the dog to make a valid match, Tommy,' she said, frustrated. 'Maybe it's in a freezer at the lab. It was evidence, right?'

'These killings occurred over a year ago, Ann,' he said defensively. 'It's doubtful if we can substantiate this even if you're right, and thinking the dog is still being held as evidence is way out of line. I have no idea what happened to the dog. I just told you.'

'Well, you have to find out,' Ann demanded, kicking a snail off the sidewalk.

'Don't start up with Delvecchio. Christ, Ann, he's dangerous . . . a monster.'

'He's in jail, Tommy. He's not going anywhere. Believe me, when I get through with him, he'll get the full boat on the rapes. Then if we put the homicides together, no more Randy Delvecchio. By the time he sees the light of day, he won't be able to walk out the front door of the joint, let alone rape and torture old ladies. They'll have to push his ass out in a wheelchair.'

Reed exploded, yelling at her, 'Let it go. Do you hear me? Let it go, Ann.'

'No,' she said, stubborn, pouty. 'Find the dog.'

'I've said it before – you're going to get yourself hurt,' Reed said. 'Correct that statement, okay? You were already shot. Next time they'll kill you.'

Ann was silent, her upper lip twitching. Tommy had been all over her for years, telling her that her habit of manipulating violent offenders would come back to haunt her one day – that one of them would get out and come looking for revenge. Now she was wondering if the detective had been right.

'Want me to take the kid out to dinner?' Reed said. 'You know, give you some time to rest up. You look bushed, Ann. You shouldn't have gone back to work so soon.'

The sun had gone down while they were talking, and it was becoming dark and chilly out. Ann hugged herself to stay warm, unable to put Estelle Summer out of her mind. Yes, what she did was dangerous, but she couldn't worry about it. How could she stop trying? How could she turn her back and just walk away? Someone had to speak up for people like Estelle who no longer had a voice.

82

'No, I don't need you to take David out to dinner,' she told the detective firmly. 'You know what you can do for me, though?'

'No,' he said, a scowl on his face, 'but I'm sure you're going to tell me.'

Ann tossed her arms around his neck, smiled, and kissed him on the cheek. Before she released him, she pulled his head down to her level and whispered in his ear, 'Find the damn dog.'

Chapter 6

Ann had been so exhausted after her first day back on the job that she'd collapsed right after dinner and slept straight through to the next morning. Spotting her calendar on the bulletin board in the kitchen, she saw that she had a doctor's appointment that morning. He'd already removed the stitches, but the doctor insisted that she return for a follow-up.

Ann called Claudette at her house and told her she would not be in until later, then yelled at David. 'Hurry up,' she said. 'You're going to be late for school.'

David was grumpy. 'I'm starving,' he said. 'I haven't had breakfast.' Then his face brightened. 'Let's stop for donuts.'

Ann put her hands on her hips. Donuts, she thought, seeing his shirt straining around his midsection. 'You can have a bran muffin, David. No donuts.'

'I don't want a bran muffin,' he whined, following Ann out the kitchen door to the garage. As he got closer to puberty, David's voice had started to change. One minute he was a soprano and the next a baritone. 'They make me fart all day.'

'Blueberry, then,' Ann said, laughing.

Leaving the doctor's office at eleven o'clock, Ann was pleased with the report. Her wound was healing properly, and in all probability the scarring would be minimal. Heading back to the office, she wondered why Glen had not called the night before. Surely he knew about Estelle Summer's death by now. Perhaps he was discouraged and had gone out drinking with some friends.

Ann was on the 101 freeway, when the traffic abruptly came to a standstill. Soon thereafter she heard sirens and knew there must be an accident up ahead. She glanced at her watch, eager to get to the office. Then she remembered Jimmy Sawyer. She'd forgotten all about him yesterday. She wanted to test him for drugs. Ann steered the Jeep to the shoulder, made her away around the string of cars, and exited the freeway.

Ten minutes later, she pulled up before a modest residence. An older abode, the house had an arched overhang over the front door, and the walkway leading to the house was lined with rose bushes. The neighborhood as a whole was quiet and shady, dotted here and there with mature trees. Ann speculated that the houses up and down the street were probably occupied by thirtysomething professionals. She saw a lot of pride of ownership – yards neatly manicured, houses freshly painted. It was similar to Ann's neighborhood, except these houses were newer and in a better state of repair.

So, this is where Jimmy lives. Mommy and Daddy got sick of him and tossed him out. Figures, Ann thought, getting out of her car and locking the door. She recalled reading in the file that Sawyer lived here with two roommates. She wondered if they were the two young men she had seen in the courtroom: the Chinese man and the blond who looked like a movie star. If Sawyer was doing drugs, his roommates were probably into drugs as well. She shrugged. She couldn't do anything about them. Opening her briefcase, Ann retrieved a paper specimen cup and a pair of rubber gloves and placed them in her purse.

Making her way to the front door, she rang the doorbell. As she waited, she noticed that the rose bushes that looked so respectable from the curb were straggly and brown when seen up close. Becoming impatient, she tried to see in the windows, but they were all covered with what looked like blankets.

Finally she noticed that the door was ajar. Knocking it open halfway, she yelled out, 'Anyone in there?'

There was no reply. From her vantage point she could see into the living room. There was very little to see. The room was mostly vacant, containing only a tattered sofa and some moving boxes. But these were single guys, Ann thought, thinking of Hank's rental house before they were married and how sparsely it had been furnished.

'I said, is anybody home?' She'd seen a blue Porsche in the driveway when she drove up, so he had to be inside. I may have come just in time, she thought, sizing up the boxes. He might be planning to abscond, leave the state, in clear violation of his probation. She stepped inside.

Passing through the living room, Ann headed to the back of the house to check out the bedrooms. Other than debris and some miscellaneous items scattered on the carpet, the rooms were empty. As far as she could tell, the house was vacant and Sawyer nowhere to be found.

The kitchen was a disaster. The floor was filthy, and in several spots the linoleum had been burned. A little free-basing? Ann wondered, looking down at the scorch marks. Walking over to the refrigerator, she pulled the latch and peered inside. It wouldn't be the first refrigerator used to store LSD. She'd once found a stash of pills frozen inside a tray of ice cubes. For a few moments, though, she just stood there and soaked up the frigid air. All the windows had been closed, and it was extremely hot inside the house.

A thick layer of ice had formed on the contents, the ice more yellow now than white. Either no one had opened the door in months, Ann thought, or the temperature had been turned down too low. Knocking some of the ice away with her hands,

Ann spotted five cans of Miller Light, then thought she saw a can of Coke situated behind several jars of pickles. Beer and pickles, she thought. What a diet.

Still, the Coke looked tempting. The house was stifling and her throat was dry. Everything was crammed inside the tight space in the small refrigerator, and to get to the soda, Ann had to take the beer and pickles out and set them on the counter. The Coke in hand, she wiped off the top, popped the tab – and slushy frozen liquid squirted out.

'Shit,' she said, looking around for a paper towel. Finally she spotted a rag on the countertop. Once she had rinsed her hands in the sink and wiped them, she turned to put the other items back in the refrigerator. Lifting a jar of pickles, Ann noticed something odd. Her Coke was frozen, but the liquid inside the jar didn't appear to be frozen at all. What could be inside? At first she thought she was looking at stalks of white asparagus. She'd seen things like that in the gourmet supermarket, but didn't they store asparagus in water?

When Ann realized what the glass jar contained, her hand involuntarily opened and the jar dropped, shattering on the linoleum floor. The contents tumbled out in a murky greenish-brown liquid.

Fingers.

She was looking at severed human fingers: a thumb, a little finger, and three other fingers. They had to have come from one hand. Bile rose in her throat and her heart pounded a staccato beat. She squatted down on her knees to get a better look at them. The fingernails were painted. Whatever color they had once been, they were now a pale orange. In some spots the pickle juice had eroded the polish and the nail was white. Ann didn't try to pick them up or touch them. She knew better than to disturb a crime scene. Already she was chastising herself for dropping the jar. They could still lift prints from glass fragments, however, so the damage might not be that bad.

Looking around the house for a phone, she found only an exposed jack. She'd have to call from a pay phone. Rushing to the front door, she flung it open and stumbled down the steps. She hardly looked where she was going. All she could picture in her mind were those grotesque fingers strewn on the dirty floor.

Ann jerked her head around, having a wild flash that Sawyer would jump out at her and drag her back in that house. The Porsche was still in the driveway. Had he been inside with her? Was he hiding right now somewhere inside that house? He might cut off more than just her fingers, she thought. He could cut her legs off, maybe hack her up entirely. No, don't panic. Although she was breaking out in a cold sweat, she willed herself to relax. Ann took several deep breaths and with trembling fingers unlocked the door to her car.

The man who had saved her life was a monster who sliced off human fingers and saved them in a pickle jar. Glen had been right. Sawyer had to be the one who had shot her. She should have never come out here alone. She was a fool, a complete idiot.

Ann fired up the Jeep and floored it, tires burning asphalt; the smell of rubber filtered in through the open window.

Heading straight to the freeway, she decided not to make a call. She was only a few minutes away from the Ventura police department. Why recite this grisly tale to a dispatcher? Half the city and all the newsrooms had police scanners. Before they could even dispatch a unit, Sawyer's house would be surrounded by reporters. It wasn't the way to start a homicide investigation. This one could be big, and Ann didn't want to make mistakes that would compromise the case.

Ann steered the Jeep into the parking lot at the police station and leaped out, jogging to the front door of the building. The receptionist was new and tried to stop her, but she flashed her ID and hurried down the hall to Tommy's office. Whatever had happened to the fingerless woman, it had happened in Reed's jurisdiction, and his unit would catch the case. She spotted him draping his jacket over the back of his chair, about to sit down.

'Ann,' he said, alarmed. 'What are you doing here? What's wrong?'

Her eyes darted around the room frantically. Two other detectives were present. 'I've got something, Tommy,' she said, collapsing in a chair and taking a breath. 'You might want Abrams and Harper to hear this. We need to move fast.'

Reed slid his chair up to the desk, and his facial muscles tensed. The other men gathered, overhearing what she'd said. 'Shoot,' he said. 'We're waiting.'

'Okay, here's what I have,' she said, speaking rapidly. 'Jimmy Sawyer has human fingers in his house. I went there for an unannounced home visit and found them in a pickle jar.'

All the color drained from the detective's face. 'Fuck. Fingers? Real fingers? You went to Sawyer's house alone with no backup?'

'I know,' Ann said. 'I should have called a unit for backup, but Tommy, I never dreamed –'

'Start from the minute you got there, Ann,' Reed said, grabbing a pen and a yellow note pad.

Ann took a breath and continued, 'Okay. There was no one there, although Jimmy's Porsche was in the driveway. He does drive a Porsche, doesn't he? Isn't that what you told me?' She looked up at Noah Abrams, and he nodded.

'Go on,' he told Ann.

'Most of the furniture and stuff is gone. He must be planning to flee. He'll come back for that car, though, so if we get out there fast –'

Abrams was already rising out of his chair.

'Please, Noah,' Ann said, 'let me finish. When I saw the

door wasn't completely closed, I just walked in. Then right before I left, I decided to check the refrigerator and see if he'd stashed his drugs in there. There were these pickle jars . . .' She stopped. They were all looking at her strangely. Suddenly she realized how bizarre this must sound. She glared at the other two detectives and continued in a flat, firm voice. 'In one of the pickle jars were five severed fingers. Women's fingers. I saw nail polish on the nails.'

'Do you have them?' Reed said.

'I dropped the pickle jar, and it broke and the fingers fell out on the floor,' Ann said, her face burning in humiliation. Why had she dropped the jar? 'I didn't want to disrupt the crime scene any more than I already had,' she quickly added, trying to save face, 'so I left and came straight here.'

Noah Abrams rushed back to his desk for his jacket. Snapping his shoulder holster into place, he said, 'Let's go before he gets rid of them.'

'Stop right there,' Reed said. He was the sergeant. If they made any mistakes, it would all come down on him. 'We can't just run out there half cocked and barge into this guy's house. Let's think of the legalities here.'

'Right, Reed,' Abrams barked, 'while he flushes the evidence down the toilet or grinds it up in the disposal.'

'Shut the fuck up,' Reed yelled. He turned to Ann. 'Look, you're a sworn peace officer. We might have a problem with search and seizure.'

'He has active search terms,' Ann quickly responded. 'Aren't we in the clear here?'

'No,' Reed said, shaking his head, thinking the matter over. 'They're not general search terms if I remember right, they're drug terms. You can search for drugs, Ann, but nothing else. Fingers are not drugs.'

Ann threw up her hands. 'This is ridiculous.'

'Hey,' Reed said, 'I don't write the laws, I only enforce

them. What you just found out there could be excluded as the fruit of an invalid search. Inadmissible, you know?'

Ann had not given thought to these issues for years. Being in investigations was totally different from being on the street as a cop. All the same, she felt certain her actions were within the law. 'I think it's legit, Tommy. It should fall under the plain view doctrine.' Both the exclusionary rule and the plain view doctrine were legal mandates that governed an officer's right to search and seizure. If an officer saw something in plain view, like a gun on the seat of a car, it was admissible evidence. But if the gun was hidden under the seat and the officer searched for it anyway, without the benefit of a search warrant, the gun would constitute evidence ultimately excluded and inadmissible in a court of law. That they were even having this discussion exemplified the absurdity of the criminal justice system, as if a person's rights could be violated when he was slicing off people's fingers.

'I think we should run it by the D.A.,' Reed said. 'Opening someone's refrigerator isn't exactly finding something in plain view.'

The other detectives, though, were getting restless. 'Let's just pop the bastard, get the fingers, and find the body,' Abrams said. 'Let the D.A. sort through the legal shit.'

Reed nodded and stood up, anxious to get the show on the road. Then he sat back down, clearly frustrated. 'Call Hopkins and run this by him,' he told Ann. 'Shit, he was right about this guy.'

'That's for sure,' Ann said. She grabbed the phone, and once she got Glen on the line, she recapitulated the details of the case. The line was silent for quite some time.

'I think you're clear here,' Hopkins finally replied. 'You weren't going out there as a police officer. It wasn't a search. You made a home visit to a probationer and just stumbled onto the fingers.'

Ann was listening carefully. She'd been in situations like this before. Glen was coaching her, telling her what to say if the case ever got to court. If she said her intent was to search, they might be in trouble without a warrant. But she had been searching for drugs in the refrigerator. That meant she'd have to lie under oath.

The detectives were staring at her, waiting for an answer. Ann would do anything to make a case, but perjury? 'Maybe we should go for a warrant then,' she told him. 'That makes it clean. With something like this, why take the chance?'

'Fine,' Glen replied. 'Give me what you've got, and I'll write it and walk it over to Judge Madsen. When he signs it, I'll fax you the copy and head that way with the original. Shouldn't take more than fifteen or twenty minutes if you give me the information right now.'

Reed was already up and making calls at Abrams's desk, advising the lieutenant and captain. Then he arranged to get some officers from patrol. Ann, in the middle of dictating the information for the search warrant to Glen, stopped and looked up at Harper. 'Please go to my car . . . the black Jeep in the parking lot. It isn't locked. Get the case file. I need it.'

Harper did as she asked and returned carrying a manila file folder. Ann immediately started reading the particulars off to Glen: Sawyer's name, the case number, the address on Henderson Avenue.

As promised, within twenty minutes the fax machine in the detective bay beeped and started spilling out the search warrant. Ann and Reed almost collided as they both raced to the machine. Tommy met her gaze, showing her how he felt about Jimmy Sawyer as he ripped off the fax. This was the man who had shot her. Ann knew it now, and so did Reed. If Jimmy Sawyer was still in the country, even if he was thousands of miles away by now, Reed was going to find him.

They formed a caravan. Ann rode with Tommy Reed in his department-issued bronze Chrysler. Behind them were four black-and-white police units, an evidence van, and the unmarked cars of Abrams, Harper, the lieutenant, and the captain.

'What if Sawyer came back to get the car?' Ann said, voicing a question that had been bothering her for the past half hour. 'When I left, he could have come back and seen the pickle jar shattered. If he's smart, he'd dump those fingers in the ocean, and then we'd have nothing.'

Reed's car fishtailed as he took a fast right and headed to the house. He glanced at Ann and then back at the road. 'We should have gone in without the warrant.'

Ann gulped and swallowed. He knew. They all must know, she decided. 'I made a mistake, didn't I? I should have gone along with the program and not insisted on the warrant.'

'You have to do what you feel is right, Ann,' Reed said, stomping on the gas and pulling ahead of the other cars.

When they reached Henderson, the cars parked at the end of the block, and officers piled out. The lieutenant stepped to the front of the group. 'Hilgard, Evans and Baumgarten, take the front of the house,' he said to the uniformed officers. 'Harper, Abrams, and Reed, head toward the back. The car's still here. He could be inside. The captain and I will take a position near the neighbors' fences where we can see on both sides. If he tries to split in our direction, we'll handle him.'

Ann was left standing, her arms dangling by her sides. She didn't have a weapon. Suddenly she felt like an outsider, and her shoulders slumped.

In another minute, Reed keyed the portable radio and asked if the officers were in position.

'Affirmative,' they replied. 'Ready and waiting.'

While the men in front rang the doorbell and announced themselves, Reed leaped over the fence and scrambled toward the back of the house, where a U-Haul truck was pulled up to the curb, its rear doors closed.

Ann, still standing in front, heard noises in the house and the sounds of a scuffle. Then one of the uniformed officers stuck his head out the back door and yelled to Reed, 'We've got Sawyer here. He's alone.'

Reed and the other detectives entered from the rear. The officers who had been waiting outside now rushed through the front door. In no time most of them were jostling elbows inside the small living room.

She could move in now, Ann thought. Just as she started up the front steps, Glen pulled to the curb and leaped out, the original warrant in his hands. Right behind him was Ray Hernandez, a man Ann recognized as an investigator from the D.A.'s office.

Glen glanced at her. 'What's happening?'

'They have Sawyer inside.'

The three of them stepped through the door and into the crowded living room. Out of the corner of her eye, she saw Harper leading a handcuffed Jimmy Sawyer out the back door. Glen quickly followed after them.

Over the sea of men Tommy yelled at her, 'Where's the fucking fingers?' His face was red and he was perspiring. It was like an oven inside even without all the policemen. Realizing this, he started shoving people aside. 'You,' he said, pointing at one of the men, 'and you . . . and you, get out of here and give us some breathing room.' Finally he made his way to the front door. 'Where did you say these fingers were?'

'The kitchen,' Ann said. 'I left them on the floor in the kitchen.'

'There's no fingers on the floor, Ann,' Reed said, a look of annoyance on his face.

The teeming mass of humanity now shifted in the direction of the kitchen. 'Over there,' Ann said, standing on her tiptoes to see over the men's heads. 'I got the jar out of the refrigerator and then dropped it. When I left, the fingers were all over the floor. There were five of them.'

Pushing and shoving the men aside, Reed and Ann made their way to the refrigerator. Reed started removing the beer cans and slamming them down on the kitchen cabinet. Then he saw a pickle jar and stopped. 'This it?' he said.

'One of them.' It wasn't the same jar she had dropped, of course, but the contents looked the same. If there were five fingers in one jar, perhaps the remaining five might be in this one. 'Yeah, yeah,' she said, unable to take her eyes off the jar. 'It was Vlasic . . . you know, the brand. It was a Vlasic pickle jar. There were two of them. This has to be the other one.'

'Get some evidence guys in here,' Reed yelled. He pulled on a pair of white latex gloves and carefully lifted the jar out of the refrigerator, holding it up to the light.

'Let me see, Tommy,' Ann exclaimed, although the contents looked different from what she had seen earlier. 'The juice is cloudy.' She moved right next to him and got up close to the jar. 'Open it. I thought they were pickles too at first. I even thought they were stalks of white asparagus or something.'

The room fell silent, and Ann felt dizzy, almost thinking she was going to be sick to her stomach. She waited as Tommy opened the lid and stuck a gloved finger inside the pickle jar. Then she held her breath and stared. Tommy held something in his hand and sniffed it. Leaning back against the counter, he glared at Ann, shoved the object into his mouth, and took a big bite. There was a unanimous intake of breath as everyone gasped.

'Pickles,' Reed said, spitting the piece back out into his hand. 'That's it,' he said. 'Everyone except crime scene people clear out. All we got here is some sour pickles. Looks like a false alarm.'

Ann looked down at the floor, too embarrassed to face the men. As she did, she realized it was clean, not filthy as it had been. 'There were human fingers, Tommy,' she said without looking up. 'I know the difference between a pickle and a finger, for chrissakes. He obviously returned and disposed of them.'

Although Reed didn't say so, he had his reservations. Ann had been thoroughly spooked by the shooting and could have simply jumped to an erroneous conclusion. She had been in this house alone, with the advance knowledge that Sawyer was considered a suspect in her shooting. Seeing something that didn't look right in the pickle jar, she had simply panicked. Reed knew the mind was a strange thing, particularly when it was under stress. He'd seen seasoned officers make serious errors in the heat of a crisis, even made a few himself.

'Listen to me, Tommy,' Ann said, talking fast. 'The floor was filthy when I saw the fingers. Look at it now – it's clean. See, he came back, saw the fingers, disposed of them, and then mopped the floor. Aren't they even going to search for more evidence? And you know, they should swab the floor. Maybe there are trace elements of blood or something they can identify in the fluid that spilled out with the fingers. Also glass fragments . . . there could be broken glass fragments that would support my story.'

Reed considered what Ann was saying. The floor *was* clean, and everything else in the place was a mess. 'We'll comb the place,' he said. 'Send a lot of stuff to the lab.' His face softened. 'Maybe we'll find something. Never know. Our guess is Sawyer and his roommates were dealing narcotics, possibly were even cookers.' He paused and gave Ann a sour look. Cookers were individuals who manufactured drugs like acid and amphetamines in homemade labs. Lately these home labs had been springing up everywhere. 'When Sawyer was originally arrested, he had a whole sheet of high-grade LSD and an envelope full of Ecstasy. According to narcotics, the streets have been flooded with this stuff lately, and the high school kids are gobbling it up like candy. My guess is this is where it was coming from – this house.'

'A lab?' Ann said, noticing that Glen had reentered the house and was coming toward them.

'As soon as he mentioned Sawyer as a suspect,' Reed said, shifting his eyes to Glen, 'we started checking him out. From what we can tell, everything points to a lab.'

'Why didn't you tell me?' Ann looked at Tommy and then at Glen, getting angrier by the second. 'He was my probationer. And that still doesn't explain why he shot me.'

'Yes, it does, Ann,' Reed said flatly. 'Sawyer must have shot you to keep you from doing exactly what you did today – show up at his doorstep and fall right into his narcotics operation.' The detective stopped and sighed, letting his shoulders fall in disappointment. 'Way it looks, they moved the lab. See that U-Haul parked in the back? Sawyer must have come back for the last few boxes, maybe the refrigerator. Bet there's nothing we want in those boxes either.'

Ann was incredulous. They were talking about drug labs, and she was talking about human life. 'What about the fingers? I saw those fingers, Reed. I'm not some moron off the street, you know. I do know what a human finger looks like. I was a cop once myself.' She peered up at Reed defiantly, daring him to challenge her.

'You can't search the moving van,' Glen said quickly. 'Not without another warrant. The present warrant specifies only the house.'

'Look, Hopkins,' Reed said, one lip curling up in distaste, 'I know you have your concerns, but what if this person without fingers is alive and bleeding to death in that van? What if Ann did see something?'

Hopkins grabbed the detective's arm. Reed jerked it away

angrily. 'Don't go near that van without a warrant,' the district attorney barked. 'Do you hear me? If you do, no matter what you find, you won't be able to use it. Wait until we do it the right way and get another warrant. Need I say more?'

'Hey,' Reed spat, 'you're the D.A.'

'Come on, Ann,' Glen said, 'I'll give you a ride back to the courthouse.'

'Not now,' Ann said, her eyes still on the detective. 'Do you think I imagined this, Tommy? Tell me. Come on, I want to hear it from your own lips.'

Again, Reed just shrugged his shoulders. 'Where's Sawyer?' he yelled out to another detective.

A disembodied voice yelled back, 'With Harper out back.'

'I saw those fingers, Tommy.'

'I didn't say I didn't believe you, kid,' Reed said, his voice lower. 'But there are no fingers here now.'

'He must have disposed of them before we got here,' Ann said, her face flushed with anger. 'Didn't I tell you he'd come back and get rid of the fingers?'

Reed, though, was eager to get outside and see what Sawyer had to say. In any case, it was time to clear out so the crime scene men could get cracking. He'd been in police work too long to sit around and ruminate over what they should or should not have done. 'Look, we're going to transport Sawyer as soon as we get things going here. I'll let you sit in on the interview.'

'Fine,' Ann said, watching as he walked away. Go on, she thought, make a fool of me in front of everyone and then toss me a bone like a damn dog. So, it was her fault for insisting on the warrant. Was that what had put a burr up Reed's ass? Was the detective blaming her for not going along with Glen's suggestion and altering the truth to suit their needs? Or did he just think she was a hysterical female who didn't know what she had seen?

Either way, Ann was boiling.

·

After instructing the officers to canvass the neighborhood and see what they could learn about the occupants of 875 Henderson, Tommy Reed drove his vehicle back alone.

He pulled into the back of the station and parked. Then he sat there staring out the windshield. The sun was setting like a huge orange persimmon, and the sky was blazing with color.

His gaze fell and he began mentally sorting through the details of the case. They'd have to get warrants issued and pick up the other two boys. The only problem was what grounds they could use for the warrants. If the crime scene unit found no signs of drug paraphernalia in the boxes or anywhere else in the house, it would be next to impossible to substantiate warrants for these other subjects. 'Oh, hell,' he said, getting out of the car.

When he entered the detective bay, Ann sprang to her feet. She'd been waiting in the chair by his desk. 'Where's Sawyer?' she asked.

'One of the patrol units is bringing him in.'

'Listen, those fingers have to belong to a female, Tommy. I saw streaks of nail polish on them. We need to check missing persons and see if there's a report out.'

Reed removed his jacket and draped it over the back of his chair. 'Even if we find a missing person report on a female, Ann, what's that going to tell us? The only thing that will substantiate your story is a stiff without fingers.'

Ann was still pissed, and Reed knew it. Her body language said it all: arms folded over her chest, chin up, a determined glare in her eyes. In response, he donned his stoic 'just the facts' look, wanting her to know that he was the homicide detective, while she was only the probation officer.

'Then check all the morgues,' Ann said. 'Then check the

missing person reports on females both locally and in Los Angeles.'

Reed bent over his desk, jotting some notes down on his yellow pad as he talked. 'In L.A. there have to be twenty-five people or more reported missing every day. Most of the missing person reports they just kiss off. They don't even write them. All they do is note it in the log book.' He continued writing, ignoring Ann completely now. A few moments later, a uniformed officer appeared with Jimmy Sawyer in tow.

'Where do you want him?' the young officer said.

Reed told the officer to take Sawyer to an interview room and then saw the captain waving to him through the glass window. Forced to wait outside, Ann looked in and saw Glen pacing back and forth, waving his hands around. Several times she saw Reed glance at her, a scowl on his face. She was dying to know what they were talking about, if they were talking about her.

When Reed came out, he was tense. 'Captain says Noah should conduct the interview.'

'Why Noah?' Ann cried. 'You're the sergeant. This is a serious case.'

'Because he's investigating your shooting, and Sawyer is now a valid suspect . . . his suspect.' He stopped and ran his fingers through his hair. 'And look, I never said I didn't believe you about the fingers. I don't know why you're so bent out of shape. They weren't there, that's all.'

'You thought it, though,' Ann said, softening. 'And the other men did too.'

'Hey,' he said, smiling, 'you can't blame me for what other people think.'

Ann returned his smile. She had more than enough enemies lately; she didn't need to alienate her friends. 'I still get to sit in on the interview, right? You said I could.'

Reed frowned. 'Why don't you go home and get some rest?

We have Sawyer in custody now. Noah could trip him up in the interview. I'll also get in touch with Melanie Chase at the lab and see if she can expedite processing whatever evidence they collected from the house.' Reed was avoiding her question, and he saw that she knew it. Frowning, he cleared his throat before continuing. 'Ann, the captain pointed out that you're basically a victim in this case, and department policy is that we don't allow victims to take part in the actual investigation.' He threw up a hand to still her protests. 'You know, there's a lot of inherent liability here. Sometimes people go out and take their own revenge, and their relatives sue the department. He'd rather you not hang around the station right now. He even chewed me out for bringing you with us when we executed the search warrant.'

Ann felt as if someone had slammed a door in her face. She was the one who had been shot, had almost bled to death on the sidewalk. All the same, she could see it was out of her hands. She could buck Reed, but she couldn't buck department policy.

'Okay,' she said, resigned. 'I guess I'll go home.'

As Ann made her way out of the police station, she purposely passed the door to the room she knew had one-way glass, and impulsively turned the knob. When she found it locked, she confirmed her suspicions that it was the room where they were holding Sawyer. Was Abrams inside now interrogating him? Placing her ear against the door, she tried to eavesdrop and then chastised herself, knowing she would look foolish if anyone walked by. It was just so difficult to walk away, knowing that the very person who had shot her was right here, right behind that door. She wanted to interrogate him herself, confront him, get to the bottom of this right this second. And she should have that right, she told herself, no matter what Reed and the others said. She might be the victim, but Sawyer was still her probationer.

Then the horrid fingers flashed in her mind, and she was relieved that she wouldn't be the one locked inside that room with Jimmy Sawyer. If he had sliced off some poor woman's fingers and saved them in a pickle jar, he was evil personified. They could never predict what he would do next, how far he would go, just as they had no idea how many other heinous crimes he may have committed. Exiting the building and getting in her car, another terrifying thought passed through her mind. If Sawyer hadn't used a gun and shot her, would he have used a butcher knife instead?

She didn't want to know.

Chapter 7

Noah Abrams stopped by his desk to pick up his tape recorder. 'Let's hope he's a braggart,' he said to Reed as they walked down the hall. 'Are you going to monitor the interview from the observation room?'

'No,' Reed said, 'but Glen Hopkins is. Sawyer's all yours, Noah. Do your stuff. I'm trying to put some other things together, get the records bureau making calls to morgues. If those really were fingers Ann saw, there's got to be a body floating around somewhere.'

When Abrams stepped inside the interview room, Jimmy Sawyer was sitting quietly with his hands folded in his lap and an innocent, expectant expression on his face, unaware that he was being watched through one-way glass. 'Jimmy Sawyer,' the detective said, loosening his tie and sliding his jacket off his shoulders. 'We meet again, huh? Not exactly the same kind of circumstances as the night Ms Carlisle was shot.'

Jimmy Sawyer smiled inappropriately and flipped his long hair behind his shoulders. His teeth were white and even, the product of years of expensive orthodontics. Then he saw the tape recorder, and the smile slid right off his face.

Taking a seat at the long table, Abrams sized up his opponent. The detective was an excellent interviewer, able to win a subject's confidence and put him at ease. Once they were nice and relaxed, he pounced.

'Last time we had a little talk, it was about your probation officer, Jim. Seems she's causing you a lot of trouble lately. Oh, is it Jim or Jimmy?'

'Whatever,' the cocky young man said. 'People call me both.'

'Well, you can call me Noah if you want,' the detective said, congenial and soft-spoken. 'Why don't we dispense with the formalities?'

'Nice tie,' Sawyer said. 'Is that James Dean?'

'Yeah,' Abrams said, holding it up to look at it. 'I have one with Marilyn Monroe on it too. I like the fifties. What about you?'

'The only thing I know about the fifties is what I saw on *Happy Days,* the TV show.'

'Then how did you know it was James Dean?'

'Give me a break,' Sawyer said, scoffing. 'Everyone knows about James Dean. I saw this movie once on the late show with him, *Rebel Without a Cause.* Pretty good. The best part was the drag race to the edge of that cliff.'

'You like dangerous things, huh?' Abrams said.

Sawyer was too smart to answer that one. 'Does this mean I'm under arrest?'

'Not necessarily. Right now we'd just like some answers.'

'Oh, I see,' Sawyer said slowly. There was a rattling noise under the table. He'd worn the boots with the chains and spurs and was resettling his feet. 'Answers, huh?'

'If you want, we can talk about this incident today and try to clear it up. If you don't, we can wait for you to retain an attorney and then discuss it. It's your decision.'

'I'll talk,' Sawyer said confidently and chuckled. 'This is so silly, you know. I can't believe it. She really told you guys I had pickled fingers in my refrigerator?'

'Yep, she sure did, Jimmy. Why do you think she would say a thing like that if it weren't true?'

Sawyer didn't hesitate for a second. 'I really hate to tell you this . . . but she's angry. She just made it up to get back at me.'

Noah Abrams could smell bullshit in the air. 'And why's she angry?'

The boy didn't blink. His eyes were cold and determined as he leaned over the table. 'Because we were lovers.'

Noah kept his face emotionless, but his stomach lurched with anger. Ann was a decent woman, a good woman. It sickened him just to sit across from this scum, knowing he might have shot her. Now what was he saying? 'Lovers, huh? You and your probation officer were lovers?'

'Just for the past two weeks,' Sawyer said tentatively, testing the waters. 'She made a move on me the first time I ever saw her, after court that day.'

'Oh, really?' Abrams said, his voice louder than he intended. 'And where did this happen?'

'In a storage room outside her office. See, I was waiting for her in the hallway. I wanted to clear some things up, some things about what the judge said.'

'Go on,' Abrams said, softening his voice. He had a piece of paper and a pencil on the table and started doodling to control his temper.

'Well, it was time to go home, I guess. In fact, I think most of the people in her office had already left. I saw them walking out before I saw Ann.' Sawyer stopped short and stared off in space, as if envisioning the scene. 'We talked. She was nice. After she explained what the judge meant, she asked if I had a girlfriend and I told her I didn't. She said we should get to know each other, since she was handling my case.' Abrams shot him a nasty look, but Sawyer took it in stride. 'Then she told me to step into this room with her for a minute so we could talk privately. That's where it happened.'

'What exactly happened, Jimmy?' Abrams said. At that moment he pressed down so hard on his pencil that the point broke off. Irritated, he cast the pencil aside.

'She told me that she could get my probation changed so I didn't have to report every month and piss in a bottle. She . . . she said she liked me, thought I was cute or something.' Sawyer looked up, pleased with himself. He'd had lots of other girls, so he knew this part rang true. 'Oh, she also told me that her husband was dead. Hey, she was flirting like mad, a real horn dog, you know.'

'No shit?' Abrams said, raising his eyebrows as if he were swallowing it all whole. Inside, though, he was burning. Sure, the man knew what had happened to Hank. When she was shot, they'd covered the whole story in the newspapers. Be cool, Abrams told himself, play the game. This was one interview he didn't want to blow. 'You're one lucky fuck, Sawyer,' he said, chuckling. 'I wouldn't mind putting it to her myself, but she's never come on to me. Anyway, then what happened?'

Sawyer smiled. This was going great. He had this cop in the palm of his hand. 'We kissed each other, okay? She's a pretty good kisser. Then she let me grab her tits. Not much there, let me tell you.' Jimmy laughed loudly, enjoying his own story. 'Anyway, after I fucked her, I left. I drove around the block and then I started thinking about her.'

'All right. Go on, I'm listening.' Abrams glanced over to make sure the tape was recording, expecting Sawyer to trip over his lies any second.

'So, I went back and drove through the parking lot, thinking she might still be there. When I didn't see her, I decided to get a hamburger at the McDonald's across the street. That's when I recognized her on the sidewalk and stopped. You know the rest.'

In a perfectly flat monotone Abrams said, 'When I first

interviewed you after the shooting, you never said you had driven through the parking lot.' Yes, he thought, knowing he had just scored the first point. Sawyer had placed himself at the scene of the crime: in the parking lot prior to the shooting.

Sawyer snapped to attention. 'Well, I didn't exactly want to tell you the truth, now, did I? The lady had been shot, so . . . I didn't want to ruin her reputation.'

Reel him in, Abrams thought, rubbing his hands on his thighs under the table, a look of phony admiration on his face. 'You're a considerate guy, Jimmy. Both a hero and a gentleman.'

'Oh,' Sawyer said, remembering the second half of his story, 'we saw each other another time too. After she got out of the hospital.' He looked back at the detective. 'I mean, I called her at the hospital first. She gave me her phone number and told me to call her.'

So far, Abrams had let Sawyer talk in generalities, but as the noose tightened, he craftily fished for specifics. 'When was this? What day did you see her the second time?'

'I don't remember the day, okay?' Sawyer said. 'It was lunchtime, maybe one o'clock. I called her to see how she was feeling, and she said she wanted to take me to lunch. She asked me to meet her in the restaurant at the Hilton. I told her I'd rather go somewhere else. The food's shit there, but she insisted.' Sawyer smiled, recalling she'd wanted to go to Marie Callender's. Then after he'd left her, he and some of his friends had continued their party in one of the rooms.

'Then what happened?'

Sawyer's gaze roamed around the room and then finally came to rest on the detective. 'When I got there, we talked. She told me how scared she was since the shooting, how thankful she was that I saved her life. She was flirting again, making all kinds of suggestive statements, saying she wanted to give me a *real* reward. Then she said she wasn't hungry and asked if I wanted to get a room. I paid for the room.'

'You paid for the room, huh?' Abrams said, cracking his knuckles. This was getting better by the second. Sawyer was lying through his teeth, and if he kept talking, he'd end up in worse shape than if he had just kept his mouth shut and demanded an attorney. 'Did you pay with a credit card?'

'Yeah, American Express. You can check my bill.' Sawyer leaned back in his chair and grinned. 'I mean, my mother always taught me to be polite, Noah. Isn't the man supposed to pay?'

Abrams laced his hands together now and placed them on the table, controlling his urge to smack the kid right in the mouth.

'Then she told me to go up to the room and wait while she bought a bottle of booze for us from that shop in the lobby. I can't buy booze, see, I'm not old enough.' He paused, searching the detective's face. 'Uh, after we had a drink was when she grabbed my crotch again.'

Abrams almost laughed at this one. Never in a million years could he imagine Ann Carlisle doing such a thing. She was demure, reserved, always a lady. 'Grabbed your crotch, huh? She just reached over and grabbed your crotch? You mean, like, grabbed your dick?'

'Yeah.'

'Did you have an erection?'

Sawyer's eyes were dancing all over the place. 'At first I didn't, but after she started stroking me and kissing me, I did. She just sort of threw herself at me. I reached under her dress and she wasn't wearing any panties. It was great.'

'Then what happened?'

'We fucked,' he said, running his tongue over his lips. 'I mean, she was wild, Noah. She sucked me. She fucked me. She wanted me to give it to her up the ass. She said she hadn't had a good fuck since her old man died or something.'

Abrams's mind skidded off track, seeing the scene Sawyer was describing in his mind: Ann Carlisle with those long legs wrapped around his neck. His neck, not this jerk's neck. Then he stopped himself. He was becoming aroused by this asinine story. Then he noticed that Sawyer was watching him intently, and he cleared his throat, 'Uh, where were we?'

'I was fucking her,' Sawyer proclaimed, winking. 'You'd like to fuck her too, wouldn't you? I can tell. I can see it on your face.' He slapped the table and laughed. 'Shit, Noah, you'd like to fuck her yourself.'

Enraged, Abrams almost leaped from his chair. Then he caught himself just in time. 'Okay, Jimmy, I'm not the one with the problem here. You are, so let's see if we can't speed this up. We can always go back for a blow-by-blow of your affair later.' He rubbed his chin as if he were thinking over all he had heard. 'What you're saying, as I hear it, is that Ann Carlisle and you were lovers. Even if this is true, what does it have to do with the fingers?'

Sawyer hit full stride, and Abrams sensed that this part had been well rehearsed in his mind. 'After we fucked, I told her I didn't think we should see each other again.' He met Abrams's gaze. 'You know, she was older, she had a kid and all. And she was my probation officer. She went ballistic, man. I guess I insulted her or something. When she left, she threatened me, saying I was going to pay . . . she was going to make me pay.'

Abrams glanced at his watch. It was time to turn up the heat. Sawyer was loose and, from all appearances, confident he was in control. Perfect. 'What you're saying, Jimmy, is Ann Carlisle got angry when you ended your relationship. Then she decided to go out to your house and manufacture this story about severed fingers to get you in trouble. Right? I mean, correct me if I'm wrong here. I don't want to put words into your mouth.'

'Exactly,' Sawyer said with satisfaction. 'She was only a

fuck. I wasn't exactly dating her or anything. Maybe she was mad that I was moving out of my house today. Shit, I was only moving back to my parents' house. It wasn't as if I was going to leave the country. One of my roommates was a prick, see, so we decided to split up.'

Abrams began to press. 'Tell me, did anyone see you together? Do you have any way to verify this relationship?'

Confused, Jimmy stared at a spot over Abrams's head. Finally he answered, 'Yes, people saw us together.'

Leaping to his feet, Abrams yelled right in his face, spit flying from his mouth, 'Who? What are their names? When exactly did they see you and Ann Carlisle, Jimmy? Where did they see you? You're nothing but a sleazy little liar. You've got no proof of this, and no one in hell's gonna believe you.'

Sawyer recoiled, pushing his chair back a few feet from the table.

Abrams circled him now, completely unleashed. Sawyer's eyes followed him warily around the table. 'She's a probation officer. What are you, bud? You're nothing. Let's talk about the narcotics lab you had set up in that house. Let's talk about that, Jimmy boy. And where did your scumbag roommates scurry off to? You didn't just have a disagreement about who was going to do the dishes. You were cookers. We know what was going on over there.'

For a moment Sawyer looked as if he was going to crack. Then he came back strong, yelling right back at the detective. 'My mother saw us.'

'Your momma, huh?'

'Yeah,' Jimmy said, composed again. 'She was having a drink with a friend in the bar at the Hilton. She spotted us in the lobby when I was checking in. You can ask her.'

Nothing was too low for this guy, Abrams thought, disgusted. He'd even drag his own mother into this mess. But the detective knew he had to back off now. When the suspect came back strong, it was time to back down. The soil had to be soft before he could plow it.

'Certainly, Jimmy,' he said calmly, walking back to his chair and taking his seat. 'Let's go back to the narcotics. Are you denying that you were manufacturing and distributing drugs from that house?'

Sawyer laughed and gave the detective a knowing glance, almost as if he were letting him in on the conspiracy. 'Of course I'm denying it. What do you think, Noah? I'm going to confess that I'm some kind of a big-time drug dealer? Pretty fucking funny, asshole.' The chains rattled under the table as Sawyer slid down farther in the seat.

So, Abrams thought, he wants to play hardball. 'And your mother is going to swear to what you've just told me in a court of law? That she saw you and your probation officer at a hotel together? She's going to perjure herself and risk prosecution?' Again the detective sprang from his chair. 'You're gonna have to do better than this, Jimmy.'

Abrams circled behind him and grabbed the back of his chair, his voice laced with sarcasm. 'You should have given this more thought. Having Mommy bail you out and cover your lousy ass ain't gonna do it.' Then he quickly walked back around the table and faced him. 'And where did you get the cash to buy that fancy Porsche? Want to tell me about that one? Are you gonna get Mommy to swear she bought it for you too? Does she have canceled checks to prove it? You're in deep shit, my man.' Abrams stopped and sucked in breath, ready to gobble Jimmy Sawyer up and spit him back out in bloody pieces. 'I'm going to crawl up your asshole, Sawyer, all the way to your throat. I'm going to find the fucking shooter you used to pop this poor woman with in the parking lot.' Abrams slammed his fist down on the table, and Sawyer jumped. 'Then I'm going to find witnesses to prove you were dealing and manufacturing drugs, drag all your little roommates in and put them through the wringer, offer them deals, whatever it takes.' Again the fist came down, and the flimsy table shook. 'By the time I'm through with you, motherfucker, you'll wish you were dead.'

'I want my attorney,' Sawyer demanded, his mouth puckered like a petulant child. Then he burst to his feet, pounding on the table as Abrams had, about to throw a full-fledged temper tantrum. 'You can't threaten me like this. I'm not saying another word until I talk to my attorney.'

Abrams hit the stop button on the tape recorder, seizing Sawyer's arm before he struck the table again and then tossing it aside. He'd played hardball, all right, but the kid had still managed to score the winning point. And he'd done it with one lousy sentence, the one every cop dreaded during an interrogation.

The minute a suspect requested an attorney, the clock stopped and the interview was over.

Noah left Sawyer stewing in the interview room after slamming a phone down on the table for him to call his attorney. Before he went in to speak with Hopkins, though, he had to make a stop in the men's room. Let the asshole wait, he thought, smiling grimly. Hopkins was probably going to tell him he'd blown the interview anyway.

After relieving himself, Abrams washed his hands and stared in the mirror. He'd lost his cool because of Ann. He was tired of eating in restaurants every night, going home to an empty apartment, never being able to have a real conversation with the women he dated. Lately, he hadn't been going out much. He was burned out on the whole singles scene, particularly now with all the AIDS. He wanted a good woman to settle down with, and Ann was it.

Heading back down the hall, Noah thought of the caustic remarks Reed had made about his failed marriages. In truth, though, the women he'd married had decided they didn't want to be married to a cop, so what could he do? According to his first wife, Rhonda, he was never home. He hadn't made enough money to give Sandra the things she wanted, while Bonnie had worried that he'd get injured on duty and she'd have to support him. Right, Noah thought facetiously, she was my last big mistake. But Ann was different. She'd been around cops all her life. She was one of them. When they were cadets together, they used to sit and talk for hours about all kinds of crazy things. He could still see her sitting there on the grass in front of the old station, knees pulled to her chest, her hair in a ponytail, laughing at his silly stories. And she was loyal, a real premium in today's world. For four years she had stayed true to Hank, he thought, amazed that she had waited so long. His ex-wives would have been dating three days after he disappeared.

If Reed had only told him Ann was starting to date again, he would be the one looking after her now instead of that cowboy Hopkins.

The detective yanked open the door to the observation room and stepped inside. 'So, what do you think?'

Hopkins had his hands pressed to the window and was staring through the glass at Jimmy Sawyer. 'I'm sorry. What did you say?'

'What do you think of his statement? Pretty wild, huh?'

'The man's a pathological liar and a drug dealer. It's obvious,' Glen spat. 'Book him.'

Abrams was taken back. He walked over to the attorney, and both of them stared through the window as they talked. 'You really think we have enough? I mean, I'm not going to argue with you. You're the one who has to try the case.' Reaching in his pocket, he pulled out a stick of gum, unwrapped it, and popped it in his mouth. Then he looked down at Hopkins's boots. 'Are those alligator? How much do a pair of boots like that cost?'

'Book the bastard,' Hopkins snarled through clenched teeth. 'There's no doubt in my mind that he's guilty.'

This wasn't the D.A. talking here, Abrams thought, this was the man. 'Uh, what's the charge?'

'Attempted murder.'

'The Carlisle shooting, right?'

'What do you think I mean?' Hopkins said, still staring through the glass. 'You can't do anything about the fingers until we prove there was an actual crime. Right now we don't have a victim. We don't have anything but Sawyer himself.'

Abrams shook his head. They could seriously compromise their case by acting prematurely. 'Maybe it is true,' he said, wanting to see the attorney's reaction. 'Think she slept with him?'

Hopkins lunged at him, ready to rip his throat out. Then he quickly reined himself in. 'You're an idiot, Abrams. You know Ann. Do you think for a moment she'd fuck a guy like this, a probationer, for chrissakes? That's ludicrous.'

'Sorry,' Abrams said, throwing up his hands. 'I'm just trying to play the devil's advocate here. Believe me, I want this guy too.'

'Just book the prisoner and let me handle the rest,' Hopkins said, quickly exiting the room.

Left alone, Abrams turned and stared at Sawyer. The kid was dirty, no doubt about it, probably up to his eyeballs in criminal activity . . . but something didn't fit here. The detective could feel it in his gut. Sure, he wanted the person who had shot Ann, but if they tried a case without doing their homework, Sawyer could be acquitted and that would be that. It always made more sense to wait out a weak case, even though he understood where the D.A. was coming from. If he'd been the one dating Ann, Sawyer would probably be in a hospital by now.

'Shit,' he said out loud while his eyes tracked Sawyer

pacing. 'Whether you know it or not, asshole, you're in for one fucking rough ride.'

Jimmy Sawyer had made a serious mistake today. He'd picked on a probation officer, someone a doctor's son would see as nothing more than a bit player. If he had accused anyone else but Ann Carlisle, his clever little defense might have worked as planned. The woman would have been discredited or at the very least intimidated enough to back off, and Sawyer's problems would be over. But he wasn't going up against a solitary woman or a small-timer, as he thought. Jimmy was going head to head with the entire police department, the district attorney's office, and the probation department.

'You stepped on the wrong fucking toes, bud,' Abrams said through the glass. The D.A. could play the heavy and file the charges, but that was only step one. Hopkins needed hard evidence to bring in a conviction, and for that he had to rely on the man in charge of the investigation. Yours truly, Abrams thought.

He thumped the glass with his finger and saw Sawyer jerk his head toward the door, thinking it was his attorney. When the door didn't open, his eyes filled with fear and he turned toward the glass. 'That's right,' Abrams said, 'someone's watching you, Sawyer. And I'm going to keep on watching until I can see right through you.'

Before he got through with him, Jimmy Sawyer would be crying for more than his attorney.

Chapter 8

Ann was playing gin rummy with David in the kitchen when he saw Reed through the glass in the back door. 'Tommy,' he yelled, rushing to let him in, his cards still in his hands. 'Look at this,' he said to the detective, grinning wickedly at his mother as he showed him his hand.

'You're in big trouble, Ann,' Reed said.

'Yeah,' she laughed, rearranging her cards. 'He's already whipped me three times in a row. I'm losing bad here.' Then she noticed the grim look on the detective's face. Placing her cards on the table, she turned to David. 'Let me talk to Tommy for a few minutes. I think he's got some information about one of my probationers.'

'But I'm going to win,' he protested. 'That isn't fair.'

Ann noticed the dishes piled in the kitchen sink. 'Why don't you be a sweetheart and wash the dishes for me? Then when Tommy leaves we'll have time to finish our game.'

Once they were in the living room, Ann didn't sit down. She stood near the front door. Because the house was small, it was hard to have a conversation without David overhearing them. 'Did you ring the doorbell?' she asked, curious. 'I didn't hear you.'

'No,' he said. 'I thought if I came to the kitchen, I might

catch you before David saw me.'

Ann knew the detective was feeling guilty that he hadn't spent more time with her son lately, but he couldn't be there for the boy all the time.

'How is he?' he asked.

'Fine, I guess,' Ann said, slowly shaking her head. 'He's wetting the bed again almost every night now, and he's having nightmares. He was better for a while, but . . .'

'Maybe you should take him back to the shrink,' Reed said.

'That's not the answer,' she said. Turning thoughtful, she went on, 'What happened to me has brought everything back. You know . . . all the fear. Time is the only cure.'

'Did Hopkins call you?' he asked.

'Yes,' Ann said. 'He said I shouldn't worry, that he gave you the green light to arrest Sawyer.' Seeing the look on Reed's face, she placed her hand over her chest. 'He is in jail, isn't he? I mean, after what I saw in his house . . .'

Reed's eyebrows went up. 'Is that all Hopkins said?'

'He said some pretty harsh things about Sawyer,' Ann said, trying to recall the conversation. 'What's going on?'

Reed proceeded to fill her in on what had happened in the interview with Sawyer. Ann was livid by the end. 'That slimy little bastard. Does he really think anyone will believe him?'

'Obviously,' Reed said, clearing his throat. 'And listen, Ann, I hate to be the bearer of bad news, but his parents are heavy hitters in the community. His father's a surgeon, and the family is active in local and state politics. This isn't your normal dirtbag off the streets. His statements could carry some weight.'

Ann suddenly felt light-headed and went to sit down in the leather recliner. Reed took a seat on the sofa across from her. Bending forward from the waist, she locked her arms down around her stomach. 'What about the fingers?'

'We're checking the morgues now. Without a body –' He stopped himself. They had already covered this earlier.

'What if he says this vile stuff about me in the courtroom? The press could get wind of it.'

Reed tried to flick this off. 'Then don't go to the hearing.'

'Right,' Ann said, jerking her head up. 'That's really the answer, Tommy. Can you imagine how it will look? The guy saved my life. He'll look like a hero and I'll look like an ungrateful bitch.'

'I wouldn't concern myself with how things look.'

'Mom,' David called from the other room.

'I'm coming,' Ann yelled back. She grabbed the detective's hand as he stood to leave, needing comfort. 'I'm scared, Tommy. Do you really think he shot me?'

'It's possible,' Reed said. 'I have to say that I'm still undecided.'

David called out again, and Reed followed her into the kitchen. Once he had said his goodbyes, he left by the kitchen door.

'All right,' David said, picking up his cards, eager to resume the game. 'I just discarded, so it's your turn.'

Ann took a card off the top of the deck and then just held it in her hand, staring out over the room. If Hank had been alive and learned about the disgusting things Sawyer had said about her, he'd have torn him apart limb by limb. All Reed had done was shrug. Six years ago when one of the bailiffs had made a snide comment about her in the courtroom, Hank had met the man in the parking lot the next night. Exactly what he'd done to him Ann didn't know, but he'd never bothered her again.

'Mom,' David said, impatient, 'you have to throw a card away now.'

Ann dropped the card on the stack, lost in her thoughts. She depended far too much on the detective. It wasn't right. Reed couldn't step into Hank's shoes and fight all her battles. He wasn't her husband, any more than Glen was her husband. Ann slumped in her chair, tears forming in her eyes.

'Gin,' David yelped, slamming his cards down on the table and startling his mother out of her thoughts. When Ann spread her hand out, David was ecstatic. 'You don't have even one pair, Mom. I bet there's forty points here.' He started adding up the total, rubbing his hands with glee. 'That's it,' he said, looking at her now. 'I won again.'

Ann quickly swiped at her eyes with the back of her hand, but David saw her.

'What's wrong, Mom?' he said, concern leaping onto his face. 'What happened? Why are you crying?'

'I'm not crying,' Ann lied, managing a smile. 'I'm just mad because you beat me.'

His fingers stretched across the table to his mother's, touching them lightly and then withdrawing. 'You miss Dad, don't you?' he said softly. 'I miss him too. Will he ever come back, Mom?'

'No,' Ann said, looking deep into her son's eyes. 'He's never coming back, honey. We have to go on with our lives.'

David's face muscles froze. A second later, he exploded, sweeping all of the cards onto the floor. 'He is coming back. I know he's coming back.'

'Pick up the cards,' Ann demanded, glaring at him.

'No,' David said, defying her. 'Not until you take it back. You have to believe, Mom.'

'I can't,' Ann said, sighing. She didn't want to have this conversation now. She started to rise from the table, but then lowered herself back down. The psychologist had instructed her to be firm with him when he got this way. He simply couldn't go on believing his father was alive. 'There's nothing to believe. He's dead. Your father died four years ago. You have to accept it.'

He stood, seething with emotion. His leg flashed out,

kicking his chair halfway across the kitchen. This was Hank, Ann thought. The explosive temper, the inability to accept the obvious, the vulnerability lurking under the surface. They were so alike, and every day the similarities in their appearance and personality grew stronger. She remained silent, knowing David had to release his anger before she could reason with him. He was just like his father, and there was nothing she could say to stop him.

'It's because of that man,' he said, pointing a finger squarely at her. 'You don't want Dad to come back because of him. That's it. I hate him. He's a prick. What do you do with him, anyway? Do you do dirty things with him? I know about sex, you know. I'm not a little kid. I see the way he looks at you, with his stupid snake eyes.'

'Stop it, David,' Ann said flatly, trying to remain calm until the tempest passed. Let him vent his feelings, the psychologist had told her. The reason he had nightmares was that he suppressed so much bitterness and rage. And there was a new source of anger now. Anger over his mother's being shot.

Seeing him subside, Ann got down on her hands and knees and started picking up the cards. She did not have to wait long before he bent beside her to help clean up. Once the cards were all retrieved, Ann scooted back against the cabinets and just sat there on the floor, too drained to get up.

'I'm sorry,' David said, eyes down.

'I know you are,' Ann answered, a strange feeling of peace coming over her. The calm after the storm, she thought. She certainly knew about that. There had been plenty of storms with Hank through the years. Extending her arm, she reached over and pulled her son closer, giving him a kiss on the top of his head. 'You're all I have,' she said. 'If your father were alive, he wouldn't tolerate your talking back to me. And he wouldn't allow you to throw things all over the place.'

'Yeah, well, he used to throw things,' David said, memories

flashing in his eyes. 'I remember him throwing a dish at you one time.'

Children saw more than people knew, Ann told herself, stiffening. She had never dreamed David remembered that night. 'That was only one time, honey,' she said, wanting to change the subject. 'We just had a fight. Married people have fights.'

He peered over at his mother and then quickly looked away. 'He wouldn't like you seeing that man. In my dream –'

Ann held up a hand to stop him. 'Dreams are only dreams, David. I have dreams too.'

'About Dad?'

'About Dad, you, the past. But we have to live for today. You can never go back, you can only go forward.'

'Does that mean you're going to keep seeing Glen?'

'I don't know,' Ann said. 'I'm being honest, David. Relationships aren't easy. One of these days you'll know what I mean. When people get married, they're together every single day. That requires a lot of give and take. Do you know what I mean?'

'Not really,' he said pensively. Then his face flushed again. 'You're not going to marry him, are you?'

'I don't know him well enough to marry him. I dated your father for five years. I've only been seeing Glen a few months.'

David's face softened and he smiled at his mother. 'Tell me again about how you met Dad.'

Ann sighed before speaking. 'I was a rookie cop, remember, and they dispatched me to a shots-fired call. When I got there, your father was already there. He'd heard the call and was in the area, so he responded, even though he wasn't supposed to.'

'Why not?' David asked.

'Because he was a highway patrol officer, and the call was in the city limits.'

'Was he handsome?'

'Of course,' Ann said, tousling his hair. 'He looked just like you. I mean, he was taller, of course. He was compact, and built like a bull, and he had this way about him. Oh, I don't know, sort of like there was nothing he couldn't handle.'

'Tough guy,' David mumbled under his breath.

'Great smile,' Ann said, seeing him in her mind. 'When he smiled, he didn't look tough at all. He looked like a big teddy bear. And he laughed. Your father loved to laugh. Every day, it seemed, he had a new joke for me.'

'Did he kiss you that night?'

'Of course not. I was on duty. Police officers don't kiss on duty.' Ann had known officers who did a lot more than kissing, but she preferred to keep her son's image of police officers intact. 'So,' she continued, 'once we made sure there wasn't a real shooting going on, we went for coffee together. That's when this man came up and started yelling for us to come outside.'

David smiled with pleasure. This was the part he liked best.

'There were these six huge apes duking it out in the parking lot,' Ann related. 'What a brawl. They were Hell's Angels, I think. You know, the motorcycle gang. I started to jump in, and your father gave me this look, like what did I think I was doing. He was old-fashioned about women in law enforcement. He never wanted me to get hurt.' Ann stopped, thinking of how crazed he would be knowing she had been shot. In a way, she was grateful he had not lived to see it. 'Anyway, he took out all six of those guys by himself and hardly broke a sweat doing it. Boy, was I impressed.'

'I couldn't beat up a puppy dog,' David said, pressing down on his flabby thighs with his fingers.

'Then start exercising,' Ann said firmly.

'No way,' he said. 'Every time I exercise I get real hungry and end up wanting to eat a dozen hamburgers. I'm starving to death right now. Do we have any ice cream left? Did Glen bring over any groceries today?'

'Nope,' she said. 'We're on our own now, kid. Back to the diet.'

While David rummaged around for something to eat, Ann went to the living room and collapsed on the sofa, meaning just to rest her eyes. In no time at all, though, she fell fast asleep. Soon she was dreaming. She was in Jimmy Sawyer's kitchen, holding up a finger and examining it, when she saw the ring – the wedding ring she'd given her husband. She screamed, dropping the finger. When it struck the floor, it changed before her eyes to a rodent and scurried off. Bolting awake in a cold sweat, Ann glanced at the clock over the stone mantel and saw that it was after midnight. The house was still, David evidently in bed.

Sawyer's arraignment would be tomorrow – no, today, she realized. That must be why she'd had that horrid dream. She would have to sit in the same courtroom with a man who had sliced off a woman's fingers, who might broadcast his lies about her to everyone present.

Ann started to get up, and something fell off her chest to the floor. She bent over to retrieve it. David had placed his father's picture, the one in highway patrol uniform that he kept in his room, right in the center of her chest.

Detective Phil Whittaker was in his late forties and getting close to retirement. Since he had left the military at age twenty-one, he'd never had any job other than as a cop. He was overweight by at least twenty pounds, and his pants hung low on his hips in order to accommodate his protruding stomach. But he was a pleasant, likable man with a jovial plump face and a hearty laugh. Unlike many other veteran members of the department, Whittaker was not bitter and disillusioned with law enforcement. Oh, there were days when he wanted to cash it in and take off to Oregon, but he knew he would never last.

Phil Whittaker was a stone-cold addict. He loved the job, fed on the excitement. When he was at home with his wife and kids, he thought of the job. On his last vacation, in Hawaii, he hadn't thought of the beautiful young bodies decorating the beach, he'd thought of the job, his mind still sorting through facts and faces, searching for that one detail that he might have missed.

Assigned to canvass the neighborhood and see what he could learn about Sawyer and his roommates, he had been knocking on doors since seven o'clock that morning, thinking he'd catch people before they left for work. All the detective had learned the night before was that the rental house needed a paint job, the yard needed water, and the boys were going to run over one of the neighborhood kids one day. Shit, Whittaker thought, from the way it sounded they were describing his own house. His yard was dead, his house needed a fresh coat of paint, and every time the detective was called out on a hot case and screamed down the street in his police unit, the neighbors called his wife and sounded off.

When he had informed the residents of Henderson Avenue that the three boys were moving out, they were all relieved. He was glad to make their day, but Whittaker needed information. When he got back to the station, Reed would be waiting like a hungry bear. Right now the only evidence he had of any illegal activity amounted to nothing more menacing than a few traffic violations. Not exactly what they were looking for.

'Shit,' he said, pulling out a wad of tissues and blowing his nose. The rug rats had brought home another damn cold. Then he looked at the house before him and sighed. He'd finally made it to the residence next door to Sawyer's. Last night the people had not been home. He hoped they'd be home this morning, because if he was going to hit pay dirt, Whittaker thought, this would be the place to do it.

He knocked on the door and waited. A few minutes later, a

scruffy toddler opened the door and looked out through the screen. The detective couldn't tell if it was a boy or a girl. The kid had short hair and big brown eyes and was dressed in a little blue tank top and flower-print shorts. 'I need to talk to your mother or father,' he said. 'Are they home?'

'My mommy's sleeping,' the child said.

'Why don't you be real sweet and go and get her for me?'

'She get mad if'n I wake her.'

'I'm a policeman, honey,' Whittaker said, reaching in his pocket for his badge, then kneeling down on one knee so the child could see it. 'See, this is my badge. Now, be a good little kid and go get your mom for me.'

'Mom,' the child screamed, taking off running down the hall, leaving the door wide open. 'There's a placeman at the door. A real placeman wid a real badge.'

Whittaker shuffled impatiently on the tiny cement porch, glancing down the street and then back at the door, coughing a few times.

'What do you want?' a woman said from somewhere inside the house.

Whittaker stepped closer to the screen. All he could make out was a dark shadow. 'Can I ask you a few questions? It won't take more than five or ten minutes max. I'm sorry if I woke you.'

'What's this about?' the woman said, still in the shadows.

'We just want to ask you some questions about the three boys renting the house next door.'

'They're moving,' the voice in the shadows said. 'I don't know anything else. I just know they're moving. They loaded all their furniture in a moving van.'

'Do you mind if I come in and talk to you for a few minutes?'

'Yes, I do,' the woman said. 'I don't know anything, Officer. All I know is the people next door are moving.'

'I see,' Whittaker said slowly, wondering why the woman

was being obstinate. Some people just didn't like cops. 'Tell you what,' he said. 'I'm going to leave my card. Then if you think of anything, you can give me a call.' He stuck the card in the metal grille of the screen door and turned away. Damn, he thought, he hadn't even gotten the woman's name. The house on the other side of Sawyer's was vacant, up for sale. He was going to have to face Reed empty-handed.

'Excuse me,' the detective said through the screen door. 'I need to get your name at least. See, my sergeant's not going to be happy when he hears I didn't get a statement from you. Can't you give me a break here?'

The pleading worked. A woman stepped out of the shadows and appeared behind the screen. She had limp shoulder-length brown hair and small hazel eyes. She was short, maybe a little over five feet, and extremely slender, almost emaciated. Her skin had a gray cast, and dark circles were etched under her eyes. She wore a pair of faded jeans and a blouse made of the same print fabric as the child's shorts, and her face was void of makeup. 'Sally Farrar,' she said. 'Why are you asking me about the people next door?'

'Oh,' he said, 'I'm really not able to give out that information right now.'

'Why?' she asked. 'What did they do?'

'They haven't been charged with a crime yet, Mrs Farrar.'

'Then why are you here?'

'Because we want to know if you saw anything suspicious.'

'What's suspicious?'

'You know, strange people coming and going at odd hours. Maybe strange sounds like someone screaming. Stuff like that.' As soon as Whittaker got the last word out, he sneezed and quickly reached for a tissue.

'You've got a cold.'

'No shit,' he said, sneezing again. 'Excuse my language. You're right. I feel terrible.'

'Did someone say something about me? Is that why you came here?'

Whittaker studied the woman. A little paranoid maybe, he thought, deciding Sally Farrar might be the neighborhood weirdo. 'No, ma'am, it's just that you live right next door. Surely you know something about what was going on over there. I mean, if anyone did, it would be –'

'They were wild, okay,' she said, stepping up closer to the screen, her voice almost provocative. 'They had girls over there every night and did disgusting things with them. Do you know what I mean, Officer?'

Whittaker blushed and put a finger inside his collar, pulling it away from his neck. It was the way she was looking at him, the tone of her voice. If she asked him to come inside now, the detective gave thought to sprinting down the street. Women used to make plays for him all the time, frustrated housewives and the like. But no one had approached him in years, not since he had stopped wearing a uniform. 'Could you be a little more specific?'

'Orgies, Officer. Do you know what an orgy is?'

'Sure, but . . . how did you know they were having orgies specifically? Maybe they were just having parties.'

'I saw them,' she said, her eyes glazing over and her mouth falling open as she pressed her entire body against the screen.

'Ah, what exactly did you see?'

'There were three of them. A Chinese boy, very handsome, a tall blond boy with a gorgeous body . . . the most beautiful body I've ever seen.' She stopped and took a breath, trailing a fingernail down the screen as she stared at him.

The detective looked down at the ground nervously. The woman was trying to seduce him. He knew it. Shit, he thought, wait till he told the guys about this. 'We're . . . interested in the dark-haired boy, the one with the long hair. His name is Jimmy Sawyer. Can you tell us anything about him?'

'He was rough. You know, with the girls. I think he had a bad temper or was more jealous than the others. They shared their women. That's the kind of thing I'm talking about. These weren't normal parties. They began when the sun went down and never stopped. Day after day . . .' Her voice trailed off and she stepped back into the shadows.

Whittaker decided to drop this line of discussion. The woman was obviously a mental case, and they couldn't arrest Sawyer and his roommates for excessive screwing. Then he thought of the fingers. Ann Carlisle had said she'd seen fingernail polish. He almost slapped himself on the forehead. The woman had said Sawyer had a bad temper. If the case got to court, this woman would be a valuable witness. 'Could you describe the girls you saw over there?'

'Possibly,' she whispered, 'if I wanted to.'

'What about drugs? Did you ever see them using drugs or anything else relating to narcotics?'

'Don't people like that use drugs?'

'Did you ever see smoke or anything along those lines? There's a possibility that they were manufacturing narcotics, running a home lab. You know, like chemical smoke?'

She laughed. 'A lab? I don't know what you're talking about.'

The door slammed in his face.

'Thanks a hell of a lot,' Whittaker mumbled, staring at the door. There was no use trying to get any more information out of this lady. They'd just issue her a subpoena when the time came.

Whatever Sawyer and his friends had been up to, he decided, they'd been having the time of their lives, and Whittaker was a tad envious. Fast cars, fast girls, easy money. Sure beats the hell out of getting doors slammed in your face. He sighed and then headed off down the street, reaching for another tissue.

Arraignment was scheduled for one o'clock. Ann met Tommy Reed outside the courtroom, and they went in and took seats in the front row. Even Reed had his reservations about filing so soon, but the case was out of their hands. Ann wanted to get it over with, get Sawyer locked up whatever it took. She was anxious about what he would say, however. If his lurid story surfaced in an open courtroom for everyone to hear, Ann knew she would be humiliated.

When the bailiffs escorted Jimmy Sawyer in, Ann couldn't help but stare. Both shackled at the ankles and handcuffed, he could walk only in small steps. His long hair was lifeless and stringy, his shoulders slumped, and his face had an unhealthy cast. In his jail-issued jumpsuit he certainly looked different from the last time he had appeared in court, she thought, feeling a measure of satisfaction. A night in the Ventura County Jail could do wonders for an inflated ego.

Harold Duke was waiting for him, and stood to allow the bailiff to seat Sawyer at the counsel table. Then the two men leaned their heads together and began to confer in hushed whispers.

Ann craned her neck around, expecting to see the entourage Jimmy had brought with him the last time, but no one was present today but his mother. After what Ann had seen in the Henderson house, she wasn't surprised that Sawyer's friends had decided to stay away.

'Where's Hopkins?' Tommy asked her.

'I called before I came over, and he was still arguing with Robert Fielder. He should be here any minute.' Ann frowned as she said this, worried that Fielder had quashed the proceedings for lack of evidence. Again she looked over her shoulder, this time checking for reporters, but the courtroom was practically empty. Just then she noticed Sawyer watching her, a glint in his eyes. When he smiled, Ann quickly looked away and inched closer to Reed. A thought kept racing through her mind: maybe Sawyer had followed her and Glen to the fire stairs, had been the one who opened the door while they were having sex. That could be the foundation for his ridiculous story. Seeing her having sex in the stairwell would give anyone food for thought.

Hopkins suddenly came barreling into the courtroom and slammed his briefcase down on the table. Removing his notes and files, he glanced back and saw Ann. 'I got the go-ahead from Fielder,' he said, smiling confidently. 'Don't worry, Ann, everything's under control.'

She got up out of her seat and met Glen in the aisle on the far side of the courtroom. 'Why didn't you tell me what Sawyer said about me last night?'

'Why?' Glen said, not happy she had been told. 'Why have you listen to something like that? I knew it would upset you, Ann. I hate to see you upset.'

Gratitude swept over her, and she quickly touched his hand with her own. 'Can you come over tonight?' she asked. 'Maybe we could visit in the backyard after David goes to bed.'

His eyes softened. 'Just take care of your son, Ann. Next week will be better. The last thing I want you to worry about right now is me. Besides, I'm burning the midnight oil on Delvecchio. Since we lost Estelle Summer's testimony, the case is not as solid.'

The two exchanged a grimace at this, and Ann slipped back into her seat, watching as Glen crossed the room to the clerk, handing her two copies of the information form, which was used in felonies to set forth the various pleadings and charges. The clerk then handed a copy to the bailiff to deliver to Sawyer's attorney and placed the judge's copy in the file. The woman's phone rang, and she picked it up. Then she yelled out to Hopkins, 'Judge Hillstorm wants to see you in chambers before we go on record.'

Glen quickly exited through the back door of the court and headed down the corridor to the judge's chambers. Hillstorm's secretary, a middle-aged woman with red hair, waved him in.

'Sit down,' Hillstorm said, looking out over a large maple desk that had seen better days. The surface was marred and scratched, and most of the desk was buried under stacks of papers and periodicals. Hillstorm collected western bronzes and odd artifacts, and his office looked more like a musty attic than a judge's chambers. On one side of his desk was a stuffed owl on a podium. Set on his credenza were several bronze sculptures of rearing horses and riders. Because of their shared love of horses, Hillstorm and Hopkins were quite chummy.

Once the D.A. was seated, Hillstorm picked up a newspaper and glanced at it. 'Is this the same man we're arraigning today for attempted murder?' He tossed the paper across the desk at Hopkins.

'Yes,' Glen said, looking at the paper and then placing it back on the judge's desk. 'You sentenced this man yourself on the narcotics case. Don't you remember him?'

Sunlight streaked in from an overhead window, and Hillstorm's white hair sparkled. But his eyes were narrow and his voice sharp. 'Of course I remember him, Counselor. They even contacted me when they did this newspaper piece. It was a nice story for a change. Man comes before the court, then saves the life of his probation officer.' Hillstorm chuckled and rested his arms over his stomach. 'Thought I made an impression on this young fellow and he cleaned up his act. Made me feel kind of special, you know?'

Hillstorm was eyeing him steadily, and Hopkins became uncomfortable. Was the old judge serious or just playing with his head? They were all hams, loved to get good publicity, particularly since most of their publicity was negative. Every day some group blasted a judge for leniency or some impropriety. 'Is this what you wanted to discuss?' he said.

'What did you think I called you in here for?'

This time Hopkins kept his mouth shut and listened.

'Bob Fielder sent over a transcript of this man's statement. Seems his parents are decent people and he has some reservations about this case in general. Think there's any truth to this man's statements about Ms Carlisle?'

'He shot the woman,' Hopkins exclaimed, leaning forward. 'If you listened to his statement, then you know he placed himself in the parking lot prior to the shooting, exactly where we feel the assailant was hiding when he fired. He must have positioned himself behind a parked car. Ann Carlisle's car was disabled. That means he flushed her out in the open so he could get a clear shot and was lying in wait for her. This was a premeditated, vicious attack. Not only that, Ms Carlisle saw human fingers in his refrigerator. We don't know what we're dealing with here. We could be dealing with a serial killer for all we know.'

'You didn't find these alleged fingers, though. Isn't that correct?' Judge Hillstorm swiveled his chair around and faced the window, not waiting for Hopkins's response. He already knew the answer. 'That will be all,' he said.

Once the bailiff had called the court to order, Hillstorm peered out over the courtroom. 'Do you have a copy of the Information, Mr Duke?'

'Yes, Your Honor,' the short attorney said, standing. 'I also have a discovery order I would like to file.' Duke walked over and handed it to the clerk for dispersal.

When the judge received his copy, he simply set it aside. To file discovery, requesting all evidence and information the other side had on the case, was routine procedure. As the case continued, more discovery orders would be filed by both parties, along with dozens of motions and petitions.

The courtroom fell silent, except for the rustling of papers by the clerk as she prepared the file. Finally Hillstorm spoke, his gaze fixed on the defendant. 'It saddens me to see your face, Mr Sawyer. You're a young man with a good family behind you, I hear. These are serious allegations you're facing.' Hillstorm shook his head and looked down at the Information, slowly sliding on his glasses before he began the arraignment. 'How does your client plead to count one, a violation of section 664/187 of the California Penal Code, attempted murder?'

'My client pleads not guilty, Your Honor,' Duke said.

'As to count two, a violation of section 12022(a) of the penal code, using a firearm in the commission of the above crime?'

'Not guilty,' Duke said again.

'As to count three, a violation of section 245(d)(1), assault with a deadly weapon on a peace officer?'

'Not guilty,' the defense attorney said, leaning over and whispering something to Sawyer, then glancing back over his shoulder at Sawyer's mother. The woman was dabbing her eyes with a tissue.

'All right,' Hillstorm said, 'as to count four, a violation of section 1203 of the penal code, violation of probation in case A5349837?'

'Not guilty.'

Suddenly, Ann realized that this was not another routine hearing, like so many others she had attended in the past. Two lives were on the line here. Not just Sawyer's but hers as well. By going to his house that day and making her grisly discovery, Ann had set this machine in motion. Even if she wanted to, she couldn't stop it now. She felt herself vacillating, thinking like a mother. Sawyer was so young, she thought, staring at his back. Maybe one of his roommates was the butcher, the one who had sliced off the fingers. As unjust as he was to accuse her of seducing him, could he have done it in retaliation? No, she thought, she couldn't allow herself to think this way.

Simply by closing her eyes, she could relive the night of the shooting, the bullet ripping into her flesh, the blood, the panic and terror. Now she knew how victims felt, sitting only a few feet away from the very person who had attacked them.

Ann knew that by law, Sawyer could be convicted of only one crime involving the shooting, plus the second count, which was considered an enhancement for the use of a firearm. If he was convicted of attempted murder, he could not be convicted of assault with a deadly weapon, basically the same crime but with nonspecific intent. Overfiling charges gave the jury an option. If the prosecution did not prove beyond a reasonable doubt that Sawyer's intent had been to kill Ann, the jury could still bring in a conviction under the lesser offense of assault with a deadly weapon. In addition, pleading multiple counts was a tactic used to provide options should the case be plea-bargained. If Sawyer was receptive to entering a plea of guilty for a prenegotiated term of imprisonment, the first count would more than likely be dismissed.

'Fine,' Judge Hillstorm said, proceeding with the arraignment. He selected a date for the preliminary hearing in three weeks and explained to the defendant what would occur then. In essence, the prosecution would have to establish only that a crime had in fact occurred and that there was probable cause to believe the defendant had perpetrated this crime. During the trial, on the other hand, the burden of proof would be more specific, and the prosecution would be charged with proving its case within a reasonable doubt.

Harold Duke stood again. 'Could we address the issue of bail at this time, Your Honor?'

'Mr Duke,' Hillstorm said sternly, 'if you'll give me just a moment here, I was about to order the probation officer to conduct a bail review. That's the way we do it.'

'I object,' Duke said quickly. 'I realize this is standard procedure, but surely you can see there is a conflict of interest here. The victim is a probation officer, and it's highly unlikely that my client will receive impartial treatment from the probation department. We feel the court should determine bail for my client independent of any other recommendation.'

Glen Hopkins was quick to object. 'Why should Mr Sawyer receive special consideration, Your Honor? Mr Duke's allegations that the probation department would act in an unethical fashion are inflammatory and downright offensive.'

Judge Hillstorm removed his glasses, wiped them with a tissue, and then slipped them back on his nose. 'I concur with Mr Duke,' he said slowly. 'I'll settle the issue of bail. Mr Hopkins, state your position.'

'The people are asking that the defendant be held without bail,' Hopkins said firmly, still irritated that Sawyer was receiving special treatment. 'He was on probation at the time of this offense, and there are circumstances to suggest he's clearly a danger to the community. Further, Ms Carlisle has been traumatized by this crime and should not be placed at further risk. Don't forget, this poor woman was shot right here, Your Honor, right outside this courtroom and only a short time after the defendant was sentenced. How can she continue her work, walk to that parking lot every night, with the knowledge that this man is back on the street?'

'Mr Duke,' Hillstorm said.

'My client has only one prior offense, a misdemeanor. He has no history of violence and has resided in the community all his life. In considering bail, the criterion is basically to address the likelihood of the defendant fleeing. There is absolutely no reason to believe my client would not return to this court as instructed.'

'Your Honor, that isn't the case at all,' Hopkins protested. 'There's concrete proof that the defendant was preparing to abscond at the time of his arrest. He rented a U-Haul van, and he moved all the furniture out of the house he was leasing. If that's not an indication he was attempting to flee, I don't know what is. He doesn't have a job or own real estate, and he's facing serious felony charges.'

'Is this true, Mr Duke?' Hillstorm said, shuffling papers but unable to find the arrest report. 'Was your client attempting to flee when arrested?'

'Not at all,' Duke rebutted. 'He was only moving back into his parents' home. There's no proof whatsoever that he intended to leave the state or even the city.' The attorney glanced back at Rosemary Sawyer, and his voice rose in indignation. 'These charges are a sham anyway. What evidence do they have linking my client to this crime? In my eyes it's unconscionable to incarcerate an innocent man when you know very well you'll never convict him.'

'I object,' Hopkins said, leaping to his feet. 'That was uncalled-for.'

'Bail is set at a hundred thousand dollars,' Hillstorm said, pounding his gavel. 'This court is hereby adjourned.'

Once the judge had left the bench, Hopkins seized his file and rushed over to Ann. 'It's a start, Ann,' he said quickly. 'The preliminary hearing's in three weeks. If he's held to answer, they'll probably revoke his bail.' Seeing she was not comforted, he lightened his tone. 'Hey, at least Hillstorm set it at a hundred G's. That's a pretty hefty amount. Sawyer might not be able to make it.'

'He'll make it,' Ann snapped, locking eyes with him. 'His father's a surgeon, remember?'

As people poured out of the courtroom, Glen said a few words to Harold Duke. Then he rushed out to return to the Delvecchio trial in another courtroom. Sawyer's family had to come up with merely ten percent, not the entire amount. Ann knew they'd never let their son sit in jail.

As she and Reed started walking out of the courtroom, she had a sudden flash of the severed fingers in the house on

Henderson. Instantly she forced it away. There was nothing to be gained by dwelling on it and making herself crazy. No matter what Sawyer had done, whom he had butchered, or how many narcotics he had peddled on the streets, he would soon be on the loose again.

'Look, Ann,' Reed said, 'I'll put a tail on him. If he gets anywhere close to your house, we'll blow his fucking head off.'

'That would help,' she answered, and then laughed nervously, trying to mask her fear. 'I mean, the surveillance.'

'We only have three weeks to put this together,' the detective told her. 'I'm going to pull every man I can and put him on this case. We've got to move fast.'

Ann nodded without speaking, deciding she would never make a recommendation for bail again, no matter what the case involved. Now she knew. She knew how they felt: the victims.

In many ways it was worse than before Sawyer had been arrested. Even though the pleadings had been filed under the name of the state of California, Sawyer knew it was Ann who was his accuser. And Ann had a face to insert behind the gun that shot her. Ironically, it was the same face she had thought was so beautiful that night on the sidewalk. Sawyer had to be deranged, twisted, the worst possible adversary. A man who would shoot you, she thought, and then stop to save you had to be a sociopath, a person with no conscience, no understanding of basic values.

What would he do now? she wondered, a sliver of fear slipping its way up her spine. If only Hank were alive, she thought sadly. But he wasn't, and Ann knew she must do what she'd been trained to do, years before her husband had entered her life. She had to protect herself. In a few short hours Jimmy Sawyer would walk out the doors of the jail, and Ann would not be safe until he walked back in again. Only three weeks, Glen had said. To Ann, three weeks sounded like a lifetime.

Chapter 9

Ann drove to her house in a driving rainstorm at nine o'clock that evening after having dinner with Claudette and her husband. She'd given David permission to stay at his friend's house. She was so exhausted and emotionally drained that she headed straight to the bedroom and peeled off her clothes, turning off the lights and crawling under the covers. Heavy rain was pelting the roof and the wind was blowing, making the old house rattle and creak. Pulling the covers over her head to shut out the noise, Ann quickly fell asleep.

Approximately fifteen minutes later, a loud clap of thunder rang out, and Ann bolted upright in her bed. Looking out over the dark room, she saw her own image quickly flash in the mirror, lit by a bolt of lightning. Yesterday she'd moved Glen's floral arrangement to the top of the safe under the window directly across from the bed, but she could smell the too-sweet odor of wilting flowers, intermingled now with the damp scent of rain.

Hearing a loud dripping sound, Ann finally forced herself to get out of bed and reached for her robe. When she couldn't find it, she decided to forget it and headed down the hall naked. No one could see into the house, and David wasn't around. When she reached the kitchen, she flipped on the overhead light. As she suspected, water was dripping from a leak in the ceiling onto the kitchen floor and collecting in a large puddle. Ann removed a metal pot and placed it under the drip, wondering how much a new roof would cost. Then she got several more pots and carried them to various locations throughout the house where she knew there were existing problems. Last year she had patched. This year she was looking at a new roof.

Ann headed down the hall to her bedroom, passing David's room. Although the lights were out and the room was dark, she felt a gust of damp air. He must have left his window open. It was probably raining in and soaking the top of his desk and all his papers. When the kid got home and saw it, he would go bonkers. 'Serves you right,' Ann said, entering the dark room. She'd told him a dozen times to shut his window before he left the house. For security reasons, Hank had installed window locks, but her silly son kept leaving his window open.

Ann touched the desktop as she leaned forward to get the window. His desk was wet, all right, and David even had several textbooks on it. Ann would have to dry them out in the microwave and try to save the expense of replacing them. She gripped the window and was trying to pull it down when something fell with a clunk onto the top of David's desk. It was a large shard of broken glass. Turning on the desk light, Ann saw that the entire window was shattered. Some of the pieces were scattered on the desk, some on the floor, and several large sections had slid between the desk and the window. Great, Ann thought, now she needed a new window as well as a new roof. She stuck her head through the window, careful to avoid the jagged glass. She saw nothing so she assumed the tree branch right outside had smashed into the window, whipped by the wind.

She pulled the desk out from the wall, wondering if she had a piece of cardboard somewhere in the garage large enough to tack in place until she could get glass installed. As she did, she became aware of the danger of the shattered glass on the floor. She stepped into a pair of David's tennis shoes, already too big for her, and grabbed his textbooks. As she was leaving the room, everything suddenly went pitch-black.

Ann screamed and fled from the room, then stopped at the door and took some deep breaths, laughing at herself. 'Don't be such an idiot,' she said aloud. 'It's just a power failure.' She wasn't used to being in the house alone, she told herself, and lately she'd become thoroughly spooked.

'Damn,' she said, feeling her way along the hallway. She couldn't see a thing, not a blasted thing. If she could just get to the kitchen, she thought, she was certain she had some candles. Just then her shoulder collided obliquely with the wall, and she decided to maintain the contact as she inched along.

'Ann,' a man's voice said in the dark. 'Ann.'

She froze, her breath trapped in her throat, her heart leaping like a jackrabbit. Quickly she spun toward the kitchen and the voice. 'Who's there? What do you want?' Dropping the books, she tried to run and slammed her shoulder into a doorframe. She could smell wet clothes, body odor, raspy breathing. The intruder was only a few feet away from her. He had to be in the bathroom. The bathroom was between David's room and the kitchen doorway.

A hand touched her arm, and Ann shrieked again, bolting at a dead run down the dark hallway toward the door to her bedroom. After only a few feet she tripped in the untied sneakers. Losing her balance, she crashed into the wall. The shock of pain brought her to her senses. She had to summon up her police training. If she stayed low to the ground, she would be a more difficult target. She had to assume the intruder had a weapon.

Holding her breath and telling herself not to panic, Ann

started crawling. She had to get to the safe in the bedroom and get her gun.

Clothes rustled and a dark image moved around her. Suddenly Ann was slapped flush against the floor as a heavy weight dropped on her. The man was on top of her, on her back. She couldn't breathe. He was crushing her. 'Get off me,' she screamed, in full panic now. 'What do you want? I don't have any money.' Was it Jimmy Sawyer? Had he come to kill her, make certain she would never testify against him?

'Just be still. It's all right,' the man said, his voice muffled. Ann pushed up with all her might, trying to throw him off her back. He was too big, too heavy. She felt something prickly and coarse brush her cheek, felt hot breath fill her ear cavity. 'Relax, Ann,' the voice said firmly. 'Don't fight. Don't you know who I am?'

As he spoke, his hands were moving over her buttocks, darting between her legs. Ann squirmed beneath him, kicking out with her legs, pushing up with all her might. 'Get off me,' she cried. Hands forced their way under her body from the sides and pinched her nipples. Ann screamed in pain. The man was going to rape her. She was naked and had never felt so helpless and vulnerable in her life. 'Stop! No! Let me up and I'll give you what you want! Please!' A horrid thought darted into her mind: Estelle Summer. The way the assailant was positioned, he could sodomize her without even turning her over.

Again the hands squeezed her nipples, and Ann clenched her eyes shut.

Who was this man? His voice . . . she tried to get a fix on the voice. It was muffled, distorted, as though he was speaking through a handkerchief or stocking mask. Did she know this person? Had she heard this voice before? Was it Sawyer? Was it some other man she had sent to prison? Hadn't Tommy always told her this would happen, that one of the men she had tricked into a confession would come after her?

Hands were still groping at her, roughly moving from her breasts down between her legs. If she couldn't get to the gun, Ann decided in that second, she would kill this man with her bare hands. She would poke her fingers in his eyes, reach down his throat, and yank out his tongue.

'Doesn't that feel good? Don't you like that?' the man said seductively. 'Where's David? Tell me where he is, Ann.'

David? She heard a rushing sound inside her eardrums. How did this animal know about David?

Consumed with fury, Ann suddenly found strength she didn't know she possessed. Adrenaline raged through her bloodstream. She would never let anyone hurt David. She would die first. 'You bastard,' she snarled from deep in her throat.

In one burst, she rose up to her hands and knees and flung the man off her back. He fell sideways, slamming into the wall. A hand seized her arm, but Ann kicked out and collided with something fleshy – the man's stomach? She didn't know, but he was groaning as though she had kicked him in the groin.

Springing to her feet, she dashed down the hall to her bedroom. Once she passed through the door, she wheeled in the direction of the safe and smashed right into the thick steel surface with her thigh, knocking the vase of flowers to the floor. Fierce pain raced up her leg, as if she'd struck a nerve, but Ann was oblivious to it, tossing the tablecloth that covered the safe up into the air, whipping the door open.

From the hallway, Ann heard banging: the man had tried to stand and had fallen back against the wall.

Patting the bottom of the safe with her palms, Ann finally felt a cold, hard surface and closed her trembling fingers around her Beretta.

Holding the gun with both hands, Ann found the safety and released it. Then she depressed the trigger and fired to make certain it was loaded. The explosion rang in her ears, reverberated inside her head, and the distinctive smell of cordite drifted to her nostrils. It smelled wonderful, Ann thought. Greatest smell in the world. She sucked it in and felt her confidence surge. 'Hear that, motherfucker?' she yelled, panting, bringing the gun up and sighting the door, her right wrist braced against her other arm. 'Come down that hall, asshole. Come and get me.'

She heard feet scurrying on floorboards.

A flash of lightning illuminated the room, and Ann realized that what she had thought was the door leading to the hall was a reflection in the dresser mirror from the bedroom window. Kicking the tennis shoes off so she wouldn't trip again, Ann sprang to her feet.

Creeping down the hall, she patted the wall and found the entrance to the bathroom. She stopped, pointing the gun into the darkness. A second later, she heard a noise in the direction of the kitchen and spun around. Was he trying to escape? Did he think she'd ever give him a second chance to hurt David? Outside the door to the kitchen, she flattened herself against the wall. On the count of three, she jumped into the doorway, her gun in her outstretched hands, ready to fire.

A gush of air suddenly struck her face, and Ann realized the back door was standing open, rain and wind rushing into the room. Moving forward cautiously, she reached the door and then broke into a run when she realized the man had fled.

Glimpsing a shadow moving rapidly down the driveway, Ann squeezed off a shot. A loud clap of thunder sounded almost the same instant as she fired, and a second later, she saw the shadow fall to the ground.

She'd shot him.

In a ray of light from a nearby streetlight, she saw his face from only a few feet away. His head was turned and he was looking back at Ann, his haunches high in the air like a sprinter, not like a man who'd been hit. Her finger was on the trigger, but she was mesmerized, unable to fire. Time stood suspended for those few seconds as they made eye contact. Ann's body shook violently. She knew this man, had seen him before. Her throat was so dry she couldn't swallow. Her heart strained against her chest.

Ann closed her eyes, wanting to block out the image, and felt for the trigger blindly. Shoot him. Now, she told herself. Opening her eyes to aim, she saw he had vanished. She let the gun fall to her side.

His reflexes had been too quick, she thought, cursing herself. Only a split second before she had fired, the man must have dropped to the ground, and the bullet had sailed right over his head. But she'd had another chance and she'd hesitated. Only a few seconds, but it was too long. Should she chase after him, or simply forget it and protect herself inside the house? She sucked in a breath and remained perfectly still, listening. There were no sounds other than the wind and rain.

Then she heard a car engine start, tires spinning on the rain-slick street, the sound of wheels skidding, a loud metallic crunch.

Ann sprinted from the driveway to the street. When she got there, she discovered only a parked car turned sideways in the road, its front wheels up over the curb. Ann knew this wasn't the suspect's car. It belonged to the man across the street. Realizing she was naked, she wrapped her arms over her chest and jerked her head to the right, hearing a car engine. All she could see was a glimmer of taillights as the car carrying her attacker fishtailed around the corner.

She ran back to her house, intending to get her car and catch him, but then she stopped herself. By the time she got the garage door up and the car started, he would be long gone.

Stepping over the glass by the kitchen door, Ann looked back and saw a hall light burning inside her neighbor's house. She then recalled seeing the intruder in the streetlight. If it was a power failure caused by the storm, the electricity would be out on the whole street. The person who had broken into her house must have turned off the current at the power box on the side of the garage. He had set her up, placed her in the most vulnerable position possible, just as on the night she'd been shot. Wet from the rain, shivering, she stood there in a daze.

Who could have done this? Why had the man seemed so familiar to her? Finding the candles and matches over the stove, Ann lit one and headed to the living room, grabbing the first garment that came to hand in the coat closet.

Shoving her gun in a pocket as she prepared to call the police, Ann felt something and pulled out a crushed pack of Marlboros. She was wearing Hank's trench coat, the London Fog she had bought him one year for Christmas. Suddenly she caught an echo of her husband's voice inside her head. The attacker's voice, she thought, trying to remember what it was about it that she'd recognized.

Once she had called the police, she dropped onto the sofa to wait, her candle flickering in her hand. In her dazed state she didn't notice it until hot wax began dripping onto her fingers. Flicking away the pain, Ann tipped the candle on its side, letting wax form in the ashtray on the end table. Then she stuck the candle into it. She pulled Hank's trench coat tight around her. Bringing her arm up close to her face, she thought she could still catch a whiff of his cologne on the fabric. But no, she decided, it was only her imagination.

Picking up the phone again, Ann called Glen and got his machine. Deciding not to leave a message, she quickly hung up. She couldn't tell him what had happened on an answering machine.

Where were the police? Already, it seemed she'd been

waiting for hours. Her feet were tapping uncontrollably as she watched the shadows, her thoughts turning again to Hank. He would have been here by now, even if she wasn't his wife. Although he mainly responded to traffic accidents, her husband had always thrown caution to the wind and driven flat-out to get to a crime scene as fast as he could. Ann had ridden along one night and scolded him, telling him he was going to get killed one day. 'They're waiting out there,' he'd told her. 'How would you like to be trapped in the wreckage of a car, hurt and waiting for someone to show up?' His dedication to people in need was one of the things Ann had always admired about him.

She reached for his picture on the end table, the one David had placed on her chest the night before. Then she saw that something was missing. On one corner of the end table was a shiny spot, devoid of dust. A picture of David had been in that spot. Thinking it had fallen down behind the table in the commotion, Ann got down to search but didn't see it. A fresh wave of panic engulfed her. The assailant had taken David's picture. During the attack she had clearly heard him state her son's name. Like the shooting, this was no random attack, no ordinary burglary.

Ann leaned forward over her knees, her head in her hands. A few moments later, though, she pulled the gun out of her pocket and clasped it tightly, pointing it at the front door.

'Come back, you bastard,' she said between clenched teeth. 'Next time I'll be waiting.'

Chapter 10

Detective Jess Rodriguez had been parked in front of the Main Street Mall since six o'clock, tailing the kid and his Porsche from Dr and Mrs Sawyer's residence on Seahorse Avenue. He had no idea what the punk was doing inside the mall, since the stores all closed at nine o'clock and it was almost ten now. Finally Rodriguez decided to go inside and see if he could spot him, but the outside doors were already locked and rain was pouring down. He returned to the car and got his raincoat out of the trunk. The guy would come back, he told himself. With a car like that one, he wasn't about to walk off. Jess slid down in the front seat of the Camaro and looked out over the parking lot. He was bushed. People didn't realize how draining it was to sit around for hours staring at a parked car.

Jess decided to work on a report before he nodded off, something he had to finish by nine the next morning or be called on the carpet. Turning on the map light and using his clipboard to write, he was about to start when he saw the Porsche lurching forward. 'Shit,' he said, springing into action. He tossed the clipboard onto the floorboard and cranked the ignition. He hadn't even seen the guy with the rain, and the windshield was fogged over. If he lost the Porsche, there'd be hell to catch from Tommy Reed.

What in the world was wrong with this guy? Jess soon wondered. He was popping the clutch, driving like an idiot. While he watched, the Porsche lunged forward, stopped, lunged forward. He could hear the transmission straining. 'You're in the wrong fucking gear, asshole,' he said. This little creep didn't know shit about driving a fine machine. Had his doctor daddy just given it to him?

The Porsche managed to get out of the parking lot and onto the rain-pelted street. It was moving slowly, but at least it wasn't lurching anymore. Navigating through the residential areas, it began ascending into the foothills, Rodriguez right on its tail. Few streetlights illuminated the area. It was dark, and with the rain, Jess figured there was no way Sawyer could see who was behind him. Again the Porsche started straining and lurching. 'Downshift, you motherfucker. You can't go up this hill in fourth gear.'

A while later, the car parked and a bulky short person stepped out. Rodriguez, stopping several doors down, looked and then did a second take as the driver walked to the front door of a house and passed under the entry light.

It wasn't Sawyer.

'Shit,' he said as the person went inside. Had he followed the wrong car like a fool? Quickly he verified the license plate on the paper next to his seat. The car was definitely Sawyer's, but where was Sawyer? He had to go back to the mall immediately and find out if his subject was still around. Right before he turned down a side street, he saw the Porsche moving in his rearview mirror. The driver hadn't engaged the parking brake, and the car was rolling right down the hill into a parked car.

'Serves you right, motherfucker,' Jess said, roaring off. 'Serves you right for switching cars on me. Hope you end up with a great big dent in your pretty little Porsche.'

•

Almost two hours had passed since the intruder had fled. Ann was standing in her bedroom, assessing the damage with Noah Abrams, as an evidence team picked its way through the house. Two narcotics officers, Greenberg and Miller, had arrived on the scene right behind the first patrol unit. Furniture was toppled, things were tossed all over the floors, and muddy footprints outlined a path from the front door to the bedroom where the police officers had traipsed in and out of the house. A war zone, Ann thought, shaking her head as she surveyed the damage.

Noah's eyes followed her as she walked around the room. She was still wearing the black trench coat, buttoned up to her neck. Her pale blond hair was damp from the rain, and she was badly shaken.

The men's heels were crunching on glass fragments as they searched the room for evidence. Abrams had already collected a mask from the driveway, like the type doctors wear in surgery, and he was showing it to Ann. She understood now that the mask was the reason the man's voice had been muffled and distorted. Because Sawyer's father was a surgeon, it also indicated that Sawyer was the culprit.

'But it can't be Sawyer,' Ann said, unable to get her frazzled nerves to settle down. 'Tommy told me you had him under surveillance, and he wouldn't get within a mile of my house.'

'Jess Rodriguez lost him,' Abrams said, grimacing. 'He says Sawyer went inside the mall around six o'clock, and Jess thought he had him in the Porsche at around ten, but the asshole switched cars on him.'

'Great,' Ann said. 'So we don't know where he is right now? What about the parked car that got rear-ended? Is there a paint transfer?'

'Maybe,' Abrams said.

'What does that mean?' Ann snapped. 'There's either a paint transfer or there's not a paint transfer. Can't you tell?'

Dropping the mask into a plastic evidence bag, Abrams moved closer. 'I'm sorry about this, Ann,' he said. 'I was home when I got the call. If I'd been working, I would have assigned a unit to watch your house.'

The guilty look on his face deflated her anger. 'I know it isn't your fault,' Ann said, lowering her voice. 'I just can't believe they lost him.'

'Well, trust me, Jess is going to catch hell.' Anger flashed in his eyes, and he slammed a fist into his open palm. Then his expression changed to concern again. 'Are you sure you're okay?'

'I'm fine,' Ann said. 'The paint transfer, Noah?'

'Oh,' he said quickly, 'we've got a tow truck en route to transport the parked car to the lab. With the rain, we'll make more headway there.'

'What about prints?'

'Ann,' the man said softly, 'why don't you let us conduct the investigation? Sit down or even lie down for a few minutes. You don't look good.' She was pale normally. Right now she looked as white as the wall behind her. 'Hey, maybe you should let me take you to the emergency room.'

'No,' Ann said, wanting Tommy, not Abrams. 'Can't anyone raise Tommy and Phil Whittaker?'

Abrams kicked a piece of glass with his shoe, stung because she didn't want him. He was the investigating officer on this case, not Reed and Whittaker. 'Guess they must be out of radio range,' he answered, shrugging. 'We tried to reach them on their cellular, but it was turned off.'

'Tommy told me he was going to Los Angeles with Phil to check out some leads,' Ann said. 'Have you been able to find out who Sawyer's roommates were? Maybe we can pick them up. They've got to know where Sawyer is.'

'Ann,' Abrams said, wanting to reassure her, 'we're doing the best we can. We have the names and descriptions of the two other boys and have already issued attempt-to-locates to pick them up for questioning. One is a Chinese guy named Peter Chen. All we know is he's never been arrested, and someone said he went to Long Beach State and studied physics or something. The other guy was a local, Brett Wilkinson. Sawyer's known him since high school.'

Ann glanced at the clock. It wasn't even eleven o'clock, yet it seemed like hours had passed since the attack. The brush with the intruder had probably lasted only a few minutes.

'I thought you said it wasn't Sawyer,' Abrams asked. 'Did you get a good look at the guy?'

'I don't know,' Ann said wearily, having been asked this before. 'All I know is the man was big, tall, you know, and he was wearing a heavy coat of some kind. It was too dark to make out the color. And he was wearing the mask you found, but I got the impression that he had a beard. I'm not certain. When he was next to me, something like hair or a beard brushed up against my face. I saw him for only a second in the light. If he did have a beard, it wasn't Sawyer. Sawyer doesn't have a beard.'

'But you're not sure, right?' Jesus, Noah thought, this woman had been a cop, and she couldn't even provide a decent description. How would she ever identify the guy in court? He wanted this guy bad, and she was giving him little or nothing to work with.

Ann suddenly remembered David and was instantly frantic. She rushed across the room to the phone while Abrams trailed behind her. 'I have to check on David,' she told him, the phone in her hand. 'He said David's name. The man was looking for David, asked for David. I should have called before.'

Abrams kept looking at Ann, eyeing her suspiciously, not sure if she was going to keel over on him. Finally he walked out into the living room while Ann called her son.

'Freddy?' she said. 'Were you guys asleep?'

'No. Who's this?'

'Ann Carlisle. Can I speak to David?'

'Hey, David,' the boy yelled. 'Your mom's on the phone.'

Ann heard giggling and a television set blasting in the background. It sounded like a rock video on MTV.

'What d'you want?' David said, as if she had embarrassed him by calling and checking up on him like a baby.

'Where are Freddy's parents?'

'In their room. Where do you think they are?'

Ann felt a wave of relief. She was close friends with Louise Litsky and her husband. 'Okay, David, how far is their room from your room?'

'Right down the hall, but we're in the living room. Why are you asking me all these stupid questions?' He stopped and yelled at Freddy, 'Turn it down. Your parents are going to come in and bust us.' Then he started giggling.

Ann could hear a woman moaning in the background. 'What is that? I hear a woman. Is something going on, David?'

'No, no,' he protested, more giggles coming out over the line. 'Nothing's going on, Mom.' David covered the phone with his hand and yelled out to his friend. 'Hey, Freddy, I said turn it down. Now. My mom can hear, man. She can hear.'

As mothers sometimes do, Ann suddenly felt she had X-ray vision and could see into the room. Hearing David's voice, knowing he was safe, was an enormous relief, but it didn't mean the kid could do anything he wanted. 'You're watching porno movies, aren't you, you little shit? That's a porno movie I'm hearing.' She knew she was right. All that phony moaning. It was one of the reasons Ann generally didn't allow him to stay overnight at people's houses. 'You're watching the Playboy Channel, aren't you?'

'No, Mom, I swear,' David whined, his voice elevating and cracking. 'It was nothing. Turn it down now, Freddy.' The sound in the background disappeared.

'I'm going to have Louise come in there right now. You hear me?' Ann was on a short fuse. People were breaking into her house, and her son was watching porno movies.

David's voice was pleading now. 'No, Mom, please don't. It's off. We turned it off. I promise we won't watch it anymore. Please, Mom, Freddy will kill me if his parents find out. They invited me to go to Magic Mountain this weekend.'

Looking over, Ann saw a tiny strawberry-blond woman in the room, bent over as she picked through glass fragments on the floor. She recognized her at once. Melanie Chase was one of the finest forensic specialists in the county. 'I have to go now. I'll pick you up in the morning.'

Ann knew Melanie well. Every law enforcement officer in the county knew the magic she could work with forensic evidence. When the highway patrol and other agencies had pulled out of the investigation into Hank's disappearance, Ann and Tommy had coerced Melanie into trying her hand at the case. After eight months of poring over documents and sorting through evidence on her own time, with no compensation, the woman had finally given up. Because the suspect or suspects had evidently jumped Hank Carlisle before he got back to his police cruiser and then transported him to another location where they had presumably committed the murder, the case was a forensic vacuum. All they had were tire marks where the suspect's vehicle had fled the scene and evidence collected on the ground, which might or might not have been left there by the suspects. According to Melanie Chase, it was the only time she had worked that hard for nothing.

Swimming in a department-issue yellow raincoat, Melanie saw Ann was off the phone and looked up. 'You okay?' she said.

'Yeah,' Ann said, 'I guess I'm okay. How have you been?'

'You know – I work and then I work some more. Such a deal, huh?'

Ann suddenly noticed Melanie's feet. She was wearing rubber galoshes, but she was so short that the top of the boots reached her knees. Combined with the raincoat, at least four sizes too big, Melanie looked like a little girl playing dress-up in her mother's clothes.

'Mel,' Ann said, 'I really appreciate your coming out tonight, particularly on a night like this one.'

'No problem,' the woman said, straightening up and then bending backward to stretch her back. 'We had a stabbing over on the west side of town, so I was already out and about.' Melanie was close to forty, how close no one knew. Diminutive in size, she was big in every other way: big mouth, big gestures, enormous smile when she felt like it. The men all loved her. Even more important was that their admiration was based on respect.

Wearing rubber gloves, she reached in the pocket of her raincoat and pulled out a Salem. A moment later, she flicked a gold lighter and fired it up. Then she let the cigarette dangle from her mouth, an unflattering and disgusting habit she had. Ann thought Melanie left her cigarette in her mouth because she wanted to keep her hands free. Every time she encountered the woman she was trying some other gimmick to quit smoking: patches, nicotine gum, devices attached to her ears. She had even gone to a hypnotist, but seeing her puffing away now, Ann had to assume the attempt had been in vain.

'How does it look?'

'Good,' Melanie said, giving Ann a quick glance and then emitting a puff. 'We have saliva on the surgical mask.'

'What about fingerprints?' Ann said.

'I don't think you're going to find any prints,' Melanie mumbled, clamping the cigarette between her teeth. She held up a plastic sack with an infinitesimal residue of white powder in the bottom. Then she removed her cigarette from her mouth and flicked the ashes into the palm of her hand. 'I lifted this off several surfaces, places I think he came in contact with.'

'What is it?' Ann was staring inside the bag. 'Looks like dust. I'm not the best housekeeper, Melanie, so don't get excited.'

'No, it's baby powder or cornstarch. Here,' she said, opening the plastic baggie so Ann could get a whiff of the contents. 'What do you think?'

'I'm not sure,' Ann said. 'It does smell a little like baby powder or talcum or something. What's baby powder got to do with anything? I don't have any powder in the house.'

'Whatever brand of rubber gloves this ape used had a residue of fine powder on them. The ones I use have cornstarch on them. It keeps the rubber soft and flexible, keeps it from cracking. Also, it makes the gloves easier to slip on.'

'So,' Ann said, disappointed, 'he wore gloves.' She recalled how inhuman his touch had felt; it was the rubber she had felt against her skin.

'Yeah,' Melanie said, a hint of that fabulous smile appearing, 'but don't worry about it. We've got plenty to work with here.' She suddenly spotted something on the wall and yelled to the young officer working with her, 'Alex, get the ladder.'

Ann followed her line of sight and saw what looked like a fly on the wall, up near the ceiling. 'What is it?'

'You fired only once in the house, right?'

'Right,' Ann said. 'And once in the driveway.'

'The first one must have struck and deflected off the mirror. That's where it went, up there.' Again she yelled, 'Get the fucking ladder and get it now, Alex.'

A young blond-haired officer stuck his head in the room, a look of exasperation on his face. 'Melanie, the ladder is at the very back of the van. We've got a ton of equipment in there. I'll have to move everything out to get to it, and it's really raining hard. Everything else will get wet.'

'So move it,' she said, taking another puff of her cigarette and then going to the bathroom to toss it into the toilet. 'If you mess up the evidence we just collected from the stick-and-run, Alex, I'll break your skinny neck. Put a tarp over it or something.'

Once the young officer had shuffled out of the room, Ann stood beside Melanie. She pulled out her pack for another cigarette and then put it back in her pocket, evidently changing her mind. 'You were here, Ann. Hey, you got any chewing gum?'

Ann shook her head. She was trying to play back the exact sequence of events. Everything had happened so fast.

'How about mints? Do you have any mints?'

'I don't think so, Mel. I have some fruit, some grapes. Would that help?'

'Grapes?' Melanie said, a funny expression on her face. 'What would I do with grapes? Forget it. Come and see what we found in the hall.'

Ann followed the woman the short distance as her rubber boots squeaked over the floor. In the center of the hall, right outside David's room, someone had placed orange highway cones in a half-moon circle out from the wall.

'Sorry,' Melanie whispered, rubbing up against Ann. 'I usually just mark it off with chalk, but they gave me that rookie to train, and the guy is either blind as a bat or a fucking moron. Every crime scene we go to, he steps right in the middle of it. It's the craziest thing I've ever seen.' She stopped and peered up at Ann. 'Don't you think they have to take an eye test at the county? I mean, how can you work in this job if you can't see?'

Ann chuckled. Melanie always had some weird tale to tell about the people she worked with. 'He's cute, though.'

'The hell with him,' Melanie said, her pale blue eyes

coming alive as her attention returned to the cones. 'This is where the suspect was when you flipped him off your back, right?'

'Right,' Ann said uncertainly. 'No, it wasn't here,' she said, correcting herself. 'I'm certain he jumped on my back right outside my bedroom door.' Ann turned and looked back at the spot where she thought the attack had occurred. It had been dark, however, and she just wasn't sure.

'Well, then,' Melanie answered, 'he must have been standing here when you fired the gun the first time.'

'Right,' Ann said, her nose assaulted with a foul odor. 'What's that smell?'

Melanie laughed. 'Scared the shit right out of that sucker, Ann. When you fired off that shot, he got a case of the runs.' She carefully stepped inside the cones and squatted down with a specimen cup and a small plastic spatula. Scraping up the runny excrement, she placed it in the cup. 'Great way to earn your living, huh?' she said. 'Rather scrape up shit than brains, though. And this is good shit,' she said, laughing again. 'Excuse the pun, but we can tell a lot from this guy's feces.' She brought the spatula up close to her face and stared at it. 'Like what he had for lunch, for instance, along with a lot of other fun things. Corn. See, that's a kernel of corn right there.'

Ann put her hand over her stomach. Melanie might make more money than she did, but she could keep her job as far as Ann was concerned. 'I think you're stirring that stuff up. God, put the lid on that thing.'

Melanie didn't react at all. 'In addition to the saliva and feces, we've got a good blood sample. When he broke out the window in your son's bedroom to get in, he must have cut himself. Because this all went down so fast, it's probably not contaminated. That means we can come up with this perp's fingerprints.'

'Wait,' Ann said. 'I thought you said he wore gloves.'

'I didn't mean that kind of fingerprint,' Melanie said, standing and putting the lid on the specimen sample. 'His genetic fingerprints. You know, do a DNA test if we need to. Of course, this isn't going to lead us to the suspect. Unfortunately, we need another blood sample from him or we don't have anything to match up with.'

Ann shook her head. What they needed now was a way to identify the suspect and track him down. What Melanie was giving her were ways to convict him.

Melanie removed her white rubber gloves, shoving them into her pocket. A few seconds later, she pulled out another cigarette and lit it, a stream of smoke exiting her mouth along with her words. 'See, a normal fingerprint is good, but not that good. We never lift a complete set. Seldom do we have anything but partial prints from one or two fingers. It tells us the suspect was in the house on some occasion, but it doesn't tell us specifically that he was in the house at the time of the crime. With DNA fingerprinting, we know it all. All you have to do is get this bastard in a courtroom.'

The woman stopped speaking and smiled, the full boat, a smile that took up half her face and instantly made the recipient a Melanie Chase fan for life. At times like this she didn't look hardened by years of working with the worst side of society, scooping up brains, guts, and human excrement. She looked just like a cherub – a little redheaded, toothy, freckle-faced cherub. Except for the cigarettes, Ann thought.

Just then the blond officer came down the hall, lugging the ladder on his back, and promptly knocked two of the cones down. Then he proceeded to pull the ladder right through the area Melanie had sectioned off. She stood shoulder to shoulder with Ann and whispered in her ear, 'Guy's blind. Didn't I tell you? Good thing I already collected the evidence. If I hadn't, we'd be scraping it off his shoes.'

While they watched, he tried to get the ladder through the

bedroom door but instead walked right into the doorframe. 'Where do you want this?' he asked Melanie, rubbing a red dent on his forehead.

'Africa, of course,' Melanie barked. Snatching the ladder from him, she slammed it up against the wall where the bullet was located. 'Where do you think I want it, Alex?'

Ann started to leave the room just as Melanie started climbing, the cigarette dangling from her mouth, her head encircled by a dense cloud of smoke. Then Ann heard Melanie screaming, a loud thump, and hurried back into the room. Evidently Alex had bumped into the ladder, for Melanie was on her back on the floor. 'Are you hurt?' the young officer said, bending down over her.

'Get away from me,' Melanie said, standing and brushing herself off. 'Don't touch me or you're dead, Alex.' Once she had picked her smoldering cigarette up off the floor and shoved it back in her mouth, she slapped the ladder back up against the wall. 'Go to the back of the van, Alex, and close the door. No, I take that back. Lock the door. Don't come out again tonight until we get to the station.'

'But, Melanie, I thought –'

She was climbing again and looked back and said to Ann, 'See, I told you it was bad. You just didn't want to believe me. No one ever believes me. Personnel doesn't believe me, my boss doesn't believe me.'

Ann began to laugh, a good feeling after the ordeal she had been through. The young officer was still standing there, refusing to leave. 'But you said you were going to let me –'

'Ann,' Melanie said, high on the ladder, digging in the plaster with some kind of metal instrument while she puffed away, 'do me a favor. Handcuff this guy for me. Lock him in a closet or something.'

Sitting on the sofa in the living room, Noah Abrams was

brooding over the case. Damn, he thought. It had to be Sawyer. The little fucker had switched cars right under their noses, probably with the express intent of coming over here and committing this attack. Correct that, he told himself. He hadn't come over here merely to hurt Ann. Whoever was after this woman wanted her stone cold dead. Anyway, that was how he saw it. This was the second explicit attack on her life, and he was the one in charge of the investigation. He had to bring this maniac in, no matter what it took.

But he was confused. He could rationalize Sawyer going after Ann to keep her from testifying, but what was this stuff with her kid?

Ann wandered into the living room and took a seat next to him on the sofa. Noah looked over at her and compressed his mouth. 'I don't like this, Ann. I don't like it at all.'

'Neither do I,' she said grimly, lacing her fingers together and then placing them in her lap.

'Isn't there anything more specific that you can tell me about the guy who did this? I mean, you did see him. Isn't that what you said?'

Ann stared off into space, forcing herself to bring forth the vision of the man in the driveway. 'He – he was . . .' she stammered, the memory filling her with terror.

'What?' Abrams said, frustrated. 'Give me something, Ann.'

At first Ann didn't respond. Why had she hesitated? Why hadn't she pulled the trigger when she'd seen him in the driveway in the light? If she had, he would be dead, and this would all be behind her. 'He looked familiar,' she finally said, cutting her eyes to him. 'I don't think it was Sawyer, Noah.'

'You know him?' Abrams said, leaping to his feet. 'Shit, you've got us jumping through hoops here, and you know who it is?'

'I know him,' Ann said weakly, dropping her eyes, 'but I

don't know him.' Realizing how ambiguous this sounded, she added, 'It was only a second, Noah. I saw him only a second, but his eyes –'

'Wonderful,' Abrams said, annoyed, turning to walk out of the room, then stopping and facing Ann again. 'What about his eyes?'

Tears slowly inched down Ann's face. 'I just don't know, Noah,' she said, the most honest statement she could make. 'Maybe it will come to me later. You know, where I've seen him before. I've handled so many cases, dealt with so many criminals through the years. It could have been any one of them.'

Ann cupped her hand over her mouth, forcing back the tears. She didn't want him to see her this way. She wanted him to see her as strong and resilient, not terrified and weak. For years she had stood in her father's shadow and fought to win the respect of men like Noah. Now she was just another terrified female, so hysterical she couldn't even give them a straight answer.

Seeing her distress, Abrams dropped down in front of the sofa, pulling her head onto his shoulder. 'We'll get him,' he said tenderly. 'I promise you, Ann, we'll get him.'

Chapter 11

By the time Reed and Whittaker finally left the Black Onion, it was last call, almost two o'clock. But they learned things they hadn't known and made a contact. They'd verified that Peter Chen and Brett Wilkinson were regulars at the dance club, even though they hadn't been seen there lately and no one knew who Jimmy Sawyer was. Evidently the Black Onion was not the type of establishment Sawyer favored. Their clientele was new-age funk. From what they'd heard, Sawyer preferred heavy metal.

Phil Whittaker's contact was a parolee from federal prison who had served four years on a narcotics bust. Phil knew he was using again and could easily get him shipped back to the joint. So they traded, a common practice in police work. The man was trading information for silence.

'Big operation,' Phil said on the walk back to the car. It had stopped raining momentarily, but water was still rushing noisily down storm drains, and huge pools had formed in depressed sections of the parking lot. 'I mean, big operation, Reed old buddy. We landed feet first in a rattlesnake nest.'

Reed nodded, his face muscles twitching. 'How did little shits like Sawyer and his buddies get in with these guys? Want to tell me that, Phil? There are two distinct breeds of cat here.'

Reed stepped off the curb right into a foot of water. 'Fuck, will you look at that?' The cuffs of his pants were soaking, his socks squishy inside his shoes. 'They just dried out, and now . . .'

Whittaker coughed a few times, feeling too miserable to care about Reed's plight. The two men continued walking down the street. Not wanting to arrive in a police car, even an unmarked one, they had parked several blocks away. 'How do I know? Maybe they were at the right place at the right time. Colombian drug dealers,' Phil said, shaking his head. 'Shit, those guys open fire with their AR-15s if you so much as sneeze on them.' Just as he finished that statement, he did sneeze and reached for a tissue in his pocket. 'Sure wouldn't want to run into those mothers right now,' he said, his nose clogged up. 'You'd be talking to a dead man.'

Reed took his car keys out and unlocked the door to the police unit. They were in downtown Los Angeles, and the nearby buildings were covered with graffiti. Reed looked around him, thinking he wouldn't want to be on the job in this area. Ventura looked squeaky clean compared to L.A.

Once he had fired up the car and pulled out, he continued the discussion. 'All right, let's assume Sawyer and his gang are financed by these Colombians from Miami. That gives us a better picture of the overall situation now. It goes like this:

'Sawyer and the rest cook the dope, and they get to distribute in their assigned territory, basically colleges and middle-class kids with some bucks, a little loose change for drugs. These guys are perfect. Wilkinson and Chen look like they just stepped out of a frat house. Sawyer works the locals, kids he probably knew in high school, kids that didn't make it to college. That accounts for his long hair and loser looks.' The rain was starting to come down again, and Reed stopped to turn on the windshield wipers. 'At least the nasty boys from Miami know what they're doing. A bunch of South American drug dealers in a small town like Ventura would stand out like a sore thumb. Every narc in town would be crawling up their assholes.'

'I agree so far,' Whittaker said, nodding. 'Keep going.'

'So, after Sawyer and company sell off their quota of goodies, they turn the rest of the product over to this drug cartel, which peddles it on the streets in Miami. Think they're shipping drugs out of the country?'

'Nah,' Whittaker said, tipping his head back and snorting nose spray up his nostrils. 'Everyone's a drug dealer in Colombia. Why do you think they come over here? We're not talking coke or smack here anyway. The stuff Sawyer and his gang are cooking is a snap to produce. All you have to know is a little basic chemistry and you're in business.'

'Exactly,' Reed said. 'My bet is they're manufacturing X, a little acid, and a ton of high-quality speed.'

Reed watched as Whittaker squirted more nose spray up his nostrils. 'You're going to get addicted to that nose spray,' Reed cautioned. 'Last year it took you a year to get off it.'

'Oh, yeah?' Whittaker said, making a show of squirting even more. 'Maybe I should contact Sawyer and see what kind of goodies he's got in his drugstore. Bet they could fix me right up.'

When Reed stopped at a light, the two men turned toward each other. 'Fucking Colombians,' Reed said, shivering like a wet dog.

'Severed fingers and Colombians,' Whittaker said, the same anxious look in his eyes as Reed's. 'Great combination, huh? Goes together like a ball and chain.'

The remainder of the ride was made in silence.

When they reached the station, Whittaker was so tired and sick that he told Reed just to leave him at the door to his car. Reed went inside the station to check with the watch commander for any new developments.

'Where you been, Reed?' the watch commander said gruffly. 'Your men lost the perp, and Ann Carlisle was attacked in her house.'

Reed's body lunged forward over the counter. 'Was she hurt? When did it happen?'

'Hours ago,' the man said. 'I think the units have already cleared. Abrams handled it.'

'Where is he?'

'Home in bed, probably.' The man shrugged.

Reed was out the door in seconds, back in his car speeding over the city streets.

Even though it was close to three in the morning, all the lights were burning when he pulled up at the curb in front of Ann's house. All the way over, Reed had been mulling over the situation. If the informant was right, Sawyer, Chen, and Wilkinson might be lightweights, but the people they were in business with were deadly. Every day that lab was out of commission, they lost a fortune in revenue. And there were other considerations. Sawyer and his friends were neophytes in the drug trade, just eager to bring in the bread, get the chicks, buy the fancy cars. To them, it was all a game. But if they were apprehended, the men behind the operation, hardened and vicious criminals, had no assurance these kids would keep their mouths shut, not turn state's evidence and cough up everything they knew. If Reed's suspicions were valid, all three boys were sitting ducks. Once they were no longer able to supply these people with narcotics, they were expendable – basically garbage.

Reed also had to consider the fingers Ann said she had seen in Sawyer's house. How did fingers fit into this equation? Did Sawyer and the rest have to do someone in, maybe to make their bones with the South American thugs? Reed was well aware that kids involved in minor crimes often proceeded to commit more serious ones. The boys could have murdered a street person, a drifter of some kind that no one had reported missing, then sliced off the fingers to provide proof of what they had done. Tommy felt a rush of excitement as he yanked open the car door. Now, this made sense. If drug dealers from Colombia knew Sawyer and his friends were tough enough to commit an actual murder, they would be more likely to accept a bunch of stupid rich boys as part of their operation.

'Yeah,' Reed muttered, feeling he was on to something as he walked up the path to Ann's house. Sawyer gets caught and placed on probation, a development his South American buddies would surely be unhappy about. To protect his operation, he shoots Ann in the parking lot, or more likely, one of the Colombians does it for him. She's out of commission long enough that they can close up the lab before she can pay them a visit.

That was the scenario – if the informant was right. Ever cautious, Reed knew how eager informants were to tell tales that would keep them out of prison. But at least it was a tale that answered some questions.

He knocked on the door and waited. When Ann didn't answer, he walked across the soaked lawn to the living-room window. Ann pressed her nose to the glass, the muzzle of her Beretta trained right at Tommy's head.

'Shit,' he said, spooking, his feet sliding in the mud. 'Let me in,' he yelled. 'What are you going to do? Blow my head off, for chrissakes?'

When the front door opened, Ann peered out from behind it. 'I wouldn't advise you to prowl around my house, Tommy. I'm a little trigger-happy right now.'

'Ann,' he said, stepping forward and embracing her, 'it's okay. I'm here now. Tell me exactly what happened.'

'Tommy,' she said, stepping back from him, the gun dangling at her side, her eyes wild, 'it was . . . it was . . .'

'Take it easy, Ann,' he said, concerned. She looked as awful as she had after Hank disappeared. 'Got any coffee?'

Ann mumbled something Tommy couldn't make out, her eyes downcast now. She was dressed in what looked like one of Hank's old shirts, white cotton panties, and a pair of white socks. She turned around and headed toward the kitchen. Then she stopped in the middle of the floor and stared into space as if she had forgotten where she was going.

'Just sit down,' Reed said, looking over at the sofa as his eyes scanned the room. He took in the candle set in the ashtray, the muddy footprints on the carpet, Ann's rubber galoshes tossed by the coat closet. Then he noticed the beige leather recliner, and he brought forth the image of Lenny Braddock sitting there, a cigarette dangling from his mouth. Glancing at the ceiling, Reed saw the ugly brown stain from the cigarette smoke was still there. Hank had painted the walls, but not the ceiling. 'I'll get the coffee myself.'

Ann took a seat on the sofa, far in one corner, pulling a throw pillow to her chest, her legs curled beneath her. Pressed into the pillow was the hand holding the gun. Ann's fingers were numb and aching from squeezing it. But she couldn't let go. The gun had become an extension of her hand.

When Reed came back in, he set the steaming cup of coffee down on the table and pointed at the gun. 'Give me that before you shoot me.'

Ann's fingers were locked tight. 'No, Tommy, I have to have it. Leave me alone. It makes me feel safe.'

Reaching over, he forcefully pried her fingers off, his mouth rigid. 'Give me the fucking thing, Ann. I'm not going to sit here and look down the barrel of a loaded gun.' Finally he pulled it out of her hand and placed it on his end of the coffee table. He rubbed his eyes, stretched out his legs, and sipped his coffee. After letting his mind clear, he turned to her. 'Tell me everything. Tell me sequentially, Ann, and talk slow so you don't leave anything out. I want to have the whole thing straight in my mind.'

Once Ann started, she couldn't stop. Words just spilled out in long rambling sentences. She told him about the man in the hallway, what the man had said, how she had got a fleeting look at him. Then she dropped the throw pillow and her eyes got even wider. 'It might have been Hank, Tommy.'

Reed did a double take. What the hell was she talking about? Then he slapped his coffee cup down on the table. The liquid sloshed onto an old *Time* magazine. Frowning, Reed rubbed his eyes with his fists. After Hank had disappeared, she'd had them running around in circles, chasing down one worthless lead after another. He'd never live down the fortune-teller episode – the time Ann talked him into digging up a vacant lot in Oxnard, convinced it was the site where he was buried. 'It was not Hank, Ann. What are you saying?'

Alone in the house, Ann had been obsessing over the missing picture. Of all the things in the world her husband had cherished, his son was the most precious. If he had staged his own disappearance as the highway patrol had originally speculated, the one thing he'd be unable to walk away from would be David.

Seeing the detective staring at her as if she'd lost her mind, Ann began to waver. 'I couldn't see him that clearly,' she said, talking fast. 'It was only a second maybe, but the man had similar features and he was the right height and body weight. There was just something about him. I know him. I'm certain I know the man who was in my house, Tommy.'

'Well, you certainly know Sawyer.'

Ann gripped his arm. 'I don't mean like that. It's different. I can't describe it. Maybe the voice . . . I don't know. It could have been his voice, and he did ask about David.'

'If it was Hank, why, Ann? Ask yourself why. Tell me, huh?' Tommy stood and started pacing in front of the sofa.

Ann felt like a scolded child. 'You're making this really tough on me, Tommy. You're supposed to be my friend.' She pulled the pillow back to her chest, hugging it tight against her body.

'Hey,' Reed said, stopping and throwing his hands in the air. 'You want to believe this shit, then convince me. I'm willing to listen, Ann. You're just not making any sense. If Hank got away from whoever grabbed him four years ago – something I think is next to impossible after this much time – why would he come here tonight and break into his own home, try to hurt you?'

'Maybe he didn't intend to hurt me.'

'Oh, really?' Reed said. 'He just broke in here and jumped you in the dark, tried to rape you, but he wasn't trying to hurt you? Sure, Ann.' While she stared at him with her mouth open, Reed continued, 'It was Jimmy Sawyer who came over here tonight. He wants to scare you into leaving town, terrify you so you'll never testify against him and the others. And if it wasn't Sawyer, it was someone worse . . . someone that would make Sawyer look like a choirboy.'

Ann wasn't really listening. 'It wasn't Sawyer. I mean, it could have been Sawyer, but the man was too big and his voice –'

'You said he was wearing a mask, Ann, that his voice was muffled and distorted. It was Sawyer. Even the surgical mask . . . can't you see how it all fits? Sawyer probably got that mask from his father's clinic.'

'I don't think so,' Ann said slowly. 'Anyone could get a mask like that, Tommy. Even manicurists wear them now.'

Again her thoughts returned to Hank. She'd been in denial all these years. Hank had hated the job. When he'd failed to get promoted to lieutenant, he'd become bitter and withdrawn. Or, she thought, maybe it wasn't even the job. Her husband could have become involved in some type of illegal activity. He'd always wanted more than he had, and for a cop the opportunities for corruption were abundant.

'It was Hank,' she said, nodding in affirmation. 'He came for David, he wanted David. He even took his picture off the end table.' She started choking up and then stopped herself. 'Don't you see? Hank wants to see his son.' Although the detective was still glaring at her, Ann saw a flicker of acknowledgment. 'How would any of this fit in with what we know about Sawyer? He's just a high-rolling rich kid in over his head with drugs.'

'Okay,' Reed said, 'if it was Hank, why didn't he just tell you who he was? Why scare you out of your mind like that?'

Ann sat upright, tossing the pillow aside and putting her feet on the floor. She looked so young sitting there, Reed thought, her long, thin legs bare except for the white ankle socks.

'What if Hank staged his own disappearance for some reason? Remember, even the highway patrol investigators had thoughts along those lines.' Ann paused, reluctant to bring up her worst fear – her husband involved in something illegal. 'He hated the job, Tommy, you know that. So what if he wanted to quit, leave me, leave everything and start all over somewhere else, but he felt guilty leaving us to survive on my income? If it looked like foul play, I would get his retirement, his insurance benefits.'

Deeply concentrating, Reed said, 'Go on.'

'Okay, Hank stages his disappearance. Everything goes well and he knows I'll eventually get the money. His plan works. Then he starts thinking about David, how he abandoned him. He tries to enjoy his new life, wherever that is. But he anguishes over David. So he decides to kidnap him and take him with him to this new life. . . .' Ann stopped. Tears were filling her eyes. What she was saying was her husband didn't want her, didn't care what happened to her.

For all she knew, Hank could have changed his identity and found a new wife, a new family. He only wanted his son.

'Ann, don't cry,' Reed said, seeing how upset she was. 'It's late. We're both tired. Why don't we just call it a night?'

'No, let me finish, Tommy.' Ann was backtracking in her mind. 'Okay, the man grabs me in the hall. He must have been already inside the house when I got home. It wasn't a power failure, by the way. Whoever did this purposely turned off the power at the box outside. He didn't want me to see him. He even wore that mask so I wouldn't be able to recognize his voice. Can't you see, Tommy? Why would a complete stranger have to disguise himself? It was dark anyway.'

Reed was silent, listening. After a few moments, he spoke. 'If he was already inside the house, Ann, how did he turn off the power outside? Wasn't the electricity working when you got home?'

'Yes,' Ann said, 'but after Melanie left, I noticed the window in my bedroom was open, and I'm almost certain that window was closed when I went to sleep. I'd never leave my window open, particularly after what's been going on.'

'Keep going,' Reed said.

'Maybe he was hiding in the house when I got home and waited until I was asleep. Then he crawled back through David's window to find the electrical panel. That could be where he cut himself, not when he came in, but when he went back out after the glass was already broken.'

Reed shook his head. 'I don't know, Ann. Are you saying that he turned off the power and then entered the house again? How did he get back in?'

'Through the bedroom window,' Ann said. 'Okay, just listen. Hank had window locks on all the windows, so there was no way to get inside the house other than to break the glass. The intruder knew this, see, once he was inside. He probably prowled around in here before I got home.' Ann's eyes expanded in fear. 'I think he was in my bedroom, Tommy. God, now that I think about it, I heard noises, but I just thought it was the wind.' When the detective nodded, Ann continued, 'So he releases the window locks and maybe even cracks my bedroom window, thinking he'll leave the house this way, or to make certain he has a ready escape route if I wake up. Then when I do wake up, he's in David's room and dives out the window, probably cutting himself on the jagged glass. Once he's killed the electricity, he comes back through the window he left open in my bedroom. He was at that end of the hall when he jumped me.'

'Okay,' Reed said, 'let's get back to Hank.'

'When he jumped me and started grabbing me,' Ann said, 'he kept telling me to relax. I think he got turned on being near me, wanted to touch me . . . wanted to . . .'

'Rape you?' Reed said.

Recalling the man's hands on her breasts, she wrapped her arms tightly around her chest. 'Maybe not rape me, but close. He could have changed his mind and decided to tell me the truth once he was here. Maybe he wanted to really make love to me, Tommy, you know, for old times' sake. This person . . . he pinched my nipples. Hank used to do that when we had sex.' Ann turned her head to the side and mumbled the rest. 'He loved to do that.'

'You never told me that,' Tommy said, a curious look on his face. 'You mean he used to hurt you in the bedroom too?'

Ann knew what he was referring to and quickly clammed up, giving him a harsh glance. Tommy knew this topic was taboo.

Letting it go, he continued, 'I still don't buy it, Ann. According to a snitch Whittaker talked to tonight, Sawyer is involved in a heavy-duty drug operation, not what we originally thought. He's involved with drug traffickers from Colombia, though he's only a bit player in the overall picture.

These people –' He stopped himself. The less she knew the better. She was terrified enough as it was. 'Let's just leave it at that. That's where you should worry, not about Hank coming back after all this time.'

'If these were ruthless drug dealers,' Ann shot back, 'they would have been armed to the hilt. Whoever broke in here tonight wasn't armed. If the guy had a gun, why didn't he return my fire?'

Reed put a hand to his face, pulling on his cheek, feeling the day-old stubble. She had a point on that one. 'If it was Sawyer, Ann, he might have tossed his gun after he shot you, then just never bought another one. There was too much heat for him to walk into a gun store and buy a weapon. He would be too afraid we'd be sitting there waiting to grab him.'

'I'm sorry I said anything,' Ann said, annoyed. She got up and headed for her bedroom, leaving Tommy standing there. The long night had taken its toll, and she fell facedown onto her bed. Was Tommy right? Was she acting foolishly, marring her husband's reputation for nothing? People were treating her the same way they had when Hank vanished and she'd acted irrationally. Well, Ann thought, grabbing a tissue and blowing her nose, maybe they'd act peculiar too if their husband or loved one disappeared without a trace.

A short time later, she smelled Tommy's after-shave and rolled over. He was leaning over her bed. 'I'll sleep on the sofa tonight and let myself out in the morning.'

'Thanks,' Ann mumbled. Then she thought of the attacker's rough hands on her body, the way he had said David's name, and sat up sharply. 'Is David safe, Tommy? Maybe we should go and get him. I'm so frightened.'

'I'm sure he's fine, Ann,' the detective reassured her. 'Aren't the boy's parents in the house?'

'Yes,' Ann said, her lower lip trembling. 'What am I going to do? What if he comes back to get David?'

Tommy's big hands gently pushed Ann back to a reclining position. 'Right now you're going to get some sleep. Put everything out of your mind. Take it one day at a time. If you don't, you won't be able to take care of yourself, let alone David.' The detective leaned down and kissed Ann chastely on the forehead. Turning off the bedroom lights, he went to the living room and promptly passed out on the sofa.

Overtired and stimulated, Ann could not sleep. Her mind was sorting and organizing, trying to find the truth. Hank liked corn, and the attacker had eaten corn. He was dense and heavy like the attacker, not lean like Sawyer. Being a cop, he was agile and would have instinctively dropped to the ground when she chased him out of the house, fearing she would come out shooting. He also knew what no one else knew – that Ann hadn't fired a gun in years. Would he have foreseen her hesitation before pulling the trigger? Of course, she thought, recalling a conversation along those lines, her telling him she didn't know if she could take another person's life.

The most convincing factor was the man's eyes. Peering out into the darkness, she could still see them staring back at her. Tommy and the others could say anything they wanted, she decided. They could call her a hysteric, even call her crazy. She knew she had looked into those eyes before, and even if it was Hank, she never wanted to look into them again.

Chapter 12

Once Ann had picked up David at his friend's house and dropped him off at school, she raced to the office and called Glen. When she told him what had happened at her house, he was appalled. 'Can I come over and talk to you?' Ann said. 'There's something about all this that you need to know.'

There was a long pause before Glen asked, 'Can't you just tell me over the phone, Ann? I'm swamped right now. I have to be in court in thirty minutes.'

Couldn't he even take a moment to listen to her? she thought, miffed. 'No,' she said. 'I don't want to talk about it over the phone. There's no privacy in my office. You know that, Glen. It won't take more than a few minutes. I'm coming over right now.' Before he could protest again, she disconnected and marched over to the adjoining building.

The Ventura County district attorney's office was set up like the probation department: one enormous space divided up into various work stations. But the assistant district attorneys had actual offices ringing the open room, all with windows. It was eight forty-five by the time Ann got there, one of the busiest times of the day. Attorneys were rushing in to go over their notes and arguments one last time before court, printers were spilling out copy, phones were jangling.

Ann stepped into Glen's office and closed the door behind her. Hearing the click, he looked up from his work. 'Sit down, Ann. Forgive me for being so abrupt on the phone. It's Friday, though, and it's been a hectic week.'

Hectic week? You should have been in my shoes, Ann thought. Her annoyance subsided, though, as she gazed at him. Dressed in a dark gray suit, a lavender shirt, and his customary cowboy boots, he looked rugged and handsome.

'Anyway,' he continued, 'I was hoping we could get together tomorrow night. You know, spend a nice evening together and put all this other stuff out of our minds.'

'Sounds nice,' Ann said, even though right now she didn't think it was possible to put what was going on out of her mind. But an evening of being held in Glen's arms seemed just what she needed. 'David's going to Magic Mountain with a friend this weekend. We can get together then. I miss you, Glen. It's been so long.'

'I know,' he said, meeting her eyes. 'I miss you too. I think about you all the time. I'm crushed over what you've been through . . . all you've suffered. It's absolutely awful.'

Ann started blinking back tears. She was fine as long as no one expressed sympathy. The moment people did, the moment she saw it in their eyes, her composure disintegrated. Just when she had started to put her life back together, it had all been ripped away. She hadn't made love with Glen since the shooting. Her body yearned for him, the way he felt, the way he smelled, the way he made her feel.

That reminded her why she had come. 'I have to tell you something. Look, I know you're going to think I'm crazy, Glen, but that man last night . . .' She was about to tell him her suspicions about Hank when his phone rang, and a strange look appeared in his eyes.

At first Glen just ignored it. 'Go on, Ann. I'm listening. What about the man last night?'

'Aren't you going to answer your phone?' The phone stopped, but immediately, it began ringing again. 'Listen, I'm sorry I came over here and bothered you when you're so busy. This can wait. Go on, answer it. It could be something important.'

'No, Ann, really,' he said anxiously. 'Whatever it is can wait.'

A feeling of warmth washed over her, seeing how much he really cared. Finally the phone stopped ringing. Ann had opened her mouth to speak when it started ringing again. 'Shit,' she said, the moment gone. 'Answer it or they'll just keep calling back. I've got a headache.' She rubbed her forehead as another ring sounded. 'I can't sit here and talk with the damn phone ringing all the time.'

Glen reached out and tried to hit the hands-free button and missed. Infuriated, he quickly swiped at the receiver, almost knocking the phone to the floor. Once he heard who it was, he swiveled his chair around with his back to Ann. 'No,' he barked into the phone, 'I already disposed of that case myself. It's right there in the file.'

Ann sat quietly, waiting. Then she stood, deciding to come back later.

Glen got up and closed the distance between them, taking Ann in his arms and leaning back against the door just in case someone tried to walk in. 'We're going to put the case together on Sawyer, Ann. Don't worry. I'll work night and day if I have to.'

For no good reason his closeness felt stifling. Ann felt herself breathing in jerky pants, the night before flashing in her mind. The way the man had smelled, the disgusting way he had touched her. Her hands were stiff at her sides, the muscles in her back like concrete. Even though it was Glen, she couldn't help recoiling from a man's touch.

'Trust me,' Glen whispered, trying to pull her closer to his body. Ann ducked and slipped away, taking a few steps back.

'Oh, and Ann, I'm finishing up on Delvecchio today. Drop by if you can, okay?'

'I will.'

Ann rushed out the door, heading down the corridor to the elevators with her head down, not looking where she was going. She was so addled, she thought, she hadn't even told Glen about Hank. She walked right into Ian McIntosh, a D.A. she knew well. A reed-thin redhead, McIntosh was a marathon runner. To Ann, he looked as if he hadn't had a decent meal in weeks.

'Ann,' he said, embarrassed. 'Sorry, I wasn't looking.'

'No,' she said, dropping her eyes. 'I think it was my fault.'

She had started to walk off when he said, 'I'm glad I ran into you. I've been meaning to call you ever since I heard what happened. God, how awful. How are you feeling?'

'Good,' she said weakly. 'Really, it wasn't that bad an injury. It's the fear more than anything.'

'I hear they caught the guy. That's got to make you sleep easier.'

'Not exactly. He's out on bail,' she said sardonically. 'Last night someone broke into my house and attacked me again.'

'No,' he said, shocked. 'You've got to be kidding. Was it the same guy?'

'I don't really know, Ian,' Ann said, sucking one corner of her lip into her mouth.

He appeared to be playing something over in his mind. 'Well, since you're here, I guess I should tell you the bad news about Carl Simmons.'

'What bad news? He's in prison.'

'The case was overturned on appeal.'

'He's out?' Ann was thunderstruck, unable to believe what she was hearing. Carl Simmons had butchered two little girls, a case she had investigated. 'What happened? It wasn't anything I did, was it?'

'No,' McIntosh said. 'The appellate court was mainly concerned with the expert testimony. Seems our Dr Adams is a real whore. He contradicted his own statements.'

'Fuck,' Ann said, ready to explode. 'I knew you shouldn't have used that bastard.' Benjamin Adams was a prominent psychiatrist who earned a sizable percentage of his income from acting as an expert witness in court hearings. The only problem was that he would sell out to the highest bidder. The doctor had evidently impeached his own testimony, and his testimony had gone a long way toward convicting Carl Simmons. Hence, the appeal. 'Are you going to refile?'

'Of course, but we want to make certain our case is solid this time. We're collecting new evidence now.' He paused and ran his hands through his hair, more concerned now than before. 'You know, Ann, when I heard about you being shot, I immediately thought of Simmons and the scene he made in the courtroom. He thinks you railroaded him. Remember? He was hurling threats at you when they hauled him off that day. I didn't say anything before, because I assumed he was still in prison. We were just notified the other day about the appeal.'

'I did railroad him,' Ann said, more thinking out loud than anything. 'I didn't say that,' she said quickly. 'You didn't hear me say that.'

'I didn't hear a thing,' McIntosh said, laughing.

Ann didn't think it was funny, and she gave the attorney a stern look before walking off. They were all hot and heavy when she came to them with the goods, but now that her life was on the line, it was something to laugh about. Shuffling off down the hall, jarred by what she'd just heard, Ann tried to bring Carl Simmons's face into focus.

He was a big man, like the person who had attacked her last night. He hated her. There was no doubt about that. Ann had been sent to interview Simmons for a routine bail review. Bail was a moot issue in a case as serious as his, a double homicide involving children, but the court followed procedure. A bail review was another way to gain information from the probation department while the other proceedings were under way. The officer handling the bail review would run rap sheets and check criminal histories, as well as accumulate other pertinent facts about the defendant.

Simmons had been responsive. Ann had played him like a violin. Before she'd walked out of the room, he had claimed that there was no way he could have committed the crime. Both the young victims were raped, and Simmons swore he was impotent and had medical records to prove it. The man mistakenly thought the investigators had not learned the truth. Although the cases had been listed in the newspapers as rapes and homicides, they were technical rapes, the penetration made with a foreign object. They'd found no sperm. A man in the prime of his life unable to engage in sex, as Simmons had just stated he was, fit the psychological profile for this type of perversity. With Dr Adams's expert opinion and other physical evidence linking him to the homicides, Simmons had been convicted on both counts.

How could they release him? Two little girls were dead, and Carl Simmons was walking the streets again. Ann felt sick to her stomach, angry at the entire disgusting system that allowed something like this to happen. How could the parents of these children sleep at night? What would she do if it had been David who had been violated and murdered?

With all the legislation over criminals' rights, Ann thought, the system had become a maze of technicalities and poorly constructed statutes. Prisoners got their sentences reduced for good behavior, received early releases for one reason or another, and all the time evidentiary rules were increasing. The injustice was simple: the system provided more protection to the individuals who perpetrated crime than to the people they victimized.

When she got back to her office, Ann got a call from Tommy Reed asking if she would like to go along when he interviewed Sawyer's father. With this new attack, they wanted to pick up Sawyer, take him back to court, and attempt to get his bail revoked. The father might be cooperative and provide them with information about his son's whereabouts.

When they arrived, Ann took out her county ID and flashed it at the receptionist. 'We're here to see Dr Sawyer.'

'Do you have an appointment?'

'No,' Ann said. 'We're police officers. Can you please tell him we're here?'

The young woman stared at Ann as if she'd seen a ghost. Then she disappeared. In no time the door opened, and she said the doctor would see them.

Dr Sawyer was an attractive older man. His skin was smooth and taut, his body as fit as that of any athlete, and he had dark hair and penetrating eyes like his son's. He looked as if he spent more time on the tennis court than in surgery. Reed introduced himself, then Ann shook his hand. 'I'm your son's probation officer, Dr Sawyer. Ann Carlisle.'

Her eyes took in the room. The drapes were drawn and only a small lamp on the surgeon's desk provided light, leaving the rest of the room in shadow. Once they were seated in front of his desk, Jimmy's father faced them, composed and in no way alarmed. The top of his mahogany desk was covered with a sheet of spotless glass. Other than a few decorative items like a crystal letter opener, a crystal pyramid clock, a framed photograph of Jimmy and another of his wife, the surface was completely clean: no stacks of papers, no messy cups of coffee. Dr Sawyer was a neat, organized man. He peered out at them with clear, intelligent blue eyes behind wire-rimmed glasses. 'I don't have a great deal of time, Officers. What can I do for you?'

They had to find support here, Ann thought, taking in the various diplomas and framed certificates on the walls. The man was a surgeon, a respected member of the community. Right behind his desk Ann saw a large plaque with a picture of Dr and Mrs Sawyer standing next to a smiling Ronald Reagan. He might be reluctant to believe his son was involved in any wrongdoing after only hearing Jimmy's side of the story, Ann told herself, but surely they could obtain his cooperation.

She took control of the conversation, leaning forward in her seat. 'Do you know what I saw in the refrigerator at your son's house? I saw human fingers, Dr Sawyer. Five human fingers. I saw a thumb and a little finger and three additional fingers. From that, I'm assuming they were from one hand.'

Dr Sawyer turned his chair sideways so they could only view him in profile. 'Yes,' he said flatly, 'I'm aware of what you said you found. I'm also aware the police responded and found nothing.' He removed his glasses and wiped them with a tissue retrieved from somewhere inside his desk. Once he had placed them back on his nose, he turned his chair to face Reed and Ann again. 'Our attorney has been looking into this situation, Ms Carlisle. He suggested we hire a private investigator, and we followed his advice. This investigator has arrived at some astonishing conclusions that I believe will support my son's statements.' Dr Sawyer leaned back in his chair and stared at Ann. As soon as she looked back, his voice dropped to a monotonous, clinical level. 'Ms Carlisle, isn't it true that your husband disappeared under very suspicious and troublesome circumstances, that you've been quite distraught over the past four years?'

Ann sat perfectly still in her seat, unsure why this had come up. 'Yes, he did, but I don't know what that has to do with your son.'

'Could you please allow me to continue?'

'Certainly,' Ann said, crossing her legs and then a second later uncrossing them again.

'Obviously, having your husband disappear as he did was a very traumatic thing, Ms Carlisle. Can I call you Ann?'

'That's fine.'

'All right,' he said, smiling warmly as if he'd known her for years. 'I'm no stranger to this type of trauma, Ann. I've had both close acquaintances and patients whose husbands or sons have been missing in action. Servicemen, of course. They tell me it's the waiting, the not knowing, that eventually wears them down. Is that the way it has been for you?'

'Yes, of course, but –'

He didn't stop. 'I'll only take a few minutes of your time, and then you can ask me anything you want. My friends say the unanswered questions are the worst. They can't sleep, can't rest, can't find peace because they just don't know the answers. How did he die? Is he dead at all? Did he suffer? And then they tell me it's the loneliness, the complete and utter loneliness. It's entirely different from a natural death. In a natural death, Ann, the circumstances are known, the situation final. A person can recover, go on with life.'

Ann was impressed with his insight – she had felt all of this and more – but why was he talking about this stuff? 'Dr Sawyer –'

He held up a hand imperiously. 'These women, women who have been in circumstances similar to yours, say they can't let go, can't have normal relationships. They want to date, want to resume normal sexual relationships, but they simply cannot. Not when they don't know, Ann. Not when their poor husband could still be alive somewhere pitifully suffering, waiting and praying for the day –'

'Please,' Ann said, interrupting him. 'What we came to talk about is urgent.'

'I'm quite interested in this type of trauma. I did my

internship in the Marines during Vietnam. Sometimes the men would crack under the pressure of waiting, just waiting for the enemy to attack, never knowing when it would happen.'

Was the doc going to keep this up all day? Ann cut her eyes to Reed as if to say, What's with this guy?

Tommy spoke up. 'Dr Sawyer, we didn't come here to discuss Ms Carlisle. We came here to discuss your son.'

'Please allow me to finish my line of thought,' Dr Sawyer said to Tommy, immediately turning his attention back to Ann. 'These people I've been speaking of, Ann, these women whose husbands have been missing in action, well, some of these women tell me they seek out physical relationships that don't demand anything from them emotionally . . . such as commitment. Have you experienced this phenomenon?'

'Don't answer that,' Reed said, glancing over at Ann. 'Dr Sawyer, I'm not sure Officer Carlisle understands where you are going with this conversation, but I do.'

'Oh, really?' Dr Sawyer said, an eyebrow shooting up. 'How astute, Detective Reed.'

Reed's face flushed, and his hands locked on the arms of the chair. This son of a bitch was no better than his lousy son. He was going after Ann's state of mind, trying to discredit her. 'What were you in 'Nam anyway? A member of the Special Forces?' Reed sneered and then spat out the rest. 'What was your specialty? Mind control?'

Reed was only an inch from flying off the handle. Turning to Ann, he said, 'Don't you realize what this prick is saying? What he's trying to imply? You're so naive, so incredibly naive. He's saying that you slept with his son because you can't handle a relationship. Isn't that right, Dr Sawyer?'

'True,' the doctor said, his voice still carefully modulated. 'Am I correct in my assessment, Ann? You see, these women I was speaking of a few minutes ago, they tell me they can't handle rejection, that rejection is similar to their husbands' failing to return to them following the war.'

Reed jerked his head toward the door. 'Let's get out of here, Ann. You don't have to listen to this shit. He's not going to give us any information.'

Dr Sawyer's face shifted into hard lines. 'Isn't that why you framed my son, made up this absurd story about fingers in a pickle jar, because you couldn't handle him rejecting you? My son saved your life. You should be grateful, appreciative, but instead you're trying to destroy him.' By now Dr Sawyer was yelling. 'Why don't you just admit that you slept with my son? Why must you lie?'

'I didn't make up anything,' Ann yelled back, for the first time seeing him for what he was: an angry, devious man who would do anything to protect his flesh and blood, not to mention his reputation in the community. 'And I certainly didn't sleep with your son.' She took a deep breath and pushed ahead. 'If your son doesn't appear in court in three weeks for the preliminary hearing, a bench warrant will be issued for his arrest. In addition to being a suspect in my shooting, there are indications that Jimmy was involved in manufacturing and distributing narcotics.' Ann pinned him with a knowing look. 'All of these are serious charges. Your son will be sentenced to prison if he's convicted. Prison, Dr Sawyer, is a very different environment from the county jail.'

'Come on,' Tommy said again, 'let's get out of here.'

'No, Tommy,' Ann insisted, 'we came for answers and I want answers. Dr Sawyer, do you know anything about the body parts I saw in your son's refrigerator?'

He looked away, refusing to answer.

Ann stood and stepped up to his desk, placing her hands purposely on the glass. 'Then listen to this. If your son resists arrest or is armed at the time we pick him up, he may die or be seriously injured.'

His eyes misted over and his face contorted with anguish. 'You mean, the police will shoot him?'

So, Ann thought, the man was human.

'Exactly,' she said. 'Can you help us?'

'Police officers like this man?'

Ann looked over at Tommy. 'Yes, Dr Sawyer, police officers like this man. And let me tell you something else. If we apprehend Jimmy actually distributing drugs, he'll be charged with each and every instance. Then he will be tried on each one of these instances as a separate and distinct crime. In a courtroom, they refer to these as counts. Do you understand?'

At the very corner of Dr Sawyer's right eye, a drop of moisture escaped and slowly made its way down the side of his face. But his jaw remained rigid, and he made no move to wipe the solitary tear away. It was actually quite sad, Ann thought. He was a father, just a parent concerned for his child.

'I'm very . . . cognizant of the law,' Dr Sawyer said, his voice straining with emotion.

In the next instant the doctor completely lost his composure. Ann had never seen a man shift gears so quickly. One moment he'd been crying and the next his eyes were bulging, his face flushed. As she was about to remove her hands from the glass, he leaped to his feet and tried to slap her in the face, but Ann quickly stepped back before he made contact.

'My son is a decent young man.' He fixed Ann with a hot stare of contempt. 'And you . . . you're a conniving tramp, a cheap slut. You sicken me. I bet your husband left you because he didn't want to be married to a whore. How many young boys have you seduced?'

Ann gasped, seizing Reed's arm. 'Let's get out of here, Tommy. You were right. Come on, let's go.'

It all happened in a flash. Reed sprang out of his seat and almost leaped over the doctor's desk. He grabbed the man's shirt and yanked him forward, pulling back his fist and belting him. Dr Sawyer didn't even struggle or attempt to fight back. Ann jumped on Tommy's back and tried to pull him off, get him to stop. 'Please, Tommy, don't –'

Reed climbed right over the desk, sending the letter opener and paperweight flying through the air, stepping on and smashing the glass in one of the picture frames. Once he was over the desk, he started shouting, 'You fucking prick. After all this woman has been through, you have the gall to say that filth.' His fist went back again, poised and ready. 'You want to slap someone,' he said, growling, 'slap me. I'll bust you for assaulting a police officer.'

'Tommy, no,' Ann said, trying to grab his arms. 'He didn't hurt me. Please, stop, it isn't worth it.'

Dr Sawyer was sitting on the floor behind his desk, a thin stream of blood running from his nose and dripping onto his white dress shirt. When Tommy stepped back, panting and out of breath, the doctor took off his broken glasses and calmly put them into the pocket of his shirt. Holding onto the edge of the desk, he pulled himself to a standing position. Once he was on his feet, he reached for the heavy crystal clock.

'The clock, Tommy,' Ann yelled, certain the doctor was going to smash Tommy over the head with it.

In a movement so fast it blurred before Ann's eyes, Reed made a fist with both hands and slammed it down on the doctor's hand before his fingers closed on the clock. Something cracked. Just then the young nurse opened the door.

'Is something wrong, Doctor? I heard . . .'

Dr Sawyer brought his hand up to his chest. Two fingers were bent at odd angles and covered with blood. 'No, Sheila,' he said flatly. 'These people are just leaving. You can show them to the door.' He looked away from the woman and sat back down behind his desk, his face flushed and gleaming with perspiration. But he didn't grimace and he didn't cry out in pain.

'But, Doctor,' the woman said, 'your hand. My God, your hand . . . and your nose is bleeding too.'

'That will be all, Sheila,' he said, removing a starched white handkerchief and dabbing his bloody nose. He turned to Reed. 'You'll be hearing from my attorney.'

'Fuck you,' Reed said, ready to jump the man again and beat him to a bloody pulp. 'Fuck you . . . fuck your son and fuck your attorney.'

They were all crowded at the door, trying to walk through at the same time, Ann pulling Reed by an arm. Finally the nurse gingerly stepped past them and Ann placed her hand on the detective's back, trying to push him forward before they ended up in a fistfight.

'Before you go, I have one more question,' Dr Sawyer said. 'Do you have any idea what a surgeon's hand is worth in a court of law?'

What a fiasco, Ann thought as she rushed to Department 17, where the Delvecchio trial was in progress. Glen had said the state would conclude its case today, and Ann wanted to hear his closing statement.

Slipping into the court, she took a seat in the back row even though there were few spectators. Judge Robert Goldstein was presiding. His hair was thinning and his face haggard, but at thirty-nine he was only recently appointed and was one of the youngest judges in the county.

Randy Delvecchio was represented by Winston Cataloni of the public defender's office. Cataloni was short and squat, his suit worn, and he was shuffling papers frantically on the counsel table, as if he was having trouble keeping track of the proceedings. Ann couldn't help but think that Delvecchio would be convicted on the basis of his legal representation alone. Cataloni was a known alcoholic. Supposedly he was on the wagon, but from the way he was acting, Ann thought he might be tossing them down again.

Walking back from the witness stand, Hopkins spotted Ann and flashed a confident smile. 'This will be people's exhibit A,' he said, a large plastic evidence bag in his hand. He handed it to the bailiff, then turned back to the witness. Ray Hernandez, the D.A.'s investigator, was testifying. A dark and distinguished man in his fifties, Hernandez had joined the D.A.'s office after twenty years with the sheriff's department, ten of them as a homicide detective.

'So,' Hopkins said, standing in front of the witness box, 'you found this overcoat in the defendant's possession. What made you suspect it was taken during the course of these crimes?'

Hernandez moved closer to the microphone. 'It wasn't in his possession exactly,' he said, a stickler for details. 'He was wearing it when we found him. On the label was a Rotary pin with the number twenty-five on it. Estelle Summer listed this as property taken from her home during the assault. It belonged to her deceased husband.'

'All right,' Hopkins said thoughtfully, glancing at the jury. 'Tell us, please, what else you found in the defendant's possession.' As soon as he finished speaking, he walked back to the counsel table.

'We found a woman's ring, a wedding ring.'

Glen snatched another plastic evidence sack off the counsel table, this one smaller, and carried it to Ray Hernandez. 'Is this the ring you found?'

'Yes,' Hernandez said after peering through the plastic. 'It was hidden in the defendant's bedroom, in a bureau drawer where he kept his underwear.'

'And who does this ring belong to?' Glen asked.

'It's Madeline Alderson's wedding ring.'

'Mrs Alderson identified it as such?'

'Yes, she did,' Hernandez said. 'She said the rapist took it off her finger before he fled.'

'The people submit this as exhibit B, Your Honor,' Hopkins said, taking his seat.

'Mr Cataloni,' Goldstein said, passing the ball to the defense.

Cataloni looked over at his client, up at the judge, and then back to his notes. 'Isn't it true, Investigator Hernandez, that the defendant would never have been arrested had it not been for this anonymous phone call?'

'Yes, that's true,' Hernandez said.

'Tell us about that phone call again.'

Hernandez appeared to be annoyed, knowing this was the weak link in the case. 'An unknown caller contacted our office and told us that Mr Delvecchio was a possible suspect in these crimes, that he'd been bragging about them on the street.'

Cataloni rubbed his forehead and glanced at the jury. 'By bragging, do you mean he was talking about how he raped these defenseless women and then stole their property?'

'More or less,' Hernandez said, no longer recalling the exact words the caller had spoken. The actual recipient of the phone call had previously testified, another D.A.'s investigator. Hernandez was only testifying to the property recovered during the search, but Cataloni wanted to nail this point home again.

'And this was the impetus for obtaining a search warrant for my client's residence, then proceeding to execute that warrant?' While Hernandez glared at him without answering, Cataloni shuffled to the box and continued speaking. 'All this you did on mere hearsay? Information obtained from a person who refused to give you a name, who even to this day has as yet to come forward?'

Hernandez's back stiffened defensively. 'A lot of information comes to us through informants. We would be remiss, Counselor, if we didn't follow through on this type of lead.'

'No further questions,' Cataloni tossed out as he walked back to the table.

Goldstein fixed his gaze on Hopkins. 'The state rests, Your Honor,' Hopkins said.

Goldstein leaned back in his chair. 'You may present your closing statements, Mr Hopkins.'

Hopkins sprang to his feet, and walked quickly to the jury box. 'I don't need to reiterate the seriousness of these crimes and the heinous acts committed against these three women,' he said clearly, holding on to the wooden railing and searching every face. 'You've heard Madeline Alderson's testimony and Lucinda Wall's testimony of the nightmare they suffered at the hands of the defendant. Estelle Summer cannot confront her attacker at this trial, because she is no longer alive to do so. But she's here,' Hopkins said, raising his eyebrows and letting the implication sink in. 'She may not be here in the flesh, but she's here in other ways. You must accept her sworn statements, as testified to previously in this courtroom. No, it wasn't her voice relating these facts, nor can you see her pain, but don't forget that she positively identified this man from a photo lineup, that he was arrested in her husband's overcoat, taken from her home during the crime.

'Mr Cataloni will soon be telling you that she was old and sick, that her death was not directly related to the defendant's actions, but you and I know that's not true.' Glen stopped, his face twisting in anguish. 'Estelle Summer died because of this man,' he said, spinning around and pointing an accusing finger at Randy Delvecchio, 'and for no other reason. She died in abject terror and humiliation. She died in fear that she would never obtain justice. But I'm confident,' he said, slowly pacing back and forth in front of the jury box, an earnest look on his face, 'I'm confident that you will not let this decent woman die unavenged.'

Hopkins turned sideways and linked eyes with Ann before continuing. 'The evidence speaks for itself. The defendant possessed property taken from Estelle Summer's home, property that he had no legal right to possess, as well as property taken from Madeline Alderson. This is not speculation, ladies and gentlemen. This is fact. You will be told by Mr Cataloni that we have not provided definitive proof, that even though his client possessed these items, they do not prove within a reasonable doubt that he committed the crimes. The defense will spin all kinds of tales explaining how Mr Delvecchio came to possess these items, attempting to plant seeds of doubt in your minds.'

Hopkins dropped his head, and the courtroom fell silent. Then he looked back up and his voice boomed. 'But I have faith in you, faith in your ability to administer justice, in your ability to see the truth.'

Ann smiled to herself. He was reining them in, praising them, emphasizing the importance of what they were doing. In addition, he was enlisting their support for the victims, telling them that they were the ones who would be responsible for a horrid miscarriage of justice if they returned a verdict other than guilty.

'These are the points to remember,' he said, circling a finger in the air as he continued to pace. 'The defendant has no alibi for the dates in question. The defendant was identified from a lineup by all three victims. The defendant was in possession of property taken from the victims.' He stopped and faced them. 'We have clearly established these facts. And these facts prove without a doubt that the defendant is guilty.'

Ann waited until Glen took his seat and Goldstein called a recess. Then she stood and tilted her head toward the back of the courtroom, indicating that she'd be waiting outside for

him. Delvecchio's back had been turned during the proceedings, but Ann was concerned that he would turn around
now and see her. She didn't want him to spot her conferring
with the district attorney. They might need her to extract more
information from him on the homicides.

When Glen burst through the double doors a few minutes
later, he was smiling. 'What do you think?'

Ann glanced up and down the hall. Seeing the corridor
empty, she quickly threw her arms around his neck and kissed
him. 'I think you're brilliant.'

'I don't feel brilliant,' he said humbly. 'I wasn't that happy
with my closing statement, but I didn't want to get too
detailed. Give them too much and they get confused.'

She started to tell him about the incident with Sawyer's
father, but then hesitated. Goldstein had called recess for only
ten minutes, and they didn't have much time to talk. 'How
long will the defense take to present their case?'

'I think it will go to the jury next week,' Hopkins said,
obviously relieved to see the end in sight. 'Cataloni doesn't
have any witnesses other than a few relatives for character. I
doubt he'd put a loser like Delvecchio on the stand.'

Ann thought of the public defender and wondered if he
was drinking. If he was, and it later came out that Delvecchio
had incompetent counsel, the case could be overturned on
appeal. Hearing about the Simmons case was enough, she
thought. They certainly didn't want to lose this one. 'Think
Cataloni's back on the booze?'

'Of course not,' Glen snapped, seizing her arm. 'Don't say a
word. Please, Ann, that's all I need.'

Ann slapped his arm away like a rattlesnake. As soon as she
did, she felt foolish. 'I'm sorry,' she said self-consciously. 'I'm
still trying to get over last night. If you don't jump at me, Glen,
I'll be okay, but when –'

'I didn't jump at you,' he protested. 'All I did was put my

hand on your arm.' Seeing the fear on her face, though, he stepped closer, his voice soft and consoling. 'Look, forgive me if I seem insensitive. Believe me, I'm worried sick about you. I know how terrifying it must have been for you last night. I'm just so caught up in this case right now I'm not thinking straight.'

'It was nothing,' she told him, turning to walk away.

His voice pulled her back. 'What about lunch? We'll be breaking at one o'clock. We could go across the street to Marie Callender's.'

'I can't,' Ann said, having no appetite. Besides, she thought he'd asked only to be kind. He was pressed for time, probably eager to get back to his office. Attorneys were always frantic when they were in trial. 'I'm going to order something in and try to play catch-up.'

'Are we going out tomorrow night?'

'As far as I know,' she said, staring out the window on the other side of the corridor. How did she know she'd even be alive by this time tomorrow? Even though it was only noon, Ann felt the night ahead all around her.

'I want Delvecchio,' Glen said, the intensity of his voice startling Ann out of her thoughts. 'He's a predator, just like Sawyer. But at least you're not seventy years old, Ann. These women were defenseless old ladies. They never had a chance.'

Staring into his eyes, Ann knew he was right. She was young and strong compared to these women. She knew how to handle a gun, had even been trained in self-defense. 'Look, I'll see you tomorrow,' she said, a weak smile on her face.

'Everything's going to be all right, Ann,' he told her. 'He knows you have a gun. He won't come back.'

With Glen watching her, she headed off down the hall, her arms locked around her body, leaning forward as if walking into a fierce wind. Yes, her attacker knew she had a gun, and in most instances this would be a great deterrent. But the attacker also knew something Glen didn't know: he knew Ann had been unable to pull the trigger.

Chapter 13

Tommy Reed was poring over a computer printout of missing persons, trying not to think of his blowup that morning. Going to see Dr Sawyer had clearly been a mistake. As soon as the brass got wind of the incident, Reed would be called on the carpet, maybe even suspended as a disciplinary measure.

Damn, he said, slamming his fist on his desk, feeling as angry as he had a few hours ago. Why had he allowed an egotistical asshole like Dr Sawyer to get to him? Sure, the doctor had taken a swing at Ann and insulted her, but they could have just walked away. But no, he chastised himself, he'd acted like a punchy, gung-ho rookie and jumped the man.

Suddenly the right word appeared in his mind: guilt. He was feeling guilty. Guilty that he hadn't been able to protect Ann from being shot. Guilty that she'd been attacked again in her home when he'd guaranteed her Sawyer would get nowhere near her house.

'How's it coming?' Noah Abrams said, striding into the detective bay in his shirtsleeves, sporting a tie with a bright blue '57 Chevy on it.

'Oh,' Reed said, looking up, and then squinting at his tie. 'Is that a car on your tie?'

'Yeah,' Abrams said. 'Isn't it great?' He leaned over Reed's shoulder and said, 'Are those the missing person reports? Is there anything in there?'

Reed slowly shook his head. 'All I've got right now is a bunch of names and dates. Nothing in Ventura County is recent enough.'

'What do you mean?' Noah said, checking his in basket and then plunking down in the chair next to Reed, his long legs stretched out in front of him.

'If Ann really saw fingers in the Henderson house, don't you think the murder took place right before she saw them, not six months or a year ago?'

'Dunno,' Noah said, noting the dark circles under the other man's eyes, the unhealthy pallor of his skin. This case was getting to him, Noah thought. 'Lab says that was only pickle juice and ordinary sour pickles. They didn't find any traces of formaldehyde or any other preserving solution. Guess you might be right.'

'But again,' Reed said, pointing at Abrams, 'that wasn't the jar with the fingers. Ann dropped that jar and it broke. How do we know for sure the fingers weren't preserved?'

Abrams shook his head, dismissing this line of thought. He didn't see the fingers as the primary thrust of their investigation. What they had to concentrate their energy on was locating Sawyer before he attacked Ann again. 'Look, Sarge, I think we should forget about the fingers and focus on the narcotics trafficking, something we can prove and use to get this guy off the street. Why waste our time when we're not even certain these fingers exist? When or if a corpse comes in with no fingers, then you worry. Right? Anyway, that's how I see it.'

'Right, we'll just forget about the fingers and wait until Ann's fingers end up in a pickle jar,' Reed said sarcastically, standing and grabbing his jacket off the back of the chair. 'I'm going to the lab to see what they've come up with.'

Abrams was stung by his words, but knew it was useless to retaliate. Reed was going to keep berating him until the case was closed.

'So, you coming or staying?'

'I'll go,' Abrams said, reluctantly getting up and following the detective down the hall.

Once they were outside in the parking lot, Reed suddenly stopped short. Abrams walked on and then looked back, wondering what was wrong. 'Are you coming?'

Reed opened his mouth to speak and then closed it, shoving both his hands in his pockets and feeling around for his antacids. Instead, he brought forth a toothpick and clamped his teeth on it. 'I blew it this morning,' he said, quickly shifting the toothpick to the other side of his mouth.

'How?'

'Thumped on Dr Sawyer.'

'You're joking?' Abrams said, his eyes coming alive. 'Jimmy's father? What did he tell you? Did he tell you where the kid is?'

Reed was staring over Abrams's head. 'I think I broke his fucking hand.'

Great, Noah thought, that would really advance their case. They couldn't find Sawyer, so Reed was beating up on his father. 'So, go on, what did he tell you?'

'Nothing,' Reed mumbled.

'Nothing?' Abrams repeated, looking at the ground and then back up at the detective's face. 'You broke his hand for nothing, Reed? What did that accomplish? Maybe the man would have came around in time and told us where Jimmy is hiding.'

Spitting the toothpick out, the detective narrowed his eyes at Abrams. 'He was insulting Ann. He even took a swing at her. I guess you would have let him say anything he wanted, huh? Just stood there and listened while he called her a tramp.'

All of Abrams's simmering resentment exploded. 'I resent that, Reed. Lay off, okay? You act like I don't give a shit about this case, that I don't care about Ann's safety.' He stopped, slapping at thin air. 'Go to the lab without me. I'm going out to find the damn suspect.' He started walking off across the parking lot and then turned to yell back at Reed. 'I think you're the one who has his priorities confused, Sergeant.' Opening the door to his unit, Abrams climbed in, slammed the door shut, and sped out of the parking lot.

'I'm sorry, but she can't see you,' Alex said.

Tommy Reed had snagged Phil Whittaker in the parking lot for the ride to the crime lab, and was now facing off Alex in the outside offices. Right through the door was the lab where Melanie Chase worked. 'Hey, Mel,' he yelled as Alex moved in front of the door to block him, 'I need to talk to you.' When the blond-haired rookie held his ground, the detectives exchanged a glance.

'There's only so much I can take,' Reed said. He positioned himself on one side of Alex, while Whittaker moved to the other. 'On three,' Reed said, counting out loud. They effortlessly picked up the slender man by the armpits and deposited him a few feet from the door.

'That wasn't nice,' Alex said huffily.

The two men strode into the laboratory. On one wall was a bank of whirring computer terminals behind glass. The rest of the room was divided up into work stations with various pieces of sophisticated equipment and microscopes set on white Formica counters. Melanie Chase, wearing a white lab coat, was perched on a high stool, sorting through some slides. 'What have you got, Reed?' she said, without looking up. 'It'd better be good.'

Reed threw his arms out. 'Me.'

'You?' she said, looking the detective up and down. Then

she winked and smiled. 'I might take you up on that offer one of these days, buddy. You'd better be careful.'

Reed smiled broadly, fingering one of Melanie's curls. 'Cute,' he said. 'Sort of like Shirley Temple.' In another instant, though, he was all business. 'What can you tell us, Mel? We're desperate here. At least give us the rundown on the Henderson house.'

'Oh,' she said, rummaging through papers on her desk, 'I was just about to dictate that report. Here it is.' Reed tried to snatch it out of her hands, but Melanie pulled it back. 'It's handwritten, asshole.' Her eyes began scanning the report. 'Okay, something fishy went on in that house. I'm not sure what, but something.'

Reed and Whittaker pulled up two stools and faced Melanie. If anyone could hand them the goods, it was she.

She continued, 'We found trace elements of dimethyl benzyl ammonium chlorides everywhere, chemicals used in commercial cleaning products. I don't know how much you remember, but here's some pictures of the inside of the house.' She stopped and handed the two men a stack of eight-by-ten photos. 'Look at all the boxes and shit. Now look in that box right there. What do you see?'

Tommy peered at the photos. 'Just a bunch of dishes and things.'

'Filthy dishes, to be specific. Dishes with caked food on them. They didn't even wash the dishes before they packed them.' Melanie didn't give them time to make a deduction before she went on. 'Sure, they were in a hurry, but they were also pigs. Why would they scrub down practically every surface of that house with a heavy-duty detergent if they didn't have anything to hide?'

'To get their deposit back,' Whittaker offered.

Melanie shook her head. 'These kids will never see their deposit. The landlord will probably sue them for damages.

Doors were ripped off hinges, holes punched in walls, nail holes all over the place. They even burned half the kitchen floor, probably when they were cooking drugs. Why would they waste their time scrubbing down every solid surface in that house?'

'You think they had a body in there?' Reed asked.

'Well,' she said, rubbing her eyes, 'I can't say a body specifically, but they had something in there that they didn't want anyone to know about.'

'The lab?'

'Possibly. But would they need to scrub the walls in the bedrooms? I doubt it. Now, if there were bloodstains or secretions of any kind, that's the kind of fastidious cleaning you'd probably see.'

Reed was thinking of the fingers. 'What about the break-in at Ann's house?'

'That,' Melanie said, bristling, 'is something else altogether.' She hated it when another officer was attacked, particularly someone she considered a friend like Ann Carlisle. 'First, I need Ann's gun to do a ballistics test. I pulled out a slug that's possibly from another shooter, but I can't confirm it without Ann's gun, and she wouldn't let me take it the other night.'

'You mean the perp shot back?' Whittaker asked, confused. 'I thought he wasn't armed.'

Melanie shook her head. 'From Ann's statements, I don't think the perp ever got near the bedroom.' She stopped and drew a little diagram on a piece of paper, holding it out for the detectives to see. 'Ann was on the north side of the room where the safe was located, right under the open window. She test-fired her gun from here and struck the door to the closet – she was disoriented by a reflection in the mirror.' Melanie stopped and looked at them. 'That was shot one. The second time she fired, she was in the driveway. Shot two. Ann only fired twice, gentlemen, and of course we couldn't find the second slug.' Melanie spun around and removed two objects from a cardboard box, holding them in the air one by one with a pair of tongs. 'But what we have here is two slugs. The path of trajectory of one of them appears to be from the open window to the dresser mirror. From there it deflected and ended up in the wall.'

Reed leaped to his feet, acid bubbling up in his throat. If he understood Melanie correctly, the case had just taken a dangerous turn. 'Then there was more than one suspect? Someone was outside shooting at Ann while she was shooting at the man in the house?'

'Bingo,' Melanie said, smiling. 'Now, I have a blood sample from the broken windowpane. It's a good one. Type O, for what good that does us. What we need for genetic finger-printing is a sample of the suspect's blood. Get me that, and we'll be off and running.' She glanced back at her notes to see if there was anything else. 'Where's Sawyer now? You can also check for any recent cuts or lacerations.'

'Good luck, Mel,' Reed said gruffly. 'Sawyer made bail and split.'

She shook her head, but she wasn't one to dwell on negatives. 'Get the D.A. to petition for a blood sample ASAP. Then the minute they pick him up, we can collect it. It takes some time to do a test for genetic fingerprinting. We send it to an outside lab. If you want the results for the trial . . .'

Reed and Whittaker started walking to the door. 'Thanks, Mel,' Reed said.

'Don't forget to bring me Ann's gun,' she said before her gaze dropped back to the microscope and she moved another slide into place.

Ann was at her desk reading through a new case, a multiple-count child abuse. After she jotted down a few notes on a yellow pad, she removed the photos in the envelope inside the file and gasped. A five-year old boy stood with his back to the camera, the clear imprint of an iron seared into his flesh between his shoulder blades. The next photo was the defendant in the case, the child's mother. Originally from Vietnam, at age nineteen the woman still looked like a child herself. Tiny, dark, with the most impassive eyes Ann had ever seen. She sighed and was setting the photos aside when the phone rang.

'Hello. Probation.'

'Ann,' a voice said, 'why does it have to be this way?'

Ann felt every muscle in her body lock in place. It was Hank's voice, her husband's voice.

'Did you hear me?' This time the voice was louder and more abrasive.

She would know that tone anywhere. She opened her mouth and closed it. Finally she managed to get out, 'Hank . . . is that you?'

'Ann,' the voice answered back.

She started shaking, feeling the past four years vanish. He had come back. Her husband was alive. She felt tears on her face. 'Where are you? Oh, God, Hank . . . tell me where you are and I'll come and get you.'

Ann held her breath and listened. There was no response. The phone went dead just as she noticed Claudette standing beside her desk.

'Who was that?' Claudette asked anxiously. 'I heard you say Hank's name. Do they have some new information?'

'It – it was Hank.' Ann looked up with a tremulous smile.

Not this again, Claudette thought, deeply concerned. When Hank had first disappeared, Ann had seen him in every face, every passing car, thought every phone call was him calling. 'It couldn't have been Hank. Honey, you're just all strung out. Look at you.' She tilted her head and studied her friend's face. 'I think you'd better go home, Ann. You don't look well. I bet you haven't had a decent night's sleep since all this happened.'

'No,' Ann said, fixing Claudette with a firm gaze, 'it was Hank. I know my own husband's voice. I knew he was alive. I kept telling everyone he was alive, but no one would believe me.'

Claudette crossed her arms over her chest. 'What did he say, then? Where is he? Where has he been for the past four years?'

'He . . . hung up. He just said, "Ann, why does it have to be this way?"'

'Sure,' Claudette said, angry that Ann was being so irrational. 'Man's been gone four years, and he calls up and says something stupid like that.'

'It was Hank,' Ann snarled, standing and shoving her chair back.

Claudette put a hand on Ann's shoulder, pulled her chair back out, and pushed her back to a sitting position. 'It was just a prank call. Don't you see? Maybe someone read all this stuff about Hank in the newspapers. When you were shot, they played out the whole story again. Probably one of your probationers read it and decided to get back at you.'

'It was Hank's voice,' Ann said, though now she wasn't so sure. What if Claudette was right? But if she was, Ann thought, how could someone imitate her husband's voice so well when he'd been dead four years?

'Look at me, girl,' Claudette said, spinning Ann's chair around and bending down on one knee in front of her. 'You're losing it.'

'I'm not going to listen to –' Ann said, ready to spring from her chair again.

Claudette cut her off. 'I know what I'm talking about. I've been watching you since this all began, and I've seen you going downhill each day. Then after that bastard broke into your house, you . . .'

Ann looked at her in a daze. Was her mind playing tricks on her? 'I might be stressed out, but I haven't lost my mind. Hank even seemed mad at me. I don't know why, but I heard it in his voice.' She arched her eyebrows. 'No one could mimic that, Claudette.'

The woman stood and straightened her jacket. 'All you have to do is think logically. If it was Hank, why did he hang up? Why didn't he tell you where he was?'

'I don't know,' Ann said, truly confused. 'Maybe he didn't hang up. Maybe he was cut off or someone hung up for him.' She reached for the phone. 'I'm going to call the highway patrol right now.'

'Don't,' Claudette said, a dark look in her eyes. 'You're going to make a fool of yourself and stir up a hornet's nest.' She watched as Ann thought through what she was saying. 'Let it be, Ann. If it really was Hank, he'll call back. With the stuff this Sawyer boy is saying about you, don't you see how bad it will look if you run around telling everyone that your dead husband is calling you? They'll think you really are a mental case . . . that Sawyer's stupid story is true.'

'I don't believe that,' Ann said emphatically.

'Believe it,' Claudette said sharply. 'Here, come with me so we can talk in private.' She led Ann to an interview room, and once they were inside, Claudette closed the door. 'People are talking, Ann. Sawyer's story is all over the courthouse.'

Her breath catching in her throat, Ann said, 'What are you saying?'

'I'm trying to explain the facts of life, woman,' Claudette said, her voice almost a whine now. 'If gossip is juicy, people want to believe it's true. It's fun, gives them something to talk about over coffee.'

A look of surprise crossed Ann's face. People were talking about her behind her back?

'You think no one's ever slept with a probationer before?' Claudette continued, her breath on Ann's face. 'Think again, Ann. Few years back there was a big scandal with Pete Hendricks and that young girl. Do you remember that?'

'Yes,' Ann said meekly. 'But that was different.'

Claudette shook her head. 'No, Ann, just because you're a woman doesn't make it different. People believe the worst, like I just said. Some people think Sawyer's a good-looking young guy. One of the typists saw him coming out of the jail the day he was released and thought he was a rock star. She was walking around telling everyone she'd do anything to meet him. Don't you see what I'm saying?'

Ann gave her a wary look. 'Do you believe it?'

Claudette gasped, placing a hand on her jaw. 'Of course I don't believe it. Anyway, go home and get some rest. If you want, take next week off and get out of town or something. Put all of this stuff about Hank and this Sawyer kid out of your mind.'

'I don't have time to take off work,' Ann said forcefully. 'In fact, I have to go to the jail and see Delvecchio right now. They called and said he was insisting that he had to see me. Maybe he's ready to confess to the homicides.'

Claudette shook her head, thinking it was useless. Ann simply could not relax. 'What happened with the dog bite?'

'I don't know,' Ann said, desperate now to get out of the confining room and away from her supervisor. 'Let me go, Claudette. I have to go.' When the woman didn't budge, Ann shoved her aside and took off down the hall.

What in the hell was going on? she asked herself. First she was shot. Then someone broke into her house and almost raped her. Now she was getting phone calls from her husband, a man who'd been missing for four years. If Hank was alive, why would he call her and speak to her that way? On the other hand, the call supported her suspicions that he'd been the man in the driveway. No wonder she hadn't been able to pull the trigger.

Reaching the doors for the elevator, Ann stopped and stabbed at the button again and again, breaking her fingernail off at the quick.

'Guess you really want to go down,' a man said, stepping into the elevator and then noticing her bleeding finger. 'Gosh,' he said, 'are you hurt?'

'Just a fingernail,' she said sweetly. 'Typical female, huh? Break a fingernail, and you'd think we'd broken a leg. Guess we don't have enough excitement in our lives.'

When the man laughed, Ann shot him a look laced with enough venom to drop an elephant.

Chapter 14

When Reed returned to the police station, he tried to get consent from the captain to put together a surveillance team to watch Ann's house. The idea that more than one person had been involved in the break-in was alarming, especially if the accomplice had taken a shot at her. The first possibility that came to Reed's mind was the Colombians. Sawyer and his friends get in a mess, and their South American friends step in to do the cleanup. If this was the case, Ann's life was in grave jeopardy, and he had to find a way to guarantee her safety.

The problem was manpower. They had a hostage situation brewing on the west side of town, two recent gang killings, and a number of men out with the same flu bug Whittaker had. Reed wasn't prepared to spring the officers watching Dr and Mrs Sawyer's house. He was certain Sawyer would return to his parents' house, and then they could pick up the tail again. Ann was at work now. By tonight they should be able to cut someone loose to keep an eye on her. Unfortunately, as the captain had clearly stated, they were not in the private protection business. It would have to be catch-as-catch-can.

A records clerk walked in and tossed something into Reed's in basket and started to leave. 'What'd you give me?' Reed asked. 'Is it related to the Sawyer case?'

'You asked for anything we had on the Henderson house. This is the only thing I could find.'

Reed picked up the paper as the records clerk left. It was an incident report filed by the traffic division several months back. Seems the neighbors had complained that the three boys were using the street as a racetrack. Of the three vehicles listed on the report, Sawyer's Porsche was the only car that he recognized. As soon as they had learned the names of his roommates, Reed had checked the computer and obtained photos from their driving records and then run a check for any vehicles registered to Brett Wilkinson and Peter Chen. What he'd come up with was a Volkswagen Jetta and an older Ford Bronco. These were the vehicles he had informed patrol the suspects would be driving.

According to the traffic division's incident report, however, Wilkinson was driving a brand-new BMW with tinted windows and skirts, gold trim on the emblems, the whole ball of wax. Chen, they said, was reportedly driving a new Lexus. Neither vehicle had hard plates, only paper dealer tags, and vehicles were not entered into the computer system until plates were issued. No wonder they hadn't been able to bring these guys in, Reed thought. They were looking for the wrong cars.

Then another thought popped into his mind: where had they gotten the cash for toys as costly as these? Of course, he thought, the answer had to be drugs, but having that in black and white would be useful in court. All they needed was for Sawyer and the rest to stroll into the courtroom, claim they were recreational drug users, and end up with nothing more substantial than another slap on the wrist. In many ways, he knew Abrams had been right when he said they should concentrate on something they could prove. The shooting and break-in might never be substantiated, along with the fingers Ann was certain she'd seen in the Henderson house. But the drug-trafficking charges looked promising.

Reed called the dealerships and learned that all three cars had been recently purchased for cash. If this didn't smack of drug money, Reed didn't know what did. He started scribbling numbers down on a piece of paper and then added up the columns. The collective price tag on the three cars was over a hundred thousand dollars. He'd like to see Sawyer explain that away on the witness stand. He certainly wouldn't be able to make up another story about his probation officer to cover himself on this one. And he doubted if even Dr Sawyer would come to his rescue. If the doctor admitted giving Jimmy that much cash to buy the Porsche, he'd end up with a shitload of IRS agents on his back. No legitimate businessperson walked around with that much green.

Reed called the radio room and gave the dispatcher the new vehicle descriptions for Wilkinson and Chen, thinking that now they would be picked up.

As soon as he hung up the phone, he started thinking about Sawyer's father and his open hostility toward Ann. What if little Jimmy ran straight to his father the moment the shit started flying, begging him to bail him out? Could the polished surgeon have backed up his son when he paid a visit to Ann? Maybe he had been waiting outside, and when he heard Ann's first shot, he panicked and fired into the house to protect his son. Reed rubbed his chin. It was possible. The man had said he'd been in Vietnam. He'd have to know how to use a firearm. Of all the scenarios Reed had come up with, he personally liked this one the best. Not that it was necessarily true, but it gave him something to look forward to: cuffing Dr Sawyer and tossing his ass in jail. Yeah, Reed said to himself, give me that one.

The phone rang and Reed grabbed it. Claudette Landers started speaking before the detective could even say his name.

'That you, Reed?' she said.

'Yes, what's going on? Hell, I haven't heard from you in

ages, Claudette. Since you got promoted, you never come around.'

'Yeah, well, you're hearing from me now,' the woman said. 'Ann is flipping out on me, Reed. She thinks Hank is calling her on the phone.'

'What in the –'

She cut him off, telling him what the caller had said and Ann's reaction. 'So, she's back to square one again, running off at the mouth about Hank. What are we going to do?'

'Maybe there's some truth to what she's saying,' Reed said, thinking out loud.

'What? Are you as wacko as she is? The only way Hank Carlisle could be alive is if the man purposely disappeared, and if he purposely disappeared, then tell me the reason why.'

Reed cleared his throat, sorting through his own thoughts. 'There was something back then. I mean, it wasn't general knowledge.'

Claudette was wound up. 'Are you going to tell me or not?'

'Right before Hank vanished, a cache of narcotics disappeared from the evidence room at the highway patrol. They decided it was an outside job, but that still doesn't mean he couldn't have been involved in some way.'

'Shit,' Claudette said, the line falling silent for some time as they both considered the implications. 'You're a jerk, you know,' she finally said. 'Why didn't you tell me this when the guy disappeared?'

'His disappearance was classified as foul play,' Reed said defensively. He was still reeling from the news of Ann's phone call, and this woman was getting on his nerves.

'I can see it,' she said slowly. 'What if –'

'Look,' Reed said quickly, 'I don't want to sit here and speculate all day. I want to call Ann and see what she has to say.'

'She's at the jail, and don't you dare hang up on me,'

Claudette said. 'What if Hank stole those drugs, and then somehow got involved with this Sawyer kid, maybe trying to unload them? Then this would all mesh, you see?'

'Let me go, Claudette,' Reed said, groaning. The picture she was painting was one he'd rather not discuss. Cops committing felonies, dealing narcotics, this sort of thing made him sick. And Hank's coming back to shoot Ann and kidnap her son was too contemptible to imagine.

'Go,' she said abruptly, immediately disconnecting.

Reed stared out over the room, taking in the cluttered steel-gray desks, the half-empty Styrofoam coffee cups, the poster of Marilyn Monroe Noah had tacked on the wall. Without conscious thought he reached down to the bottom file drawer in his desk and pulled out a bulging file. Reed had courted his own suspicions about Hank Carlisle at the time he vanished, but as the years clicked off and the man never surfaced, he had set them aside.

Reed knew things that the highway patrol investigation had failed to uncover about Ann's husband, things Ann had kept carefully concealed. Hank's childhood had been traumatic, bad enough to damage a person for life. In addition, the perfect marriage everyone had assumed simply did not exist. Oh, they had had their good times, and they had both adored the boy, but there had been plenty of times when Reed had asked himself why Ann stayed.

Rubbing his eyes, he recalled the early days following Hank's disappearance. For the first month Ann had been unable to sleep and had staggered around like a zombie, trying to push her way through the days. By the second month her thinking had become so illogical that Reed had been forced to carry her physically to the emergency room, terrified she was on the verge of a nervous breakdown. The doctors had classified it as sleep deprivation and prescribed sleeping pills. What followed was even worse – Ann drugged most of the time, contacting psychics and all kinds of lunatics. On one occasion she'd even let a psychic claiming to have information about Hank take up residence in the house. She insisted the woman had to be close to Hank's belongings in order to pick up the right vibes. It had taken Reed two weeks to persuade Ann to throw her out.

Damn, he thought, opening the file. Although he was no fan of Glen Hopkins, he'd felt a measure of relief when Ann finally had started dating. Now he just didn't know. Was she tumbling back into the abyss again from lack of sleep and stress? Or was Hank Carlisle really a monster?

Reed rummaged through the paperwork until he reached the inventory of all the items the highway patrol officer had had in his possession at the time he disappeared. In particular, his eye rested on Hank's revolver. As adversaries go, Reed thought, Hank Carlisle and that punk Jimmy Sawyer were worlds apart. He prayed Ann's suspicions that her husband had surfaced were not valid. Hank was a trained police officer, a crack shot, and a shrewd man. He would balk at nothing, back down for nothing, and stop at nothing to get what he wanted.

Reed felt a shiver of strong dislike ripple through him. He had only feigned friendship with the man for Ann's sake. For all they knew, Hank's death had been a professional hit of some kind stemming from illegal activity. The incident had that distinctive odor to it: the lack of evidence, the car just sitting there with the doors open, not even a matchbook on the road to track down. Nothing. Too clean. Too neat. Professional, Reed had told himself. Even Melanie Chase had agreed with him, but they had also agreed that it was not right to voice their opinions to Ann. Such a burden would just make her loss more difficult to bear.

Reed was jolted out of his thoughts by a ruckus outside in the hall.

'Get the hell in there, you fucking asshole. Now,' Phil Whittaker was yelling, his voice nasal from his cold. 'I have to get off my deathbed to track down scum like you.'

Phil shoved his prisoner, a young man in his early twenties, through the double doors leading into the detective bay. The man was handcuffed behind his back.

'Who you got there?' Reed said.

'Don't say I never gave you anything,' Phil boasted. 'Tommy Reed, meet Brett Wilkinson. Hard to recognize him from his DMV photo, but I found the little fucker up at U.C. Santa Barbara. Of course, he's not enrolled in the university. Tells me he's just visiting some friends, trying to decide if he wants to enroll in January.' Phil stopped and sneezed, immediately reaching for his handkerchief. 'Fuck this cold. And fuck you, Reed. You wanted him, you got him.'

Reed jumped up and pulled Whittaker to a corner of the room, leaving Brett Wilkinson standing there, looking around as if he didn't know what he was supposed to do. 'Why is he cuffed? I said I only wanted him brought in for questioning, not hooked and booked.'

Again the chunky detective sneezed. He pulled out his handkerchief, took one look at it, and tossed it into the trash can. 'Wait a damn minute,' he told Reed, going for the nose spray in his pocket. 'Wait a minute. I can't breathe.'

Once he had medicated himself, Phil reached into his pocket and brought out a plastic bag filled with a variety of colored capsules. 'Let's see, we've got some speed here, some X – guaranteed to make you fuck for four days – and, let's see, some 'ludes, a few Seconal, a few hits of LSD. Shit, we have a regular little drugstore right in this bag. Ain't that right, Brett? You a pharmacist, man?'

The man in handcuffs sneered. 'Fuck you, asshole.'

'You wish,' Whittaker retorted, turning and shaking his ample ass at him. 'Wait till you get to the joint, buddy. They'll be plenty to fuck you there. They'll just love your pretty little tight ass.' Whittaker looked over and pursed his lips, making kissing sounds at his prisoner.

Reed shook his head and smiled. Old Phil hadn't lost his touch. 'How did you peg him for Santa Barbara?'

'You know, did some legwork, made some calls, asked a few favors from some friends. I didn't want to mention anything until I had him in custody. Thought I'd surprise you. Seems they had a pretty clean campus up there, no problems with anything heavier than a little pot. Then along comes Jones over here, and suddenly they got a big drug problem on campus.'

'How did you know it was Wilkinson?' Reed asked, keeping his voice low so the prisoner couldn't hear.

'Snitch,' Whittaker tossed out and then started coughing. 'Paid him out of my own pocket, Reed.'

Reed was already walking back toward Wilkinson. The boy was over six feet tall, well-built and fairly clean-cut when stacked up against Sawyer and his long hair. He must be the outside man, Reed thought, the dispenser in their drug operation. Therefore he had to look the part – like a college man. His hair was a honey color and his eyes were hazel. Wearing a blue button-down shirt and a pressed pair of slacks, he looked good enough to walk right into a courtroom. 'Did you test him? Is he loaded?'

'Yeah, I tested him. The guy filled two cups, but he's not on anything. Go figure.'

Reed opened his desk drawer and removed his tape recorder, preparing to take his suspect to an interview room and grill him about Jimmy Sawyer. This was the type of opportunity he loved. Brett was in deep trouble, looking at a felony possession for sale. And he wouldn't fare as well in court as his cohort Sawyer. Reed knew he had a prior arrest for selling narcotics. The clean-cut preppie standing there in handcuffs was staring at a prison sentence. Reed popped his knuckles and smiled. The setup was perfect.

'Okay, Brett,' he said, 'you and I have to get to know each other, have a nice long talk.' Grabbing the man from behind by the handcuffs, Reed started pushing him across the floor.

'Thank you, Phil,' Whittaker said, his legs tossed up on his desk, a wad of tissue clutched in his hand. 'I appreciate your hard work there, Phil. Especially when you're sick, Phil.'

Reed looked over and smiled at the detective. 'You did good, buddy. Thanks.'

''Bout time,' Whittaker said. 'Now I can fucking die, huh? Do I have your permission?'

Reed beamed, overjoyed with Wilkinson's arrest. His right shoulder started twitching and he was grinning like a Cheshire cat. 'Well, there's still Sawyer and Chen, Phil. I gave the radio room the right vehicles this time, so picking up Chen should be a piece of cake for a guy as slick as you. We need all the players. Kind of know what I mean?'

Whittaker pushed himself to his feet and grabbed his jacket. 'I hate you, Reed,' he said, heading for the door. 'I mean it, and I don't just consider you an inconsiderate prick, if that's what you're thinking. I really hate you. Got it? Hate you. Hate you.'

As Whittaker shuffled back down the hall, still mumbling under his breath like a lunatic, Wilkinson spat, 'I hate you too, asshole.'

'Oh, really?' Reed said, seeing red. With a cruel shove he twisted the boy's hands toward his body, causing him to cry out in pain.

'Shit, you're hurting me.'

'One false move,' the detective snarled, 'and I'll teach you the real meaning of pain. Bad things have been happening, Brett baby, and someone's gonna pay.'

Ann crossed the courtyard to the jail, her mind so abstracted by the shock of Hank's call that she couldn't think straight.

She just couldn't imagine it. Claudette was right. If Hank was alive, he'd call back, manage to get to her some way. And even though the voice had sounded exactly like Hank, something about it just wasn't right. Ann couldn't put her finger on it. She was too shook up now, but eventually that something would come to her.

Like a robot she tossed her badge into the bin and waited for the jailer to buzz her through the security doors. 'You wanted a face-to-face, right?' he asked as they walked through a maze of corridors.

Ann heard her own footsteps on the floor, heard the men talking in the cells, but the noises seemed remote. All she could hear was her husband's voice. Had she already forgotten the sound of the man on the phone? Was she bringing forth Hank's real voice now when she thought of the call?

'I take it that means yes,' the jailer said, unlocking a door to a small interview room. As soon as Ann stepped inside, he went to get Randy Delvecchio.

Ann had her head down on the table when Delvecchio stepped into the room. 'Are you sick?' he said softly.

'No, no,' Ann said, straightening up in her chair. 'What did you want to see me about?' Suddenly she remembered the trial. Glen had thought they would have a verdict by now.

Randy Delvecchio shuffled over and took a seat. 'I called you 'cause I thought you'd help me.'

Right, Ann said to herself. She couldn't help herself, much less a vicious criminal like Delvecchio. What she wanted to do was nail him to the wall and watch him bleed. 'How can I help you? I'm only a probation officer, Randy.'

Reaching into the pocket of his jumpsuit, he pulled out an envelope and placed it on the table. 'This proves I didn't hurt those women.'

Ann fingered the envelope dubiously, wanting to toss it back in his face. She'd come anticipating a confession, not another proclamation of innocence. 'What is this?'

Delvecchio rubbed his palms on his jumpsuit nervously and then placed them on the table. 'They sent it to my mother, see. I told them when they arrested me that I was working the day that one woman was raped, but they didn't believe me. This here is the proof.'

Proof, Ann thought, wondering what the hell he was talking about. What kind of proof could he possibly have to support his innocence? She eyed the contents of the envelope. The first paper she pulled out was a statement of earnings, listing his federal and state income taxes. The name of the company on the 1099 form was Video Vendors. Ann set that paper aside and examined the other papers. In a big sloppy scrawl, Randy's mother had written to the company four months ago asking them to verify his hours. The address listed on the letter was a post office box. The next paper was an employee time sheet showing the hours Delvecchio had worked for the company during the past year. 'This wasn't a full-time job,' Ann said. 'It says here you only worked eighty-three hours all year.'

Delvecchio said earnestly, 'See, the people at the unemployment office send me out on jobs. If I don't go, I don't get my unemployment benefits. This company I found myself, and they gave me some hours.'

'That's all well and good, Randy,' Ann said, folding up the papers to give back to him, 'but I don't think it proves your innocence. There were three crimes here. Are you saying you were working at the time of all three crimes?'

'No,' he said, shaking his head, his dark eyes flashing, 'I'm saying I was working the day that Estelle woman was hurt. The other days I don't know where I was, but I know where I was that day, and that there is the proof.'

'I'll check it out,' Ann said, standing and ringing for the

buzzer, wishing she'd never wasted her time by coming over here.

'Aren't you gonna take the papers?' Delvecchio said, picking them up and extending them to her, a pathetic look on his face. 'Please help me. I don't want to go to prison. The other inmates say they're gonna charge me with murder now that the lady died. I didn't do these things. Can't someone help me?'

Ann fell back against the door and regarded him warily. The chances of Delvecchio's being innocent were a million to one. The public thought innocent people were convicted all the time, but it just wasn't true. It was hard enough to get a guilty person convicted, let alone an innocent one.

His eyes were so big and pleading, so full of need, that Ann suddenly felt compassion for him, as a mother would. She reached out and accepted the envelope from his hands before she even fully realized she had done so. 'I'll see what I can do.'

When Brett Wilkinson was situated in an interview room, Reed started the tape recorder whirring. 'My attorney is on the way,' Brett said, nodding at the recorder.

'Oh, really?' Reed said calmly. He should have known Wilkinson would have legal representation right from the starting gate. That meant anything even vaguely resembling a confession would have to be obtained in the next few minutes. 'Well, you and I can talk or we can wait for your attorney. That's up to you, Brett.'

The young man's eyes flashed with fear and indecision. He looked around the room, but he didn't speak.

Reed sensed the boy's fear and adjusted tactics accordingly. With a strong suspect, his method was to befriend him and catch him off guard. But when the suspect was afraid, he went the opposite direction, feeding into their fear. 'You're facing a prison term here,' he said sharply. 'Your attorney isn't the one who'll be riding that bus to the joint.'

Brett's face was ashen. 'But if I talk, I'll go to jail for sure.'

'Jail?' Reed said, laughing. 'You're worried about jail? Wait until you get to the big house.' He cut his eyes to the boy. 'You know, you might just make it in the joint. You're willing to put out, aren't you, become some hairy con's lady?'

'You shut up,' Brett yelled, beads of perspiration popping out on his forehead. 'They'd have to kill me. I won't fuck a guy. I'm not a faggot.'

This rich boy was going to crack, Reed thought, smiling. 'You will, Brett. You've got that look, you know. I've seen it dozens of times. You could even take a shine to it. Hey, don't knock something you haven't tried.' This time he threw back his head and emitted an even louder burst of laughter.

Brett was fidgeting in his seat, trying to free his hands from the handcuffs. 'Let me out of these things. I'm claustrophobic, man.'

'What?' Reed said, still laughing. 'You don't like confinement? How you going to survive in the joint if you're claustrophobic?'

Sweat was streaming down the boy's face now, his chest and armpits starting to show stains. Somehow he'd managed to get his hands up over the back of the chair and then ended up with the handcuffs on the other side, stretching the muscles in his arms to the limit. 'Help me, please,' he cried.

Reed stood and walked behind him, watching as the boy tried to crane his neck around to see him. With one fluid motion Reed kicked the chair legs, and the chair tumbled over backward, crashing onto Wilkinson's hands. 'I'm so sorry, Brett,' Reed said. 'That was an accident. Here, let me help you.' Bending down, he yanked Brett up by his shirt, the chair with him.

'I'll talk,' Brett said, crying. 'Please, just take the handcuffs off.'

Reed sprang to life, unlocking the handcuffs and shoving

them in his back pocket. Brett rubbed his wrists, a wave of relief passing over his face.

'Okay, let's talk about Jimmy Sawyer,' Reed said, quickly taking his seat.

Brett wiped his sweaty face with his shirttail. 'What about him?'

Reed was in no mood for games. 'He's a bad actor, a real bad actor. We have no idea what all he's involved in. I bet you don't either . . . not all of it, anyway.' Reed paused, forcing himself to slow down. If he seemed too eager, Brett would clam up. 'See, I just don't want you paying for his crimes, and that's exactly what's going to happen here. Sawyer's going to spill his guts to save his own neck, then he's going to walk and you're down for the fall.'

'What're you talking about?'

Reed gritted his teeth and popped his knuckles. 'First one to cut a deal, Brett. That's how it goes down.'

The boy sensed an advantage. 'Are you offering me a deal?'

'No,' Reed said. 'I'm not offering you anything. Only the district attorney can negotiate a plea agreement. But who do you think puts the pressure on them to do a thing like that?'

'You,' Brett said, studying the detective's face.

Reed smiled warmly. Now was the time to win him over. 'You're a smart boy, Brett, even if you don't know how to pick your friends. Now, we know you were running a drug operation from that house. From the price of the cars you guys were driving, it was a pretty big one.'

Brett shrugged this off, his confidence returning. 'What cars? I wasn't even driving a car today. Ask that asshole who arrested me.'

Reed leaned back in his chair, irritated. If Brett had been arrested in his BMW with a stash of narcotics, the car could have been legally seized as the profit of drug trafficking. These boys knew too much about the system for kids not long out of high school. When they made a play for girls, they drove their flashy cars, but when they dealt drugs, they knew enough to maintain a low profile.

'I got you on the car, Brett,' Reed said, looking him straight in the eye. 'Those cars were purchased in one day, and all three were bought with cash. Not many honest people walking around with over a hundred grand in their pocket, all green. So let's not fence about that. That's something we know for sure, Brett. In fact, I'm not even going to ask you a lot of questions about that lab. All I want to know is the name of the chemist. Is it Peter Chen?'

Brett hesitated, knowing he was at the crossroads. Once he rolled over on his own, there would be no turning back. But his friends weren't sitting here with this hard-nosed detective hammering away at them. If they were in his shoes, he thought, they'd give him up in a second. 'Yes,' he said, his voice low. 'It was Peter.'

Reed moved the tape recorder closer. 'Say it again, Brett.'

'It was Peter,' he said, his voice louder.

'Okay,' Reed said, 'that's a start. Keep going.'

'It's just all so messed up. I don't know where to start.' The tough veneer had vanished. He looked as if he was about to cry. 'There are awful people out there. . . . Things got so fucked up. My parents are going to die. My father has a heart condition.'

'Okay,' Reed said, unable to tell if Brett's emotion was real or simply staged for his behalf. 'Where did you move the lab?'

Brett shook his head, his lips clamped shut.

'Does that mean you won't tell me, or the lab is no more?'

'Gone,' Brett said, looking away. 'Everything's gone.'

'I see. Decided to close up shop temporarily,' Reed said, trying to contain his excitement. Brett's response had just given them the narcotics operation. 'Okay, Brett, you're doing good. Real good. I'm proud of you, buddy. Now, let's move on, if you don't mind. Let's talk about the contents of that refrigerator of yours.'

Once Brett Wilkinson's attorney showed up, the interview was terminated and Wilkinson was booked into Ventura County Jail on charges of manufacturing and distributing controlled substances. Any satisfaction Reed felt was cut short, though, by a call from the chief. 'Get your ass in here, right away!' Rosemary Sawyer had called the mayor, claiming Ann Carlisle had seduced her son, Reed had beaten up her husband, and the police were harassing her entire family for absolutely no reason. Apparently the Sawyers had contributed a bundle to the mayor's last campaign. Of course, the mayor had called the chief, and Reed got an earful.

The police association would provide him with legal representation if he was sued, but it would still be a hassle, and, as the chief pointed out, bad press for the entire department. But at least when Reed explained how Dr Sawyer had provoked him, almost striking Ann, the chief did not mention any disciplinary action. Reed knew his pristine record was a definite plus at this point. An officer who lost his cool in an isolated incident was not the same as an officer who did it repeatedly. On the other hand, if the Sawyers continued to press, the department would have no choice but to order a full investigation. In the long run, it could even end up worse than a civil suit. They could insist on charging the detective with assault and battery.

Once Reed returned to his desk, he reviewed the status of the case. Brett Wilkinson had rolled over on his friends. He had admitted that Sawyer and Chen were manufacturing narcotics in the house on Henderson, admitted that Peter Chen was the chemist and mastermind, and then admitted that Sawyer was dispensing sundry pills to his social contacts within the local community. He didn't, however, seem to know anything whatsoever about any drug runners from South America, and Reed had thought that was strange. Either he was scared of retaliation or Phil Whittaker's snitch had conned them. Brett had said they did have a financial backer, though, basically a silent partner. He swore the person's identity was known only to one person: Jimmy Sawyer.

So, Reed thought, there were more players than just the drug trio.

Every time Sawyer's name had come up, Brett had started zigzagging all over the place. He had denied any information regarding Ann's shooting, denied that Sawyer owned any firearms. As to the fingers, the young man had simply laughed. 'What in the hell are you talking about? You mean, fingers off a real person? Don't think so, asshole. Drugs, yes. Fingers, no way.'

So much for Ann and the finger sighting, Reed thought. On second thought, though, he realized Wilkinson wasn't stupid enough to confess to something that serious. He might get sentenced to a few years in the slammer on the drug charges, granted, but even possession for sale was a far cry from attempted murder – or, in the case of the mysterious fingers, mutilation and murder. For the drug case he'd get maybe four years at the max. With what they called good time and work time, Brett would hit the streets in less than two years, about the time it would take to graduate from junior college.

The way the case looked right now, all roads led back to Jimmy Sawyer. At any rate, Reed thought, once he was apprehended, he could kiss his freedom and fast-wheeling life-style goodbye. Even if they couldn't nail him for Ann's shooting, the drug offense would violate his original proba-tion, and Sawyer would certainly go to prison.

An idea suddenly flitted through the detective's mind. Could Jimmy's father be the financial backer? Surgeons didn't make the money today they used to, not with the cost of malpractice insurance. If Dr Sawyer was the silent partner in the drug operation, the supposition that he could have acted as Jimmy's accomplice during the break-in at Ann's house was not that farfetched. Granted, the idea that the doctor would risk arrest simply to bail his son out of a sticky situation didn't fit. What seemed feasible, though, was that the doctor would do whatever was required to protect his investment.

Glancing at his watch, Reed saw that the day was almost over. Soon it would be night, and Ann would be alone and vulnerable. Did Jimmy's father own a gun? Reed decided it was time to find out.

Chapter 15

That evening, after downing a few beers and taking a cold shower, Reed called to check on Ann. All he had managed to come up with for protection was advising patrol to make frequent drive-bys. He could handle the surveillance himself, but he was too exhausted to remain alert, and for that reason Ann would be better off without him. If she thought he was protecting her, she would develop a false sense of security. Would they come back tonight? Reed knew there was a possibility, a slim one, but with Wilkinson in custody, Sawyer had to be nervous as hell.

'Hey, David,' he said when the boy answered. 'What's happening, big guy?'

'Nothing,' he whispered. 'I think my mom's asleep.'

'No,' Ann said, cutting into their conversation from the extension phone. 'I'm just resting, Tommy.'

'I've been trying to reach you all afternoon,' Reed said, eager to hear her version of the phone call from Hank. 'Claudette told me what happened in the office.'

'What happened, Mom?' David said, concerned. 'Did something bad happen today?'

Ann was furious at Reed for bringing this up with David on the line. 'Nothing bad happened, honey,' she said quickly. 'I'm hanging up now, Tommy. I'll call you later.'

Once his mother was off the phone, David's voice elevated and cracked. 'Why can't you find the person who shot my mom?' he pleaded. 'She's so scared, Tommy. I don't think she wants to be alone.'

'Well, son,' Reed said softly, 'that's why she has you.'

David lowered his voice to a whisper again. 'When I came home today, you should have seen the house. I don't know what she did here, but it looks like she had a big party or something.'

Not quite a party, Reed thought. 'She needs you now, David. You're the man of the house. Isn't that what I always tell you? My pop died when I was about your age, and I had to more or less take over. You gotta stand tough, you know? Be mature.'

'Yeah, I know,' David said.

'I know this has been hard on you,' Reed said, wanting to console him, 'but it's going to be okay. No one's going to hurt you or your mother. Understand? Not as long as old Tommy is around.'

As David was prone to do, as soon as the subject moved close to the subject of fear, he wanted no part of it. 'Sure. Hey, I gotta go. I'm watching this great video movie. It's about this guy everyone thought was dead and then he comes back. He was just hiding out to get the insurance money.'

'David,' Reed said, 'you're not still harboring thoughts that your dad is coming back? It's not good for you to think that way. It's what they call unrealistic expectations.'

'Oh, yeah, well, they also call it false hope,' David said. 'That's all the stupid shrink ever talked about. But see, I don't have false hope or unrealistic expectations. I know, Tommy. My dad's coming back. I don't know when, but I know he's coming back. And when he does, Mom and I will be happy again.'

Before Reed could say anything else, David had hung up the phone.

Ann was in the bedroom, staring at the ceiling. She had to tell David the truth about last night, but she couldn't force herself to do so. First someone had shot his mother, and now she had to tell the poor kid that somebody had broken into his home.

Slipping on her robe, Ann went to check on him. 'You're watching a movie, huh?' she said, finding him sprawled on the sofa, his head propped up with pillows.

'Be quiet,' David said. 'It's almost over.'

'Look at this mess,' she said, running her fingers through her hair. His schoolbooks were in the middle of the floor, and his nylon parka and five or six comic books, as well as an empty sack of microwave popcorn. 'I've told you a dozen times not to leave your stuff in the living room.'

'Mom,' he yelled. 'You're standing right in front of the television. I can't see.'

Ann bent over and started picking up his things. 'I just want to clean –'

'Great, Mom,' he said sarcastically. 'I'm missing the end of the movie. Thanks a lot.' He stormed out of the room and slammed the door to the bathroom down the hall.

'It's just a video, David,' Ann said through the bathroom door. 'You can rewind it.'

When he opened the door a few minutes later, he found his mother hovering outside. 'What are you doing?' David said.

'Nothing,' Ann said self-consciously, following him back to the living room. 'How about some cookies?'

'We don't have any,' David said.

'Maybe I can make some peanut butter cookies. Stay here, I'll see what we have. I should have some flour and some . . .' Her voice trailed off as she wandered into the kitchen.

Shaking his head at her peculiar behavior, David cleaned

up his mess and carried it all to his room. Returning back down the hall, he peered around the corner into the kitchen to see what his mother was doing. Offering to make cookies for him when she was always all over him about his weight struck the boy as strange. But it wasn't half as weird as seeing his mother dropping spoonfuls of peanut butter straight from the jar onto the cookie sheet. 'Mom, don't you have to make dough first?'

'Oh,' Ann said, without turning around. 'I don't have any flour.'

Okay, David thought, tiptoeing off. His mother had gone completely bonkers again, just as she had after his father disappeared. What he had to do was get out of the house before she forced him to eat whatever it was she was making.

All the same, the mere mention of food had his stomach growling. If he hurried, he could get to the video store on the corner before it closed and rent another movie. While he was there, he could sneak in a candy bar. He grinned. If he was going to eat something fattening, he decided he'd rather eat a candy bar than burned peanut butter.

'This is stupid,' Ann said in the kitchen some minutes later, scraping off the peanut butter and dumping the pan in the sink to soak. She'd take David for an ice cream instead.

When she didn't see him in the living room, she instantly panicked. Then she saw the VCR was empty. He must have walked to the corner to return the movie. She'd always allowed him to walk to the corner, but not tonight. Racing to the garage, Ann backed out the Jeep and sped down the street.

There he was, just ambling along with a sack in his hands on his way back to the house. She slammed on the brakes. 'Get in,' she yelled out the window, throwing the passenger door open. 'I didn't give you permission to leave the house.'

'You're not dressed, Mom,' David said, frowning as he

opened the door and got into the passenger seat. Ann's robe was open in the front, and her underwear was showing.

Pulling the robe shut, Ann shouted, 'Don't leave the house again, you hear me?'

David cowered in the corner. 'I'm sorry, Mom,' he said. 'You always let me walk to the video store. I just wanted to get another movie.'

Ann pulled the car into the garage and just sat there, taking several deep breaths to calm her raging fear. 'David,' she said, looking over at him, 'someone broke into our house last night. I didn't want to tell you, but you have to know.'

'Who?' he said, his mouth falling open in shock.

'I don't know who it was. Tommy thinks somebody's just trying to scare me to keep me from testifying against him. It's called intimidating a witness.'

David's body became rigid, and he got out of the car, slamming the door behind him. Ann followed him into the house, and they stopped in the kitchen together, facing each other. 'Come here, honey,' Ann said, opening her arms.

'No,' he said, shaking his head, his shoulders twitching and his face flushed. 'I'm not a baby. I'm not scared. If anyone comes here again, I'll beat him up. I won't let anyone hurt you, Mom. No one's gonna hurt you again.'

Ann walked over and put her arms around her son, holding him tight. In a low and reassuring voice she said, 'It's okay to be afraid, David. Even I'm afraid. But everything's going to be all right. No one's going to hurt us.' Ann pulled back and smiled at him. 'I almost killed the guy last night. I got my gun and shot at him. He was so scared, he crapped right in his pants. I mean it, right in the hall.' She paused, managing a chuckle. 'Your mother's pretty tough, you know. I'm not going to let anyone hurt us.'

'You don't have to say this stuff to me. I'm not afraid,' David lied, jerking away from his mother and heading to his room.

'That's why my window was broken out, right? And that's why my book report was ruined, right? It wasn't the tree like you said. Why don't you just tell me the truth?'

Ann followed her son down the hall, but he slammed his door in her face. She just stood there staring at it. Then she leaned her forehead against the wood and spoke through the door. 'I'm not going to come in, okay?' she said softly. 'I know you have to work this out yourself. But please believe me, David, everything is going to be all right. If things don't get better soon, we'll just pick up and move away somewhere.'

A few moments later, the door opened and David looked out. 'Can we really move away?'

'I promise,' Ann said.

'When?'

'I don't know exactly when, David. I'd have to get a job and find us a place to live.'

'You're not going to move. You're just saying that, just like you said the tree broke the window.'

When David got angry a vein stood out in his neck, exactly like his father. Every day her son looked and acted more like his father. When he slammed the door in her face again, Ann gave up trying to reason with him. She'd never been able to reason with her husband, so why would she think she could with his son? Walking to her room, down the same dark hall where she had been attacked, Ann felt a wave of depression she knew well by now. Just as before, someone had pulled a string, and her entire life had begun to unravel. She fell on the bed face first. Soon dark memories of the past were flooding her mind, against her will. Life hadn't been that great with Hank. All those times he had exploded. . . .

One that was seared into her mind had happened when David was four months old and Ann was still employed at the police department as an officer. Walking out of the station late one night with her partner, she had been laughing at a joke the young officer had made when she suddenly saw something out of the corner of her eye. 'Quick, Bobby,' she said, pulling the other officer behind a parked patrol unit. 'Look,' she whispered, reaching for her gun as they crouched behind the car. 'Someone's hiding over there in the bushes.'

'Shit,' the officer said, removing his own weapon from his holster as he dropped to his knees. 'It's a man. I can see his legs. He must have been waiting to ambush us.'

Ann scooted over next to him. 'Come out,' she yelled as loud as she could. 'Come out or we'll fire. If you have a weapon, throw it down on the ground. Keep your hands where we can see them.'

When the man stepped out of the bushes, his arms over his head, Ann was flabbergasted. She was pointing her gun at her husband.

Sending her bewildered partner on his way, she lit into Hank. 'What in the hell were you doing? I almost shot you, for God's sake. And Bobby thinks you're nuts now, hiding in the bushes like an idiot.'

Hank seized her roughly by the arms, practically lifting her off the ground. 'You're screwing him,' he growled like a rabid dog. 'I won't have my wife screwing some damn rookie.'

Ann twisted away from him, appalled by the accusation. 'I am not,' she screamed back. 'What's wrong with you? Bobby has a girlfriend. He's my partner, Hank.'

'I want you to quit the department,' he said, still panting. 'I don't want my wife working nights with strange men.'

'Where's David?' she asked, suddenly alarmed. 'You didn't leave him home alone, did you?'

'He's with the sitter,' Hank said, glaring at her. He would never neglect his child.

Relieved, Ann looked around the parking lot and sighed. At least David was all right, she thought, and as far as she knew, no one had seen them. Most of the evening watch had already left for the night, and the graveyard watch was already on the street. Ann had stayed late with her partner to finish a report in the squad room, probably one of the reasons Hank had gone crazy. He insisted that she be home ten minutes after her shift ended – just enough time to drive to the house. Ann had let the time get away from her, and had forgotten to call.

'I'm going home,' she said, turning to walk to her car.

'I mean it, Ann,' Hank said, following behind her. 'I don't want you to work anymore. I want you to stay home where you belong. David needs you.'

'I have to work,' Ann said flatly, still annoyed at his behavior. 'You don't make enough money to support us.'

She saw the explosion coming, but there was nothing she could do to stop it. She hadn't meant to say that to him. She was angry, and it had just slipped out. His face got inflamed, his mouth tightened. Then the arm went back. The next thing she knew, his eyes had rolled so far back in his head that all she could see was the white. She kept her eyes focused on him, refusing to duck, refusing to look away. There, Ann thought. It was almost over. The arm was whipping through the air. She braced herself for the impact.

With a loud, sickening smack, Hank slapped her right across the face.

'I dare you to say I don't earn enough money to support my family!' For a moment his face went blank, as he realized what he had just done. Then the tirade continued. Pacing back and forth in front of Ann, he spat words at her like bullets, flailing his arms around. 'I work night and day at that lousy fucking job. People spit on me, puke on me, and that's not counting those that want to blow my frigging head off.' He stopped and caught his breath, then continued ranting. 'Maybe I'll just throw in the towel, walk away from the whole thing.'

The longer Hank raged, the more agitated and out of control he got. 'You can support me, huh? We already live in your father's house. Why don't you just support me, huh? You gonna support me, huh?'

Ann was silent, her hand cupped over her mouth. It made her ill to see her husband this way. But she wouldn't cry. She refused to cry. They had been down this road before, even gone to a family counselor. All day long on her job, Ann dealt with domestic violence, but at home she was still the victim.

People didn't understand, and she certainly couldn't confide in their friends, since most of them were police officers. They all thought Ann and Hank were a perfect couple. They didn't know the pressure her husband was under, how he hated the job, hated the hours, even claimed he hated half the highway patrolmen he worked with. He simply wasn't meant for the profession. What he needed was a job without stress, a position that didn't require him to deal with other people's suffering.

Ann saw her husband's head lower as he rushed toward her again, the same look on his face as before, but this time he was moving fast, almost charging her, about to butt into her like a bull on a rampage.

'Don't hit me again, Hank,' Ann screamed, stepping sideways and ducking. 'I won't allow it. I'll leave you . . . file for divorce.'

He stopped and stood perfectly still.

'Did you hear me, Hank?' Ann said. 'If you ever hit me again, I'll file for divorce.'

'Divorce me,' Hank said, yelling back at her. 'Just leave me. Go on and leave me. Everyone else in my life always leaves me.'

Ann sat up in bed, her head pounding, her body damp with perspiration. Why had she let this memory surface? She wanted only the good memories. The bad times she had simply erased as if they had never occurred.

After the first time her husband hit her, Ann had insisted

they go to a family counselor. The therapist had told Ann her husband had unresolved conflicts, and the terrible truth had finally come out.

When Hank was only a chubby little four-year-old, his parents, drifters and alcoholics, had been residing in South Dakota. For reasons Hank never uncovered, they had driven him out to a spot on the interstate in the dead of winter, told him to get out of the car, and then ordered him to hold on to the fence until they came back to get him. The temperature was below freezing. By the time the authorities rescued him, Hank's fingers had frozen to the metal fence. For the first day or so, it was touch and go whether the child's fingers would have to be amputated. But Hank had recovered from the physical injuries and was placed in foster care. He had been shuttled from one place to the other, never having a real home of his own. Finally, when he was in his teens, he was adopted by an elderly couple. They weren't well off, but they tried to give Hank a decent home and love. It just wasn't enough. They never located his parents, and Hank grew into a bitter and confused young man. According to the therapist, he had so much suppressed rage that he was a walking time bomb.

In therapy, Hank was sullen and closed, refusing to deal with his tragic past. Finally he stopped going, and there was nothing Ann could do but try to understand and love him. With enough love, she told herself, Hank's anger would one day subside.

In his favor, the one thing Hank Carlisle had never stooped to, the one thing he knew Ann would simply not allow, was venting his anger on his son. It was one of the reasons Ann tolerated as much as she did. Whatever else Hank Carlisle was, he was an excellent father to David.

How many times had Hank hit her? More times than she could remember. The incident in the house, the one he had wanted to buy her, had been a particularly brutal one. When she'd told him they couldn't afford it, he'd knocked her to the ground. His attacks had gone on for a few years, until the night he threw a plate at her, cutting her forehead so badly she required seven stitches. That was the last. After that Ann had hit back. And when that didn't stop him, she attacked. One night she struck her husband in the legs with a baseball bat when it looked like he was going to slug her. That had put an end to the outbursts.

But ending the outbursts hadn't ended the fear. Every day she had lived with it, never knowing when he would explode. By this time Tommy Reed had entered the picture. After one blowup he had spotted Ann with a black eye and had come unglued. Ann had covered for Hank – she told the detective she had walked into the bathroom door during the night. Tommy Reed, however, was an astute man. He knew Ann was lying. He also knew Hank had a vile and explosive temper, because he had seen it on numerous occasions with his own eyes. Several times Reed even tried to talk Ann into leaving. Other than the one instance when she had threatened to file for divorce, however, Ann had never seriously considered leaving her husband. How could she leave a man who had already suffered the ultimate injustice, rejection by his own parents? Underneath the tough-cop facade he presented to the world, her husband was still that little child on the freeway, still clinging desperately to the fence.

Things improved for three or four years before Hank set his sights on getting promoted to lieutenant. If he could just get promoted, he kept telling Ann, then they would have enough money to move to a bigger house, maybe buy some new furniture or take a much-needed vacation. He studied and studied, sitting at the dining-room table far into the night, eventually scoring one of the highest grades ever on the lieutenant's exam. Hank was certain he would make it.

But he didn't. Too many instances in his personnel file of

excessive force, they said. Too many citizen's complaints. Hank was devastated. In the months before he vanished, he didn't make love to his wife. He didn't socialize with his friends at the department. The only person he appeared to have any interest in at all was his son.

The phone began ringing, stirring Ann from her thoughts.

'Ann,' the voice said.

'Yes?' she said, the phone still several inches from her ear.

'Ann, why don't you go get David so we can leave?'

She gasped and gripped the phone with both hands. 'Who is this?' It was Hank's voice again. Her heart began hammering against her ribs. 'Hank, is that you? Oh, God, Hank, don't hang up on –'

She heard a click and then the dial tone.

'No,' Ann cried, throwing the receiver violently against the wall. 'Don't do this to me. You can't do this to me.' She was so distraught that she couldn't think. Digging her fingers into her temples, she tried to bring back the sound of the voice. Had she really heard it? Was she hallucinating again, suffering from sleep deprivation? What had he said? What were his exact words? But they were gone, nothing now but an echo floating around in her head.

The one thing she distinctly remembered the voice saying was her son's name.

Chapter 16

Sally Farrar was standing on the back porch, watching her children play, when she saw a red car pull into the driveway next door. She assumed they were the new tenants and looked away, not wanting to have to introduce herself and make small talk. Since the three boys had moved away, Sally had been plunged in depression, sitting and staring for hours on end, barely saying more than three or four words all day. Dishes were piled high in the sink, and she refused to wash them.

The voyeurism had started so innocently. When Sally and her husband had first moved to Henderson Street, they found that the former occupants had covered the kitchen window with frilly curtains. Everyone on the block, Sally soon learned, had been gossiping about the boys and complained about them speeding up and down the street where there were so many children playing. Sally didn't allow her children out in the front yard, so she wasn't concerned. Besides, she was not into socializing with her neighbors. All her life people had picked on her for one reason or another: her clothes were weird, she was too skinny. She'd attended special education classes and the other kids called her a retard. People were cruel and malicious. Sally had learned to keep to herself and mind her own business. If you started poking into other people's lives, they would start poking into yours.

One day she removed the kitchen curtains, and that evening, as she was washing dishes, she realized she could see directly into the master bedroom of the house next door. What she saw took her breath away. She saw young naked bodies, both male and female, the most beautiful bodies she had ever seen. And the sex . . . Sally knew things like this went on, but seeing it with her own eyes was shocking. Sometimes two of the boys would have sex with one girl at the same time. Sometimes there were girls having sex with each other, the boys watching while rock music blasted out the window. At first Sally was disgusted. The neighbors were right, she'd thought. These were evil, wicked boys, perverts and drug users. Sally wasn't stupid. She knew they were using drugs. She saw them sniffing stuff up their noses, smelled bitter smoke she knew wasn't from cigarettes, saw one boy with a pipe far too small for tobacco.

But the disgust turned to fascination. She began to look forward to washing the dishes. Sally would position herself at the kitchen window, breathing shallowly in anticipation. She would fantasize that she herself was part of the exotic scenes she saw playing out only twenty feet away. Sex with her husband, a routine she had always thought more a chore than a pleasure, Sally now looked forward to all day, just as she looked forward to spying on the people next door through the window.

Then the entertainment had all just stopped.

She saw other things happening in the house next door. Strange things. Things Sally didn't understand.

Giving up on the window now that nothing was happening in the bedroom, Sally had taken to prowling outside the house next door after her husband was asleep. Even though the rest of the windows in the house were covered with blankets, some of them were still open for air, and sometimes she could hear what the boys were saying. There were arguments. She recognized the voice of the boy with the long dark hair. He was always rough with the girls, slapping them around in the bedroom, though the girls never seemed to mind.

Sally became obsessed, no longer connected to her own life, hopelessly mired in the more intriguing lives of the young men next door. Prowling at night turned to spying during the day. Enormous stacks of dirty laundry spilled over the top of her laundry basket next to the washing machine. The children had to wear the same dirty clothes days in a row. The house was a pigsty. Sally hadn't cleaned it in weeks. Right before Earl got home from work every evening, she would leap in her car and pick up something for them to eat at a fast-food restaurant, telling Earl she had a headache, the cramps, the flu, whatever she could think of.

She watched and she listened.

Every time one of the boys went out, Sally knew it. Every time one came back, Sally was right there watching through the trees, the windows, peeking through a hole she'd made in the fence. Once she even managed to slip inside the garage when they left it open. She'd run her fingers over the hoods of the fancy cars. Carefully opening the door to one that belonged to her favorite, the blond boy, she had stuck her head inside and inhaled the wonderful aroma of expensive leather. Then she put her hand on the seat, the very seat where he had sat, where that part of his body had been. It was almost like touching him. Sally had shivered in delight.

Then she'd looked over and peered through the windows of the Chinese boy's car, seeing something in the backseat. Sally preferred the blond, but the Chinese boy was the best lover of the three. She had watched him many times, almost felt what he was doing to those girls. She tried to open the car door and look inside, but it was locked.

Sally smiled. That was just like him, to lock the car in the garage. He was always so particular with his things, so neat and orderly. When she'd gotten up to make the children's breakfast the night after one of their arguments, never expecting to see anything through the window that early, knowing the boys always slept until noon if not later, she was shocked to see the Chinese boy already awake and in the bedroom cleaning. She stood there and watched while he put new sheets on the bed, carefully folding and tucking in the corners, watched as he scrubbed down the walls, the furniture, almost everything in the room.

'Mommy, I'm hungry,' Sally's oldest boy said. 'When are we going to have dinner?'

'I don't know,' Sally said, staring at the house next door and the red car, standing on her tiptoes to see over the fence. Then she dropped down to the steps. She didn't care about the new neighbors.

'Mommy, please make us some dinner,' the boy insisted, tugging on her sleeve. 'Where's Daddy?'

'Stop that,' Sally snapped, jerking her arm away and glaring at her son. 'Your father is working late tonight. Eat some crackers and leave me alone.'

'I ate crackers for lunch.'

Sally didn't answer. She was lost in her thoughts. When the police officer had come to the door the other day, she'd been terrified, certain the boys had reported her spying on them and the police had come to arrest her like a common criminal, some kind of crazy person. She even thought the boys had moved away because of her.

But she was safe now.

The policeman had never come back and the boys were gone. It was over. Henderson would never be the same now, and Sally would never be the same. She didn't want Earl. She didn't want a bunch of screaming kids anymore.

Sally Farrar wanted what she had seen through the kitchen window.

As soon as Ann woke up Saturday morning, she called Freddy's mother, Louise Litsky, and asked if they were still planning to take the boys to Magic Mountain the following day.

'Of course,' the woman said. 'That is, if it doesn't rain.'

Ann explained what had happened two nights before and her fears that David could be in danger. Louise expressed her sympathy and asked if there was anything she could do to help. 'Actually, there is,' Ann said. 'Would you mind if David slept over there tonight? I just have to get him out of the house, Louise.'

'I'll have to think about that, Ann,' she answered, reluctant to get involved. 'You know I want to help. I just don't want to put my own family in danger.'

'Forget it,' Ann said quickly. 'You've done enough all these years. I understand, Louise.'

'Say, I've got an idea. Charles and I will take the boys to a hotel over near the amusement park and spend the night tonight. To make certain no one knows where David is, why don't you drop him off at Charles's office downtown? I'll have Charles meet you there. If you meet him in the underground parking lot, no one will be able to follow him. They wouldn't know what kind of car to look for.'

Ann wasn't sure all the secretiveness was necessary, but she was relieved anyway. 'You don't know how much I appreciate this, Louise,' she said.

'Ann, why don't you go with us? Why would you want to stay alone in that house after all this?'

Louise had a point, but Ann didn't intend to be alone. She

was going out with Glen, was going to forget all this insanity for a few hours. 'No, Louise, but thanks. Really, thanks for everything. I'll bring David over to Charles's office at five o'clock.'

Right before lunch, Reed headed to the records bureau. The case was coming together nicely. He'd talked to Hopkins a short time ago, and the district attorney felt certain they would have a warrant for Peter Chen in a few hours. Even though it was Saturday, Hopkins insisted on handling it at once. Picking up Chen could easily lead them to Sawyer. Not only that, once Chen realized Wilkinson had rolled over, he might spill the beans on all of them, including Sawyer.

Standing at the counter, he checked heads. 'Angie,' he called to a pretty brunette, 'come here a minute. I've got something for you.'

Angie Reynolds was quiet socially, but on the job she was as aggressive as any officer on the force. Her dark hair was tied back in a ponytail, and she was wearing a red sweater, a black short skirt, and tennis shoes. In fact, Angie looked like a high school kid, but Tommy knew she had four small children at home.

'Here's what we have,' he said. 'We think we may have a possible homicide, but as yet we have no body and no ID. What I want you to do is get a printout of all the missing persons in the last ninety days. I know you gave me a whole stack of stuff yesterday, but we have to narrow it down. Let's start with females in their late teens or early twenties. Get the actual reports faxed to us, with any photographs. Also, did you find out anything from the morgues?'

'No,' she said, smiling at him fondly. Tommy Reed was at the top of her list of good guys. 'There's a few Jane Doe bodies in Los Angeles, but they have all their fingers. I'm going to send out a query letter all over the state. If that doesn't work, I'll go to neighboring states.'

He handed her a piece of paper with the license number of the red Honda Jimmy Sawyer had traded his Porsche for when Rodriguez had lost him at the mall. The owner of the Honda was a young woman in her late teens named Jennifer Daniels. She'd known Sawyer for some time but had no idea where he was now. All he'd done was walk into the clothing store where she worked and asked to trade cars for a few days. A Porsche for a Honda, the girl had said, her eyes gleaming. Too good to pass up.

'Make certain you note that Sawyer and Chen may be armed and dangerous. Also, be sure to cross-reference the warrant with the Honda, and get Peter Chen in the system ASAP.'

Reed had started walking off down the hall when she called out, 'Hey, knucklehead, get back here. I need a full description on these people.'

Reed turned around and headed back. 'You want everything, don't you?'

'You bet,' Angie said, reaching over to adjust his tie while she was talking. 'See, I can get a lot from their DMV records, but without their date of birth I don't even have that. Then I'll need the license plate on this Chen guy's car. Besides, Reed, they enter the warrants at the courthouse.' She eyed his tie, cocking her head to see if it was centered.

'Look,' Reed said, 'it sometimes takes thirty days or longer for the court to get warrants in the system. I want them in now. I'll get you all the information, Angie, even the warrant numbers. I have everything you need in my office.'

'These are the suspects in the Carlisle case, aren't they?' she said, seeing the strain on his face. 'How is Ann holding up?'

'You know,' Reed said, making a wavy motion with his hand. 'Fair.'

As Reed walked off, she thought of Ann Carlisle and all the horrid things the woman had been through. Not long after her husband had vanished, Angie had seen her walking down the road late at night. Thinking her car had broken down, Angie had offered her a ride. But Ann had said she just couldn't stay in the house any longer and wait, so she had taken up the habit of walking at all hours of the night. They had gone for coffee, and Angie had tried her best to console her. Then she'd given her the phone number of a psychic they'd used once at the police station, thinking the woman might be able to help. What a mess that had been, Angie thought. She'd certainly never thought Ann would get so carried away that she'd let the woman move into her house. Tommy Reed had been hopping mad.

When Reed got back to his desk, he couldn't find Sawyer's file. He knew he had it, unless Abrams had taken it. Abrams was the department's hostage negotiator, and the captain had called him out to try to talk down a psycho. The lunatic was holding three nurses and a doctor hostage at the local hospital, claiming they had given his wife the wrong baby.

In his search his eyes fell on the inventory list he had pulled out of Hank Carlisle's file, and he studied it again. A missing link – what could it be? The one item they had felt certain would eventually show up was Hank's revolver. It was doubtful that the person or persons who had killed him had buried the gun with the body. Guns were interesting that way. They always surfaced somewhere. Weapons used in one homicide would turn up in another, sometimes years later. Police officers had a rule of thumb for this: the kind of person who used a gun seldom destroyed it, even when the gun might be the only link to the crime.

Still musing, Reed dropped the paper and finally located Sawyer's file on Abrams's desk. As he started to leave the detective bay, though, a light flashed in his mind and he backtracked. On an impulse he picked up the piece of paper with the serial number of Hank's Smith & Wesson service revolver.

'Here you go, Angie,' Reed said, handing her the information she needed on Sawyer and Chen. 'And could you run this serial number for me? I'll wait.'

She sat down at a computer terminal and punched in the numbers. 'It's clear,' she reported seconds later.

'It can't be clear,' Reed exclaimed. 'That gun belonged to Hank Carlisle. Every flag in the world should pop up with that serial number.'

'Maybe I made a mistake,' she said quickly. 'I'll run it again.'

Reed hurried around the counter and pulled up a chair right next to the woman.

She tapped the screen. 'See, it's clear. There's nothing at all. Maybe someone accidentally deleted it. It's been four years, right?'

'Right,' Reed said sourly. This was the exact reason he had decided to run it. Sometimes even cops forgot that items entered into the system could be removed or deleted by error, and no one ever checked. 'Call the highway patrol and tell them about this. Have them get that gun back in the system. It's the only hope we have of ever catching his killer.'

'Wait, there is a flag,' Angie said, staring at the screen. 'It's not entered into the system as stolen, but it looks like it might have been pawned. Hold on while I pull up that file.' She started tapping the keys, and another screen appeared.

'Where was it pawned?' Reed said eagerly. 'This might be it.'

'See the AZ in that little box?' she said, pointing. 'That's the code for Arizona. I'm sorry, but we just got a national hookup on this system. No one really knows how to use it yet, or I

246

would have caught it the first time.' Angie took out a thick manual and started flipping through the pages while she spoke. 'See, in the past we kept records on pawned items, but only locally, and it was really sporadic. Every computer entry had to be backed up with a hard copy from the pawnshop. You know, copies of the original receipts. For that reason the pawnshop guys purposely stalled as long as they could.' She stopped and looked in his eyes. 'Now we do it all by modem, or if they don't have a computer, all they have to do is fax it. When the kinks are out of the system, it should be great. Think of all the stolen property we're going to recover. Shit, I can't find the section.' She threw the book down and started playing with the computer.

'The reason we finally got funding for this,' she mumbled, fingers flying over the keys, 'is we have to move fast. The pawnshops can sell the stuff after a certain amount of time if we don't advise them it's stolen.'

'What are you doing?' Reed said anxiously. 'Can't you figure it out?'

Angie finished punching a series of numbers and letters in the computer, and the screen filled with data. 'Hot damn,' she said. 'Isn't this neat? See, here's the person who pawned it, the date it was pawned, the address and store where it was pawned, and the subject's driver's license number. Now wait, there's another page.' She tapped a command. 'It should be the subject's photo ID.'

Reed was amazed by what appeared next. The picture was not photo-quality, but it was in color and pretty darn good. This could be the actual killer. Then he looked again, shocked. The man in the computer-generated photo bore an uncanny resemblance to Hank Carlisle. Reed almost nudged Angie out of the way so he could get a better look at the screen. Was it his imagination? Was he as crazy as Ann? No, he thought, staring at the image. Although the man had dark skin, it could be only a deep tan. He had an abundance of facial hair which obscured the lower half of his face, a full beard and bushy mustache, but the nose could easily be Carlisle's, and the bone structure was similar, rather broad across the midsection of the face. For the photo the man had worn tinted glasses. That was a bad break, since it eliminated one of the most accurate means of visual identification: the eyes.

But whoever it was, Reed was excited. If they recovered the gun, they were on the way to finding out what had happened to Hank Carlisle. This was the first major break in the case after four years.

Seeing that Angie was waiting for him to tell her what to do next, he said, 'Can you print it?'

'Sure,' she said, springing back into action. 'I'll print the whole thing. This gun was pawned six weeks ago. If you don't want the shop to sell it to someone else, you'd better call right away.'

'You better believe I'll call,' Reed said, grabbing the papers as they spilled out of the printer one at a time.

'Okay, while you do that, I'll get on the horn to the highway patrol and tell them what we found.' Angie picked up the phone and started dialing the number from memory.

Reed suddenly jumped up and depressed the button on the phone. 'Don't,' he said.

Angie gave him an annoyed look. 'But why? This is a good lead, isn't it? I mean, it's the gun he had when he was kidnapped. This guy that pawned it could be involved in the kidnapping itself. Surely you know that?'

'Don't do anything, Angie,' Reed said slowly, turning to look over his shoulder, checking to see if anyone had been listening to their conversation. 'I'll handle it myself, okay?'

'Here, then,' she said, 'let me give you the number for the highway patrol.' She scribbled the number on a piece of paper and turned to hand it to Reed, but the detective was already halfway down the hall.

Glen called Ann at four o'clock that afternoon. 'Are we still going out tonight?' he asked cheerfully.

Ann didn't respond at first.

'Ann,' he said, 'did you hear me?'

'Some strange things have been happening,' she said, deciding she had to tell him. 'I was going to tell you about it the other day, but I didn't have time.'

'My God, are you all right?'

'Yes,' Ann said slowly. 'I'm fine.' Standing in the kitchen talking on the portable phone, she was pacing back and forth, the phone call from Hank still the foremost thing on her mind. 'I've been getting these phone calls, Glen. I'm not certain, but the voice sounds just like my husband.'

'No,' he said, incredulous. 'What are you saying?'

'I know it's crazy,' Ann said, desperately wanting him to believe her. 'But I'm telling you, the voice sounds just like Hank. Not only that, he may have been the man who broke into my house and assaulted me.'

'Why would you think that?'

'When I saw him in the light, I recognized him.'

'As your husband?' he said. 'You recognized him as your husband? The man is dead, Ann. How could that be?'

She was getting impatient. 'I didn't recognize him specifically as my husband,' she said, not certain how to explain it. 'His eyes . . . Glen, I recognized the man's eyes. They were familiar to me. I know I've seen those eyes before.'

'So,' he said calmly, 'it was just Sawyer. Remember when you were shot, you thought your husband was at the scene. Isn't that what you told me?'

'Of course, but –'

'Well, that explains it. If Sawyer made you think of your

husband when you were shot, they must share some common feature.' Glen's voice became low and condescending. 'His eyes, maybe?'

'I don't think so,' Ann said. 'I was delusional the night of the shooting. This isn't the same.'

'Just think about what I said, okay?'

'Fine,' Ann responded, thinking she should have never mentioned it. All she needed was another person telling her how stupid she sounded.

'Anyway, how's eight o'clock?' Glen said. 'Want to meet me at the Bristol?'

'That's fine,' she answered.

Once she had hung up, she headed to the bathroom to take a shower and make herself presentable. When she stood in front of the mirror, she was aghast at what she saw. She looked a thousand years old. Her hair was limp and lifeless, her lips cracked, and her normally clear skin was covered in a rash of some sort that made it feel like sandpaper. Touching her face with her fingers, Ann felt dozens of tiny bumps just under the surface.

'I have to push ahead,' she told herself. Even if the man calling was Hank, from what she could tell thus far, he was not calling to tell her he loved her. He was calling to terrify her; he had come back to take her son away. After all these years Hank Carlisle was still making her life miserable.

Giving her image a last sour look, Ann shed her clothes and stepped into the shower. Scrubbing her body, she vowed that she wouldn't let Hank's phone calls, real or not, destroy her relationship with Glen. If she lost Glen, she would never forgive herself. She had finally found a man she respected, a man who transported her with his lust for life, a man who seemed to know how to make her happy.

Already she felt better. She'd drop David off, come home,

and get dressed in something nice for a change, and possibly, just possibly, she could manage to have a normal evening.

The restaurant, specializing in Belgian cuisine, was situated in a lovely, quaint Victorian house. Glen was already waiting at a table when Ann walked in. She was wearing a short black dress, a lightweight knit, with only a strand of pearls around her long, graceful neck. Her look was one of simplicity, with her face fully exposed by her short haircut, but she was striking and heads turned as she crossed the floor to Glen's table. Ann always wore sensible shoes to work, but tonight she was wearing high heels. They made her long legs appear more shapely than they actually were, her walk more seductive, as her hips moved from side to side beneath the clinging fabric.

Glen stood, a hesitant smile on his face. 'You look wonderful, Ann,' he said. 'I mean it, you look absolutely fabulous.'

Ann kissed him lightly and then took a seat at the table, basking in his praise. 'I've decided to go on with my life, you know. No matter what's going on.'

Glen had no sooner taken his seat than he leaned forward over the table, his voice low and tense. 'After we talked, Ann, I started thinking about the things you told me about your husband. It isn't right for me to tell you what to do, what to think. If you believe it's Hank, then it must be Hank.' He looked away, as if too overcome by emotion to face her. 'What if it is him? What happens to us then?'

Ann twisted her napkin in her lap. 'Let's not talk about it,' she said. 'Not tonight, Glen.'

'No,' he said adamantly, slapping the table and causing the silverware to jangle. 'I need to know now, Ann. How can we go on if you're just going to throw it all away if he comes back?'

Ann met his gaze and held it. Finally she answered, her voice firm, 'I'm not going to throw it away, Glen.'

All the tension left his face. 'All right,' he said, smiling as he signaled the waiter. 'Let's eat.'

Ann picked up the menu and studied it, settling on a chicken crepe with a mushroom cream sauce. Her diet had been atrocious lately, and she knew she was losing weight. Tonight she felt as if she could eat everything in sight.

Glen ordered a bottle of wine with dinner, then sighed, leaning back in his seat. 'So we have the whole evening to ourselves.'

'Great, isn't it?' Ann said, diving into her salad the moment the waiter placed her plate on the table. 'This is delicious. How's yours?'

He stretched his fingers across the table. 'I've missed you, Ann.'

'I've missed you too.'

'I want to devour you,' he said, rubbing his leg against hers under the table. 'That's what I'm really hungry for.'

Ann dropped her fork as she felt the contact, her face flushing a bright shade of pink. She could feel it already – the aching between her legs. 'You're a sex maniac,' she said playfully. 'You should be ashamed of yourself.'

'I'm never ashamed,' Glen said, his eyes dancing, his voice low and seductive. 'The only thing I would be ashamed of is not being able to please you.'

Responding in kind, Ann slipped her shoe off and scooted her chair closer to the table. Then she found his crotch with her stocking foot. 'Oh, really?' she said. 'So far I don't have any complaints.'

The waiter brought their wine to the table, and Ann straightened up in her seat self-consciously, placing both her feet back on the floor. When the waiter had finished pouring, she said, 'We could leave if you want . . .'

'That's exactly what I want.' His eyes tracked the waiter until he was a good distance away. When he turned back to Ann, his lids were half closed with lust. 'Unless you want to get under the table with me right here. We could put on a dinner show. You know,' he said, laughing, 'give these nice people a little entertainment.'

'No,' Ann said quickly, not certain if he was joking. 'Let's get out of here. I'm not hungry anyway.'

He called the waiter over and asked for the check, much to his surprise. 'We'll go to my house, Ann. Then nothing will distract us.'

'You're on,' she said, smiling brilliantly.

From the outside, Glen's house looked fairly unassuming. It was approximately ten years old, and the front was almost obscured with dense shrubbery and towering trees. But the first time Glen had taken Ann inside, she had been pleasantly surprised. The interior was filled with opulent furnishings she wouldn't have expected a bachelor to own. He collected antiques, and most of the pieces were massive. In the living room he had an overstuffed sofa covered in a tapestry-type fabric. Every other table bore a sculpture or art object of some kind. Every piece had its place. No glasses stood around without coasters, no dirty dishes in the sink, no unmade beds and towels tossed on the floor.

Glen lit a fire in the fireplace and went to get them a bottle of wine. Ann already felt a little woozy, what with the lack of sleep lately and her meager diet.

'I think I'm going to get drunk,' she said when Glen came back and handed her a long-stemmed crystal glass.

'Maybe that's just what you need,' he said, smiling and pulling her into his arms.

Ann kissed him and then pulled away to set the glass on the mantel. 'You're what I need.'

'Oh, really?' he said, massaging her buttocks through her clothing. 'You feel good, Ann, really good. It's been too long.'

Gently he pushed the neckline of her dress down until her shoulders were exposed. Then he kissed each of her shoulders and ran his finger along her collarbone. 'You're so delicate,' he whispered. 'Your skin, your bone structure, your nose, even your mouth.'

'How can I be delicate?' Ann said. 'I'm so tall, I look like a giraffe.'

He continued pushing the knit dress down. Ann hadn't worn a bra, and she was soon standing nude from the waist up, the fire against her back. Her fingers fumbled with the buttons on his shirt. She was so nervous and excited that she couldn't get them open and finally dropped her hands to her sides and watched while Glen removed the shirt himself. His upper body was laced with sinewy muscles, and his chest hair was dark and thick. She stared at him in the dim light of the fire and then stepped closer until her chest was pressing against him.

'My breasts are too small,' she said shyly.

'No,' he said, pushing her back to look at them, 'they're perfect. If they were bigger, they would sag like an old woman's. I hate sagging breasts. My mother's breasts sag.'

In one easy movement he took Ann's hand and pulled her down onto the plush carpet. Then he carefully pulled her dress off and tossed it aside. Ann was wearing a garter belt and hose with no underwear. Glen had told her several times how much this excited him. He'd even bought her the very garter belt she was wearing, but until tonight she hadn't had an occasion to wear it.

Ann lay on her back as his hands roamed, her eyes closed, listening to the fire crack and pop only a few feet away, the wine making her feel far removed from what had been happening in her life, loose and uninhibited. A handsome, exciting man was making love to her, and nothing else seemed to matter.

When he spread her legs and bent his head between them, though, Ann tried to sit up and protest. She'd never done this with Hank, and she was embarrassed, but Glen pushed her back down, holding her in place with his arms. After the first, soothing strokes, Ann relaxed, allowing her body to respond. She began tossing her head from side to side and moaning. Not sure she could take it any longer, she tried to pull Glen on top of her, but he wouldn't budge.

'Just be still,' he whispered. 'I want to make you feel like you've never felt before. I want to show you what real pleasure is.'

Ann heard his words, but they were disconnected and floating. The pleasure was overwhelming, building somewhere deep inside her body. She felt tears on her cheeks and was powerless to stop them. Feeling this good was both alien and wonderful. 'Please, Glen,' she begged, 'I want to feel you inside me.'

She waited, expecting him to get on top of her, but he did not. Stretching out on the floor next to her, he pulled her on top of him instead. 'Ride me,' he said, his eyes filled with passion.

Ann pressed her lips to his and felt him plunge inside her. His hands grabbed her buttocks, forcing her to rock with him. Her inner muscles were in spasms, gripping him tightly and then releasing him over and over again. Glen would move her up until they were almost disconnected. Then he would push her back down. Ann sat up and arched her body backward, feeling his soft hands graze her breasts, the tender flesh of her abdomen. Then his fingers were stroking the very place where their bodies met.

'Oh God,' she cried, throwing herself down to his chest and riding him fast, hard, their bodies wet with perspiration. 'I love you,' she said.

When she collapsed on his chest, spent, he rolled with her,

still connected, until he was on top and she was looking up at him.

He picked up her legs and draped them over his shoulders, plunging inside her again and again, his face contorted, his eyes shut, all power and force now, like a man possessed. 'Yes, yes,' he cried, his whole body trembling and jerking as he exploded inside her.

At last he collapsed on top of her, a dead weight. After some five minutes, Ann felt she couldn't breathe and was certain he had fallen asleep. She finally managed to slip out from under him. 'Where are you going?' he said, reaching out a hand. 'Come back to me.'

Ann laughed, and they faced each other on their sides, only an inch apart. 'I'm embarrassed,' she said. 'I've never been so . . . you know . . . carried away.'

Glen smiled at her, pressing a nipple between his thumb and forefinger until Ann yelped. 'What's wrong?' he said. 'Don't you like that?'

'Not if it hurts,' she said, doing it back to him. 'See, that hurts. If you do it softly, it feels sexy. If you do it hard, it hurts like a bitch.' She started to tell him that it repulsed her especially now because the man who had attacked her had touched her in that way. Then she thought better of it. Mentioning that night would lead to more talk of Hank. What would that accomplish?

'Oh, now you're an expert on pleasure,' Glen said, his eyes boring into hers. 'Don't you know pain and pleasure are closely related? Without pain, there would be no such thing as pleasure?'

Ann sensed his pride had been wounded, and she chuckled. 'Maybe, but I'll just take the pleasure.'

In a rapid movement Glen leaped on top of her and pinned her hands to the floor. 'Now you're powerless,' he said. 'Completely under my control.'

Ann giggled, but she didn't like it. She tried to wrench her arms free. 'Let me go. I don't . . .'

'What?' Glen said lightly. 'Are you one of those women that has to be in control, Ann?'

'It's not control . . . it's . . . let go of my arms. I want to get up.' Didn't he know that she'd just been attacked? Didn't he know how it had made her feel to be pinned on the floor by a man again? Perhaps it was because of the attack that he felt some need to reassert control.

A black intensity appeared in his eyes, but he released her arms. 'There,' he said, standing and reaching up to the mantel for his wineglass. 'I didn't mean anything.'

Ann stood as well and wrapped her arms around his waist, kissing him on the nape of his neck. Then she moved her hands to his shoulders and felt the rigid muscles. He was tense over the situation with Hank, she told herself, fearful that he might lose her. 'There're some things I just don't like, Glen. But I want to make love to you. You made me feel fantastic tonight.'

When he didn't respond, Ann pulled away, knowing there was nothing she could say to reassure him. Their relationship was young, and as yet they had not learned to trust each other. Possibly, she thought, he was comparing their lovemaking to what she had shared with Hank. She almost laughed, thinking he had nothing to worry about in that department. Sex with Hank had been fast and rough, and she had seldom been satisfied.

Walking around his living room, Ann began looking at the art objects, the photographs on top of the sleek grand piano. Of course, as a district attorney he made more money than she did, but she knew there was family money. His fancy car, his European clothes, the antiques. She picked up a picture in a silver frame and gazed at it. 'Is this your mother? She looks so young. I mean, being a judge, I expected her to be a lot older.'

Glen took the picture out of her hand and placed it back on the piano. 'I don't want to talk about my mother, okay? Any more than I want to talk about your husband. Come with me.'

He led her in the direction of the bedroom. As they were walking down the hall, a shiver of fear raced through her body. The hall was dark, and memories of the night she had been attacked returned. Ann slammed back against the wall, lost in panic.

'What's wrong?' Glen said, his hand sliding out of hers.

Ann could hear the man's voice now: 'Don't you like that? Doesn't that feel good?' After the attack was over, so much of what had happened in that hall had vanished from her mind. Now she remembered everything: the way he smelled, the way he had sat on her back.

'I – I feel sick,' Ann stammered, already sidestepping down the hall toward the living room, knowing she had to get some fresh air. 'The food . . . the wine . . . I have to go.'

'Wait,' Glen said, following her. 'If you don't feel well, lie down until you feel better. If you want, I can even drive you home, and you can pick up your car tomorrow.'

'No,' Ann said, seizing her clothes off the floor and quickly dressing. 'Please, Glen, I want to go home. I don't feel well. Everything was great, but . . .'

He tossed his hands in the air in frustration. 'Whatever.'

Ann stepped into her shoes and then raced out the door.

Once she was inside the Jeep, Ann put her head down on the steering wheel in despair. She had to take control of her life and stop the madness once and for all, or she was going to lose this man and the happiness he had brought her. Raising her head, she stared back at the house, longing to return but knowing she couldn't.

Her thoughts turned to the telephone conversation with Glen earlier in the day. He was the only person who had made any sense of the situation. Perhaps there *was* something about

Jimmy Sawyer's eyes that reminded her of Hank. As Glen had pointed out so logically, on both occasions when she had been in Sawyer's presence, she had instantly thought of Hank. Was it cruelty she saw in his eyes? Was Sawyer as explosive as Hank? Was that something she would instantly recognize after all the years of abuse? Ann knew it was possible.

How many times had she actually seen Sawyer? The first day in the courtroom, the night of the shooting, the time they met for lunch. On all those occasions she had been either injured or distracted by other concerns. And the day of his arraignment, she had been worried that he was about to slander her reputation in the courtroom. Appearances had always meant so much to her. It was one of the reasons she had never told anyone about Hank's abusive behavior.

Sawyer wasn't merely a drug dealer, not with human fingers in his refrigerator. Yes, she thought, cranking the engine and pulling away from the curb, Glen had to be right.

Chapter 17

Sunday morning brought a new determination. Ann got out all the information she had collected on the Sawyer case, as well as the information relating to her shooting, and stacked it in neat piles on the kitchen table. The only way to reclaim her life, she had decided the moment she woke up, was to find the person or persons responsible for terrorizing her. She couldn't let her relationship with Glen be destroyed by some clever mutt with a talent for impersonating voices.

Ann got David's blackboard from his room, lugged it down the hall, and propped it up on the kitchen counter. All morning and into the afternoon she worked, making notes on the blackboard when a detail caught her eye or when she saw a hole in the case that had not been filled. One large gap that emerged was any background information on Peter Chen. Because he had no prior criminal record, other than a few parking citations, they really knew next to nothing about him. So how were they supposed to locate him? He wasn't living on Henderson anymore, but it was doubtful that he had left the area. He was simply too young to leave his family and contacts in the community behind. He was also Chinese, and Ann knew the importance most of them placed on family.

Rubbing her chin, she flipped back through her notes.

Someone had learned that Chen had attended Long Beach State at one time and studied chemistry. But the note in the file indicated that all the information the university had provided them had led nowhere. No wonder, Ann thought, studying the fax from the registrar's office. The student in question was named Peter Chen, all right, but he was the wrong one. At the time they had checked, they'd only had Chen's name and not his date of birth. The date of birth on the school records was not the same as Chen's, and Noah Abrams had failed to contact the school again once he had the correct information.

Glancing at the clock, Ann was reminded that it was Sunday. No one would be in the registrar's office on the weekend. Then she had another idea. She picked up the phone and dialed information. 'I need the number for the dean's office at Long Beach State,' she told the operator.

After seven unproductive phone calls, Ann finally called the computer lab and got an answer. She asked the student who picked up the phone if the dean lived on or near the campus. He advised Ann he did. She then informed the student that she was a deputy probation officer and needed to speak to him regarding a dire emergency involving a student. The boy agreed to go to the dean's house and have him call Ann right back.

She waited, tapping her fingers on the kitchen table.

Fifteen minutes later, the phone rang, and Ann seized it. The voice said, 'Get David.'

The voice on the phone was her husband's, but Ann refused to be deceived. 'If that's you, Sawyer, you're making a serious mistake,' she said forcefully. 'The next time you get within five feet of me, I'm going to blow your fucking head off.'

She waited, holding her breath and listening. She heard something on the line, but she wasn't certain what, some kind of clicking noise. 'You're not going to talk, are you? You're just going to keep calling and calling. Whoever you are, you're not going to get to me.' Ann didn't wait for the person to hang up this time. She slammed down the receiver. If it wasn't Hank and some jerk was trying to rattle her cage, she wasn't going to give him the satisfaction. From now on, she decided, the moment she heard that voice, she would simply hang up. Once the caller realized Ann wasn't buying it, the game would be over.

A few minutes later, the dean of students called, and Ann tried to talk him into going down to his office and getting the information on Peter Chen out of the school's computer banks.

'I don't have to do that,' the man said. 'I'm linked to the university's system through my own computer. Wait, let me see what I can find.' He left the line open, and Ann heard computer keys tapping. A minute later, he came back on the line. 'That's such a common name. You know, we have a lot of Chens here. We certainly tried to cooperate with the police when they called. Hold on,' he said again. 'I think I have it.' He rattled off Chen's physical description and date of birth. Ann verified it from the driving records. 'Would you like me to fax his complete student profile, everything we have?'

'Super,' Ann said.

'I have to fax it to a legitimate agency, Ms Carlisle. You do understand, don't you?'

'No problem,' Ann said, giving him the fax number at the probation department and thanking him profusely. As soon as she hung up the phone, she grabbed her jacket, shoved her Beretta into her purse, and took off.

Sunday-evening traffic was light on the 405 Freeway headed to Huntington Beach, and Ann was making good time. Checking her map and the list of addresses she had jotted down on a yellow note pad, she took the Beach Boulevard exit and watched for the right cross street. Finally she found it and searched for the numbers on the houses. According to the school records, Peter Chen's uncle lived here.

It was a small, neat house, the lawn perfectly manicured. Ann knocked, waited, looked around the back, and then finally left. There were several days' worth of newspapers in the driveway. The people had to be out of town.

The next stop was one of Peter Chen's character references on his college application. At least someone came to the door, but he wasn't Chinese and claimed he had never heard of Peter Chen. A new tenant, Ann decided.

After another stop four miles away in Redondo Beach, Ann backtracked to Huntington Beach again and checked her map. Of all the places she had checked, 1845 Orangewood had to be the biggest long shot. It was Chen's parents' home, and the boy was unlikely to hide there. As she drove through the neighborhood of houses worth three or four hundred thousand dollars, she couldn't help but think what a waste it was that all three of these boys had become involved in criminal activity. Unlike inner-city kids, they'd had all the advantages: decent homes, good families, money for college. Peter Chen's academic history at Long Beach State had shown him to be an outstanding student. Why did a boy so bright have to throw it all away?

She knocked on the front door and waited. A young Chinese boy cracked open the door and peered out. He was so small, Ann thought at first that he was only about ten, but on further inspection she decided he must be fourteen or fifteen. 'Hi,' she said. 'I'm here to speak to Peter. Are you his brother?'

'He doesn't live here anymore.'

'I see,' Ann said. 'Are your parents home?'

'No.'

'Do you know where Peter's staying, by any chance?'

'He lives in Ventura now.' The boy glanced behind him and

then pulled the door nearly closed so that nothing more than a narrow swatch of his face was visible.

'Would that be Henderson? Is the address on Henderson?'

'Yes,' the boy said politely. 'What's this about?'

Ann sighed in disappointment. 'Nothing,' she said, walking back down the steps and getting into the car to leave. She was turning on the map light to locate her next stop when something caught her eye. The drapes in the front window moved. Okay, she said, cranking the engine and driving slowly around the block. She parked at the end of the street, then again walked up to the front door and knocked. There might be something going on here. The same young boy answered.

'Sorry to bother you again,' Ann said, 'but I'm with the Stanford University scholarship fund. Your brother has been awarded a full scholarship, but we haven't been able to locate him.' The door opened an inch. Quickly she engaged the boy in eye contact and placed her foot in the door without him realizing it. 'It's a shame, really. We have rules, you know. After a certain period the scholarship is retracted and awarded to another individual.'

Ann watched the boy's face. He was about to bite. A smile still plastered on her face, she slipped her hand inside her purse and found her gun. 'Stanford, of course, is a very prestigious school.'

'Peter,' she heard the boy calling as he disappeared from the door, 'you won a scholarship to Stanford.'

This was it.

Ann kicked the door open and jerked her Beretta out of her purse. 'Get down,' she yelled at the boy, seeing a dark figure in the background. 'Now,' she shouted, advancing quickly and shoving the boy to the ground herself, 'Peter Chen, you're under arrest. If you move even one muscle, I'll shoot you. I'm serious. I'll kill you without a second thought.'

A handsome, well-built young man stepped out of the

shadows, his hands over his head. 'Who in the hell are you?' he said, looking Ann up and down. She was dressed in Levi's and a denim jacket, looking more like a model for Guess jeans than a cop.

The young man was perfectly calm. Not a single bead of sweat appeared on his forehead, and he looked as fresh and relaxed as someone who had just stepped out of a shower. Staring down the muzzle of a loaded gun, his eyes reflected a cold defiance and superiority. Somehow Peter Chen managed to look elegant standing with his hands over his head.

'I guess you could say I'm your worst nightmare,' Ann said, grabbing his wrists and shoving him toward the door.

'You,' Chen said, recognizing her. 'You're the probation officer, aren't you? The one who was shot?' Then he laughed. 'Where are the cops?'

'They take Sunday nights off,' Ann said, her Beretta pressed against his back. While Chen was as cool as an arctic wind, she was drenched in sweat: her shirt, her pants, her hair, every inch of skin on her body. She was almost afraid the gun was going to slide right out of her hands. Walking around to the front of her prisoner, Ann unbuckled his belt.

'No, Peter,' she whispered right in his face, 'I'm not going to give you a blow job.' Then she yanked his belt out of the pants loops, spun him around, and crisscrossed his hands behind his back, securing them tightly with the belt.

Before she left, she turned around and spoke softly to his brother. 'What's your name, guy?'

'Sean,' he said meekly. 'You're taking my brother to jail, aren't you? You tricked me.'

'Sean, I want you to call your parents and tell them what happened here. Tell them your brother was arrested on a warrant for manufacturing and dispensing narcotics. He'll be booked into the Ventura County Jail. They can call there or

Peter will be able to call them in a few hours. Okay? Can you remember all that?'

'He didn't really win a scholarship, did he?' the boy said, avoiding his brother's hard stare.

'Of course not, idiot,' Peter snapped.

Ann kneed the older boy in the back and then turned to his brother. 'Sean, listen to me. You're the one who's going to get a scholarship one of these days. Learn something from what happened here tonight. Earn your money the legitimate way, the way I'm sure your parents did. You hear me?'

'Yeah,' he said, his face downcast. A second later, he became excited and animated. 'If you go to jail, Peter, do I get your Lexus? That's so bitching.'

Peter Chen didn't answer.

'Kids,' Ann said, shoving the older boy out the front door. Never make a sincere speech to a kid. All Peter's brother was interested in was his car.

On the ride back to the police station, Ann tried to get her prisoner to talk, but he was too smart. He sat there in total silence, his face set in granite. To cover herself, Ann read him his Miranda rights off a little card she kept in her wallet. One of the nice things about being a probation officer, as she saw it, was having full powers of arrest while not having to work shifts or walk around in a tacky uniform.

At stoplights, she measured the man sitting next to her. He had thick dark hair, perfectly cut, every strand falling exactly correct, hooded lids over intelligent and fiercely determined eyes. He was dressed in an expensive silk shirt and slacks, all black except for an intricate hand-embroidered design that covered the buttons and the tips of his collar. In his right ear was at least a two-carat diamond stud. He was an extremely handsome and confident young man, not the type of customer they generally received at the jail.

'How long did you go to Long Beach?' Ann asked, thinking he might not answer questions about the case but might be coaxed into small talk.

His head remained motionless, but his eyes shifted to Ann. She could see his tongue, pink and smooth inside his mouth as it slid across his teeth. Ann shivered in spite of herself. Peter Chen was good-looking and he might be smart, but he had a mean streak a mile long. Ann could sense it, almost smell it. This wasn't the man who had crapped on the floor in her hall the night she'd started shooting. Ann was convinced she could stick her gun right in his ear and he wouldn't blink.

Chen could very well be the one, though, who had sliced off some poor girl's fingers. What had the girl done? Ann wondered, feeling an evil cloud emanating from the young man seated next to her. Had she reached for something she wasn't supposed to, done something to offend his masculinity? Had he simply sliced off her fingers for the hell of it?

The rest of the ride passed in silence.

Ann didn't call ahead. She wanted to walk into the Ventura police department with her prisoner. Her father would have been proud of her.

Ann's grand entrance was not exactly what she had in mind. Detectives Reed and Whittaker were out in the field, Noah Abrams had gone home, and the only uniformed officer in the station was the acting desk sergeant, a motorcycle cop on desk duty with a bum leg. Ann had never seen him before. She handed over Peter Chen, advised him of the status and nature of the warrant, and then walked out of the station without so much as a pat on the back or a solitary word of praise.

The only good aspect about it, Ann told herself, was that she didn't have to listen to Tommy Reed lecture her about how dangerous and impulsive she was. Besides, she'd delivered the goods. That was the name of the game.

•

'Alone? You went out there alone?' Glen Hopkins said. He had called her the moment she walked in the house. 'He could have killed you.'

'Glen,' Ann said, 'what's done is done. With what's been happening lately, I had to immerse myself in work. Besides, I've survived everything else. I decided I could survive Peter Chen.'

'Did he talk?'

'I wish,' Ann said. 'Maybe you could make some headway with him if you're willing to bargain. This guy's cold, Glen. If I were to place my bets on the most violent member of the threesome, I'd go for Chen. If anyone sliced off a woman's fingers, it was probably him.'

Glen fell silent. 'I want to see you, Ann,' he finally said. 'I was very concerned last night, the way you ran out of the house.'

'I can't,' Ann said. 'David should be home from Magic Mountain any minute.'

'Are you angry at me for some reason? Did I do something last night to upset you?'

'No, no,' Ann said quickly. 'I just didn't feel well. And listen, Glen, you really helped me. I mean it. What you said about Sawyer resembling Hank could be true.'

'Have you told anyone else?' he said, his voice low. 'I've been thinking about it, and you should inform the officers working the case, even let the highway patrol know what has been happening.'

Ann took a seat on the sofa. 'It's nothing, Glen,' she said. 'Things are coming together on the Sawyer case, so . . .' Then her thoughts turned to Delvecchio, to the envelope he'd given her. She'd completely forgotten about it. 'What's happening with the trial? You know, Delvecchio.'

'Looks good,' he said confidently. 'The defense concluded their case. Monday the jury will begin deliberations. Why do you ask?'

'He called me the other day, asking to see me.'

'Oh, really? Why would he want to see you?' Glen said, contempt in his voice.

'I guess I gave him the impression that I was his pal or something.' Ann laughed. 'Pretty funny, huh?'

'Don't go over there again,' Glen said angrily. 'I'm telling you. Delvecchio is devious. He's a fucking animal, a killer, for God's sake.'

'Hey, calm down,' she said. She started to tell him about Delvecchio's proclamation of innocence, but decided it would just annoy him further. 'He's in jail, remember?'

'Just stay away from him,' he snapped.

'I'll talk to you tomorrow,' Ann said. 'I think I hear David at the door.'

Monday morning at the office, Ann was grabbing a file to go to court for a sentencing hearing when she spied the envelope given to her by Randy Delvecchio. She'd promised the man she would check the dates on his time sheet against the dates of the crimes, but she'd forgotten to do so. Out of idle curiosity she opened the envelope and compared the dates. 'Oh, my God . . .'

There it was, in black and white. On the day Estelle Summer had been raped, Randy Delvecchio had been working. It was a mistake, she told herself. Ann glanced at her watch. She had only fifteen minutes, but she had to find out. She called the company's number and got a disconnect. Then she checked the address on the envelope and saw it was from an accounting firm. Ann got the firm's number from information, and when she reached it, she quickly explained her position and why the information was so crucial.

'Well, we're only an accounting firm,' an older woman's voice said. 'Video Vendors filed bankruptcy some time ago.'

Ann assumed this was the reason Delvecchio had not been

able to contact the company previously. 'But you evidently have the employee records. Listen, it's absolutely imperative that I confirm if this man was working on a specific day.'

The woman put Ann on hold and came back a few minutes later. 'According to the time sheets he was at work that day.'

'It has to be a mistake,' Ann said. 'Maybe he came to work and left, but no one clocked him out.'

'Doubt that,' the woman laughed. 'The owners of this business were very tight with their money. I mean, they were going under, but even before they got in trouble, they were sticklers for certain things. Let me tell you, no one got paid if he didn't do the work. They didn't even pay for lunch breaks or give their employees mandatory coffee breaks.'

'Great,' Ann said, irritated by this new development. Glen was killing himself to get the man convicted. She should have left well enough alone.

'They're being investigated by the Labor Department right now, because a number of employees filed complaints,' the woman continued. 'In any case, they used time clocks. Mr Delvecchio clocked in at eight in the morning and clocked out at five that evening. He was a temporary employee, more along the lines of piecework.'

Still Ann couldn't believe it. Then she recalled that Estelle had been raped at three o'clock in the afternoon. 'How about lunch? He could have taken a long lunch hour.'

'No,' the woman said, 'he didn't clock out for lunch. Most of the low-end workers never took a lunch break. They ate a sandwich off the truck outside or something. Like I told you, they didn't get paid for lunch breaks.'

There had to be a logical explanation, Ann thought. 'Did he work alone somewhere? Like possibly in the back storeroom where he could have slipped out and no one knew about it?'

The woman dismissed this idea. 'According to the file, Mr Delvecchio worked in the warehouse with all the other employees. The company brokered used video movies. They used day laborers to unpack the movies, clean them up, and stack them on the shelves. That's what Mr Delvecchio was hired to do.'

Once Ann had thanked the woman for her help, she hurried around the partition to Claudette's office. 'I have something incredible to tell you, but I have to be in court right now. Will you be available around lunch?'

'Tell me now,' Claudette said, her curiosity piqued.

'I can't,' Ann said, darting out of the office and sprinting down the hall to court.

Because Ann was late, the case she was appearing on had been shuffled to the end of the afternoon calendar by the time she arrived. Judge Hillstorm glared at her, along with opposing counsel, when Ann walked in after they were already in progress. Because she had no idea how fast the other matters would be resolved, she had to remain in the courtroom. If she left and they called the case and again she wasn't present, all hell would break loose.

Taking a seat next to the public defender, Ann turned her thoughts to Randy Delvecchio. Were they about to convict an innocent man? She wasn't aware of anything else about the case that would support such an assumption. But she hadn't had time to read every document. She'd spent more time concentrating on Delvecchio's criminal record, his psychological profile, and ways she could aggravate his sentence by linking him to the homicides.

There was no positive ID, even though Glen had tried to convince the jury otherwise. Ann knew the rapist had worn a stocking mask over his face, and the victims had made only a general ID based on height and body weight. He'd also worn a condom, so there were no seminal fluids available. As more sophisticated police technology was implemented, criminals were becoming smarter. The crimes against persons unit was seeing more rapists with condoms, men who knew that ejaculating inside their victims could be the very act that could convict them. Semen was one of the bodily fluids they could use for genetic fingerprinting.

The state's entire case, as she understood it, rested on the fact that Delvecchio had property in his possession that belonged to the victims. Ann shook her head in puzzlement, oblivious to what was going on in the courtroom, asking herself if Randy Delvecchio was a burglar and had simply stolen the items. Or possibly the real rapist had discarded the property and Delvecchio had simply found it.

'Ms Carlisle,' the judge said, 'would you like to state your agency's position regarding sentencing?'

Ann looked up and started flipping wildly through her notes. She had been so deep in her thoughts she had not even heard them call the case.

Chapter 18

Angie Reynolds dropped her children off at her mother's house in Simi Valley on her way to the records bureau on Monday morning.

'Why are you going to work now?' her mother asked as the children streaked past her into the house. 'I thought you were working the three-to-midnight shift this month.'

'I need to check on some things, so I thought I'd go in early. You don't mind, do you?'

'No, of course I don't mind. But I worry about you, honey. You work too hard.'

Angie kissed her mother on the cheek and took off. All night long she had thought of Ann Carlisle and the disappearance of her husband. Angie knew what it was like to lose your husband, although she knew exactly where hers was – shacked up in Thousand Oaks with an ugly fat blonde. He had just walked out one day three years ago and never returned, leaving Angie with the full responsibility for the children and a pile of unpaid bills.

As soon as Angie got to the records bureau, she booted up the computer, tapped in a series of codes on the keyboard, and pulled up the program they used to generate computer composites of suspects. Scanning all the stored files next, she found the one she was looking for, the image of Hank Carlisle the highway patrol had transmitted via computer to every law enforcement agency in the country. Then she blanked the screen and pulled up the data from the day before, the photo identification of the man who had pawned the Smith & Wesson revolver in Arizona. Although she had never met Hank Carlisle, Angie had read all the newspaper articles and bulletins relating to his disappearance. The moment the pawnshop record had popped up, she had seen the similarities in the two men's appearances, even though she'd kept her mouth shut. Reed was the detective, and she didn't want to appear disrespectful. But Angie felt an affinity with Ann Carlisle. If Angie's husband could desert his family with no advance warning, Hank Carlisle could have done the same.

Opening the relevant manual, Angie tried to figure out how to compare the images. She had to superimpose one image over the other, and she'd never been trained in this particular program. The only person who used it was the department's composite artist. Finally she found the right page and scanned it quickly, moving her finger down each line. Then she followed the directions, and poof, there it was: one face on top of the other. She clapped her hands softly and then brought up a grid. Separating the face into sections, she transferred one of the sections to a clean screen. Now all she had to do was move the image from the pawnshop on top of this one and repeat the same procedure until she had superimposed both images.

Picking up her stylus, Angie outlined the combined images on her pad. Then she used her mouse to eliminate the hair. As best she could tell, the man who had pawned the gun had a thinner face than Hank Carlisle's, but Angie knew a different hairstyle could make a face appear thinner. So far so good, she thought.

She now transferred the lower half of the grid. The facial hair was a problem, but she could fix that too. She erased the beard and bushy mustache, then went back to the composite board and tried a dozen or more faces on for size. The lower lip was visible in the pawnshop photo, but the upper lip was partially covered by the mustache, so in this area of the face she had to speculate. She knew the image would be her creation and not actual, but it was as close as she could get. Soon her handiwork was finished.

'What are you doing here this early?' the other records clerk asked, leaning over her shoulder.

'Just playing,' Angie said.

'Man, don't you get enough of this stuff?' the man said, walking away. 'I sure don't consider this place fun. Get a life, Angie.'

She ignored him, her eyes riveted to the computer screen. How close was the match? Was it close enough to call the highway patrol? Not really. After making a few more adjustments and comparisons, Angie went back to the pawnshop records. Now she had to think like an investigator.

The identification the man had given was an Arizona driver's license. Storing and saving her other work, Angie entered the DMV records in the Arizona system.

Turning the pages slowly, she jotted down all the particulars: the man's name, date of birth, place of birth. The date of issuance was six months after Carlisle had vanished, and the name listed was Bill Collins. If ever there was a generic name, this was it. Suddenly she saw something that caught her eye. In the box where applicants were asked to list their previous driver's license number, Collins had marked none. According to the man's date of birth, he would be fifty-two years old. Angie felt her heart do a little jump. He was fifty-two and had never had a driver's license? 'I bet, buster,' she said out loud, smiling. 'Sure, tell me more. If you're fifty-two, I'm eighty.'

They saw fake identification all the time. People with one too many drunk-driving convictions, criminals with convictions to hide. All they had to do was go to the DMV and take the driver's test, provide a phony birth certificate, and bingo, their checkered past disappeared. Police often arrested people with five, even ten different driver's licenses in their wallets. Paper hangers, people who wrote bad checks, were notorious for this. Their MO was to get a fresh ID, open a new checking account with a lousy hundred bucks, and end up walking away with thousands of dollars in merchandise before anyone was the wiser.

Angie took the man's name and date of birth just to be certain and ran it through the national system. This would take some time, she knew. Some less sophisticated states didn't have access to the national system, or if they did, their people were not trained to check the computer. Sometimes the computer was down, overwhelmed with the sheer number of queries.

She waited. The computer answered after a five-minute search. There were 2,453 people named Bill Collins in the national system who had valid driver's licenses. Of those, forty-eight had the same date of birth. Now she had to input the physical description to try to narrow it down. The task was impossible, though. The name and age were just too common for the computer to make an accurate sort. Whoever had come up with this new identity knew the system all too well. The largest section of the driving public fell right in this age bracket.

Frustrated, Angie decided to cross-check Carlisle's actual driving records against those of Bill Collins. She knew human nature. People were smart, but they were also lazy. Many criminals gave themselves new names and still used other legitimate identifying factors, such as place of birth, middle names, the same numbers on an address connected to a different street. They'd use their actual day of birth and then switch the month or year. Sometimes their reason was more caution than laziness. When asked to rattle off details by a police officer, they found it a lot easier to put on a credible performance when a portion of the data was legitimate.

Angie was getting tired. It was almost lunchtime, and her regular shift started at three. She began inputting all comparable data into the computer as fast as she could: Hank and Ann's home address, Ann's birthday, David's birthday, their Social Security numbers, Hank's badge number at the highway patrol, any and all number sequences she could find that he might have memorized.

She finally finished at two-thirty. Leaning back in her chair and rubbing her eyes, she stretched her arms over her head. With a swan-dive finger she reached forward and pushed the enter button, hearing the computer hum as it gobbled up the data.

'Do your stuff, baby,' she said, patting the beige metal box as if it were human.

When Ann came rushing out of the courtroom, she ran right into Tommy Reed. 'We have to talk,' he said, a stern look on his face.

'What's wrong?' Ann said, tagging along behind him. 'Where are we going?'

'Outside.'

Ann stopped short, trying to figure out why the detective was so peeved. Was he annoyed that she hadn't called him back Friday night after he spoke to David? 'You're angry, right? Because I didn't call you back.'

Reed turned around and scowled. 'Among other things.'

Ann was confused. 'What other things?'

'Try Peter Chen.'

'Oh, that,' she said, smiling, thinking his ego was just bruised. 'Aren't you pleased I got him?'

'Yeah,' Reed said, his anger subsiding as they continued

down the corridor. 'The captain reamed Noah's asshole out this morning. You found Peter Chen when we had half the city looking for him.' He turned to her. 'Want to explain how you accomplished this little feat?'

Ann shook her head and winked. 'Trade secret. Look and you find things. Have you interviewed him?'

'Fuck, are you kidding? This guy hasn't said a word since you picked him up. He just sits in his cell and stares at the wall like he's in a coma.'

Once outside in the sunshine, they took a seat on the concrete ledge around the fountain. 'I'm sorry I didn't call you back,' she said. 'I just didn't want David to hear me talking about the phone calls and Hank.'

'That's why rooms have doors,' he retorted, his annoyance at her flaring again.

Ann continued, undaunted, 'The same person called again Friday night at the house, and then again yesterday. The last time he called, I hung up on him.'

'And you're certain it was Hank?'

Ann stared out over the courtyard, watching as several unsavory-looking characters passed on their way to the jail. 'No, Tommy, I'm not certain.'

He was surprised. 'That's not what you told Claudette.'

'That woman,' Ann said, angry that Claudette was talking to Tommy behind her back. 'Look,' she said, 'I don't know who it is, but it does sound like Hank.' Then she voiced a worry that had been nagging at her ever since that last call. 'What if David picks up the phone the next time this person calls? It would destroy him, Tommy. I could never convince him it wasn't his father. The voice is just like Hank's.'

Remembering how confident the boy had been that his father was coming back, Reed felt a similar alarm. 'I suppose we could try a tap.'

'Yes,' Ann said eagerly, seeing where this could take them.

'Then if it is Sawyer, we can trace the call and pick him up.'
She slapped her forehead, feeling like a fool. 'Why didn't I
think of that?'

'Well, I did,' Reed said, standing, a smug expression on
his face. 'I even drove over to your house Saturday night, but
you were out. Anyway, give me your key and I'll get a crew
over there now.'

Ann fished her key out of her purse and handed it to him.
As her gaze drifted past the windows of the jail, she was
reminded of Delvecchio. She proceeded to tell the detective
the new developments in the case. When she was finished,
he just shrugged, as if to say the rape case was out of his
hands.

'Wait,' Ann said, stopping him before he walked away.
'Did they ever check that dog bite?'

'It wasn't a dog bite,' he said, giving her a surly look.
'We're not incompetent, Ann. We checked that mark on his
leg when he was first booked.'

Ann watched the detective as he headed across the parking
lot, mired in confusion. Delvecchio had told her it was a dog
bite. Why would he lie about something like that?

'Ray Hernandez,' Ann said to a pretty blond receptionist.
'Tell him Ann Carlisle is here to see him.'

Adjacent to the D.A.'s office, the investigative unit was set
up like the probation department. The investigators didn't
have actual offices, they had partitioned cubicles like Ann's.
Once the receptionist called Hernandez, she nodded, and
Ann made her way to his desk.

'Ray,' she said, flopping in a chair and meeting his gaze,
'you know I'll be preparing the presentence report on Randy
Delvecchio. I have a few questions for you.' Ann paused,
thinking through the facts. She knew the first lead to
Delvecchio had come from an anonymous phone call, but

she also knew it could have been a police informant. 'The person that fingered him – was he a snitch?'

'No,' Hernandez said. 'What made you think that?'

Another dead end, Ann thought in disappointment. Even if the informant had refused to testify, she'd hoped to obtain more explicit information. 'Can you tell me exactly how this all went down?'

Hernandez put his hands behind his back as he recited the facts. 'An unknown person called and informed us that Delvecchio was bragging on the street about raping several old women. The informant proceeded to tell us what he looked like and where he lived. We then requested a search warrant.' He stopped, finished with the part he had memorized for the trial. 'Hopkins didn't want to simply pick him up for questioning,' he added, his admiration for the attorney obvious. 'He wanted to do it up right.'

Ann was thinking that to obtain a warrant on the basis of such flimsy evidence was a credit to Glen's expertise, but it was precisely the manner in which Delvecchio was apprehended that troubled her the most. 'Ray, do you really believe that anyone in his right mind would boast about raping old women?'

'Hey,' he said defensively, 'assholes like Delvecchio love to shoot off their mouths. Happens all the time.'

Ann made a wry face. 'Just how many cases have you handled where a rapist targeting older women bragged about it?'

'Aw shucks, there's got to be –' He abruptly stopped, trying to search his memory.

'Did I hear you say none?' Ann said sarcastically.

'I can't think of anything right now, but –'

'Rapists aren't the most popular people in the neighborhood,' Ann continued, 'even if the neighborhood is San Quentin. And raping old women is almost as bad as raping little kids. Everyone has a mother. Are you following me?'

'I see your point,' he said slowly.

Ann wanted everything clear in her mind. 'So, you got the warrant and went directly to his house. Who made the actual arrest?'

'I did. Well, I wasn't alone, if that's what you mean. Hopkins went along and . . . let me think here a second. Oh, Martin Gathers was there too.' Gathers was another D.A.'s investigator. 'He's the one who found the ring.'

'Gathers?'

'No, Hopkins. He found it in Delvecchio's bedroom, in his drawer. There were other things taken during the rapes as well, but Delvecchio must have already sold them.' He pushed his chair up to the desk and started shuffling through his phone messages, trying to give Ann a hint that he needed to get back to work.

'The overcoat?' she asked.

'Sucker was wearing the overcoat.' Hernandez looked up and smiled, letting Ann know that for him, this had been the clincher. 'Actually came to the door in it. Guess he was so proud of that coat he even wore the damn thing in the house.'

'And this was the whole case? There was never a positive identification by any of the victims? I recall Glen alluding to this, but it never occurred, right?'

Ray Hernandez frowned, annoyed by Ann's implication. 'We put Delvecchio in a lineup and made all the men wear stocking masks. The Summer woman and the Alderson woman made an ID based on his size and build, his voice, things like that. That's an identification, you know,' he said, defending Hopkins for taking it a few steps forward in the courtroom. Then he laughed. 'We must have done something right. They just convicted him about thirty minutes ago.'

Ann gasped. 'You're certain?'

'Yep,' he said with pride. 'We do good work around here. Glen called me himself from the courtroom. Says we might file homicide charges now that the Summer woman is dead. If he can substantiate that her death was a direct result of the crime, this guy's headed to the gas chamber.'

Ann could almost hear the clock ticking inside her head. Delvecchio had several strikes against him, including race and inadequate representation. That meant things could move fast. Her intervention was critical. 'What about fingerprints?'

'No prints, Ann. Lab determined the rapist wore gloves. There wasn't a lot of physical evidence left at the scenes. This man's clever. There's no telling how many other crimes he's committed.'

Ann thanked him for his time and headed back to her office. Clever, he had said. Delvecchio wasn't clever at all. In fact, she suspected that he was borderline retarded or learning-disabled. He'd even told Ann that he'd dropped out of school because he'd had no shoes to wear. No wonder he was so attached to that overcoat, she thought, thinking he was more childish than cunning. And gloves? Ann couldn't see it. Delvecchio had been convicted on circumstantial evidence, primarily the victims' possessions.

Then another thought crossed her mind, so mind-boggling that she stopped and took a seat on one of the benches outside a courtroom. Why hadn't she made the connection before? The person who had broken into her house had worn gloves. He'd also worn a mask, maybe not a stocking mask but nonetheless a mask. And Ann had formed the distinct impression that the man in the hallway was about to rape her. In addition, she was getting strange phone calls, and a phone call had been used to point the finger at Delvecchio. Could this person be one and the same?

She sprang to her feet, wanting to tell Glen at once. Then she stopped herself. How could she tell him he might have convicted an innocent man? And on the same day he had brought in the conviction. He was probably whooping it up in his office right now, celebrating his victory. The man would be devastated. Before she brought him down, she decided, she'd better make damn sure she knew what she was saying.

Ann took a seat across from Randy Delvecchio in an interview room at the jail. 'Randy,' she said, 'I've decided to help you, but there's something you have to do for me or I'll just walk away and let you go to prison.'

'What?' he said, his eyes expanding. 'I'll do anything. Please . . .'

'You have to be completely honest with me,' Ann said, looking him in the eye. 'No matter what I ask you, you have to tell the truth. Do you understand? Are we perfectly clear on this?'

He nodded, licking his dry lips before he answered. 'I promise on my mother's life.'

What an odd comment, Ann thought, for someone accused of raping women around his mother's age. If he was guilty, he sure didn't know how to choose his words. 'Did you rape any of these women?'

Fear shot from his eyes. 'No, I – I swear.'

'Did you break into their homes and take some of their possessions? Don't lie, Randy. Burglary is a crime, but not like the crime you've been convicted of.'

'I never broke into no one's home.'

Ann opened her file and took out his rap sheet, sliding it across the table to him. 'What does that say, Randy?'

'It's just a bunch of numbers.'

'It says 459. That's the penal code section for burglary. You're on probation in that case right now. You're lying to me, Randy, and I told you –'

'Wait,' he exclaimed. 'I didn't break into no one's home that time. That was a grocery store. My mother lost her job. We was hungry, so I got us some food.'

Ann stared at him intently. She couldn't confirm what he was saying without the original crime report. 'Let's set that aside for now. I'll verify if what you're telling me is the truth. Now, tell me why you had Estelle Summer's husband's overcoat and Madeline Alderson's ring if you'd never been in their houses.'

'I didn't have no ring. I swear. They said it was in my room at my house, but I don't know how it got there. I never saw that lady's ring. Please believe me.'

'The overcoat?' Ann sat back in her chair, eager to see how he was going to explain this one.

Delvecchio dropped his chin to his chest, mumbling under his breath, 'I had the coat, but I didn't steal it. Someone gave it to me.'

Ann shook the table with her hands, causing him to bolt upright. 'When? Where? Who? I have to know everything.'

Delvecchio cowered, pushing his chair back from the table. 'I don't remember. Maybe a few days before they came to my house to get me.'

Ann frowned. 'You've got to do better than that.'

'A man gave me that coat,' he said, searching his memory. 'I was standing down on Alvarado. That's where we stand sometimes when we want day work. The people come by in their cars and pick us up. This man stopped and I asked if he wanted me to work for him. He says no. He wanted me to have a warm coat 'cause it was getting cold.'

Surely, she thought, if it was Chen, Delvecchio would remember him. 'What did this man look like?'

Delvecchio scratched his arm, a dull look on his face. 'I dunno. He was just a man. My memory ain't so good. I forget things a lot.'

And this was a clever man, Ann thought. Not hardly.

'Randy, this is extremely important. Can't you remember anything?'

'He had a really big car. I don't know what kind it was, but it was big and black. I'd never seen a car like that. It was like a box. Kinda like one of those old cars.'

'What about his face?'

'I don't remember. He was wearing sunglasses, and he just handed me the coat out the window and drove off. Oh, he had dark hair.'

'Did you tell your public defender that you were working when Estelle Summer was raped?'

'Yeah, I told him,' Delvecchio said angrily. 'He didn't believe me, though. Says I ain't got no proof. Wouldn't even let me testify. Said it would just make things worse.'

'Why didn't you have him verify your alibi?' Ann shot back.

Delvecchio was back to scratching his arm nervously. 'See, I told you I tried to call that video place and their phone was cut off. My mother thought of the letter, but they just answered us the other day.'

Ann closed the file and weighed what she had just heard. The details he had given her seemed too odd to have been made up. The man's memory was so poor that he couldn't even tell her the make of the black car.

'Randy,' she finally said, 'I believe you.'

His face brightened. Hope sprang into his eyes.

The world was not a nice place, Ann thought. The jail was full of men like Randy, men who weren't that smart, who had ended up involved in criminal activity as a result of their lack of skills, their backgrounds of poverty and hardship. Ann felt compassion for some of these men. How did she know what she would be today if she'd been in their shoes? Maybe she would have turned to gangs and crime as well.

If her suspicions were right in this case, however, Randy

Delvecchio wasn't a criminal at all. He was an innocent man a step away from the gas chamber.

'I'll come back as soon as I know something,' Ann told him. 'Until then, just keep your mouth shut and stay to yourself.'

Just one last thing, Ann thought as she returned to her office. She rang up Melanie Chase.

'I've been swamped, Ann,' she said rapid-fire. 'If you're calling about the evidence from your house, I simply haven't had time to process it yet. It's slated for tomorrow.'

'No, Melanie,' Ann said. 'I mean, I want to know what you found, but I also need to ask you about the Delvecchio case. You responded on the rapes, didn't you?'

'Yes,' she said shortly. 'What's this about? Delvecchio's been convicted, Ann. Didn't you hear?'

'Did you find any prints?'

Melanie sighed, eager to move on to more pressing matters. 'None that didn't belong to the victim or her friends. We checked it out completely.'

'But surely you collected other evidence.'

'Well, of course, we collected all kinds of shit. We vacuumed the house, went over everything. Most of the actual physical evidence came from the victims themselves in the rape exams. Do you want me to get the file?' she asked wearily, sensing the determination in Ann's voice.

'Please,' Ann said. 'It's really urgent, Mel. I wouldn't bother you if it wasn't.'

A few minutes later, Melanie came back on the line. 'Okay, they found some hairs that we were certain had to belong to the suspect . . . some other cloth fibers, a few other things. As far as the hairs were concerned, they didn't match up with Delvecchio's hair. They weren't even human hairs. They were from a synthetic wig.'

'I thought the rapist wore a stocking over his head.'

'That's what they say.'

'Why would he wear a wig?'

'Look, I don't know, Ann. Maybe the wig belonged to the old lady. When it didn't match the suspect and the rest of the case came together, we just dropped it. There didn't seem to be a reason to pursue it. Hopkins himself told me to drop it. He said he didn't need it, and it would only confuse the jury.'

'I see,' Ann said, dark thoughts of Glen passing through her mind. 'If you had the wig, could you match the hair?'

'I don't think so, Ann. We could determine it was synthetic hair like we found on the victim and even possibly determine the wig manufacturer, but I doubt if we could get any closer than that. It's all the same stuff, you know. It's not like natural hair.'

Ann was silent, thinking. If there was anyone she'd ever wanted to nail in her life, it was the person behind this. Right now she'd do anything to learn the truth. 'No other evidence?'

Melanie flicked her lighter. 'Let me look again.' Puffing out the smoke with the words, she said, 'Well, yes, there was, but it didn't pan out either. We found some pubic hairs on Florence Green.'

'Did you try to match them to Delvecchio?'

'They didn't match.'

'What?'

'I said they didn't match. What else do you want me to say!'

Ann was so agitated that she stood up and started to pace. 'If the pubic hair didn't match, how did Randy Delvecchio get convicted? Jesus Christ, this old lady wasn't exactly a hot ticket. Any pubic hair that you found had to be from the rapist.'

'Look,' Melanie snapped back, 'I don't try the cases. Talk to the frigging D.A. All I do is just work up the evidence.

How would I know what this woman did or didn't do? Maybe she did have lovers, Ann. Shit, it's not impossible. She was only sixty or so.'

'Sixty-eight,' Ann said.

Melanie laughed. 'Well, bless her heart, maybe she still liked a good roll in the hay now and then.'

'I don't think so,' Ann said sarcastically, 'but thanks anyway.'

Chapter 19

As soon as Ann hung up the phone with Melanie Chase, Reed called her. 'You'd better come home right away,' he said without preamble. 'I'm at your house with David.'

'David?' she said, instantly terrified. 'He's supposed to be in school. Oh, my God –'

'He's fine, Ann,' Reed said quickly, not wanting to alarm her. 'When we got here to install the wiretap, he was already here. He said he got out of school early for some reason. Just come to the house and I'll tell you what's going on.'

When Ann pulled up to the curb ten minutes later, she spotted a surveillance van a few doors down. The minute she walked in, David rushed to meet her, his face flushed with excitement. 'I talked to Dad,' he said, grabbing Ann's arm, digging in his fingernails. 'He's alive. He called me on the phone. I swear, he's alive. He's alive, Mom.'

'No,' Ann said, shaking her head. As Tommy Reed appeared from the kitchen, she asked, 'Were you here?'

'No,' he said, 'but I heard the tape.'

'It's true, Mom,' David cried. 'It's true. I always told you he'd come back. He's alive. Dad is alive.'

'David,' Ann said, all the blood draining from her face, 'please, honey, don't get all worked up. It sounds like him, I

289

know, but that doesn't mean it's him.' She looked at Reed for help, her voice shaking. 'Were they able to trace the call?'

'Not enough time, Ann. They have to get the DAV number first.'

'What's that?' David asked eagerly.

'Digital Analog Viatrace. Next time he calls, you have to keep him on the phone longer.'

'He'll be here tomorrow,' David said. 'You don't need to trace the call. He's coming home tomorrow. He told me he was.'

'Come here and sit down, big guy,' Reed said to David, patting a spot on the sofa.

'No. You're just going to tell me it isn't true, and it is. He called, Mom. He's alive.'

Ann exchanged glances with Tommy. At least she wasn't the only one who thought the voice sounded like Hank's. That gave her some measure of relief. 'What exactly did the person say, David?'

'He said, "I'll see you tomorrow, kid."' David tried to mimic his father's deep voice. 'Just like that, Mom. Just like he always used to say at night when he left for work.'

'That's all?' Ann said.

'No,' David said. 'First he called and said, "What's up, David?"'

Something was floating around in Ann's mind, but she couldn't nail it down. She rubbed her forehead, trying to get a fix on what was bothering her, but it flitted away again. 'Did you try to talk to him? You know, ask him where he's been, ask him what happened?'

'Yeah,' David said, frowning. 'I said all kinds of things, but he just hung up. I guess he can't talk now or he got cut off. Hey, maybe he just wants to talk to you first. Yeah, that's it, he looks really weird and skinny or something. He's been locked up somewhere all this time.' The boy was puzzled, trying to figure it out, but then his face brightened. 'But he did say he'd see me tomorrow. That's what he said, you know?' He had turned around and was speaking to Tommy.

'Why couldn't he see us right now?' Ann said, stepping in front of her son.

David's face flushed with anger. 'I don't know. How would I know? I told you he was coming back. You just wouldn't believe me. It's because of Glen,' he shouted, a vein protruding in his neck. 'You don't want Dad anymore. You want that awful man. I hate you.'

Ann stepped back and cupped her hand over her face, reeling at her son's words.

'Ann,' Reed said calmly, 'why don't you go into the other room and let David and me talk.'

As soon as Ann had left, Reed pulled the boy down beside him on the sofa. For a few minutes they sat side by side in silence, David's chest still heaving with emotion. 'I didn't mean it,' he said softly, choking back tears. 'I hurt my mom.'

'She understands,' Reed answered, draping his arm over David's shoulder. 'Moms always understand.'

'I've waited so long for Dad to come back. Why isn't she happy too?'

'Well, kid,' Reed said, meeting his pleading look, 'she doesn't want you to be disappointed. It may not be your father. That's what we've been trying to tell you.'

'It is my dad, Tommy. I know what my dad sounds like, and it was my dad.'

'This is what we're going to do,' Reed said. 'We're going to take that tape of the person who called down to the lab and compare it to your father's voice. That's called a voice analysis. Then we'll know if it's your father or not.'

'Okay,' David said. 'That's a great idea. How long will it take?'

'It shouldn't take long. I'll have to see if your mother has a tape of your father's voice, though. Without that, we can't make a comparison.'

'I have one,' David said, springing to his feet. 'I saved the old tape from our answering machine, the one that was in there when he was kidnapped. I also have our old home-movie videotapes. Want me to get them?'

'Sounds like a plan,' Reed said. As the boy dashed off, the detective went to the kitchen to check on Ann.

Her face was pale and drawn, the short hairs on her head sticking straight up. 'Tommy,' she said, 'this is destroying David. Who's making these phone calls? We have to find out.'

'Here,' David said, bursting into the kitchen and handing Reed the cassette from the answering machine. 'This is all I could find. I don't know where the other tapes are.' He gave his mother a puzzled look, but she didn't respond.

'This should do it,' Tommy said, sticking it in his pocket. 'I'll drive it down to the lab right now. Melanie's still working. She'll get right on it.' On his way out, he locked David in a bear hug. 'You gonna be good to your mom while I'm gone?'

'Yeah,' David said meekly.

'Okay, then,' the detective said, exiting through the kitchen door.

Ann finally headed for bed at one o'clock in the morning. She'd called Melanie Chase earlier to see if she'd made any progress on the tape, but the woman had never called her back. All evening she had waited for the call. At midnight she had called again, and they'd told her Melanie had been dispatched on an armed robbery. Ann knew it might be four in the morning before she got back to the lab.

David had fallen asleep on the sofa. Ann decided not to wake him. Going back to his room, she got a cover off his bed and placed it over him on the sofa, bending down to kiss his forehead. The poor kid had expended every ounce of energy he possessed in excitement over his father coming back. It broke her heart.

Once Ann had shed her clothes, she got into bed, and turned the lights off. She knew she would never sleep. When the phone rang, she lunged for it, praying it was Melanie Chase. 'Yes?' she said.

'Where's David?'

'Hank? Is that you? God, Hank, you have to stop . . .'

She started sobbing so hard she could barely hear him. His voice sounded far away and close at the same time, too close, almost as if he were calling from somewhere inside the house.

'Get David, Ann.'

'Hank, please tell me where you are. Tell me what happened.'

A moment passed before Ann realized she was listening to a dead phone. She fumbled in her purse for the number of the surveillance van, hoping the officer hadn't fallen asleep. Her efforts weren't necessary, though, for the phone rang right away.

'Was that your husband? He wasn't on the line long enough to get a trace.'

'Yes,' Ann said. 'I mean, it was his voice.'

The officer repeated that Ann had to keep the caller on the phone longer, and she felt like screaming. 'I don't know how to keep him on the phone. What am I supposed to do?'

'Next time,' the officer said calmly, 'pick up the phone but don't say anything. Do anything you can to stall for time.'

Ann accepted this, though it bothered her she wasn't certain who she was speaking to. 'Who is this?'

'Phil Whittaker. I guess you don't recognize my voice. I have a bear of a cold.'

'Oh,' Ann said. 'Thanks, Phil.' Turning out the lights, she settled back and stared into the darkness, trying to empty her mind of all thoughts. Finally, sheer exhaustion defeated her, and she closed her eyes and slept.

Ann awoke to morning sun streaking through the crack in the drapes. She was aching all over and felt as if she hadn't slept more than an hour. Her eyes were puffy and scratchy from crying, and the sheets were damp with perspiration. For a few minutes she remained perfectly still in the bed, looking at the ceiling, trying to decide if she could make it to work. Then she heard the sound of clothes rustling in the room with her and bolted upright in bed.

David was sitting in a chair, watching her, waiting for her to wake up. The boy's normally tousled hair was still damp from a shower and combed carefully away from his face. He was wearing one of his two dress shirts and a pair of black slacks. He had even put on his black shoes reserved only for special occasions. The last time Ann had insisted that he wear them, he had told her they were too small.

'What time is it?' Ann asked, concerned.

'Seven.'

'How long have you been sitting here?'

'Since six o'clock.'

Ann took in his formal clothes again and felt her heart sink. He was waiting for his father. 'Come here,' she said softly, patting a spot next to her on the bed.

'No,' David said. 'I don't want to mess my shirt up. You know how Dad hates wrinkles. I want to look really good, you know. I want him to know that I'm all grown up now, that I've been doing everything he told me to do.'

'Hand me my robe,' Ann said. 'I'll make you some breakfast.'

'No,' David said, finding her robe on the hook on the door and handing it to her. 'I don't want to eat until Dad gets here. Then we can all eat like a family.'

Like a family, she thought sadly. He didn't know how bad it had been at the end. 'Honey, we don't really know for sure it was even him. I thought about it last night, David, and the man who came to the house and attacked me was wearing a mask to disguise his voice. He took your picture. He even said your name. Someone could be mimicking your father's voice. Maybe it's a computer or something.'

'What do you mean?'

'Don't you see, honey? Everyone knows what happened to your father. When I got shot, they put the whole story back in the paper. Whoever has been doing all these things to me could be trying to imitate your father's voice, saying things he knows will make us think it's Dad. It's a way to hurt us.' Ann turned her head away. If what she had said was true, there was no doubt as to how much it would hurt. Seeing David like this, his hopes raised so high, was almost more than she could take.

'I don't believe that,' he said, waiting for his mother as she put her arms through her terry-cloth robe and got out of bed. 'It was my dad. I know my own dad, Mom. That's just silly. Why would anyone do that?'

'Well,' Ann said, 'maybe someone wants to upset me, confuse me, make me think I'm going crazy. David, there's a lot about this situation that you don't know.'

'It was Dad,' he snapped angrily. Then he turned around and stomped out of the room, screaming back at her, his voice echoing in the hall. 'You're just saying all this because you don't want Dad to come back. I know how you used to fight with him.'

So he did know, Ann thought. Even so, he still blamed her instead of his father. Was his attitude inherited from Hank, like his explosive temper? Did her own son believe that she had deserved the abuse, had somehow asked for it? Heading to the kitchen to make a pot of coffee, she passed David in the living room. He was sitting on the floor in front of the television, as still as a statue, watching cartoons. Ann shook her head. David hadn't watched cartoons for years now. He preferred the science features on public television. She dumped coffee in the filter and was ready to shove it into the coffee maker when the phone rang. She reached for it, heard David rushing across the floor at the same time. When she said hello, she heard him yelling into the phone: 'Dad, Dad, is that you? We're waiting for you. When are you coming?'

'David,' Reed's deep voice said, 'this is Tommy. I just called to see how you're doing, and to tell you that they're working on your tape.'

'Why isn't he here, Tommy?' David said. 'He told me he would be here today.'

'Hang tight, guy,' Reed said. 'We're going to get to the bottom of this thing. Is your mother with you?'

'Yeah,' he said, downcast. 'She's here.'

'I'm on the line,' Ann spoke up. 'David, hang up and let me talk to Tommy. Please, honey.' She waited until she heard the click, and then her voice turned to desperation. 'We're going crazy over here. Why hasn't Melanie finished the voice analysis? David's sitting here all dressed up like it's Christmas, waiting for his father to walk through the door. The poor kid's —'

'Take it easy, Ann,' Reed said, consoling her. 'Melanie was buried in work last night. She can only do so much.'

'So?' Ann cried. 'Get someone else to do it! Get that Alex guy. Hell, get someone. We have to know who's behind this.'

'I'll call her again and see what I can do,' Reed said, quickly disconnecting.

Ann clicked off the portable phone in the kitchen and rushed to the living room to comfort her son. She wasn't thinking now, just reacting, her emotions too out of control for coherent thought. She crushed her son to her chest. 'I want you to go to school, honey. You can't sit here and wait all day.'

'No, I can't go to school,' he said, tears spilling out of his eyes. 'Dad might come while I'm gone.'

'Please, honey, don't cry. Go to the bathroom and get a cold washrag for your face. Please, David, it will make you feel better.'

'No,' he said, jerking away from his mother. 'I talked to him. I'm not going to school. I don't care what you do to me, I'm waiting right here for my dad.'

David ran to his room and slammed the door.

Ann knew she couldn't send David to school, nor could she go to work until the situation was resolved. She called Claudette and told her that she was taking the day off.

She waited. Minutes turned into hours. Finally, at twelve o'clock, Melanie Chase called.

'The two voices are the same, Ann. This is your husband, isn't it?'

'They're . . . the same?' Ann stammered. 'Then it is Hank who's calling me?'

'I'm not certain about that. I just know the voiceprints are the same on the two recordings.'

Ann was confused. 'If it's Hank's voice, then it has to be Hank calling me. I don't understand what you're saying.'

'The police tape of your phone call is a lot higher-quality than the one on the answering machine. With our sound equipment we detected some technical noise mixed in with the voice.'

'What kind of technical noise?'

'Some kind of machinery . . . whirs and clicks. It's almost impossible to differentiate what was on the original tape and what's coming from the police's recording equipment. I need another recording from the police before I can identify the sounds. Can one of the guys bring one over?'

'Sure,' Ann said. 'They're still monitoring my calls. I'll get them to bring over the tape of our conversation. How's that?'

'That'll do. Let me go now,' Melanie said.

As soon as she terminated the call, Ann called the officer in the surveillance van, Oscar Chapa, and asked him to edit out her call to Melanie and take the tape to her.

'Does that mean your husband is alive, Ann?' Chapa said.

So, he had been listening. 'You heard the tape, Oscar. I don't know what it means, to tell you the truth. Will you get someone from patrol to take it over right away?'

'No problem,' he said.

As lunch had come and gone and David was still locked in his room, Ann made him a sandwich and knocked on his door. 'Let me in,' she said. 'You have to eat, honey.'

'Go away. I'm not hungry.'

'David, please . . . at least let me come in and talk to you. Don't shut me out like this.'

'Go away. Just leave me alone.'

Ann set the plate down by his door and returned to the living room to wait. She tried reading the newspaper, tried watching television, but she couldn't concentrate. Finally she started cleaning the house, scrubbing the kitchen floor on her hands and knees, trying to get out the old stains in the grout on the counter with a toothbrush, rearranging all the china in the cabinet.

At five o'clock, Ann had resorted to cleaning silver when she heard a knock at the front door. This is it, she thought, breaking out in a cold sweat. Peering through the peephole, she saw a strange woman standing on her doorstep. 'Who is it? What do you want?'

'Ann Carlisle,' the woman said through the door, 'my name is Connie Davidson. I'm a reporter with the *Star Free Press*. I'd like to talk to you.'

Ann slammed the bolts back and threw the door open. Did they have news of Hank? 'What do you want?'

A photographer stepped out of the shadows and started snapping pictures of Ann. Instantly she threw her hands over her face. 'Stop that. No pictures or I'll close the door right now.'

The reporter waved the photographer away. 'Do you mind if I come inside? I just want to ask you a few questions.'

'What kind of questions?' Ann said, eyeing the woman suspiciously.

'I . . . Mrs Carlisle, I'd rather we talk inside, if you don't mind.'

'My son isn't feeling well. What's this about?'

'We've been contacted by a Dr Sawyer regarding your relationship with his son. Can I just ask you a few questions, get a statement?'

Ann felt as if a ball of cotton were stuck in her throat. She wasn't going to give in to this, try to defend herself. Anything she said would only add fuel to the flames. 'No,' she said. 'Print whatever you want. If you slander my reputation, I'll sue. I'm Jimmy Sawyer's probation officer. There's no other relationship.' Ann started to close the door, but the woman had stepped into the doorway.

'Is it true Sawyer saved your life because you were having an affair with him? Did you manufacture that story about severed fingers to get back at him? Is this the first time you've been involved with one of your probationers?'

Ann began determinedly pushing the door shut, squeezing the woman's foot until she finally stepped back, allowing Ann to close it all the way. Then Ann leaned against the door and tried to catch her breath. Of all the things she needed right now . . .

'It's not going to go away, you know,' the reporter called back through the door. 'Don't you want to give us your side of the story before we print it?'

'Get off my property,' Ann said, shaking.

Once she heard the woman's footsteps receding, she walked down the hall, so distraught that she couldn't see where she was going. 'David,' she said, seeing the door to his room open.

The boy was sitting on the edge of the bed, just staring into space. His round face was drawn, and his eyes were filled with despair. He was no longer dressed in his best clothing. He was wearing jeans and a sweatshirt. He had finally given up.

'Oh, David,' Ann said as her son crossed the floor into her arms.

'Why didn't he come, Mom? He said he'd come.'

'Don't talk,' Ann said. 'Let's say a prayer for your dad, that wherever he is, he's at peace and not in pain. That's all we should wish for, honey.'

They just stood there and held each other.

'I love you,' David said, his voice a choked whisper. 'I'm sorry I said those ugly things to you.'

'Oh, David,' Ann said, stroking his hair, 'I'll always love you no matter what you say to me.' Then she tilted his head up and looked him square in the eye. 'Do you believe that? Are we a team like always?'

'Yeah,' he said weakly. 'We're a team, Mom, but we're not a family without Dad.'

Ann pulled him back into her embrace. 'You're wrong, David. My mother died when I was really young, and my father raised me. We were a family. Do you understand? A real family. Just because Dad isn't with us doesn't mean we aren't a family. A family is built on love and respect.'

David didn't answer. Ann continued to hold him until he finally pulled away and went to the living room to watch television.

When the doorbell rang again later that night, Ann was playing gin rummy with David on the kitchen table. He lurched to his feet, but Ann rushed to the door ahead of him and found Tommy Reed with a grim look on his face. He ignored Ann, seeing David standing behind her. 'David,' he said, 'I have a treat for you. Go down the street to the surveillance van. Oscar's going to show you how the equipment works.'

'Cool,' David said. 'What's in that thing, anyway?'

'Every kind of electronic device you can imagine. Run along now. Oscar's waiting to show you.'

Once David had left, Reed turned to Ann. 'I have something to tell you. I think you'd better sit down.'

He took her hand and led her to the couch, pushing her down with his hands on her shoulders. 'There's been a new development in Hank's case.'

Ann was numb. She couldn't think of anything worse than what she'd already been through with David.

'I notified the highway patrol late yesterday, and they flew some men to Arizona to investigate.' He stopped and cleared his throat. 'They've got a suspect in custody, Ann.'

'No,' she said, bending over at the waist and wrapping her arms around herself. 'Hank . . .'

'We don't know all the details yet. All they know is this individual was in possession of Hank's gun. Then one of our records clerks at the department did some investigating on her own and discovered that the man had used Hank's badge number for a date of birth. I guess he carried that badge around all these years and memorized the numbers without even realizing it. When they arrested him and printed him, they found out his real identity. His name is Wayne Coffer, and there's a warrant out for his arrest for murder. It was issued by the Texas authorities over six years ago. The man's been living under an assumed name.'

'Then they think he's the man who abducted Hank?' she said. She'd waited so long to know the truth, but now that she was hearing it, it didn't seem real. Was what she was hearing no different from the phone calls? Was it all just a mirage, an awful dream?

'It looks that way,' Reed said. 'This was what we speculated all along, that Hank stopped someone who was wanted and the person jumped him when he went back to call in the information.'

Ann was still holding herself, rocking back and forth, trying to assimilate what she was hearing. 'But we still don't know if Hank is dead or alive, right?'

'Top-ranking investigators for the highway patrol are there now, along with local FBI agents. They've been grilling the suspect since last night, trying to get him to crack. Seems he's an alcoholic and suffering from liver disease. We're just lucky we found him before he croaked. The man's in bad shape.'

Inside, Ann wanted to scream. They were so close, but they still didn't know. 'What happens now?'

'They'll work on him a little longer, then transfer him back here. They'll have to build the case quick, however, because Texas will start extradition proceedings at once.'

Melanie had just told her the man on the phone was her husband. She couldn't believe what Tommy was saying. If it wasn't true, she'd lose her mind. 'Is there any chance that Hank escaped? Can he possibly be alive? Melanie said it was Hank's voice, Tommy. Something's wrong.'

'Well, there's always that chance, Ann, but it doesn't appear likely. As for the phone calls –'

Persistent as always, Ann said, 'Maybe he was injured. That could explain the phone calls. It sounds just like Hank's voice, but he always hangs up and his speech is erratic. Say this Coffer guy hit Hank on the head and left him for dead somewhere. Hank could have a brain injury and not remember who he is.'

Reed pulled her into his arms. 'I'm sorry. But at least we have a suspect in custody. Isn't that worth something?'

'No,' Ann said, wrenching away, her mouth set. 'I can't accept it until they find his body. Until they do, he could still be alive.'

Just then Ann saw David standing in the kitchen door, his mouth open and his face a ghastly shade of gray.

'How long have you been listening?' she asked, her heart beating so loud she could barely hear herself speaking.

'He's dead,' David said bitterly. 'My dad is dead. That man killed him. He never was coming back.' Huge tears streamed down his face. 'How could he call me? How could Dad call me if he was dead?'

Both Ann and Reed stood and crossed the floor, standing on either side of the boy. 'David,' Reed said hesitantly, 'there's a slim possibility that your father is still alive. It wouldn't be right to tell you otherwise, son. But we should have some firm answers soon.'

'Honey,' Ann said, brushing his hair off his forehead, 'we're coming down to the end now. It's almost over. If we can just hold on a little while longer, we're going to know for sure.'

'He's dead,' David said flatly.

Ann and Reed looked at each other. What more could they say? David had finally crossed the line.

Chapter 20

On Wednesday morning, Ann drove David to school and then, weak and shaky from the night before, headed to the government center. Reed had stayed until after ten, when the investigators in Arizona notified him that they were calling it a night. Thus far, the suspect had refused to confess. Ann knew that they would be executing a search warrant on his apartment in the hopes of finding additional evidence, but for the present, there was nothing to do but wait.

Once Reed had gone home, Ann had sat with David until after midnight, looking through the old photo albums, telling him detailed stories about his father. They had laughed and they had cried, but Ann felt it was necessary. David was about to bury his father. She wanted the memories to be fresh in his mind.

Walking across the courtyard to the cafeteria for their morning break, Claudette kept bumping into Ann. 'Why do you always do that?' Ann snapped. The tension had given her a nasty disposition and a throbbing headache. 'Do you realize you do that, Claudette? Do you have any idea how annoying that is?'

'What?' Claudette said. 'What'd I do?'

'Every time we walk somewhere together, you constantly

bump into me. You don't walk straight. You sort of weave all over the place like a drunk.'

'Well, thanks for sharing that with me,' Claudette said good-naturedly. Then she saw the strain on Ann's face and fell serious again. 'Did you tell Tommy to call you at work when he heard something?'

'Certainly,' Ann said.

'Shit,' Claudette said. 'This thing is getting real spooky. All this stuff about Hank. Did you find out about Carl Simmons?'

'He was still in prison when I got shot, but he was released the following week. I don't think we're talking about two separate people here, Claudette. Whoever shot me has to be the person terrorizing me. Noah Abrams has hammered that point home to me.'

'I don't know, Ann. Maybe Simmons planned it that way.'

'What do you mean?'

'He's an educated man, Ann, if I remember correctly. He might be crazy, but he's not dumb. He could have hired someone from inside the joint to shoot you, knowing he would have an air-tight alibi. Then when the shooter failed to kill you, he started stalking you himself.'

A man stepped out of the shadows and approached them. 'Ann Carlisle?' he said. 'Are you Ann Carlisle?'

Claudette grabbed Ann's arm and pulled her close, her dark eyes wide with alarm. 'What do you want?' she said.

The man gave Claudette a hasty once-over and handed a paper to Ann. 'Ms Carlisle, please sign your name where the red X is.'

Ann looked down at the paper and then back up at Claudette. 'He's just a process server, Claudette. Someone's serving me with a subpoena, probably a defense lawyer on one of my cases.' Ann scribbled her name, shoved the subpoena into her purse, and handed the man the form. As soon as he had the paper in his hand, he scurried off to find another victim.

Ann pulled on the heavy doors leading to the main building of the courthouse. Claudette had insisted they go for a coffee break. And when Claudette insisted, it was better to just go along.

'Aren't you even gonna look at the damn thing?' Claudette said, curious.

'No,' Ann said, her mind on other things. 'I'll look at it later.'

Claudette stopped in the middle of the reception hall, people streaming past her on their way to court. She had that look in her eyes that said she had to know and she had to know right that second. 'Oh, come on, Ann, look at it. Let's see which case it is.'

'No, Claudette,' Ann said, forging ahead without looking back.

Footsteps scurried behind her, and Claudette once more reached Ann's side, her shoulder butting up against her. 'You'll tell me later, then? Right after we have our coffee?'

'Maybe,' Ann said with a coy smile. 'You buying, Claudette?'

'I'll buy,' Claudette snapped. 'I'll buy the damn coffee. I'll even buy you a damn donut.'

They joined the food line at the cafeteria. Ann looked out over the room, searching for Glen.

'Are you going to give me the dirt on Delvecchio?' Claudette asked, when they were seated at a table with their coffee. 'Didn't you tell me something was going on?'

Ann choked at the mention of Delvecchio. As soon as she cleared her throat, she answered, 'I have to talk to Glen. There's something I don't understand about the pleading.'

'Well, take care of it,' Claudette said. 'Now that he's been convicted, we have to get that report done.'

The cafeteria was crowded and noisy, attorneys conferring with one another, arguing their cases over coffee, others sitting alone poring over briefs, their bulging litigation cases open before them. Here and there rough-looking defendants, tattoos and all, were sipping coffee and waiting for their turn in the courtroom. Right next to one particularly nasty character was a table full of men Ann recognized as assistant district attorneys.

She leaned across the table to Claudette, whispering, 'Do you ever think how dangerous it is to have us all in this complex together?'

'Not really,' Claudette said, stabbing her sweet roll with her fork and shoving it at Ann's face. 'Take a bite. I thought you were going to have a donut. I've gained ten pounds. God, how am I ever gonna lose it?'

Ann pushed the fork away. 'I'm not hungry, Claudette. See that guy over there sitting next to the table of D.A.s?'

'Yeah,' Claudette said, craning her neck around. 'What about him? Looks like a killer.'

'What keeps him from pulling out a gun and shooting one of those guys? How do we know one of those men isn't the very district attorney that's prosecuting him?'

Claudette was chewing, her sweet roll almost gone. When she swallowed, she dabbed her mouth with a napkin. 'You're getting paranoid, Ann. Even in the old building, defendants and prosecutors intermingled. If you have a restaurant of any kind near the courts and it's open to the public, that kind of thing's bound to happen.'

Ann knew she was right. It just seemed too close to her, too tight. All around her she saw menacing faces. 'Look at that guy,' she said without thinking. 'A real sweetheart, huh? Looks like he could rip your heart out and eat it for breakfast.'

Claudette laughed. 'He's an attorney, Ann.'

'See, I told you he was vicious.' Ann laughed too, and the paranoia faded.

'Come on, let's look at that subpoena.'

Ann smiled despite herself. Claudette just couldn't hold out any longer. Pulling the paper out of her purse, Ann spread it out on the table, moving her coffee cup out of the way. 'Shit, it's Sawyer,' she exclaimed, her face flushing with anger. 'He's suing me for false arrest, defamation of character, and harassment.'

'No,' Claudette said. She hated it when one of her people got sued. Since she was the supervisor, she always had the ultimate responsibility. 'I told you it was Sawyer all along. Now with this new development, you know for sure. It's obvious. This guy will do anything, absolutely anything, to stay out of jail. Slimy, no-good piece of dog shit.'

Claudette's curiosity was satisfied, and her mind instantly returned to work. 'Take care of Delvecchio, Ann,' she said, getting up. 'You can deal with Sawyer later.'

When Ann got up herself, she did not head for the probation department. Instead she took the elevator to the third floor, where the D.A.'s office was located. Glen would have to reopen the case, as she saw it, and make an honest effort to get Delvecchio cleared. Of course, Ann thought, there was another serious issue involved: if Delvecchio was innocent, the real rapist was free.

Once she had been buzzed through the security doors, she spotted Glen in the hallway, laughing and chatting with a pretty brunette. 'Ann,' he said, pushing himself away from the wall, 'what are you doing over here?'

'I'll see you at lunch,' the woman said, smiling flirtatiously at Glen as she walked away.

'Do you know Linda Weinstein?' Hopkins asked, a strained smile on his face. 'She's in the sex crimes unit. Delvecchio was her case initially. After I told her how strongly I felt about the case, she agreed to let me try it.'

Ann felt a twinge of jealousy. Linda Weinstein was glamorous, with her long hair, her expensive blue suit, her polished nails. Ann's nails were ragged and unpolished, and she'd grabbed the first thing she'd seen in her closet this morning: a white blouse frayed around the collar, a simple black skirt, a well-worn pair of flats. She looked like a schoolteacher. 'Why did you insist on trying Delvecchio, anyway?' Ann said. 'I mean, the crimes were awful, but you have so many other cases, and you're always complaining how overworked you are.'

'Oh, well –' he said, and then stopped, looking behind him nervously.

'Glen . . .'

'Yeah,' he said quickly, taking Ann's hand to lead her to his office.

Ann pulled back. 'Was Estelle Summer really your teacher? What school did you go to?'

'Yes,' he said gruffly. 'Let's talk in my office.'

Glen was off balance, Ann realized, and annoyed with her for some reason. What had she said? All she'd been doing was discussing a case. Had he been making a play for that woman when she walked in and interrupted?

Insisting she come with him, he squeezed her hand even tighter. As Ann flinched away, she felt something raised and abraded above his wrist. Quickly she brought it out in front of her so she could see what it was. On his right hand was a jagged cut, already scabbing over. 'What did you do to your hand?'

'Nothing,' he said, his teeth clenched. 'What's wrong with you? You're making me feel like a cad, like I've been carrying on behind your back with Linda Weinstein. I was only chatting with a coworker.' He stopped, and the look in his eyes became vicious. 'You're letting these phone calls make you crazy. Get some help for yourself. Go see a shrink or something.'

Ann's mouth fell open in shock. It must be true, she thought, he was probably seeing that woman. He wouldn't be so defensive if she hadn't touched on something. She started to tell him about Hank, tell him it was over, but was unable to do so. An irrational, instinctive fear had seized her. Unable to pull her eyes away, Ann started shaking her head in denial. What was she seeing in his eyes? What had he said to her? Who was this person?

She knew she couldn't be with him another second.

'I – I have to go,' she stammered, taking off briskly down the hall, shoving people out of her way. Passing through the security doors, she broke into a sprint. She continued running until she reached the ladies' rest room and rushed inside.

When Ann walked out fifteen minutes later, unable to stop thinking about that cut, she heard her name being paged over the intercom and returned to her desk to take the call.

'I have some information for you,' Melanie Chase said. 'I tried to call Reed, but he's tied up on another call. I'm sorry I took so long, Ann, but it's been a madhouse around here.'

'What have you got?' Ann said with a horrid sense of foreboding.

'I finished the analysis of that paint transfer from the break-in at your house,' Melanie said. 'The car's black, Ann, and the make's probably a Rolls-Royce. This was an easy one. They're the only people who use this kind of sealant. I mean, Rolls or Bentley. It's one or the other.'

Ann slapped back in her chair, unable to believe her ears. 'A Rolls-Royce?' she said. 'You're certain the paint came from a black Rolls-Royce?'

'No, Ann,' Melanie said firmly, 'I didn't say that. I said it came from a Bentley or a Rolls. The same company makes both cars, so it could be either.'

Ann could see Glen's black Rolls-Royce in her mind. He loved that car, was so proud of it. She felt the room reeling, as if it were about to capsize. Then everything came together at once. 'Don't hang up,' Ann said frantically. 'Didn't you say the man who broke into my house would have a cut somewhere? Where would it be?'

'I can't believe you're asking me this,' Melanie said, annoyed. The flick of a cigarette lighter came over the line, and she inhaled. 'How in the hell would I know where he cut himself?' she said, emitting a puff. 'I didn't see the guy, you know? You people think I'm a fucking magician or something.'

'I thought –'

'Forget it,' Melanie said, her voice softening. 'I've had a rough couple of days.'

Even though the cut didn't prove anything, Glen was the right build, and Ann had recognized the eyes.

The mask! Delvecchio had been picked out of a lineup of men of similar build wearing masks. According to Delvecchio, the man who had given him the coat had been driving a black car that he hadn't recognized. Something boxy like a Rolls-Royce.

'You have pubic hairs from the rapist in the Delvecchio case? Right? Isn't that what you said?'

'Of course, Ann,' Melanie said, confused. 'I thought we were talking about the break-in at your house.'

'We are,' she answered, gasping for breath. She felt as if a boa constrictor had wrapped around her chest and was squeezing the life out of her. Glen was the man who had attacked her. He had raped and brutalized three helpless old women. How could it be true? He had no reason. And why would Glen have driven a car as distinctive as the Rolls-Royce to break into her house? That was a foolish error, and Glen was not foolish. Besides, he had a motorcycle. Then Ann remembered the thunderstorm and heavy downpour the night she was attacked. Now it made sense.

But that couldn't explain everything. Why would a man as

attractive as Glen have to rape? Then Ann corrected herself. She knew better. Rape had to do with power, aggression, hatred. It had nothing to do with sex.

Once Ann said goodbye and hung up the phone, she laid her head down on the desk. She had to remain calm, think logically. Delvecchio hadn't been able to identify the car. If she showed him a picture of Glen's Rolls-Royce, however, he might be able to. For all she knew, the car still had body damage from the collision. Glen was too smart to take it into a body shop so soon after the crime. He would wait it out, wait until interest died down.

She suddenly felt a firm hand on her shoulder and jerked her head up.

'Ann,' Glen said softly, 'I'm sorry we had a disagreement. Linda and I are old friends. I was going to buy her lunch because she let me try Delvecchio. I guess I was angry that you doubted me.'

'It's fine,' Ann said, forcing a smile, feeling the heat from his touch through her blouse and wanting to knock his hand away. But she couldn't show her fear. If Glen was a rapist, he would lap it up, feed on it. 'It's just these phone calls,' she lied. 'They're making me crazy.'

'You asked about my hand,' he said, showing it to her. 'It's only a scratch. I must have done it when I was working on my motorcycle the other day. To be honest, I didn't even notice it until you said something.'

Ann took hold of his hand, seeing the irregular manner in which it was cut, consistent with broken glass. Did Glen know she knew? Feeling a spasm in the side of her neck, she forced herself to let the hand go. 'All I was going to do is suggest a Band-Aid, Glen,' she said, sighing as if it were nothing. 'You know, it's the mother in me. I'm always afraid of infection.'

Glen laughed, confident again. 'How's David?'

'Great,' she said. 'Everything's great except for those phone calls. I just can't figure out who's making them.'

'Can you sneak away for a few hours tonight?' he said, winking suggestively. 'I'll make it worth your while.'

'Oh, no,' Ann said, shaking her head. 'I really can't, Glen. I promised David I'd take him to a movie.'

His eyes turned suddenly wary. 'On a weeknight? Doesn't he have school tomorrow?'

'Early movie,' Ann said quickly. 'Anyway, forgive me, but I have an appointment any minute. A probationer, you know?'

'No problem,' he said, standing and tousling her hair before he left. 'Call me later, okay?'

'Sure,' she said, holding her breath until his footsteps receded. How could anyone be so cruel, so heartless? How could she have fallen for him? Was she this bad a judge of character? Where did she go from here?

The Rolls, she decided.

By late afternoon, Tommy Reed had not contacted her, and Ann was a nervous wreck. She had a plan in mind regarding her suspicions about Glen that might be viable, but she couldn't leave the building until she heard the news about Hank. Finally, at five o'clock, the phone rang.

'The suspect confessed,' Reed said. 'It's over, Ann.'

She cupped her hand over her mouth, unable to reply coherently.

'From what the highway patrol investigators told me, they found Hank's badge in the suspect's apartment. When they confronted him, he confessed. He knew it was over at that point. He'd rather face prosecution for Hank's murder in California than be returned to Texas. The legal system's a lot harsher there, and he could get the death penalty.'

'Did . . . he tell them where Hank is buried?'

'They're on their way out there now.'

An overwhelming feeling of relief swept through her. 'Then it's really over.'

'Yes, Ann,' Reed said softly, 'it's over.'

By seven o'clock that evening, Ann was in her bedroom on the bed. David had taken the news better than she'd expected. Like Ann, he too was relieved that they finally knew the truth.

The phone rang and Ann grabbed it, thinking it was Reed with the flight information. They had found Hank's body and were flying it back tomorrow. She had already told David that they would have a funeral, and she needed to make the arrangements.

'Ann,' Glen said, 'how was the movie? Which one did you see, anyway?'

'Oh,' Ann said, immediately on guard, 'we didn't go. David isn't feeling well.' Stay calm, she told herself. 'So, what's going on?'

'I'm sitting here all alone,' he said pensively. 'I miss you, Ann. Can't you come over after David goes to sleep? I haven't felt right since this morning.' He laughed. 'Was that our first fight?'

The first and the last, Ann thought bitterly. 'I guess,' she said instead. 'Had to happen sometime. Look, I have an idea. Why don't I meet you at the Sail Loft in thirty minutes? David will be asleep by then.'

'Super,' he said. 'You don't know how much better this makes me feel. I hate to have arguments with people I love.'

Love? Ann thought. Up until today he'd never uttered the word. 'You really love me, Glen?' she said, unable to resist.

'I think I've loved you from the moment I saw you.'

How touching, she thought, trying to sound as sultry as she could. 'I'll see you soon, then. You can tell me more.'

'I'll be waiting.'

Ann hung up the phone, a cold ball of rage forming in her

stomach. Because of Glen, she couldn't allow herself even a moment to reflect on Hank's passing, a few hours to comfort her son, arrange his funeral.

She had to move fast.

After telling David that she had to go out, under the pretext of contacting a funeral home, Ann walked down to the surveillance van and knocked on the door. A few moments later, an enormous, slack-jawed officer in his middle fifties peered out at her. Oscar Chapa moved slow, talked slow, and would scare a person to death in a dark alley. He had that type of face. He was a Native American, a Sioux, Ann had heard, and his looks were deceiving. He was the kindest man she had ever known.

'Oscar,' she said, 'do you think you could stay in the house with my son for a few hours? I don't want to leave him alone, and I have to go out.'

'Sure,' the man said.

When she pulled up in front of Glen's house, she parked the car and stared at it, trying to get the nerve to go in. Lights were burning inside, but Ann was certain Glen was waiting for her at the Sail Loft.

She went to the door and rang the bell to be certain, quickly rubbing her sweaty palms on her pants. As she waited, minutes seemed like hours. Nothing. In all her life Ann had never broken the law. Not really broken the law, she told herself. Oh, as a kid, she had stolen a toy once from another kid, but that was it. Her father had whipped her so hard she couldn't sit down for a week. That had put a stop to the stealing.

But this was different. If she broke into Glen's house, she would be committing a felony, a burglary. Her whole career could go up in a puff of smoke. A part of her said to walk away from this. She'd tell Tommy and let him handle it.

Another voice, though, told her, Now is the time. She

couldn't walk away. She'd never walked away no matter how dangerous the situation was if someone's life was at stake. The life in this situation could be her own.

She decided to do it.

Creeping around the back of the house, Ann tried to stay low so the neighbors wouldn't spot her and call the police. She knew Glen had an alarm system, and she didn't know the code. That meant the alarm would sound at the security company as soon as she opened a door or window. But having been a cop, Ann knew it would be a considerable time before anyone responded. The area where Glen lived restricted the residents from using audible alarms. Too often these alarms were triggered by the wind, a cat, or some other freak thing, and police would respond for nothing while the neighbors raised all holy hell, having to listen to an ear-shattering alarm until someone managed to disconnect it.

She should have time to get in the house, get what she needed, and get out before the police were even dispatched. First the alarm company would be dispatched, and their patrol car might be on the other side of town. The alarm company only called the police if they noted any signs of forced entry.

Ann thought of her car parked on the street and decided that wouldn't do. Returning to it, she drove around to the alley and parked a few houses down. Then she dug in the trunk for something to put over her clothes, a makeshift disguise of some kind just in case someone saw her. Also, Glen's garage was in the back of the house. If he came home, he would come in through the garage. Entering through the back of the house, Ann would have a better chance of seeing him if he drove up. She found an old parka that she'd worn to the beach the past summer and put it on. Then she saw her Polaroid camera. Quickly she checked and saw there was enough film for four shots. Last, she palmed a large rock she had brought along.

Returning to the house, she checked all the windows and

found them locked. She slipped inside the backyard, feeling a bit less exposed within the privacy of the stockade fence. She took off the parka, wrapped her hand in it, and quickly smashed out the back window with the rock. Raising the wooden frame, she stepped inside, trying not to cut herself on the glass. Right at this minute, she knew, the alarm company was getting the signal. She had to hurry.

Racing to the bathroom next to the master bedroom, she found Glen's hairbrush and shoved it into her back pocket. She started to look for a comb to be certain, but she was afraid to take the time. Walking back down the hall, she passed an open door to a room she had never been inside before. Every time she had visited Glen's house, the door to this room had been closed.

Stepping inside, she saw that it was a study. Numerous certificates and framed photos hung on the walls, a desk was situated in one corner, and a mounted gun rack covered the back wall. Ann's eyes were drawn to the photos. In one, Glen was a young boy. He was holding an enormous rifle in his hands. The next photo showed Glen again as a boy, possibly ten or twelve. He was standing next to a calf at a 4-H event, and there were tears in his eyes. Had they been about to auction off his treasured pet for slaughter? She saw photos of Glen with his mother, a stern expression on her face. Glen had been a sensitive child, she thought, with an overbearing mother. Was that what had made him rape?

Another was a group picture of the Boulder High School graduating class, and she spotted Glen's face. He'd even lied about this, she thought, snatching the photo off the wall to take with her. Estelle Summer couldn't have been his high school English teacher. Even though Glen had attended college at Berkeley, he'd obviously attended high school in Colorado. Lies, Ann thought. Everything about him amounted to lies.

The house was so quiet, deathly quiet.

Ann searched his desk, her hands flying through the papers. Mostly bills. She opened the desk drawer and started rummaging inside. Something fell out of an envelope with a metallic jangle, landing in the bottom of the drawer. A silver charm bracelet. Ann seized it and saw a charm that was engraved 'To Grandma from Billy.' The date was 1965. She shoved the bracelet in her front pocket. It had to be from one of the victims in the rapes. Knowing she had to get to the garage and then get out of the house, Ann rushed to the gun rack.

Shotguns, high-powered assault rifles with scopes, handguns. Glen had never once mentioned that he was a gun collector. Of course, he knew Ann hated firearms. The one with the scope, she thought, her breath catching in her throat. Should she take it? Had he used it to shoot her?

No, she'd stayed too long already. Besides, she quickly decided, if Glen had used a rifle with a scope, she would be dead. Any minute, either Glen would come back or the police would come screaming up and arrest her. She had to get out of the house. Dropping the photograph of Glen's high school class, she hurried to the garage.

There it was, under a canvas tarp: Glen's black 1979 Rolls-Royce. He had to be driving the Harley Davidson motorcycle now as it wasn't in the garage. Yanking the canvas tarp off, Ann spotted the damage on the right front, and proceeded to photograph it. Then she used all four shots in order to get as complete a record of the car as she could in the few remaining seconds she felt she had left.

She shoved the photos into her back pocket and was about to leave when the garage door opened. Ann's heart began racing as she saw the motorcycle turn into the driveway. Quickly she dropped the camera behind a bunch of ski equipment and then dropped her parka on top of it. Patting down her hair, she tried to quiet her breathing. What was she going to say? How could she explain this? God, he could kill her right here.

'Ann,' Glen said, stopping the bike and removing his helmet, a dark look in his eyes. 'What are you doing in my garage? I've been waiting at the Sail Loft.'

'Oh . . . Glen, I'm so glad you're here,' Ann said. 'I ran out of gas just a few blocks away. When I couldn't find a pay phone, I decided to walk to your house and see if you'd come back.' She was talking so fast her words were running together. She forced herself to slow down. She had to get out of here, get away from him. 'When I got here, I saw your back window broken out. I thought you might be hurt and crawled inside to check. Then I just came out here to see if your car was here.'

He was still on the motorcycle, his hands clasping and unclasping the handlebars. 'That's bullshit,' he said, fury in his eyes.

Ann stepped backward, her eyes darting around the garage. Glen's motorcycle was in front of her, so she couldn't escape through the open door. If she ran back inside the house, though, he could catch her, kill her. No one even knew she was here.

The fingers. How could she have forgotten the severed fingers? Was Glen responsible for that as well? He had framed Delvecchio. Had he framed Sawyer too? Butchered some innocent woman and then planted the fingers in the Henderson house? She had been sleeping with a monster.

He was walking toward her. Ann forced herself not to recoil. The closer he got, the better chance she would have to defend herself, take him down. Let him come, she told herself, her muscles stiffening in preparation. He might lift weights, but he didn't know much about self-defense.

'What are you trying to do to me?' he spat, his breath hot on her face. 'You're like all the others.'

'No, Glen,' Ann pleaded, giving him what he wanted now.

'Don't hurt me. Please, don't hurt me.' As soon as she expressed the fear, his head went back and a milky look appeared in his eyes.

He was momentarily off guard, drunk on her fear. Now was the time. Placing her hands on his shoulders, Ann pulled him closer, as if she were about to embrace him. Suddenly she brought her knee up hard into his groin.

'Fuck,' he screamed in pain, his face twisted. His head fell to her chest as his pelvis jerked backward.

As Ann jumped to one side, Glen slid to the garage floor, his knees to his chest. In one swipe she collected her parka and camera. She took off running toward the alley, hearing him scramble to his feet. The hairbrush was dislodged from her pocket and hit the concrete in the driveway. She heard Glen stopping for it, only a few feet behind her. Let it go, she told herself. But she couldn't. She had to have proof. She'd risked her life to get it. She wasn't leaving without it.

Just as Glen's fingers closed on the brush, Ann stomped on his hand with her full body weight. Bending over, she snatched the brush. If only she'd brought her gun, she thought, she would kill him right that second. Their eyes met, and Ann saw that the tables had turned. He was the terrified one now, the defenseless one. She refused to remove her foot from his hand. 'Don't come near me,' she spat, saliva flying from her mouth. 'If you get within three feet of me, I'll blow your fucking head off.'

With his free hand he lunged for her ankle, but Ann was too fast. She tore off down the driveway, into the alley. Leaping in her car, she cranked the engine and burned off, passing a patrol car on the main street en route to Glen's house.

Chapter 21

I have to see Melanie this instant.' Ann was at the crime lab, beating her fists on the counter as she shouted at Alex. 'I told you it was an emergency.'

'Ann,' Melanie said from the doorway, a puzzled expression on her face. 'Come in. What's going on? You look awful.'

Ann glanced at Alex and then looked away, taking a deep breath and trying to calm herself. 'Not as bad as I feel, Mel,' she said, smoothing her hair down as she entered the lab. Once Melanie had taken a seat on a stool, Ann handed her the hairbrush. 'I need you to make a comparison of the hair in this right now. See if it matches the pubic hairs from the Delvecchio case.'

'What's going on?' the forensic expert said, deeply concerned. With her foot she nudged a stool next to her, indicating that Ann should sit down. 'I'm not doing anything until I know what this is about.'

Ann proceeded to relate all the connections she'd made. She'd rather deal with a woman right now than have to tell her story to a man. Once she had told her everything she had learned, she chastised herself. 'I was sleeping with him,' she said, wringing her hands. 'How could I be such a fool? Why couldn't I see it, sense it?'

Melanie slid off her stool and embraced her. 'Honey, men are assholes. I mean, any man, and this was far from any man.'

'But why?' Ann said, her shoulders shaking. 'Why would he shoot me, attack me? I just don't understand, Melanie. If I only understood –'

'He's a rapist, Ann,' Melanie said, her own voice strained and cracking, her eyes blazing with intensity. 'He thrives on –the sick bastard – seeing women suffer. It sexually excites him. I bet he wouldn't have been able to have sex with you any other way.'

Ann still could not grasp it. 'But Melanie, I was seeing him before this all started happening. He was having sex with me then. I wasn't afraid then, and he had no trouble, believe me.' She suddenly remembered Glen's fetish for having sex in public places, risking exposure. What had seemed exciting then now seemed revealing. Once she had divulged this information to Melanie, the woman pulled away and perched back on her stool, lighting a cigarette.

'You were already a victim,' Melanie said, her mouth compressed in growing outrage, the cigarette burning in the ashtray and smoke swirling up to her face. 'I hate to say this, Ann,' she said, waving the smoke away, 'and please don't take it the wrong way, but the word *victim* was engraved on your forehead. Hank . . .'

Ann felt her stomach lurch. Did Melanie know Hank had beaten her? Did everyone know? 'You mean that's why Glen began dating me to begin with?'

'Probably,' she said, taking a quick puff and then setting the cigarette back in the ashtray. 'You'd already been primed, you know, by what happened with Hank.' Then she thought of something else. 'Tell me, how do they assign cases at your agency?'

'What do you mean?'

'Well, didn't everything come to a head when Hopkins learned you'd be handling the Delvecchio case?'

Ann searched her memory. The night she was shot, she'd told Glen she would be handling the presentence report on Delvecchio, but at the time she had already been assigned the violation of probation report anyway. 'They always give me the multiple-count cases. Glen knows that. I'm the only one who can figure out the bingo sheet. But I don't see your point, Melanie. You think he shot me because he thought I might discover the truth?'

'That's a possibility, but I don't think so,' Melanie said thoughtfully. 'I think it was just the opposite, Ann. He was excited by the fact that you'd be dealing with Delvecchio. That made him even more sexually aroused. Rape is about control, but it's also about risk. This was the ultimate game he was playing. A man like Glen is different from an ordinary rapist.'

'In what way?' Ann said, as always wary of psychological interpretations. Some of the things David's therapist had said were way off.

Melanie looked over Ann's head as she talked, piecing her thoughts together as she went along. 'He's smart, see,' she said, taking another drag on her cigarette and then stubbing it out. 'But he probably doesn't feel smart. Maybe his mother's being so high-placed in the legal world makes him feel unimportant. For all we know, she could belittle him, tell him he'll never rise to her level of accomplishment. By out-smarting the judicial system, the system he associates with his mother, he's outsmarting his mother too. Can't you see? Symbolically, you became his mother and therefore the target of his rage.'

Ann looked up. 'You mean because I had a child or something?'

'Exactly,' Melanie said. 'You're idealistic when it comes to your work, Ann. You're determined and strong, a trained police officer. Someone shoots you and you hardly miss a stride. This reminds him of his mother.'

'Go on,' Ann said.

'But on the other hand, he sees you as the perfect mother to David, kind and understanding. His own mother is probably demanding and critical of everything he tries to do to please her.' Melanie paused and leaned forward, taking Ann's hands. 'See, Ann, you're both everything he hates and everything he desires. What he really wants is to take David's place, get rid of David. Then he can be the one basking in your love.'

Ann felt a jolt of fear and leaped off the stool. 'David. He wants to hurt David?'

Picking up the hairbrush, Melanie pointed at the phone. 'Go on. Call him and make certain he's all right.'

'Will you start on the hairs?'

'Sure,' Melanie said, turning to her microscope.

Once Ann had talked to Oscar Chapa and confirmed that David was asleep and safe, she leaned over Melanie's shoulder. 'How does it look?'

'Ann, you brought me head hairs. I didn't want to say anything when you first came in, but the samples we collected were pubic hairs. There's a difference.'

Ann gripped the back of her chair, about to scream. 'You've got to match it, Melanie.'

'Calm down,' Melanie said, a hand in the air as her eye remained pressed to the microscope. 'Some of the cellular/ translucent configurations are similar. To make a valid comparison, though, I need actual pubic hair.'

'God,' Ann said. 'Pubic hairs.' She'd gone over there and broken into Glen's home for nothing. The only way she could get what Melanie needed would be to sleep with Glen again, and that was clearly out of the question.

'Shit,' Melanie said, looking up. 'I should have noted this when the evidence first came in on the rapes. Because Glen said it wasn't necessary, I more or less skipped over this sample.

The pubic hairs found on the victims are from a Caucasian. Isn't Delvecchio black?'

'Yes,' Ann said.

'Well, he's not the rapist.'

'We already know that,' Ann shot back, becoming more frustrated by the second. 'We have to prove it's Glen's pubic hair.'

'I can't help you, Ann,' Melanie answered, equally discouraged. 'I'm sorry, but as I said, head hairs and pubic hairs are different. With enough time, I could study the cell structure, even do a DNA test, but right now –'

The charm bracelet. Ann stuffed her hand in her pocket and pulled it out. 'I found this in his house. Quick, Mel, get the reports and see if it was taken from one of the victims.'

While Melanie went to the other room to get the file, Ann studied each charm. There were lockets with pictures of children, engraved hearts, tiny icons of various objects: a piano, miniature praying hands, a cross, a unicorn. She was holding a lifetime of treasured memories.

'Estelle Summer,' Melanie said, a smile on her face, waving the report in the air. 'It was taken during the rape. It's right here in black and white. We got him.'

Ann opened her mouth to respond, her fingers closing on the bracelet. Then she saw the smile disappear from Melanie's face.

'You broke into his house to get that,' she said, shaking her head, her red curls spilling onto her forehead. 'Can't use it. Shouldn't have taken it, Ann. That's illegally obtained evidence, inadmissible in court.'

'But –' she protested, opening her hand and staring at the bracelet. 'What are we going to do, then?'

Seeing Ann crumbling before her eyes, Melanie grabbed her by the shoulders forcefully. 'Look at me, Ann,' she said. 'What's done is done. Can you be strong?'

Ann just stared at her, unable to speak.

'No,' Melanie said, 'right now you're acting like a victim. Stop it. You have to force him to make a move. That's the only way you're going to catch Hopkins and get him to court.'

'How?' Ann said, her voice shaking. 'He could harm David. I can't put David in that kind of –'

'Stash the kid,' Melanie said curtly, dropping her hands and pacing back and forth in front of Ann. 'Tell Reed everything and have him back you up every second of the day. Act like nothing has happened, like the scene in the garage never occurred. Drive Glen crazy. He'll have to make a move then. Don't you see? If you catch him in the act, catch him trying to harm you in some way, you'll have him cold.'

Ann knew what she was saying. She could possibly get Glen arrested on what she had and what she knew, but she couldn't keep him behind bars. He'd make bail like all the others, and once he did, they'd never see him again. He certainly had enough money to flee the country. His house was loaded with art and valuables he could sell. Or, even worse, he could make bail, go underground, but continue to stalk Ann until he killed her. If she did what Melanie suggested and refused to back down, it would be Glen on the defensive, Glen who would be forced to risk everything to stop her.

'I can do it.'

'Thatta girl,' the woman said, patting her on the back.

A half hour later, Ann stepped out on the front porch of her house to speak with Oscar Chapa. He was the perfect person to protect her son. He lived alone, was single, and had a trailer somewhere in the mountains in Ojai, not far from Ventura. 'Oscar,' she said, 'I need your help.' She then proceeded to tell him what was going on, asking if he would take David for a few days.

'I have to work, you know?' he said, a blank look in his eyes. He couldn't take time off to baby-sit her kid for her.

'This is work,' Ann answered, her voice louder than she intended. 'I'm going to clear it with Reed and the department, Oscar. I just wanted to ask you personally before I did.'

'Sure.' Oscar smiled. 'He's a nice enough kid. I won't let anything happen to him.'

Ann leaned over and pecked the big man on the cheek. 'I know you won't, Oscar. That's why I picked you.'

Ann called Reed and gave him a summary of what she'd learned, refusing to spend much time fielding his questions. When he got here, she'd go over what she had step by step.

Once he said he was on the way over, Ann got David out of bed and threw some of his belongings into a duffel bag while he was in the bathroom putting on his clothes. She'd lied and told him that she had to fly to Arizona to identify Hank's body, that the authorities there wouldn't release it until she did so.

Next, she insisted that Oscar take the boy to his trailer in Ojai immediately. Ann wasn't going to wait for daylight. She'd seen the arsenal of high-powered weapons Glen possessed. He could slip past their surveillance and kill them both during the night.

Once David came out in his clothes, sleepy and disoriented, Ann pushed him out the door with Oscar. 'Reed will be here any second,' she told the officer, closing the door and shoving the deadbolts into place.

Taking a seat on the sofa, Ann laced her fingers together and placed them in her lap to control the trembling, but her eyes kept straying to the phone. The bastard, she thought, suddenly grabbing it and dialing his number. When he answered, she listened and then hung up. Let him sweat, she decided. Let him see what it was like to have someone calling him all hours of the day and night. How had he imitated Hank's voice, though? It was the only aspect of the case she couldn't figure out.

Then she thought of the voice analysis and Melanie's statement that it was Hank's voice. She'd mentioned technical noise. Ann herself distinctly remembered hearing a strange noise during the calls: a clicking sound or something. Of course, she thought, a light coming on in her head. It sounded like Hank's voice because it was Hank's voice. Racing to David's room, she dug in the bottom of his closet for the old videotapes. Then she recalled that he had kept them in a shoe box on top of his desk. Ann found the box, but it was empty. Glancing at the window, she knew now what had occurred. Glen had broken into the house looking for something he could use to make her crazy, make her think she was losing her mind. If her credibility was destroyed, no one would believe her if she ever suspected the truth and tried to point a finger at him. All he had done was steal the videotapes and then play them back over the phone. She'd thought the phrases the voice had uttered had sounded familiar. After Hank had disappeared, David had played those tapes dozens of times. Ann had finally insisted that he put them away.

'Where's David?' the hostile voice had said. 'Go get David.' Yes, she realized, her thoughts racing. One of the tapes had been made at a park. Hank had suddenly been called in to work that day, spoiling their picnic, and he'd promptly flown into a rage. Ann remembered him screaming at her to get David, even knocking her to the grass. David had asked her many times why the tape just stopped, why there were images of nothing but lopsided scenery. The child had been on the other side of the park, playing on the swing set. He hadn't seen his father blow up, thank God.

Maybe Glen had thought he could push her over the edge,

Ann thought, that she would end up in a mental institution. Everyone knew how crazy she had acted when Hank had vanished, all the foolish things she had done. As Melanie had said, Glen Hopkins had selected her for these very reasons. Victim. Victim. Victim. Like an animal, the predator he was, he had caught the scent of prey.

Hearing Reed pounding on the front door and yelling, Ann dropped the shoe box and headed to the door, her courage fueled by utter hatred. She would never back down, never let him frighten her again. If it was the last thing she ever did, she was going to make Glen Hopkins pay.

Both Reed and Noah Abrams remained at Ann's house all night, taking turns sleeping while the other one maintained surveillance. Ann didn't sleep more than an hour. She maintained a post in the back of the house, letting the detectives cover the front from the living room. At first Reed had been skeptical, refusing to believe Ann's suspicions. But his dislike of Hopkins, coupled with the evidence Ann had provided, caused him eventually to come around.

Just as the sun was rising, Abrams came into the kitchen and pulled up a chair next to Ann. 'You should sleep some more,' he said softly. 'You've hardly slept all night. Reed's awake and I'm here. Go on. It's almost daylight. He's not going to make a move now.'

'I can't,' Ann said weakly, her hands locked on her gun, her face haggard and her eyes bloodshot. Right next to her on the kitchen table was the portable phone. Unknown to the detectives, Ann had hit the auto dial all night, every fifteen minutes or so, always hanging up the minute Glen picked up. The payback wasn't much, but it gave her a certain sense of satisfaction.

Noah and Ann sat silently in the kitchen, watching through the windows as the sky turned gray, then orange. Outside in the trees, the birds were chirping and lights were coming on in some of the houses as people prepared to go to work, mothers made breakfast for their children and got them ready for school.

'Even without all this,' Noah said thoughtfully, 'he wasn't good enough for you, Ann.'

Ann met his gaze, the kindness she saw there deeply touching. She hadn't seen Noah this serious in years, not since they had been cadets. Back then they used to have long talks about their hopes and dreams for the future. Bathed in the morning light, his hair looked almost red, and Ann smiled at the freckles covering his face, thinking how innocent they made him look. Normally, he was dressed in a suit and one of his eye-catching ties, but this morning he looked just as he had all those years ago. In his jeans and T-shirt, he looked guileless and youthful.

'We didn't do very well, did we, Noah?' she said in a melancholy voice.

'What do you mean?' he said self-consciously.

'Remember how we were both going to marry someone wonderful and live happily ever after with a houseful of kids?'

Noah's eyes dropped to his lap. 'Yeah,' he said. 'I always thought Hank was your Mr Wonderful, Ann. I thought he had what I never found.'

'Well, he wasn't Mr Wonderful,' Ann said, sighing with regret. 'He was a confused and bitter man, Noah.' She wondered how much he knew about her relationship with Hank, how much Reed had told him. Noah had gone through three failed marriages, and Ann had fallen for a maniac like Glen. How had they gone so far off course? she thought. When she was young, she'd been infatuated with Noah, even fantasized that they would get together one day. 'Why didn't you ever ask me out?' she asked him, curious now.

'Oh,' he said, keeping his eyes averted, 'I didn't think you liked me. I mean, not that way. You were so pretty and confident, Ann. I was just a skinny little nerd.'

She'd been a handful back then, all right. A spoiled brat was more like it. Her father had been a captain, and that had given her special privileges around the station. All the men knew her and made way for her, giving in to her all the time, letting her get away with things the other cadets would be disciplined for.

'But I liked you,' Ann told him, watching as his eyes lit up. 'I mean it, Noah. I would have gone out with you in a second if you'd only asked.'

'Really?' he said, smiling broadly, his right shoulder twitching with excitement.

All at once they both burst out laughing. Ann kept looking at Noah and starting up again. She kept laughing until tears were streaming down her face, the tension balled up inside finally finding an outlet. 'You know, Noah,' she said, swiping at her eyes with her hands, 'we could have saved each other a lot of heartache if you'd just had the balls to ask me out.'

'Yeah,' he said, chuckling nervously. 'I guess so. I really fucked up, didn't I?' He rose to go into the other room, hearing Reed calling, but instead stood directly over Ann's chair. 'Can I do something I've wanted to do for years?' he said haltingly.

Ann looked up, uncertain what he meant. He didn't wait for her to answer. Bending down, he pressed his lips to hers in an awkward kiss. It lasted only a second, but Ann felt a jolt of recognition, a rush of warmth, and the intervening years seemed to vanish. The world around them had changed and they'd both seen their share of shattered dreams, but Noah hadn't really changed at all, and inside, Ann knew she was still the same girl from years past.

Goodness endured, she thought, her heart swelling with affection for this man, watching as he headed to the living room to see what Reed wanted. Evil, by its very nature, was constantly changing, shifting, darting in and out of the shadows, like Glen, but the basic goodness that Noah possessed remained constant.

Fortified with renewed strength and hope, Ann returned to her vigil.

At nine o'clock, Noah parked in front of the jail. 'I should come in with you,' he said.

'No,' Ann insisted. 'Just cover me until I'm inside. Nothing can happen once I'm inside the jail. If we want Glen to make a move, he can't know you're on to him. He's got to think I'm still compiling evidence, afraid that without it, no one will believe me. That's how he planned it all along. Let's let him think he's still in control a little longer. It can only work to our advantage.'

'You're right,' Noah said, picking up her hand and squeezing it. 'It's just, now that we've —'

Ann shot him a stern look. Whatever had passed between them this morning had to wait. An innocent man was in jail, and a very dangerous man was free. 'It shouldn't take more than a few minutes, Noah.'

He reluctantly released her hand, and Ann walked rapidly to the jail entrance, her eyes darting up to the windows of the D.A.'s office.

If she could plant enough doubt, she thought, the court might be able to declare a mistrial in Delvecchio's case. And she had to do something to help him right now. Her conscience wouldn't allow her to let an innocent man remain in custody a moment longer. Not only had Glen framed him, but the man's attorney had failed to defend him. Ann thought that even without Glen's involvement, she could get the case overturned on appeal, but that would take time, and during that time Delvecchio would remain in prison.

There were two ways to look at it, however, and blaming the public defender at this point was premature. He had filed the appropriate discovery motions to obtain all the information the prosecution possessed against his client. Since Glen was behind these atrocities, he could easily have eliminated some of the lab findings when responding to the discovery. As to the employment records, Ann knew how that went. Every man that walked into the courtroom had something he swore would prove his innocence if he could just find it. The public defender, like so many others in the system, had simply become jaded.

A ting rang out when Ann plunked her county identification in the metal bin to pass to the jailer. 'Face to face,' she said flatly. She was punchy and scattered, barely able to go through the motions. So much had happened in such a short time.

As Ann walked down the corridor past the open quads, a man teased and whistled, yelling out, 'Come here, baby. Show me your fucking tits.'

Ann flipped the prisoner the finger, unable to control herself. 'Go fuck yourself.'

The man sneered and rattled the bars. Then he broke out cackling. Soon the whole quad was in an uproar, the prisoners banging their cups on the bars, whistling and screaming.

The jailer glared at Ann. 'If you just ignore them, they'll stop. If you respond at all, they go crazy.'

'I'm sorry,' Ann said, hanging her head. 'I'm not in a very tolerant mood today.'

The door to the interview room was opened, and Ann saw Delvecchio sitting vacantly, slouched low in his chair. As soon as he saw the tall blond probation officer, his eyes came alive and he straightened to an upright position.

'Well, Randy,' she said, sitting down, 'I've made a little progress, but not enough. I want you to look at some pictures of a car and tell me what you think.' Ann took out the Polaroids and slid them across the table.

Delvecchio recognized it in a second. 'That's the car. That's the car the man was driving that gave me the coat. How did you find it?'

Ann leaned over the table, her palms down, getting right in his face. 'You're certain, Randy? We're talking dead certain? Anything you tell me now you'll have to testify to in a courtroom. Are we clear?' At this point the man would identify his own mother's car to get out of jail. She had to be certain. Even if she did know it was Glen, she wanted Delvecchio's testimony to be truthful, not perjured.

Delvecchio was fidgeting excitedly. 'I swear,' he said. 'See, I know cars, but I never seen a car like this one before.'

Ann snatched the pictures back.

'What's wrong?' Delvecchio said. 'Don't you believe me? Please, man, I swear. I wouldn't lie to you.'

'Why did you tell me a dog bit you?' Ann said, recalling the first interview. 'A white poodle with a bow in its hair. Isn't that what you told me?'

Delvecchio hung his head. 'I dunno. We was talking and I wanted you to like me. I just said it. You're the one who wanted to talk about poodles.'

'What else have you lied about?'

'Nothing, lady, I promise. If you don't help me, they're gonna kill me. They're gonna send me to the gas chamber now that woman done died.'

Watery dark eyes pleaded with her. Ann probed there, refusing to look away. She didn't see evil or malice. She didn't see deception and cunning. All she saw in Randy Delvecchio's eyes was the same thing she saw when she looked in her own mirror.

Raw fear.

She watched as the muscles in Delvecchio's face twitched. Suddenly she heard something tinkling on the floor.

Ann bent down sideways, glancing under the table. Delvecchio had urinated on the floor. He'd pissed in his pants.

Feeling a prickle of fear herself, Ann quickly rang the buzzer and waited at the door until the jailer opened it.

Noah had told her he would be waiting outside the back entrance to the jail, where there were more parking spaces. Ann made her way through the crowded waiting room, down the back corridors, and then suddenly stopped in her tracks, every muscle in her body locking.

Glen was standing in the middle of the hallway, blocking her passage with his body.

'Get out of my way, Glen,' she said firmly.

'No,' he said, lunging at her with his hands, trying to grab her. 'You're sick, Ann. Everyone knows it. You're mentally ill.'

Ann stepped back, but she didn't run. She had to stand her ground, show him she wasn't afraid. 'Get out of my way.'

'Please,' he said, refusing to move. 'I don't look down on you, Ann. I know what it's like to have problems. There's a hospital right down the road that can help you. I'll drive you there myself.'

Ann almost felt compassion for him. He was insane, completely insane. Did he really think he could cart her off to a mental institution and get away with it? Walking backward as fast as she could, she finally reached the lobby. Glen was still in the corridor. Then she jogged out the front of the building, crossing outside to the rear, and leaped into the waiting car.

At six o'clock that evening, Ann, Reed, and Abrams were sharing a pizza in the kitchen and discussing how to proceed with the case. Reed had just informed Ann of the rape exam performed after she was shot, and she was ecstatic. 'They'll have pubic hairs, Tommy,' she exclaimed. 'All Melanie has to do is match them with the ones found in the rape case, and we can take this to Fielder. That's proof,' she said, lifting her glass to toast them. 'What else do we need? We'll arrest him, get him held without bail, and then I can get my son back.'

When the phone rang, Noah wanted to answer it, but Ann waved him away. 'Yes?' she said, thinking it was David.

'Is this Ann Carlisle, the probation officer?'

'Yes,' she said. 'Who is this?'

'I need to see you,' the voice said. 'It's important.'

Ann thought she recognized the voice, but she wasn't certain. 'Jimmy,' she said, keeping her voice calm, looking over at Reed and Abrams and pointing at the door. Noah quickly took the cue and raced out the back door to go to the surveillance van. Intent in their pursuit of Hopkins, they had forgotten all about the phone calls. But they certainly wanted to trace this one. 'Where are you, Jimmy?' Ann asked.

'I know the police are looking for me. I'm never going back to that jail.' He was talking fast, in a high-pitched voice. 'I spent six days in that stink hole when they arrested me the first time. I didn't shoot you, Ann, I swear. Yes, I was involved in drugs, and I said things about you to cover my ass, but I didn't hurt anyone.'

'Jimmy,' Ann said slowly, trying to engage him in conversation long enough for them to trace the call, 'why did you say those things? Did you really think people would believe you over me?'

'I saw you fucking him in the stairwell,' he said, his voice dropping to a whisper. 'If you fucked him, I thought people would believe you fucked me too.'

Ann felt as if something were stuck in her throat and she couldn't swallow. She'd been right. Sawyer was the one who had opened the door in the stairwell. Was she wrong about the tapes? She had to know. 'Have you been calling me, disguising your voice?'

'What do you mean?'

'You know what I mean,' she said, looking in Reed's eyes as

she spoke. 'Someone's been calling me and disguising his voice, pretending he's my husband.'

'Look, I'll tell you everything I know if you'll meet me,' Sawyer said, his voice getting stronger. 'But no cops and no district attorneys. If you bring those assholes, you'll never hear from me again.'

'District attorney?' Ann said, arching her eyebrows at Reed. 'Did you say something about a district attorney?' Reed went in the other room to pick up on the extension phone.

'He's trying to double-cross me,' Sawyer said quickly. 'My father told me to call you. He said they'll kill me if they find me.'

Ann was incredulous. They'd almost eliminated Sawyer and his cohorts from any involvement in the case. Was he saying he was a co-conspirator, that he had been working with Glen? 'Who's trying to double-cross you?' she said firmly, slapping the wall with her palm. 'Say his name, Jimmy.'

'Not over the phone. I'll tell you everything when you come. I'm a witness. If you promise to help me and not let them throw me in jail, I'll testify for you.'

Ann felt her heart pounding. The whole thing was mind-boggling. Glen involved with Sawyer? Glen was the man who had insisted on Sawyer's arrest, who had filed the case when no one thought they had enough evidence. 'Did Glen Hopkins kill someone and store the body at your house?' she asked, thinking this might be what he had witnessed. 'The fingers, Jimmy. If you want to tell me something, tell me about the fingers.'

The phone went dead.

A moment later, Reed was back in the kitchen, hopping mad. 'Why did you antagonize him? When you named Hopkins, he panicked, thinking he had nothing to use as leverage. That was stupid, Ann.' He ran his fingers through his hair. 'I take it back. It wasn't stupid, it was fucking dumb.'

'I'm sorry, all right?' she cried defensively. 'What if Glen did butcher some poor woman? Don't you want to know? Christ, Tommy,' Ann said, 'the fingers are gone. Sawyer might be our only link to this murder.'

'If there was a murder,' Reed tossed back at her.

Noah came back into the house, shaking his head. There hadn't been enough time to trace the call. A few moments later, the phone rang again. 'Answer it,' he said. 'The equipment is set up. Keep him talking.'

'Where do you want to meet?' Ann said, knowing it was Sawyer. 'Why don't you just tell me everything on the phone? How do I know you don't want to get me somewhere where you can hurt me?'

'Hey,' Sawyer said, far more confident than he had been before. 'I'll tell you about the fingers. And yes, they were real fingers. But you have to meet me at Marina Park in an hour. Wear something white and sit on the bench near the jungle gym. Don't be late. I'm not going to wait.'

'No,' Ann said, trying to keep him on the line. 'Don't hang up. What about the fingers? Why would I meet someone like you, Jimmy? You could be a killer.'

'Because I'm going to tell you what you want to know.'

He hung up, and she slammed the phone down.

'Next time, Ann,' Noah said for the umpteenth time, 'you have to keep him talking longer.'

'There's not going to be a next time. He wants to meet me,' Ann said, her voice fluttering. 'Didn't you hear him? He's ready to turn himself in, even testify against Glen.' She stopped and glared at the two detectives. 'Get some men together. I'm going to meet Sawyer. I have to know what's going on. If you don't, I'm going in alone. And tell them to step on it. We only have an hour.'

Reed grabbed her and shook her, shouting right in her face.

'I'm not letting you go out there. He could shoot you. Maybe we're wrong about Hopkins.'

Noah pulled Reed back. 'Let's not start fighting with each other,' he said. Then he turned to Ann. 'Reed's right, Ann. You shouldn't go out there.'

'No,' Ann roared. 'I'm going. When I don't show up, he'll flee and we'll never know the truth. Those were human fingers.'

They both knew what she was referring to, the possibility that Glen had committed a homicide, and without Sawyer's information, they might never be able to prove it. As she stormed out of the room, Reed growled and banged the table with his fist. 'All right, Noah,' he said wearily, 'contact the radio dispatcher and have her begin assembling the necessary men and equipment.'

Chapter 22

Seven unmarked units from the narcotics pool pulled up and parked behind the Alpha Beta grocery store six blocks from Marina Park, along with several additional units from the sheriff's department. Noah Abrams leaped out and handed Ann the wire, while Reed and the other men huddled together on the opposite side of the parking lot. Ann immediately pulled up the white parka and her sweater underneath, holding the microphone to her flesh while Abrams taped it down. Although it was chilly, Ann was perspiring. 'Better put more tape on there,' she told him. 'I'm sweating and it's going to slide.'

Abrams took the masking tape and started to position the rest of the apparatus in the small of Ann's back. Then he felt the Beretta. 'You're packing a piece,' he said. 'Shit, what if the guy frisks you?'

'I'm not going to let him frisk me,' Ann answered, turning to face him once the unit was in place. 'If he does, he'll find the wire.'

'I really care about you,' Abrams said softly, holding her by the shoulders. 'I wish you wouldn't do this.'

Ann looked deep into his eyes.

The detective caressed her cheek tenderly with the palm of

his hand. 'We could have a life together, a good life. I've always been crazy about you, Ann, and I've always wanted a family. Hey, when Hank vanished, I'm embarrassed to say it, but I was glad.' He dropped his eyes in shame. 'Pretty contemptible, huh? Reed didn't want me to approach you, though. He was adamant about it.' He finally raised his eyes. 'I guess he thought I would hurt you. He was wrong.'

Ann was so touched she was speechless. All this time he had been afraid to say something to her. If she'd only known.

'Anyway, we'd better get going,' Abrams said awkwardly, seeing her searching for words. 'Here's the earpiece.'

'I can't wear the earpiece,' Ann said, handing it back to him.

Noah's face contorted. 'But, Ann, you have to wear it. We can't talk to you without the earpiece.'

'So, you won't talk to me. You can still hear me,' Ann responded, anxious to get going before she lost her nerve. 'See my hair, Noah? It's too short to cover my ear. He'll see it the minute I walk up to him. He'll never tell me the truth if he thinks I'm wearing a wire.'

'This is so dangerous,' Abrams said, walking around in small circles. 'Sawyer could be armed to the hilt. He might be coming out here just to blow you away.' He stopped and stared at Ann. 'He even admitted the fingers were real. Don't you see, Ann? We have no idea what's really going on with this guy.'

Ann ignored him, stepping a few feet away and speaking into the microphone, 'Testing, one, two, three. You got It, Noah?' She turned around, and he nodded somberly. Then she stood there jiggling her hands and shuffling her feet, trying to relieve the tension.

At last she let out a deep breath. 'I'm ready,' she told him. She climbed in the driver's seat of a borrowed Range Rover and roared off.

Detective Reed was instructing a group of officers when Abrams joined them. 'I don't want Sawyer to get within a mile of Marina Park,' he told them. 'Are we perfectly clear here?'

Captain Mathews walked up just as Reed completed his sentence. 'Hold it right there,' he barked, the men already walking off to their units, high-powered shotguns with scopes in their arms. 'What are you talking about, Reed?'

'Just what I said,' Reed snapped. Then he realized he was speaking to his commanding officer and changed his tone of voice. 'Look, Captain, Ann thinks Sawyer's coming to spill his guts or provide us with information about Hopkins, but we don't know what all this guy's really involved in. If we take him before he gets to the park –'

The captain glared at him. 'When you say take him, we're talking taking the man into custody, right?' When Reed just shrugged, the captain turned to address the men. 'You will not fire unless you are fired upon or Ann Carlisle is fired upon. We came out here to obtain information. I have no intention of turning this into a bloodbath.'

Reed pulled Abrams aside. 'Did you verify where Hopkins is?'

'Yeah,' Abrams said, 'he's at his house. I called to verify he was at home before we even left Ann's house. Then I called him again on my cellular phone just a few minutes ago, and Hopkins answered the phone again. There's no way he could get over here now without us seeing him. He lives all the way up in the foothills. Besides, we have units positioned on every street leading into the park.'

'Good,' Reed said, nodding. 'But let's not take any chances. Have a patrol unit park in front of Hopkins's house. As soon as we find out what Sawyer has to say, we're going to pop him anyway. I want to make damn certain this bastard doesn't show up tonight. That's all we need right now.' He started to walk off and then stopped. 'And I want you to monitor Ann yourself, Noah. Is she on the auxiliary channel? If she isn't, any transmission she makes could get buried under other radio traffic.'

'Yes, she is,' Abrams said. 'I've got my portable tuned to her frequency right now.' He jerked a black portable radio up to his ear and listened. 'She just notified us that she was walking into the park. Central dispatch is monitoring her transmissions as well. If anything goes wrong, they'll broadcast it over both frequencies.'

Reed stared off into space, thinking. 'Okay,' he said a few moments later, feeling confident they'd covered all the bases. 'Get a unit over to Hopkins's house at once,' he repeated. 'Advise them not to make contact unless he tries to leave. And call Hopkins again to make certain he's still at his house. We don't want him slipping out before the surveillance unit gets there.'

Reed walked to his unit and jerked his shotgun from the holder, checking the ammo. If the captain wanted to be obstinate and play by the rules, he thought, so be it. If he had to, he'd take Sawyer down himself. For all they knew, Sawyer was a murderer and butcher. No way was Reed going to let him get to Ann.

Just then the detective looked up and saw a flash of red out of the corner of his eye speeding down the road toward Marina Park. Squinting until he made out the license plate, Reed immediately cranked the engine and screamed out of the parking lot, fishtailing around the parked police units. The plate on the red Honda was Jinny, the girl Sawyer had switched cars with in the mall. Reed grabbed the microphone off the seat and shouted into it, 'I'm in pursuit. I have the red Honda and I'm almost certain Sawyer's behind the wheel. We're headed west from Alpha Beta on Tradewinds now. Get the units ahead of me to cut him off before he gets to the park.'

*

Marina Park was located in the beach area of Ventura not far from Dr and Mrs Sawyer's house. After numerous problems with juveniles congregating, drinking, and using drugs, the city had closed the park to the public during the evening hours. Ann pulled up and killed her engine, noting that there were no lights in the park itself. A street lamp was located close to the entrance, however, and cast a narrow beam of light across the playground. To Ann, the park looked desolate and terrifying. She stepped out of the car and closed her white jacket. Then she spoke to the surveillance officers via the concealed microphone: 'I'm about to walk in.'

Bracing herself, she began walking. She tried to keep her head straight and resist the urge to look behind her, but her fear was raging. First she walked on grass. As she got to the playground area, her feet sank in the sand. A short distance away, she could hear the waves crashing on the shore, and the air was heavy and damp. She saw what looked like a wooden fort for the children to play in, and then she spotted the jungle gym.

Taking a seat on the bench, she waited.

Minutes passed in agonizing slow motion. Ann had never felt so alone in her life. Somewhere off in the distance she heard sirens, wondering what type of incident they were responding to, then telling herself it was probably a fire or an injury accident.

She knew the officers were listening, ready to come to her rescue at the slightest indication of trouble. It didn't help. By the time they got to her, Sawyer could kill her. Quickly she placed her hand behind her and touched the cold steel of her Beretta.

Hearing a noise nearby, Ann tensed, but she couldn't tell where it was coming from. Then she almost screamed when she saw a head emerge from the wooden fort, followed directly by a man's body. 'Jimmy?' she said, hoping some drunk or homeless person hadn't crawled in there to sleep.

Ann was standing, trying to see the man's face and verify it was Sawyer when the man leaped from the shadows like a wild animal and knocked her to the ground. Instinctively Ann flipped over onto her stomach, reaching behind her for her gun. She came up empty-handed. The gun had fallen out when he had jumped her, and was now lost somewhere in the sand.

The next second Ann felt the man's knee press into her lower back, and a hand closed tightly over her mouth. Her screams were muffled inside his palm. She sank her teeth into the skin, but the man didn't react. Struggling against him, Ann knew the assailant was too strong. With what seemed like herculean strength, he pinned one hand behind her back, holding her other arm on the ground with his body. Fingernails scraped her skin near her chest, and Ann was certain he was going to rape her. But he only ripped the wire off her chest and tossed it somewhere in the darkness.

Ann rolled sideways into his body, knocking him off balance, but he grabbed her and they started rolling together, ending up in the section of the park illuminated by the street lamp. For the first time Ann could see the man's face.

It was Glen.

'You,' she said, screaming wildly, certain the surveillance officers would be here any second.

She was on her back, Glen on top of her, both her hands pinned now over her head. 'They're not coming for you,' Glen said, smirking. 'They're too busy arresting Jimmy.'

Ann heard something coming from the fort now, heavy radio traffic and police jargon. 'A scanner?' she said. 'You have a police scanner? That's how you knew I was meeting Sawyer.'

'What?' he said, his eyes lit by a strange glow. 'Do you

345

think I'd let a piece of shit like Sawyer destroy me? Or a stupid woman like you?'

'No,' she yelled frantically. 'They're coming. They're right down the street. They'll shoot you . . . kill you.'

'Poor Ann,' he said, a maniacal grin on his face. 'You were so perfect, you know. I really cared about you, but you took the game too far, tried to make it your game.' The grin disappeared and Glen's face turned hard and cold, an ugly, evil visage that defied description. 'Now you want to take all the credit, get all the praise,' he continued. 'But you're not going to do it. I'm the one the legal community will look up to and admire. I'm the one who brought in the convictions on Delvecchio. You know how proud my mother is right now? You think winning just any case would impress her? No, only an impossible case would do.'

'The police know everything,' Ann shouted. 'I've already told them, given them evidence. If you kill me, they'll arrest you, track you down, send you to the gas chamber.'

For a moment he paused, a flicker of reason appearing in his eyes, then it was gone, and all Ann could see was the madness. Hands of steel locked around her throat, and she felt him squeezing. Ann was gulping and gagging, clawing at his hands with her own. Where were the men? Then she remembered the missing wire. They couldn't hear her.

In that instant Ann knew she was going to die.

He was going to kill her. And like everything else, he was going to get away with it. Rage suddenly filled her, driving her like a powerful engine. Finding his little finger on her throat, Ann bent it backward with all her strength, an old police tactic to break a suspect's grip. The pressure released long enough for Ann to pry his other hand off her neck and scramble a few feet away. She was on her hands and knees when she felt him on her back, the hard object poking between her shoulder blades

346

unmistakable. A gun. Ann froze and every muscle in her body locked into place.

'I don't like using guns, Ann. They're too loud.' Glen was panting, his face right by her ear. 'I did enjoy shooting you, though,' he said with pleasure. 'I never hunted a human being before.'

'Why?' Ann cried. 'Why did you want to kill me?' She had to stall him, keep him talking, anything until the men came to her rescue.

'If I had wanted to kill you,' Hopkins said, nipping her ear with his teeth, 'I would have done so. I only wanted to put you out of commission. You were a threat.'

'I didn't threaten you,' Ann whimpered. 'We'd just made love.'

'You were going to destroy my business,' he continued. 'I worked hard to build that business. For the first time I had real money of my own . . . more money than most people see in a lifetime.'

Ann felt the gun press firmly between her shoulders and screamed. Then the pressure disappeared momentarily as Glen stood and used the toe of his boot to flip her over onto her back again. She pushed herself to a sitting position, ready to lunge at his legs and try to knock him off balance, when she suddenly stopped and became perfectly still.

The gun in his hands looked like a cannon. Only inches from her face, Ann found herself staring down the dark, seemingly bottomless barrel. Never in her entire life had she been this afraid. Her bladder emptied, and warm urine soaked through her jeans. Glen stood over her, quickly seizing a handful of her hair and pulling her to a kneeling position. When he yanked her head toward the gun, Ann opened her mouth to scream, certain it would be her last sound before death.

The cold metal entered her mouth, lodging deep in her

throat. She gagged, her mouth filling with fluid. A few moments later, the gag reflex died under the weight of her terror, and she became as still as a statue.

'That should shut you up,' he said, laughing as he pushed on the back of her head, forcing the gun even farther down her throat.

She began praying. Then she felt tears gushing out of her eyes. Tears for her precious child, she thought, but she knew she was grieving for more than David. She was mourning her own death, imagining what it would feel like when he pulled the trigger. She'd seen numerous suicides who'd swallowed a gun. Ann knew she could never survive it. The bullet would blow the back of her head off, her brain along with it.

Glen's eyes were searching the area, and he appeared to be noticing how close they were to the parking lot and the streetlight. Too much time had passed now, and he couldn't take a chance. Sliding the gun out of Ann's mouth, he said fiercely, 'Stand and start walking.'

Ann struggled to her feet, forcing back the urge to vomit. A horrid metallic taste was in her mouth, and she brought one hand up to rub her throat. Why didn't he just kill her, pull the trigger and get it over with? It must thrill him to see her helpless and terrified, pleading for her life. Once he killed her, this awesome power he held over her would be gone. He was enjoying himself, so insane that he thought he was invincible.

Glen nudged her with the gun, and Ann stumbled forward. Should she run for it, she asked herself, make an attempt to escape? No, she decided, knowing he would only shoot her in the back. She wasn't going to give him the satisfaction. When he killed her, she wanted him to look her straight in the eye.

'Hurry up,' he commanded, forcing her in the direction of the surf.

Ann looked off into the darkness, catching a reflection on the water. What was he going to do to her now? she thought in horror. Was he going to drown her instead of shooting her? It didn't really matter, she decided, resigning herself to her fate. Whatever means he used to accomplish it, Ann knew when it was over, she would be dead.

The red Honda was parked sideways in the center of the street, the passenger door standing open. One side of the vehicle had sustained substantial body damage. At least a dozen police cars were parked on either side of it, some with their wheels up on the curbs and lawns.

Jimmy Sawyer was prostrate on the ground in the center of the street in the glaring lights from the police units.

'Throw out your weapon,' Reed barked over a loudspeaker from one of the units.

Sawyer pleaded, 'I swear I don't have a gun. Don't shoot me. Please, don't shoot me.'

Reed glanced over at Abrams. 'Call Ann and tell her we have Sawyer. She doesn't have to wait any longer.'

Abrams scowled. 'She doesn't have an earpiece, Sarge. We'll have to go get her.'

'You have been monitoring the surveillance channel?' Reed asked quickly, arching his eyebrows. 'She hasn't called for help and we didn't hear her?'

'Of course not,' Abrams answered. 'She's got to be just sitting out there wondering what happened to Sawyer.'

Reed turned back to the prisoner. The past fifteen minutes had been chaotic. Sawyer had been traveling at such a high rate of speed when Reed first spotted him that a dangerous high-speed pursuit had ensued, Reed in the lead, with other units joining the chase from various side streets. Finally, Sawyer's Honda had spun out of control and crashed into a tree.

Reed picked up the microphone again and addressed

Sawyer. 'Stand up slowly with your hands out from your body. Then strip. Keep your hands where we can see them.'

Sawyer pushed himself to his feet, his hands out at his sides. He was wearing a sweatshirt and quickly pulled it over his head, immediately showing the officers his open palms.

'The pants too,' Reed ordered, turning back to speak to Abrams again. 'Go get Ann. I don't want her sitting down at that park alone.'

While Jimmy Sawyer was removing his jeans and kicking them aside, Abrams spotted his unmarked unit, but it was blocked by several of the black-and-whites. 'I'm going to have to wait until we take him into custody,' he told Reed. 'I can't get my car out.'

'Then walk,' Reed said flatly, picking up the microphone again. 'Take off your shorts too,' he told Sawyer, watching while the boy removed this last item of clothing. Now he was standing completely naked in the glaring lights, and he instinctively placed a hand at his groin to cover his genitals.

Abrams moved in to cuff him, along with several other officers, thinking that now he could get the officers to move their units and head to Marina Park to pick up Ann. Sawyer had switched directions during the pursuit and led them away from the park. If Abrams tried to walk it, he knew it would take too long.

Once Sawyer was cuffed, Abrams handed him over to Reed, and the detective started shoving him in the direction of his unit while Abrams tried to find the men driving the police cruisers that were blocking his own.

'I'm freezing,' Sawyer said in the passenger seat of Reed's unit. 'I mean, I came here to turn myself in. Every time I try to do something right, it turns into a fucking nightmare. Can't you at least let me put my clothes back on?'

'Not until I get some answers,' Reed told him gruffly. 'And

for your information, your roommates rolled over on you. You're staring down some serious drug charges, Jim-boy.'

Sawyer was silent, a muscle in his face twitching.

Reed turned to him, looking him squarely in the eye. 'Were you working with Hopkins?'

'Sort of,' Sawyer replied. 'I mean, I liked to think we were working for ourselves, but it didn't turn out that way.'

Reed was confused. 'Are you talking about the drug lab?'

'Yeah,' Sawyer said, leaning forward and trying to get comfortable with his hands cuffed behind his back. 'He was our financial backer, see. Someone Peter knew on the street told us about this guy who would put up ten grand for us to set up a home lab. They said he would give us all the chemicals we needed to cook the stuff too and we'd make a ton of bread. How the hell did I know the guy was a fucking district attorney?' He started struggling again. 'Shit, these handcuffs are killing me.'

Reed couldn't believe his ears. Hopkins was dirtier than they'd ever imagined. Feeling a measure of sympathy for the boy, the detective reached over and unlocked the handcuffs. Then he removed his own jacket and tossed it over to him. 'When did you first hook up with Hopkins?'

'I don't remember the exact date,' the boy said, slipping his arms into Reed's jacket. 'Maybe eight months ago or something. Look, he guaranteed us we wouldn't go to jail, and the money was great. We cooked the drugs, delivered them to this warehouse he had in L.A., then sold the rest of them on the street. We bought the cars, some new threads. Then when I got busted, things went crazy.'

'You're talking about the first arrest, right?' Reed said, rubbing his chin, cursing himself for buying Whittaker's informant's tale about Colombian drug dealers. But never would he have connected Glen Hopkins to a drug operation. 'Did you shoot Ann Carlisle?'

'No, I swear,' Sawyer said earnestly. 'Hopkins shot her. I even saw him. I mean, I didn't see him actually pull the trigger or anything, but I saw him running across the parking lot and he had something in his hand.' When Reed just stared at him, Sawyer continued. 'He promised I would only get court probation, see. He said he would fix it. Then when I got to court, Ann messed everything up. I was scared she was going to come out and find the lab, so I tried to talk to Hopkins and ask him what he wanted us to do, but I couldn't because he was with her. I left and then drove back later to find him. That's when I heard the shots and saw him running across the parking lot.'

'Why did you stop to help her, then?' Reed asked, fearful Sawyer was feeding him a line of bullshit and might actually have shot Ann himself.

'Look,' Sawyer said, an indignant expression on his face, 'I might be a drug dealer and all, but I don't kill people, and I wouldn't let someone bleed to death like that. Shit, he would, though. He just stood there and stared at her. Then when the paramedics got there, he pulled me over and told me to move the lab, that he shot her so she wouldn't bust us.'

'Didn't he realize that if he killed her, they'd just appoint another probation officer?'

'Hey, how do I know?' Sawyer snapped. He paused and then continued, 'Wait, he did say something. He said if she was only out a few weeks, the case would just sit around dead. And he was right. No one else came around, and we had enough time to rent another house and get it set up. But, of course, when she found the fingers, Hopkins told us to shut down for good.'

Reed's thoughts turned to Ann, and he picked up the microphone to try to raise Abrams. When Abrams answered, he roared at him with impatience, 'Where the hell are you? Where's Ann? I thought you would be back by now.'

'I'm almost at the park,' Abrams said, the radio cackling with static. 'I could have never walked it, Reed. You have no idea how faraway we were, but listen, Ann hasn't made a peep all night. She's fine. I even confirmed it with the dispatcher.'

Reed dropped the microphone on the seat and stared out the windshield. A funny feeling came over him, the kind he got when something wasn't right. Ann would never sit down there without a word all this time. At least twenty minutes had passed since she walked into that park. Ignoring his prisoner now, he drove forward a few feet and then stopped in front of several officers, reaching past Sawyer to open the passenger door. 'Take this guy in,' he told the men, instantly shoving Sawyer out the door.

Before the men could react, Reed had roared off, the passenger door of his unit still open. He gunned the engine and the speedometer started climbing, the door slamming shut when he whipped the car around the corner and headed to Marina Park.

Ann was back on her knees at the water's edge, pleading with Glen to let her go, the gun trained at her head. 'Glen, please,' she begged, 'don't do this. If you did these things because you're sick, then you can get help. We cared about each other. I have a child. Don't do this to me.'

'Should have thought of that before you started poking around in places you didn't belong,' he said, wiping his sweaty face with his shirttail.

Ann's eyes were darting all over. Far off in the distance, she saw what had to be headlights pulling into the parking lot. It could be a total stranger and not one of the officers, but Ann didn't care. She was filled with such utter hatred that she no longer cared if she lived or died, as long as she could be assured Glen would pay. What she simply couldn't tolerate was the thought that he would escape without punishment.

Suddenly Ann stared at the barrel of the gun, and something darted through her mind. Any second he would pull the trigger. Anything she did in her own defense would be better than nothing. If she made an attempt to escape and failed, the outcome would be the same anyway. Cutting her eyes to the parking lot, she saw a dark figure step out of a car and head toward the playground area. If Glen was going to kill her, Ann wanted him to do it now.

She had her witness.

But she also had one chance. Not a good one, but a chance. When she had been a police cadet, her father used to practice a trick with her, a way to disarm a person aiming a weapon at close range. She closed her eyes and tried to bring back the exact moves that her father had taught her.

In a flash she went for it, seizing the barrel of the gun with both hands, twisting his wrist sideways with every ounce of strength she possessed. Once the gun was pointing away from her, Ann used her ribs and body weight to apply more pressure against Glen's wrist. He yelled in pain and she heard what sounded like bone cracking. With lightning speed Ann slid her fingers between Glen's and suddenly found his gun in her hand as they toppled over backward.

'Now,' she said, gritting her teeth as she stared up into his eyes, the gun flush against his forehead, 'make a move, Glen. Go ahead. If you so much as hiccup, you're a dead man.'

Ann looked to the side and saw Noah Abrams sprinting across the sand. 'Over here,' she called out to him. 'We're near the water.'

'Jesus Christ,' Abrams said, seeing Ann on the ground with Hopkins. Immediately he pulled him off her. 'Are you okay?' he said quickly, reaching in his back pocket for his handcuffs and clamping them roughly on Hopkins's wrists.

At first Ann didn't answer. Flat on her back, staring at the sky, she stretched her arms out from her body and let the revolver fall from her fingers onto the sand.

She was alive.

'I'm fine,' she finally said, standing and dusting the sand off her clothes. But there was sand in her hair, sand in her mouth, sand in her eyes, and sand inside her clothing. Ann started scratching as if a million fire ants were attacking her. Then she saw Abrams staring at her and narrowed her eyes at him. 'Where were you guys, by the way? It's a good thing I didn't have a problem out here or anything. I mean, it's nice to know you've got such great backup. Gives a person a real feeling of security.'

Abrams looked miserable. 'I'm sorry, Ann. Really, I feel terrible. I don't know what happened. As soon as we set up down the street, I called this bastard's house and he answered the phone. We even dispatched a patrol unit to watch his house, and I called him again to verify he was still there only a few minutes after you said you were walking into the park.' With Hopkins in a choke hold, Abrams yanked his head back and screamed in his face, 'How did you pull this off, asshole?'

'He has a scanner,' Ann said. 'I heard it coming from the fort.'

Abrams was perplexed. 'That doesn't explain how he could answer his phone, though. How could he be in two places at the same time, Ann?'

'Answering machine,' Ann offered. 'Maybe when you called, you got his answering machine and thought it was him.'

'No way. It was a real voice on the phone. I don't know how, but it was him.' Shoving Hopkins to the ground, Abrams moved to kick him. 'Tell me, motherfucker, or I'm going to break every bone in your body.'

'Call-forwarding,' Hopkins mumbled, moaning in pain. 'I

just forwarded my home number to my car phone. My wrist is broken. I need medical treatment. I'm in severe pain.'

'Shut the fuck up,' Abrams said, 'or I'll break your frigging neck.'

Off in the distance, they both saw Reed jogging toward them. 'Reed's the one who fucked everything up,' Abrams told Ann. 'We popped Sawyer on the way over here, or we would have come back to check on you sooner.'

Reed reached them and, quickly sizing up the situation, rushed over to embrace Ann. 'It's over now,' he said tenderly. 'Sawyer and Hopkins are both in custody, as well as the others. Everything is going to be okay now.'

Ann pulled back and retrieved Glen's gun, handing it to the detective. 'You might want this,' she said. 'It's probably the gun he used the night he shot me. My gun fell out when he jumped me. It's back there somewhere in the sand.'

'Shit,' Reed said, turning the .9mm Ruger over in his hands. 'You disarmed him yourself?' When he looked up, Ann was already walking back to the parking lot. 'Hey,' Reed yelled out, 'wait and I'll drive you home. I don't want you going home alone.'

Ann glanced back over her shoulder, then continued walking.

'Where are you going?' Abrams called after her. 'Maybe you should be checked by a doctor.'

Ann stopped and faced them, speaking from several feet away. 'I don't think that will be necessary, gentlemen.' She spun around and called out the rest, making her way to the parking lot. 'I'm going to get my son, and then I'm going to take a shower. I don't think I need your assistance to do that.'

Reaching the Range Rover in the parking lot, Ann just stood there, leaning back against the car, the sheer joy of being alive causing her entire body to tingle with pleasure. For a few minutes she stared up at the sky, letting the cool evening breezes caress her face, inhaling the salty sea air. She felt her father's presence surround her. Somehow he had known, had experienced some type of premonition. Years ago, when he had taught her the maneuver she had used to disarm Hopkins, he had told her she might be forced to use it one day, and that it would be the most courageous moment in her life. The gun could have easily discharged and killed her, but her father had known. He had known that if his daughter were ever in a situation that grave, she would be facing certain death anyway.

Ann watched as Reed and Abrams trudged across the sand with Hopkins in tow. After all this, the two detectives were still trying to protect her, offering to drive her home. After what had just occurred, it was so ridiculous, it was almost comical.

But Ann had learned a valuable lesson tonight, one she would never forget. When it came down to the wire, all the armies in the world couldn't protect you. Man, woman, child, it was all the same, she told herself.

There was only one person in the world who would never let her down, never make an error in judgment, never fail to appear when she needed them. With her fist she tapped her chest, acknowledging herself.

Then she got in the car and sped off.

Chapter 23

Ann slipped into the courtroom and the first empty seat in the back row. Jimmy Sawyer was on the witness stand, and the courtroom was packed with spectators.

'Did Mr Hopkins ever come to the Henderson house?' Harold Duke asked.

'Yes,' Sawyer said. 'The first time was right after I was arrested.'

'Was this the night Sally Farrar saw him through her window?'

'I guess so,' Sawyer said. 'See, we were having a party. Hopkins talked to me and then he started talking to the chicks. He dropped some Ecstasy with us like he was one of the guys. Then he just partied with the girls the rest of the night.'

Ann knew Sally Farrar had already testified earlier, positively identifying Glen as one of the men she had seen at the Henderson house, but the fact that he had used drugs and engaged in group sex was utterly appalling. This was the man she'd been sleeping with, the man she had thought she could love. She also couldn't understand why he would take such a blatant risk. But Ann had seen this type of behavior with other multiple offenders: serial killers, serial rapists. They started out cautious, but as they continued to commit crimes and get away with them, they became sloppy, almost as if they were taunting the authorities to apprehend them. Glen was committing atrocious crimes, raping old women around the time he went to the Henderson house. Subconsciously, Ann decided, he must have been crying out for someone to stop him and put an end to his madness. She shook her head, turning her attention back to the proceedings.

Duke paused, walking back to the table, then quickly spinning around to face his client. 'Ms Farrar testified that she saw a large object in the back of Peter Chen's Lexus. Can you tell the court what this object was?'

Sawyer brushed his hair out of his face, and moved closer to the microphone. 'We were moving the lab then, so I guess it was a piece of equipment or something.'

'It wasn't a body, was it?' Duke said, smiling.

'Of course not,' Sawyer said adamantly.

'When was the next time you spoke to Mr Hopkins?'

'It was at the house on Henderson. The officers were searching after she found the fingers, and Hopkins came outside where I was being held. The other officer went in the house for something, and that's when Hopkins told me that he would have to file charges against me. He said I was basically a fuck-up and a disgrace.' Jimmy stopped, looking up at the judge. 'I'm sorry. I didn't mean to use profanity, but that's what he said. He said he had to file charges against me in Ms Carlisle's shooting and for violating my probation, and that if he filed the charges, it would be better for me in the long run. He said I'd get bail and he'd make sure I'd never be convicted of anything. Once I was tried and found not guilty, he said they could never try me again. He said that would be double jeopardy.'

'I see,' Duke said, walking back to the table and sitting down. 'Were you comfortable with this, even knowing that you might be sent to jail for something you didn't do?'

'He was a district attorney,' Sawyer said intently. 'I thought he knew what he was doing. And I didn't shoot her anyway. I was also scared out of my mind. See, he found out we were dealing on the side and pocketing the money. I thought he would kill me if I didn't do everything he said. He was angry too because of what she found in the house. He said I might end up convicted of murder if I didn't do exactly what he said.'

'Who is she? Are you speaking of Ms Carlisle?'

'Yes. She found the fingers.'

'What fingers?'

Sawyer dropped his eyes. 'The ones in my refrigerator.'

'Where did these fingers come from?'

'We didn't kill anyone. We got the fingers from a Chinese guy that Peter knew in Los Angeles. The guy had just come over from China and was working for one of those cheap burial societies. He said he could get us anything we wanted.'

'What does that mean exactly? What kind of society?'

'You pay a couple hundred dollars and they cremate the person.' Sawyer shrugged his shoulders as if to say he didn't know about these kinds of things.

'So how did you come by these fingers?'

'We bought them.'

Several people in the courtroom gasped, and others began whispering. Judge Hillstorm looked out over the room sternly, and the noise died down.

Duke continued, 'This Chinese guy, as you called him, he was the one who sold these fingers to you? Not his own fingers, right, but fingers off a corpse?'

'Right,' Sawyer said. 'He said they had bodies stacked all over the place, that they didn't even know who half of the corpses were anymore. We were going to get a hand, but then Peter said we couldn't preserve it as easy as the fingers.'

Harold Duke walked up to the witness stand. 'Why did you want severed fingers?'

'Because once we started dealing on our own,' Sawyer said, his eyes scanning the courtroom and then returning to rest on Duke, 'all these local gangbangers went after us. They said we were dealing in their territory, that they owned it. We thought if we scared them, they'd leave us alone. So we got the fingers and flashed them around on the street and said we'd killed the last guy who tried to interfere in our operation. I mean, the fingers came from an old lady, I think, but no one ever looked at them close enough to figure that out. A gang still took a shot at Brett one day, but they missed. That's when we decided not to deal in their area anymore. Instead we started dealing at colleges, malls, and places like that.'

'When did you see Mr Hopkins again?'

'He called me and told me to meet him the day I got out on bail. When I met him, he wanted me to break into Ann Carlisle's house. He said we needed something regarding her son or her husband that we could use against her. He said we needed to make her crazy and really scare her so whatever she said about us wouldn't be believable, you know, about the fingers and all.'

'Did you do what he asked?'

'I was already in enough trouble,' Sawyer said, his voice strained. 'I wanted out. On the phone he told me to bring the Porsche. I couldn't figure out why he wanted me to do that unless he wanted to set me up. I knew the police were tailing me, so I switched cars with a friend in the mall. When I met Hopkins, I told him I wasn't going to do it.'

'Do what?' Duke asked.

'Break into her house.'

'What kind of car was Mr Hopkins driving?'

'A black Rolls-Royce,' Sawyer answered.

'What happened after you met him?'

'We drove to Ms Carlisle's house and parked a few houses down on the street. He had a gun, a Ruger. He handed me the gun and told me if I wouldn't break into her house, I had to cover him from the outside.' Sawyer paused, thinking through his next statement. 'He'd been inside her house before, see. He said she had locks on all the windows, but once he was inside, he would open the window in the front of the house. If I saw anyone drive up, I was supposed to turn off the power at the box outside. He even showed me where it was.'

'And did you do this?' Duke asked. 'Did you see Ms Carlisle drive up?'

'Yes, I did, but I didn't turn the lights off right away. I didn't know what to do, really. It was pouring down rain and I just wanted to go home.'

'And what other instructions did Mr Hopkins give you?'

'If I heard a struggle or something, I was supposed to come through the other window and help him.'

'Did you do that?'

'No,' Sawyer said, shaking his head. 'After she drove up, she went inside and I guess she went to bed, because all the lights went off. Then I prowled around the house to see where he was and try to tell him she was back. That's when I saw him.'

'Where did you see him?'

'Coming out the window, the window he broke to get in. He handed me these things, and told me to turn off the power, that he was going back inside, that he wanted to scare her good.'

'What did he hand you?'

'I think it was a picture and some videotapes.'

'What happened next?' Duke said.

'I turned off the power like he told me.'

'Did Mr Hopkins go back inside the house?'

'He must have gone through the other window. Then a few minutes later, I heard someone shooting inside the house. I thought he was killing her and ran to the window. That's when I fired the gun.'

'What were you shooting at?'

'I thought I was shooting at him,' Sawyer said, frustrated. 'You know, Hopkins? It was raining and dark. I was certain I hit him, but I guess I didn't.'

'Then what did you do?'

'I ran back to his car and panicked. When I tried to drive off, I was so excited and scared that I crashed into a car parked on the street. I really thought I had shot someone then. I didn't know I'd missed.'

'After you collided with the parked car, what did you do?'

'I just kept driving.'

'In Mr Hopkins's Rolls-Royce?'

'Yes.'

'And where was Mr Hopkins?'

'I don't know. I guess he ran down the street or something and hid.'

'What did you do then?'

'I wiped down the Ruger and left it in the car, along with the things he had given me. I even left the keys in the car, but I wiped them down too. Then I left the car along the side of the road near where I had parked my car. It was maybe six blocks from Ann Carlisle's house.'

'Did you ever see Mr Hopkins again?'

'No, but I guess he found his car and got away in it.' Jimmy laughed, as if he had said something comical.

Duke grimaced, and Sawyer became serious again. 'Did you speak to him on the phone?'

'No. I've been hiding in my parents' yacht. Before that I was staying in the house on Henderson. No one knew where I was, except I guess that Farrar lady next door, but she didn't call the cops.'

'Why did you ask to meet Ann Carlisle at Marina Park?'

'To tell her the truth and turn myself in. I finally told my father the truth about what we'd been doing, the drugs and all.

He said if I didn't turn myself in, the police would kill me. He was the one who told me to call Ann Carlisle. He said if anyone would help me, she would. I certainly wasn't going to call the district attorney's office, and I didn't know if the police were in with Hopkins or not.'

'You didn't call Glen Hopkins and tell him you were going to Marina Park?'

'No. I never thought he'd have a police scanner and show up,' Sawyer said, his face muscles twitching at the memory of that night. 'He was the last person I wanted to see, let me tell you.'

'No further questions, Your Honor,' Duke said.

Judge Hillstorm looked at the clock and saw it was three o'clock. 'Why don't we take a fifteen-minute recess? Mr Duke, how many more witnesses will you be calling?'

'None,' Duke said.

'Fine,' Hillstorm said, 'then we'll conclude this matter when we return from recess.'

When Jimmy Sawyer's hearing resumed, Robert Fielder, the district attorney himself, stood to address the court. The courtroom was even more crowded and noisy than before the break.

'The people are prepared to dismiss counts one through three,' Fielder said, 'relating to the shooting of Ann Carlisle. But Mr Sawyer's own statements make it clear that he has violated the terms of his probation by continuing to distribute narcotics and should be held to answer on a violation of probation on the underlying offense. In addition, the defendant should be held to answer on section 11366.5 of the Health and Safety Code, management of a location used for unlawful manufacture or storage of controlled substances; 11366.6 of the Health and Safety Code, using this location to suppress law enforcement entry in order to sell; and 11383 of the Health and Safety Code, possession for manufacturing purposes.'

Fielder took his seat and Judge Hillstorm said, 'Mr Duke.'

Ann knew that Sawyer was still in deep trouble. The majority of the code sections he had been held to answer on required a mandatory prison term if convicted. This was due to the fact that Sawyer and his roommates had not only been distributing narcotics but manufacturing them, and the penalties for this type of activity were severe. If it had only been possession for sale, the judge would have the option of sending Sawyer to the county jail in lieu of prison. Probably in exchange for Sawyer's testimony against Glen Hopkins, Ann thought, a far more serious case where his testimony would be invaluable, the district attorney would dismiss one or more of the stated charges. But Jimmy Sawyer was facing a stint in prison. There was no doubt about it. He could cooperate all day and night, and he would still end up on a bus to prison. The only thing his cooperation would accomplish was a shorter term.

Duke addressed the court: 'My client has cooperated fully with the authorities. This is evidenced by his candor in the courtroom today. Even knowing he was incriminating himself and with full knowledge that he is facing a prison sentence, Mr Sawyer chose to tell the truth.' Duke paused and looked straight at Hillstorm before continuing. 'For this reason I'd like to request that the court reinstate the previously ordered bail.'

Hillstorm nodded and placed his glasses on his nose, shuffling papers around. Then he looked up and began speaking. 'Counts one, two, and three will be dismissed at the people's motion. On count four, a violation of probation, there appears to be probable cause to hold the defendant to answer, as well as counts five, six, and seven, relating to manufacturing and distributing of controlled substances for sale.' The judge proceeded to set the matter over for trial and selected a date that both attorneys agreed upon.

When finished with the formalities, he looked out at Jimmy Sawyer. 'Mr Sawyer, it's a sad thing to see a young man like yourself drawn into the world of crime. Hopefully, what has happened to you as a result of your criminal activities will be a lesson you won't soon forget. I will not be the trial judge, but if you are convicted, you can still recover and become a contributing member of society. You are a young man, and you have a decent family behind you. Many people in your position do not have these advantages.' Hillstorm paused and looked over at Dr and Mrs Sawyer, his tired eyes full of compassion. 'All right,' he said, sighing heavily while he pondered his next move. 'Because you stepped to the line here today and appeared to be forthright with this court, I will honor Mr Duke's request to reinstate your bail forthwith.' Hillstorm took his glasses off and struck his gavel one time. 'This court is adjourned.'

Newspaper reporters started running out the back doors to reach their editors. Jimmy Sawyer's parents surrounded him, and Ann watched as Dr Sawyer embraced his son. She couldn't help but think of all the hopes and dreams the surgeon had held for his only child. The boy could recover, but neither he nor his family would ever be the same. Once a person went to prison, it left a permanent scar.

Waiting until most of the courtroom had cleared, Ann walked over and stood there until Jimmy saw her. Dr Sawyer stepped back, and Ann reached out to shake Jimmy's hand. 'I'll always be grateful to you for stopping that night,' she said. 'I just wanted you to know that. If you didn't have something good inside, you would have never stopped.'

Dr Sawyer glanced at Ann and then looked away self-consciously.

'How's your hand?' Ann asked politely.

The doctor held it up, and Ann saw the splints on two fingers. 'Not so bad. It will be fine in a few weeks. I guess I got carried away that day. Please accept my apology. It was my son, I just –'

'I have a son too, Dr Sawyer,' Ann said, meeting his gaze. 'You don't have to explain yourself. I understand.' With that, she turned around and walked out of the courtroom.

When Ann got home from work, she took David out to his favorite restaurant, Bob's Big Boy. They ate hamburgers and french fries and still managed to find room for a sundae. Finally David leaned back in his seat and put his hand over his stomach. 'I'm stuffed. Ugh.'

'That's for sure,' Ann said, smiling at her son. 'Hey, you wanted the sundae, big guy.'

They walked out to the car, their arms linked together. Once David got in the passenger seat, Ann turned to him and took his hands in her own. 'Honey, the service for your father will be really nice. All the highway patrol officers will come in their dress uniforms from all over the state. Your father would like that, don't you think?'

'Yes,' David said softly, 'he'd like that.'

By the time Ann got to the courthouse the following morning, Tommy Reed and Noah Abrams were waiting in her office. 'They searched his house last night.'

'Glen's?' she asked.

'Yes,' Reed answered. 'They found the wig he used in the rapes. I guess he wanted to be certain that he would never be identified forensically from hair samples. It also served to obscure his identity even further.'

Ann nodded. In many ways Glen had been shrewd and devious. In other ways he had been reckless and foolish. All that trouble with the wig, and the condoms. He should have realized that there could be pubic hairs. He'd prosecuted dozens of rape cases. But he also knew, she realized, that he was in the perfect position to correct his mistakes, cover his errors. Having the power to manipulate the system must have played into his madness, and the more he got away with, the bolder he became.

Ann looked at the detectives. 'How long had he been involved in narcotics trafficking? Do we know?'

'According to the rental receipts for the warehouse where the drugs were stored, Hopkins rented it two years ago,' Reed said. 'It wasn't only Sawyer and his pals, Ann. We're almost certain Hopkins was behind a number of these home labs.'

'But why?' Ann said, shaking her head.

Abrams rubbed his thumb and forefinger together. 'Green,' he said. 'Lots of green. He had over a half-million dollars stashed in an offshore account. We found the bank books in his house. And there may be more. We haven't gone through his safety deposit boxes yet.'

'But his family is wealthy,' Ann said. 'Why deal drugs?'

'His mother flew in today,' Abrams said. 'We met her at the house. She's a tough old bird, let me tell you. She claims she had a falling-out with her son when he took the job as a county prosecutor. Because of it she cut him off financially, even threatened to cut him out of her will. She wanted him to affiliate with a fancy law firm back East, but they all turned him down. Seems his academic record was not the greatest.' Abrams shrugged his shoulders. 'I guess he thought he could impress her if he made a lot of money, just like he wanted to try Delvecchio and bring in the conviction to win her approval.'

'And we also know about the phone calls,' Reed interjected. 'You were right, Ann.'

'The home videos,' she said quickly.

'Bingo,' Abrams said. 'We found them in his house. Your suspicions were right, Ann. He merely edited out a few sections, transferring them to a high-quality audio tape, and then played them back over the phone when he called you.'

'Bastard,' Ann said, wanting to strangle him with her bare hands. Making David think his father was alive was the ultimate cruelty. 'He should go to the gas chamber for that alone.' Then Ann recalled the unsolved homicides. 'What about the murders? What did Melanie find out?'

'The fingerprints obtained from the homicides aren't Glen's,' Reed said. 'The only similarities were the fact that the victims were older women. Because the murders occurred prior to the rapes, we think Hopkins purposefully wanted us to believe the same individual was responsible. You know, sort of a copy-cat crime.'

Ann was just staring out her window, her eyes on the spot in the shrubbery.

As if he could read her thoughts, Abrams said, 'Hopkins is down, Ann. Last night we got together a lineup, and Delvecchio positively identified him. We're going to get the surviving rape victims in and see if they can identify him as well. They may not be able to identify his face, but I bet they'll never forget his voice. And Melanie has a blood sample from your house. Once we get one from Hopkins, they can positively identify him through genetic finger-printing.'

'But wait,' Ann exclaimed, Abrams touching on the one point that still disturbed her. 'Delvecchio saw Glen dozens of times in the courtroom. Why didn't he recognize him then?'

'I think it was seeing him out of context,' Abrams said, placing a hand on Ann's shoulder. 'You know, he just never dreamed the district attorney was the man who gave him the coat. I mean, Delvecchio is a pretty dull fellow. We made the men in the lineup wear dark glasses like Glen wore that day in the car. Sometimes it's a detail that small.'

Ann said she needed some fresh air. They walked outside

369

and took a seat on the ledge around the fountain. 'What's Fielder going to do about Delvecchio?'

Abrams looked behind him at the jail and smiled. 'I think your answer is right there, Ann.'

Walking across the courtyard was Randy Delvecchio himself.

'But they have to officially set aside the convictions,' Ann said, standing. 'How did he get out so soon?'

'Nothing says an innocent man has to remain incarcerated,' Reed said, a smug smile on his face. 'Fielder got him released on bail. By the way, Melanie invited me over for Thanksgiving. She wants you and David to come too. Hell, she even invited Noah. I kind of like that woman. She's a feisty little thing.'

'You and Melanie Chase?' Ann said, shocked. 'God, Tommy, are you serious?'

'Yeah,' he said, a flush spreading across his face. Then he looked over at Abrams and sneered. 'You got a problem with that, Noah?'

'Me?' Abrams said, pointing at his chest. 'Hey, Sarge, you can go out with anyone you want. Of course, it would be nice if you'd let me do the same.' He tilted his head toward Ann.

She smiled at them and pecked both men on the cheek. 'I don't know how I would have made it through this without you guys,' she said fondly. 'But then again –'

Reed and Abrams both frowned, knowing she was referring to the fiasco at Marina Park. She was never going to let them live that one down. 'Hey,' Reed said, wanting to change the subject fast, 'are you coming to Mel's for Thanksgiving or not?'

With so much going on, Ann had forgotten all about the impending holiday, but seeing Delvecchio out of the corner of her eye, she decided at least one person had cause to celebrate.

Delvecchio saw Ann and started walking toward her. He grabbed her hand, bringing it to his lips and kissing it. 'You're my lady,' he said, bowing at the waist. 'I knew there was a God the minute you walked in my cell. The other inmates told me I was crazy. They said you were nothin' but poison. But I heard His voice in my head. He said, "Randy, this is the woman who'll save you." '

Ann took his hand and pulled the young man to her. Throwing her arms around his neck, she hugged him as she would hug her son. 'I'm so sorry for all your suffering,' she said softly. How many months had he sat in jail? How many days of his life had been cruelly stolen? He could sue the county, but no amount of money could give him back the portion of his life that had been lost.

When she released him, he took off across the courtyard walking briskly, the sun at his back. Then he stopped and yelled out over the parking lot, as excited as a five-year-old, 'I'm gonna have my mama's roast turkey next week. She's the best cook in town.'

Ann smiled and waved at him as he leaped into a car filled with people and drove off. Instead of going to prison, a young man was going home for Thanksgiving. 'God,' she said to the detectives, 'he doesn't even seem bitter. If that had been me, I think I'd be out for blood.' As soon as she said it, she recognized the irony of her words. Look at what she'd been through, not just the past few months but the entire four years she had waited to know the truth about Hank. Was she bitter? No, she decided, smiling at the detectives. She knew how Delvecchio felt: an overwhelming feeling of relief, so intense that it left no room for bitterness, no room for hatred.

They headed back to the courthouse. Ann walked slowly, savoring the warmth of the sun on her skin, the company of two good friends, the fragrant fresh air. So many little things she had taken for granted, she thought. But having been only seconds away from death had left her with a renewed appreciation of life, and for that she would always be thankful.

Over and over the same thought played in her mind, and her eyes turned to the sky in a moment of gratitude.

'I'm alive,' she suddenly said. 'By the grace of God, I survived. Do you know how great it feels just to be alive?'

'I think we do,' Reed said, a smile stretching across his rugged face.

Reaching the double doors to the courthouse, Reed held one door open while Abrams held the other, and Ann stepped through. Then the two men followed, the doors slowly closing behind them.

All Orion/Phoenix titles are available at your local bookshop or from the following address:

Littlehampton Book Services
Cash Sales Department L
14 Eldon Way, Lineside Industrial Estate
Littlehampton
West Sussex BN17 7HE
telephone 01903 721596, *facsimile* 01903 730914

Payment can either be made by credit card (Visa and Mastercard accepted) or by sending a cheque or postal order made payable to *Littlehampton Book Services*.
DO NOT SEND CASH OR CURRENCY.

Please add the following to cover postage and packing

UK and BFPO:
£1.50 for the first book, and 50P for each additional book to a maximum of £3.50

Overseas and Eire:
£2.50 for the first book plus £1.00 for the second book and 50p for each additional book ordered

----

BLOCK CAPITALS PLEASE

name of cardholder ....

address of cardholder ....

postcode ....

delivery address
(if different from cardholder)

....

postcode ....

☐ I enclose my remittance for £. ....

☐ please debit my Mastercard/Visa (delete as appropriate)

card number ☐☐☐☐☐☐☐☐☐☐☐☐☐☐☐☐☐☐

expiry date ☐☐☐☐

signature ....

prices and availability are subject to change without notice